DARK CONTACT

The Dragons of Earth

Mark S. Wojcik

ISBN: 9798417424045

Cover Design by Skottie O'Mahony

Printed in the United States of America

Dedicated to family and friends.

TABLE OF CONTENTS

PART ONE
Revelations

PART TWO
Invasion

PART THREE
NEVER GIVE UP

Smoke sometimes has more substance than what we are led to believe.

PART ONE
Revelations

Chapter 1
Meeting the Enemy

"Embedded self-destructs! That certainly presents a whole series of nasty problems for us, Colonel," Danny felt nauseous, his face still pasty white after finding out all the defensive ships provided by the Stickmen could all be destroyed by them.

"So many, I don't even know where to start," Duval replied bitterly as his mind raced, trying to get a grasp of all the ramifications.

"Okay, now that we know those Stickmen are the assholes who tried to kill us, why did they bother to pursue us? Why didn't they just detonate our ships' self-destruct devices when they chased us off Mars?" Karlson argued, still not wanting to accept what they just learned.

"I think there can only be one answer to that question," Danny responded dejectedly.

Karlson and Duval stared at him, unable to see what he alluded to.

"One signal fits all. It would have to be that way. Think about it! They've given us millions of ships. It would be nuts for them to have to send separate signals to every ship! How would they know which specific signal to send?"

He let Duval and Karlson chew on that for a moment and then added miserably, "You know this also means we don't dare go home. We can't even risk sending a warning. They have to be monitoring the entire damned solar system just like the EDF does. If so, then we can't take the chance of them destroying all of our ships if they find us reappearing again in the middle of the solar system. They'll know we're on to them."

Duval pondered that one too for a moment and grimly nodded in agreement. "Murphy's right. They obviously plan to destroy our ships anyway if the EDF ever discovers the Stickmen are just using us to fight against the Ghosts. It keeps us from turning on them. With all of our Dragons destroyed, Earth will be wide open for the Stickmen to take over."

"It was wide open anyway, but it still makes sense," Karlson said. "It's diabolically clever. This way, with our people and the Ghost people fighting each other, they're killing two birds with one stone. It's a win-win for the Stickmen. Hell, they probably plan to blow up the Dragons anyway if we manage to wipe out the Ghost ships for them!"

Pat then put out a burst of heat that Jake's disk interpreted. "Pat: Why do the Destroyers seek to kill two of your birds with one stone? I am

1

unable to comprehend why they would want to do this!" All of the men ignored Pat's question.

Wide-eyed and looking deathly ill, Jake Bennings hung onto every word of the conversation. "Pat has been telling me from the beginning I can never go home. He said I would die if they took me back, but he never explained why. Now I understand why!"

"Pat: The inevitable attack on your world is indeed the reason we informed Jake he will certainly die if we take him home.

"No offense, Whitey," Karlson snarled, but why should we believe our planet isn't just a bone that two dogs are fighting over?"

"Pat: Who is Whitey? How is it you believe a planet can become a bone? What are dogs?"

"Karlson has a point," Duval agreed, eyeing the Ghost skeptically and ignoring Pat's increasingly annoying questions once more. "We've been fooled once already."

"Pat: I do not understand."

Jake enlightened the Ghost being. "Our new friends now realize that the beings they refer to as the Stickmen are their true enemies. However, they need to know if the Ghost people are also their enemies competing with the Stickmen for the domination Earth."

The Ghost remained silent while soft pink patterns rippled all over his body without translation, a sign he was communicating with other Ghosts.

Before long, Pat responded, "Pat: Did not Duval agree with Danny's speculation that their attempt to go home might cause the detonation of the explosive devices in all the ships given to you humans?"

Duval shot Danny a look of pure fury for speculating about enemy intentions in front of yet another potential enemy, speculation the Ghosts might yet use to their advantage. He felt just as angry with himself for making the same error. Also realizing the blunder, Karlson had a deer-in-the-headlights look on his face. Danny's face reddened with shame for making such an obvious mistake.

"Pat: If we Ghosts are your enemies too, then we would simply release you immediately. Once you are detected, the Stickmen would eliminate all of the ships the humans would send against us. However, we Ghosts will never do that. We will face your human warriors who will come to destroy us, as well as those of the Stickmen in our efforts to gather our seeds."

Duval glared at Murphy and Karlson. "In the future, gentlemen, we must strive to discuss potentially sensitive information among ourselves in private!"

2

"What did you mean by seeds?" Murphy asked the Ghost, puzzled by their constant reference to them.

"Later, Murphy! Who gives a rat's ass about plants? We have more important matters to resolve! But before we discuss anything further . . . Pat, will you take us to the captured ship you just showed us?"

They felt another burst of heat that translated to, "Pat: Follow please."

As the Ghost began to lead them, Duval and his men marveled at how the being glided silently from one place to another.

"Look at that thing move!" Karlson marveled. "It never turns or rotates to change direction."

"I know," Duval agreed, "it just seems to flow in whatever direction it wants to go. I wonder what propels it under that fleshy skirt."

"I'd be willing to bet that it's still pointed in the original direction it faced when it was born," Murphy speculated.

"Lieutenant Commander Murphy is probably right. I've studied them since they captured me," Jake told them as they followed the alien being. "I've at least figured out they have three-hundred-sixty-degree vision. That being the case, they don't need to turn around. They face every direction at the same time."

Pat led them several hundred feet across the chamber to a bulkhead where another portal opened ahead of the being into an equally large hangar, for the lack of a better name for it. The Stickman spacecraft they viewed in the earlier projected images rested in the center of the bay.

Though the Dragon fighter pilots fought a desperate battle with ships like this a short while earlier, this was their first opportunity to get a good, up-close look at one. The ship, twice the length of the spherical Dragon ships Duval and his team flew, also rested on the deck instead of floating above it.

Its size and shape presented a more menacing and deadly nature than a Dragon. Torpedo-shaped, thirty feet in diameter at its center and sixty feet long, its ends tapered to rounded tips ten feet in diameter. Four hemispherical bulges protruded from each end of the ship, two on each side.

"Stay here, everyone. I'm going to check it out."

"Pat: Duval, why do you wish to approach alone? Do not all four of you humans wish to examine this ship?"

"Human commanders find it more prudent to expose as few warriors as possible to potential danger until any possible risk is fully assessed," Duval answered. "As the officer responsible for the lives of my men, I must make this assessment myself."

"Pat: Again, an example of human disregard for self-preservation in favor of ensuring no harm coming to others." His body rippled with pink patterns and sent out another burst of heat that went untranslated, another one of his constant ongoing reports to his people.

"While we Ghosts find it exciting to witness yet another verification of this human characteristic, please be aware, Duval, that there is no danger present within the captured ship. We found no personal weapons in their possession, and we rendered their ship has as harmless as we rendered yours. The Ghost people would never permit anything capable of causing harm to ourselves or other beings to remain functional. Did we not remove your weapons?"

"Well, that explains that," Duval commented to his men. "Okay . . . Pat," he still found it difficult calling a nine-foot-tall monster 'Pat,' "I'll take your word that it's safe. Gentlemen, let's all go take a look then, but keep your eyes open in case the Stickmen have any tricks up their sleeves."

"Pat: Our nanite examination of this ship and these beings indicate there are no objects hidden within the garments of these Stickmen, as you refer to them."

With Duval leading the way, the group of humans still approached the alien ship with caution despite Pat's assurances.

"If the occupants manage to pop open any exit portals, be ready for a fight."

The four men circled the vehicle slowly as they investigated it. Duval and Jake went around one way, while Karlson, with Danny wheeling behind in his chair, went the other way. Pat waited at the point where the men split up.

"Except for the shape, there's no doubt it's a Stickman ship, Colonel," came Danny's assessment when reassembled at their starting point. "I don't think there's any question that it's made of the same mirrored stuff that make up Dragon hulls."

"I agree, Colonel," came Karlson's support of the evaluation.

Far from satisfied, Duval told them. "Fine, but we need to know a lot more than that. Jake, the Earth Defense Force back home has had hundreds of thousands of ships like ours for many weeks now, and we have yet to find any tool in our possession that can even scratch the skin of these ships, let alone allow us to penetrate it for study. Your Ghost buddies had no problem getting us out of our ships. Can they open up this one for us so we can go inside? I would love to have an up-close and personal 'discussion' with the guys inside this thing." He chose his words carefully so Pat would not interpret them as the promised mayhem they really meant.

"Pat: Duval would like to enter the captured ship to engage in a meeting?"

"Yes, I certainly would. Can you make an opening in the hull of this ship?" Duval's neck started to ache from talking to the Ghost. He found it increasingly uncomfortable to look up at Pat for too long, the alien's 'head' easily three feet higher than his. He also found himself wishing the Ghost being had a face on his upsidedown bowl-shaped head, unable to accustom himself to the fact it had no front or back to it.

Pat's body rippled with pink patterns and emitted another burst of heat. A moment later, the deck in front of the Stickman ship began to rise out of the hangar floor, and a ramp began to form. As it extended toward the ship, a small opening appeared on the hull above it that quickly grew larger.

"Pat: Our small, small machines, the ones Jake calls nanites, can pass through any substance, no matter how hard the material. They are carrying away small structural elements of the hull material to create an opening through which you will be able to enter shortly," the Ghost explained. "This is how we helped you to exit your ships."

Fascinated, the four men watched the size of the hole expand while Jake enlightened his companions further. "The Ghosts make use of infinitesimally tiny machines to manufacture almost everything they need. I suspect they are likely to be as small as individual molecules, maybe even smaller. Our scientists on Earth have just begun to pioneer a field called nanotechnology with the goal of creating similar machines. From what I've been able to figure out, I believe the Ghost nanites can manipulate the very atoms of a material."

"This is so damned amazing!" a wide-eyed and very impressed Murphy remarked as he rolled his chair closer to the ship to get a better view of the hole. "There's no sound and no debris, just a hole that keeps growing larger."

"Get back from there before it gets big enough for one of those assholes to get out!" Duval ordered sharply.

"Yes, sir," Danny replied as he reluctantly rolled his chair back from the expanding opening. A moment later, the hole stopped growing.

Chapter 2
The Crew of the Eradicator

The Stickmen referred to the type of ship they sent to pursue Duval and his men as 'Eradicators.' Capable of speeds even faster than a Swarm ship, they were sent to overtake and destroy the meddlesome humans who discovered their hidden Martian base.

As expected, the powerful ships sent against the six small swarm vehicles rapidly caught up to the humans. However, what should have been a simple extermination of the filthy human life forms infesting those ships turned into a catastrophe of epic proportions.

Against all logic and reason, the six ships executed insane maneuvers and tactics that enabled the humans to destroy far too many of their fellow pursuers, seemingly without effort when they should not have been capable of destroying any at all!

Once reinforcements arrived, the destruction of the human-infested Swarm ships should have been inevitable until the surviving Eradicator ships began to vanish one by one.

They knew then there could be only one cause for such a phenomenon, and their ship's tactical system confirmed it. One of the ships of their ancient enemy appeared out of nowhere, bearing down on them from behind! By the time they made the alarming discovery, it was too late to elude their pursuer. Inexplicably, instead of being destroyed, their ship abruptly became inactive, unresponsive, and blind, the result of an unheard-of cascade of system failures.

At this moment within the captured vessel, its Stickman crew worked frantically to reactivate their ship. Three of them focused their efforts on the ship's power compartment, which they could access through a dome in the middle of the main deck. The shipmaster sat in the command chair at the fore end of the ship and sent numerous but unsuccessful mental commands to the ship's control systems to try to get any of their functions to respond. The fifth crew member nearby carefully manipulated a lighted

6

wand within the volume of space above the deck where the tactical hologram should have been.

The ship's gravity control and life support systems still functioned, but its tactical hologram and viewing field did not. Blind to the outside of their vessel, their ship still floated disabled and derelict in space as far as the crew knew.

All five Eradicator crewmen knew no rescue ships would come for them. Any single ship and its crew had no value to the Hive to make such an attempt worthwhile. The crew members knew their only hope for survival lay in their ability to restore their ship's functionality themselves. For these Stickmen, self-preservation wasn't what drove their efforts to survive; what did drive them was a genetically crafted, almost rabid need to live on to contribute to their race's objective to exterminate all forms of alien life.

An urgent, mentally delivered warning issued by one of his crew members pulled the shipmaster's attention away from his work. In close quarters, they communicated telepathically, the thought transfer systems being needed only to communicate ship to ship and across vast distances. The crewman frantically emphasized his alarm with a surprising vocal hiss, a sound rarely employed by the Hive race.

The shipmaster snapped his attention to where the crewman indicated and, to his horror, saw the hull dissolving far from where the location of the ship's exit portal should be. The loss of the hull integrity should be causing the ship's internal air pressure to blow them all explosively out into space, yet that wasn't happening! The hole continued to expand, but instead of the blackness of space beyond, light filtered into the cabin.

∿ ∿ ∿

Outside the Eradicator ship, the opening the Ghosts created and the ramp before it finished forming just above where the flight deck should be, the breach just large enough for a man to pass through.

"If Pat knows what he's talking about, they should be as unarmed as we are," Duval whispered to Karlson, hoping Pat's translator wouldn't pick up his voice.

"They're taller than us, but with those skinny bodies of theirs, we should be able to throw them across the ship like spears!" came Karlson's low opinion.

"Snakes are skinny too, but they're still deadly." Duval reminded him.

He pointed up at the opening. "Go up the ramp on the left side without exposing yourself to them. I'll take the other side."

"Roger that."

7

His inability to join his friends left Murphy frustrated. Even if Duval permitted him to board with them, Danny knew he wouldn't have been able to get his wheelchair to roll up the steep ramp without tipping. Forced to stand by and watch helplessly, this was one of the rare times his disability frustrated him.

The ramp's width allowed Duval and Karson to stand at either side of the opening without exposing themselves to the occupants inside. Duval reached the top of the ramp and stole a quick peek inside, then turned, gave Karlson an evil grin, and whispered, "I think you might be right. They're just walking toothpicks. We can take them! Are you ready for this?"

"Just say the word."

"On three."

Duval held up his hand, raising one finger at a time to give the count. On three, Duval stormed through the opening with Karlson right on his heels.

There were five Stickmen scattered about a relatively spacious deck, all of them turned toward the humans who, from their point of view, somehow found a way to breach their hull and board their ship. When they saw the humans rushing at them, their reaction brought the men's charge to an abrupt halt. All five began to wail in shrieking hisses, every one of them shrinking back from the two Earthmen in obvious terror as if two demons boarded their ship instead of two of their so-called human allies.

"What the hell, Colonel?"

"They look terrified," Duval responded, equally bewildered, "but terrified or not, I want answers from them!"

Knowing the Stickmen who came back with the astronauts always seemed to understand what was said to them, Duval menacingly crossed the short distance to the closest one, grabbed it roughly by the arm, and demanded, "We're supposed to be allies, you assholes! Why did you try to kill us?"

～ ～ ～

The shipmaster's mind reeled! None of this should be happening! How could his Eradicator no longer be in outer space? Moreover, the two beings rushing through the breach in his ship's hull were two of the primitive Earth creatures who couldn't possibly have the technology to create an opening in the hull of his Eradicator! Yet here they were, irrevocably polluting his ship with their presence! He heard the hisses of abhorrence coming from his other four warriors adding to his own.

The two beings within his ship made a reality of the worst nightmare any member of the Hive race could have. Their presence rendered him, his crew, and his Eradicator forever corrupted and useless by the contamination caused by their filthy human presence.

The shipmaster shrieked again with horror, disgust, and despair. Then, to his unbearable horror, the desecration of all desecrations happened when one of the alien creatures shouted a series of sharp sounds and charged at him, not just touching him but clamping its hand painfully around his arm.

The intense disgust and loathing the shipmaster felt went far beyond his ability to endure it. He died instantly from the trauma of such an unspeakable repelling act perpetrated upon him. The four remaining creatures collapsed to the floor one by one, dying of shock from just witnessing such a revolting and horrifying act.

∿ ∿ ∿

To Duval's amazement, when he grabbed the creature's arm, it collapsed to the floor and lay motionless. When he looked up at the remaining aliens, they too sank lifeless to the deck, one of them twitching for several seconds before becoming still.

"Damn, Colonel! What kind of crazy Vulcan nerve pinch crap did you pull?" a dumbfounded but thoroughly impressed Karlson asked.

Stunned himself, Duval ignored the question and stared down at the body at his feet. It occurred to him to try to find a pulse, and he knelt to take the skinny wrist of the dead alien in his hand to try to detect one.

Karlson rolled his eyes and threw up his hands. "What the hell are you trying to do, Colonel? You don't even know if these things have a heart, let alone a pulse!"

Duval let the creature's wrist fall from his grasp. "You're right . . . for once. It doesn't matter, though. I don't think there's any doubt this one is dead. Help me check these other four for some sign of life."

"This one over here is already as cold as a corpse," Karlson reported after he lightly slapped the side of its face and rolled the head back and forth to try to make it regain consciousness.

"This one is too," Duval replied as he knelt over a second Stickman crewman. "They can't have cooled off that quickly. Their natural body temperature must be low, to begin with."

This was their first, up-close look at a Stickman outside of what they'd seen from Earth's news broadcasts. They were grotesque with hairless, grayish skins, large lidless black eyes, and ragged slits for a nose. An involuntary shiver ran through Duval. He hoped he never found a reason or need to touch another one of them ever again. The dead alien would not have understood the irony of the human wiping his hand vigorously on the pant leg of his flight suit after touching its corpse.

Jake Bennings appeared out of nowhere, startling the Colonel. "Pat says they're all dead." He glanced down at the nearest alien corpse.

"Geez, these things are ugly. I see why you call them Stickmen." He continued to stare, wide-eyed, at the dead beings, the first Stickmen he ever saw.

"Did the Ghost nanites take them out?" Duval asked.

Mesmerized by the sight of the dead aliens, the question didn't register with Jake.

"Jake!" Jake's head jerked up. "I asked you if the nanites killed these beings."

"No." He shook his head and forced himself to look away from the corpse to concentrate on answering Duval's question. "No. The nanites just performed the evaluation. They didn't kill these beings."

Duval sighed, shaking his head. "Whatever killed them prevented us from getting answers to a long list of some very pressing questions."

He rose to his feet and carefully studied the ship's interior for the first time, finding its construction very much like the inside of a Dragon, only much longer and wider. While any part of the spherically shaped Dragon became the forward side of the ship simply by changing direction, this elongated ship had well-defined fore and aft ends to it.

"Look around and see if you can figure anything out," Duval ordered Karlson. "Jake, you too!"

"What's going on in there?" Danny called loudly from outside the opening. There could be no mistaking his tone of frustration and concern for not being able to join his companions.

"We have five dead Stickmen in here," Duval responded loud enough for Danny to hear him.

"Dead? What happened? How did you kill them so quickly?" Danny called back.

"We didn't kill them," Duval answered irritably. "Be quiet and sit tight!" With a belated presence of mind, he winced at spitting out such a poor choice of words with Danny needing a wheelchair. "We're going to take a good look around."

Duval and Karlson each went to a control station where command seats were still in place. Duval noted that the crew's frozen seats still retained their shape to accommodate the Stickman physique. No joystick controls extended from them like the Dragon ship command chairs, and he remembered from his training that the Stickmen didn't need the same kind of placebo controls as the ships they made for humans.

Jake, never having seen any type of Stickman ship before, wandered slowly around the deck trying to figure out how he could possibly identify anything at all in this featureless cabin as he examined the walls and floors of the craft everywhere for anything standing out from the rest of the ship.

"This place seems as clean as an operating room ... probably even cleaner. There's nothing here but that bulge of a dome in the center of the cabin. Hey, there's a hole in the side of it, though!"

That drew the attention of the two EDF officers, and they rushed over to see it for themselves. The hole was about two feet wide, enough to expose whatever it contained.

"Damn, this is the first time we've ever seen an opening to the drive compartment of a ship!" Karlson told Jake excitedly. Duval crouched on the floor, trying to peer inside it.

"Damn, I wish I had a flashlight. I can't see a damned thing!"

He took a coin out of one of the pockets of his flight suit and dropped it, listening for the sound of it hitting something solid below.

"Sounds like it went to the bottom without bouncing off anything. We'll look into this later if and when we get another chance."

They inspected the ship for several minutes more, unsuccessfully sending mental commands to its systems before exiting without knowing very much more about it than they did before they entered it.

"Nanites, ships without controls, translator devices . . ." Duval rattled off the list of alien devices they'd encountered just in the last hour, all of which were beyond his understanding. "We are truly infants in the realm of physics and technology compared to either of these two alien races. How can humanity possibly triumph against it all? How will we be able to survive?"

"Pat: We Ghosts will take heavy losses, but we will still be able to save many of your people when we gather our seeds from your planet. Your race will survive. Your planet will not."

"I don't know what the hell is so important about seeds, but we can't just sit back and let our people kill innocent Ghost beings!" Karlson protested.

"Pat: My people and I see no other solution. Even though your defending warriors will destroy many of us, we will not harm them now that we know their aggression will be driven by a need for self-preservation and the preservation of your species."

Pat's human guests stood by in stunned silence as they absorbed the enormity of his revelation. Much of the human race would die in the end, but thousands of the Ghost people would also sacrifice themselves willingly to save whatever humans they could.

Duval broke the silence, "Would it be possible to speak to your leaders? The Stickmen must have found us so adept at warfare that we must be the first civilization they've encountered whom they didn't immediately destroy. Work with us! Convince your people to make use of our martial talents just as the Stickmen intend to! Perhaps, together, we can find a solution to save our world and its people without the need for your people to sacrifice themselves for our sake!"

Pat put out yet another burst of untranslated heat. Minutes went by, the survival of Earth teetering on the answer to Duval's request.

Finally, "Pat: Our expeditionary council will meet with you. They cannot dismiss the fact that, despite our physical and behavioral differences, the single trait our people share, the willingness to risk ourselves to save others, makes you our brethren in spirit, the first we have ever encountered. Be assured we will not turn away from you. This meeting will take time to arrange. From our studies of Jake, we know your people need periodic rest. Now would be a good time for you and your men to acquire rest while you wait.

∿ ∿ ∿

Five months earlier:

The mission was over. Hermes and Mercury knew they carried out their assignment flawlessly, succeeding in all the Hive expected of them. They successfully convinced the remarkable beings of this world of the necessity to defend their planet against a coming invasion. Even better, because of their extraordinary battle skills, these humans would destroy far more of the enemy than the Hive swarm fighters could ever hope to. If the Hive's grand experiment succeeded, Swarm ships would soon be able to move on to other worlds while the Hive used the humans as tools to engage the enemy repeatedly to the point of total destruction of one or both of the races.

Now the revolting contact and exposure to the vermin of this star system were over at last. Specially bred to withstand the contamination that exposure to the presence of humans inflicted upon them, Hermes and Mercury became the only two beings among the entire Hive population capable of withstanding brief interaction with them. Their reprogramming from birth to resist their instinctive revulsion of alien life forms succeeded only by means of enhancing their one greater instinct to sacrifice themselves willingly for the good of the Hive.

However, despite the lifelong brainwashing they endured, the abhorrence of the Hive race for alien life forms was too deeply embedded in their DNA to be neutralized completely. Freed of their obligation to the Hive, Mercury and Hermes rushed back to their ship outside the UN building. They took care not to touch each other; neither one could stand further corruption by coming in contact with yet another contaminated by contact with the humans.

Hermes and Mercury took pride in their success and drew comfort from the fact that no additional interaction with humans would ever be necessary again for them. Thanks to them, the uncanny martial abilities of these humans were ready for harvesting to serve the Hive race.

Only moments ago, they finished providing their final holographic narrative to the human leaders assembled within the strange building. The humans radiated emotions of distress from their departure, but with their mission completed, the two Stickmen felt the overpowering need to board their ship and savor their longed-for isolation from the humans that it achieved. Two chairs rose out of the cabin deck as they entered the ship's portal, and they both seated themselves, one the passenger, the other the pilot.

The pilot engaged the ship's drives and accelerated at maximum atmospheric speed straight up into the Earth's sky as quickly as possible.

The Earth's moon zipped past as a brief glimmer of light in the viewing field as they zoomed past it at the near-light speed they'd achieved. Even though the mission of the two beings originated from the moon, they would never go back to it again.

At the velocity they traveled, Hermes and Mercury reached the asteroid belt in forty-three minutes and took less than two minutes more to close on their destination, a mountain-sized asteroid. The pilot slowed his approach to guide the ship toward a camouflaged portal deep inside one of its craters that slowly opened to receive them, the soft glow of its interior light beckoning. After they landed and exited their ship, the spacecraft took off again, unmanned, on a preprogrammed course.

As expected, no one greeted the two envoys. Hermes and Mercury felt fulfilled that their success represented one of the most extraordinary contributions ever made to the Hive race by any of their cast. However, the nature of their mission left them with an overwhelming need to cleanse themselves.

Almost desperate to purify themselves after their rank corruption from human contact, the two Stickmen sought only one reward. A small chamber awaited them in the hangar a very short distance from where their ship deposited them. Hermes and Mercury practically raced to it, their need to be cleansed an overpowering one. Gratefully they stepped inside, still careful not to touch one another. The portal closed behind them, and the brief flash that followed within the chamber incinerated them to ashes in a microsecond, mercifully and without pain. A second flash rendered their ashes into component atoms that the decontamination system afterward bled outward into the vacuum of space as a faint mist.

Their swarm ship, traveling on a preprogrammed path, raced the millions of miles toward its goal of decontamination via incineration by the sun of this solar system.

Chapter 3
Accommodation Marvels

Duval, Murphy, and Karlson felt exhausted and drained, having been awake for nearly thirty hours. Duval asked for a place where they could all get some sleep, so Jake and Pat obligingly led the three Dragon pilots through featureless, unadorned metal corridors with ceilings high enough for the Ghost beings to comfortably pass beneath.

Duval looked forward to the chance to get some much-needed rest before their upcoming critical meeting with the Ghost Council. Being the senior officer and the one who would speak for them all, he wanted to be clearheaded when the time came. The three Dragon pilots felt drained not only from battle but by the extreme ranges of emotions they all experienced from their dogfight with the enemy ships, their subsequent capture, and from the stunning revelations they'd been exposed to since. Fatigued or not, though, they marveled at the corridor lights forming in the dark tunnel yards ahead of them that shrunk back into non-existence again yards behind them.

When they reached Jake's living quarters Jake, no longer surprised by anything the Ghosts could accomplish, found three new chambers established next to his room. Three more Ghost beings waited there for the humans to arrive. Using one tentacle, one of them held three translator disks precisely like the one Jake possessed, all of them dangling from cords. Jake took the disks from the Ghost and handed one to each of his new friends.

"Pat: These Ghosts are of those among us who study your planet and your species. They wish only to learn from you as I have learned from Jake. If you permit their company while you are with us, they will serve as your guides and see to your needs as well."

Duval looked up at the one nearest him, a being indistinguishable from Jake's Ghost friend, Pat, and shrugged indifferently. "I'm okay with it, I guess," he said wearily. "I'm too tired to care one way or another right now."

"I'm good with it, too," Karlson responded half-heartedly. He had doubts about keeping company with aliens he thought of as white columns of gelatin, and it showed by the look on his face despite the apparent evidence they were not Earth's enemies. Remembering the Stickman propaganda holograms driven into his head, he couldn't help thinking that the Ghosts might somehow still be lying too. However, his commanding officer already set the example for them to follow.

Murphy, fascinated by everything he saw, rolled himself closer to the Ghost nearest him and said, "What's your name?"

"We have not yet been given human names. We would very much appreciate it if you would assign names to us." This time, Jake's simulated voice came only from the disk Danny wore around his neck.

"Pat: Human names are unknown to us, but it will make communication among us less cumbersome if you would provide my associates with names too."

Pat's voice came from Danny's disk this time too. Only the disk worn by the person the Ghosts addressed carried the voice, and at the moment, only Jake's translator disk had a voice when a Ghost spoke to all four men simultaneously.

"After all these weeks with them, I can barely tell the Ghosts apart, if at all," Jake confessed with a frustrated sigh. "The only one I can truly recognize all the time is Pat. I don't know why; I just can. Remember, though, when one of the translator disks speaks, it will always begin with the Ghost's name speaking through it, so we know which one is doing the talking. I've given names to several of the others I've worked with. Since my translator disk uses only an imitation of my voice no matter which of them is speaking, I wouldn't know who the hell was talking to me without the name prefix the translator disk puts out first. By the way, the disks are also the equivalent of radios. The Ghosts may not be in sight when they talk to you, but you can call them through the disk if they're not around just as if they were radios."

Karlson scrutinized the four Ghosts closely, frowning as he tried unsuccessfully to discern any differences at all. "Jake, you have a better eye for detail than I do. I can't tell any of them apart. No political incorrectness intended; they all look alike to me. How do we even know if they are male or female?"

"Believe it or not, gender determination is not something I've bothered to figure out yet or discussed with them. It never seemed important since I've been working mainly with Pat and forgot all about the subject. For

16

that very reason, though, I've been giving them names that would fit either a man or a woman."

Duval, bleary-eyed, wearily looked up at his assigned companion towering over him. "How about Jan? Is the name Jan acceptable to you?"

After a delay of five seconds, Duval felt a burst of heat radiate from the Ghost. The translator disk around his neck said, "Jan: I accept Jan as my name, and I thank you, Duval." Once again, the disk emitted a perfect imitation of Jake's voice.

Murphy gave his companion the name of Jacky, while Karlson, breaking from the gender-neutral name trend, dubbed his companion Odin. Oddly enough, the act of naming a Ghost himself made Karlson feel more at ease around them. To him, it was like bestowing a name on some sort of weird, super-smart pet, although he dared not voice that impression aloud.

"Pat: We have briefed our council on the events leading to your presence here as well as everything you have told us so far. The information disturbs them greatly, and there is much more they urgently wish to know."

"We share the same sense of urgency," Duval replied. "We have many questions for them too. How long will it be before we can meet them? I presume we'll be stuck here while we wait for them to arrive?"

"Jan: It is we who have arrived in the solar system where they await us. They are ready to meet with you even as we speak, but they recognize and honor your need for rest.

The four humans glanced uncomfortably at each other at this unexpected piece of news. They didn't let on though how disturbed they felt by it.

Danny Murphy was the only one among them whose thirst for knowledge outweighed his exhaustion. He couldn't wait to find out how they'd traveled to another solar system in such a short time. Once outside the solar system, even their Dragon ships would take months to reach the nearest star at full mini-jump speed. He realized, though, this was not the time to be asking questions.

"After we rest then," Duval continued, "and before this meeting takes place, I would like to take a short amount of time to confer with Jake and my other human companions, in private, if you will permit us."

His companion's translator disk responded, "Jan: We will provide you with whatever amount of time you require, and I assure you that will have the privacy you require."

Duval was in no mood to thank the Ghost. Instead, he said, "If you don't mind then, we would like to withdraw to the quarters you've provided for us."

"Jan: Please feel free to do so."

Even though the humans were ready to retire to their new rooms, the Ghosts made no effort to leave. Duval leaned close to Jake and whispered, "Are these things going to crawl into bed with us too?"

"Of course not!" Jake told him. "I suspect, though, that with their insatiable need to know everything about us, they'll continue to observe you right up until the door closes behind you."

Duval glared up at the four Ghosts standing there motionless, silent, and providing no hint when they would ever leave, and just shook his head. He then picked the nearest chamber and disappeared inside.

Taking Duval's lead, Karlson did the same, both men relieved to see that their new Ghost companions didn't try to follow. After the openings of their chambers closed behind them, Jake, too, took his leave.

~ ~ ~

Danny found himself alone in the corridor with four of the Ghost companions. Having no choice of rooms left, he rolled himself into the last one, its portal already open and awaiting his entrance. Exhausted and unable to move as easily as his two friends, he rolled his chair sluggishly through the opening.

Surprisingly, he found the room furnished in the fashion of a typical and very human-style efficiency apartment. It consisted of a living room, a bedroom, a bathroom containing a toilet, sink, shower, a larger chamber with standard kitchen appliances, and a table and chairs. Cabinets on one wall of the room held utensils, cups, bowls, and plates.

Chalking up the room's design to Jake's influence, he rolled himself into the bathroom. He made use of the toilet but was too tired to try to use the shower despite the fact he knew he desperately needed one. Rolling his chair back into the main chamber, he was startled and alarmed to find that the four Ghosts were still present in his room.

When none of them spoke, he asked apprehensively, "Is there something you want from me?"

The translator disk Danny wore said, "Jacky: Why does Danny make use of a chair with wheels?"

"Odin: Why does Danny not walk like Jake and the other humans?

Forewarned now, not only by Jake but also by his exposure so far to the Ghosts' unquenchable curiosity and need to learn, Danny felt relieved to know that information was all they wanted. He could even sympathize with them since he had just as much curiosity about them and their abilities. He saw no harm in answering the question, especially if the answer would get rid of them sooner.

"An accident damaged my body a long time ago. It doesn't function properly. I am no longer able to control my legs. They have no feeling, and the chair is the tool I use to enable me to move about."

This revelation caused the generation of multiple bursts of heat and pink body patterns among the four Ghosts. No translation of their infrared conversation came back through Danny's translation disk.

"Would you all kindly leave so I can get some sleep?" he asked irritably. Without waiting for their answer, he wheeled himself closer to the bed, pulled up alongside it, and dragged himself out of the chair onto it.

The Ghosts still didn't leave. Propping himself up on one elbow, Danny glared at the four Ghosts, his patience fading fast. "What do you still want?" he demanded testily.

"Jacky: We wish to examine you to understand the non-functionality of your lower body."

"Whoa," Danny said, holding up his free hand with a halting gesture. I don't want to be a lab rat for a bunch of alien mad scientists."

"Odin: You are mistaken. There is no Ghost here with the assigned name, 'Whoa.'"

"Jacky: What is a lab?"

"Pat: What is a rat?"

"Jan: We are indeed scientists, as we understand your term, but we are not angry."

Danny's lips compressed in frustration and, by counting to ten, he managed to pull a smidgeon of patience from somewhere deep inside to help him get control of his rising temper, then patiently searched for a more precise way to express himself.

"I do not wish to be harmed by your examinations or experiments or by anything else for that matter," he said simply.

"Jacky: We assure you no harm will come to you, nor will you be discomforted by, or even be aware of our examination taking place.

"Odin: We simply wish to try to learn as much as we can about beings whom we gather into our care. The knowledge we will gain from you may help us comprehend potential damage that can come to the bodies of other humans."

"Pat: We gathered much knowledge from one of Jake's human companions at the place where Jake discovered us. Back on your planet, when life left the body of the human called Marley the moment we

19

confronted him, we could not help him because of our lack of knowledge. We studied his body afterward and learned much about human biological components. However, the many types of damage that can come to a human body are still a mystery to us. Only our examination of actual damages such as that which your body bears will help us determine the abilities we will need to develop to provide future aid.

"We ask your permission to do this as we wish very much to know how it can be possible for half of a human body to be nonfunctional without causing death."

"How do I know your examination will not cause my body further damage?" Danny asked.

"Jan: We have already made such examinations with Jake's healthy human body. Small, small machines that Jake calls nanites will make the examination while you sleep."

"While I'm sleeping!" Danny yelped in surprise. "Is that why I can't get rid of you? You all want to stand around here conducting experiments while I'm sleeping?"

"Jacky: We remained only to make this request."

"I don't want to feel things crawling around inside me while I'm sleeping!" Danny protested irritably. "For that matter, I don't want to feel things crawling around inside me while I'm awake either!"

"Nanites do not crawl. They are tiny, small enough to pass through the spaces between the smallest elements of matter. You will not feel, nor even remotely sense their presence."

Exhausted and defeated, Danny just wanted to get rid of this alien quartet of pests. He didn't know whether it was due to exhaustion or something else, but he found he no longer felt the slightest fear or distrust of Ghosts. From everything he'd seen and heard, he began to believe that Jake's Ghosts might genuinely be the good guys in this nightmare of a space soap opera.

The very fact they asked for his permission reassured him that his instincts were probably correct about them. If they wanted to, they could have made their examination anyway without his knowing it. He didn't particularly care for the idea of an examination but could no longer believe the Ghosts would let any harm come to him.

With a deep sigh, he caved. "Will you please let me sleep in private if I agree to this?"

"Jacky: As we promised, we will leave. When you awaken, the examination will be concluded, and the knowledge we gain from it will be recorded for the future benefit of others of your kind."

"I hope I don't regret this, but you have my permission. Can I get some sleep now?"

"Jacky: You may sleep, and we will leave you isolated as you humans seem to prefer."

"Thanks a bunch!" Danny laid back and shoved himself with his arm to roll over on his side to present a turned back to his unwelcome guests. He no longer cared whether they left or not. He fell asleep before his head hit the pillow.

∾ ∾ ∾

An intense pain startled Danny awake four hours later. He cried out against it, his legs feeling like a thousand needles were pricking them. Terrified and wide-awake, he cursed himself for trusting the Ghosts. He frantically rubbed his legs, trying to ease the pain before it dawned on him that these were the first sensations he had felt in his legs since his accident so many years earlier.

The pain soon subsided, and he remembered feeling a similar but less intense sensation the times when one of his legs would 'fall asleep' from sitting with his weight on it for too long, thus cutting off the circulation.

Hoping against hope, he slowly reached down again and touched one leg, then the other, and found he could feel the pressure of his probing fingers on each of them. He tried to remember how to move his legs and feet and succeeded in wiggling his toes, first on one foot, then the other. The responses were weak, but they were undoubtedly successful ones.

Experimenting further, Danny found he could bend his ankle too, but when it came to lifting one of his legs, he couldn't quite achieve it. The muscles were too atrophied from lack of use over the years. It didn't matter, though; he could move again, and he could feel his entire lower body! He buried his face in his hands and wept with joy.

Chapter 4
Search Failure

In his office at the Earth Defense Headquarters in Hong Kong, Ling Wu read the report while his four fleet admirals sat across from him, their deep concern showing on their faces as they waited for him to finish. Dr. Ling was a human information sponge, constantly absorbing and analyzing all the data he received without letting emotion distract him from his concentration. Eventually, he put the report down.

"We currently have more than ten thousand, five-warrior scout teams on patrol at any given time with their numbers increasing every day," Ling Wu said, airing his thoughts aloud. "No other ships have gone missing, and none of our patrols reported finding anything unusual after an intensive search for your people. Fleet Admiral McKay, your staff officers vanished without so much as a single cry for help despite their extensive training, excellent judgment, and reflexes, and despite the availability of their instantaneous communication systems.

"We have no idea what our new allies think about this, but they must surely know of the disappearance. However, they remain their silent, introverted selves.

"I believe we can only conclude that, somehow, an enemy vessel took our men by surprise before they could call out and caused their ships to cease to exist as we've seen happen to the Stickman Swarm ships. From the power signature anomaly recorded after their disappearance, we must presume it belonged to an enemy ship and that our people are dead."

"Regretfully, we agree," Ruark said, speaking for all of them.

"I feel personally responsible," a disheveled Lee McKay said dejectedly. He'd barely slept since the search for his people began the day before. "I was the one who gave them permission to continue their exploration of Mars for a short period."

"I see no reason why you should have denied them such permission. I would have given it myself," Ling Wu dismissed. "However, we will take a lesson from this unfortunate incident and immediately put out a mandate that all scouting and sentry missions must report directly back to their home base at the end of their tour without exception. There are to be no further explorations or experiments with their ships that exceed the boundaries of their immediate orders.

"I will also order more frequent in-flight status reports from the time our people leave their bases until the time they return. We will double the patrols in the area of Mars where Colonel Duval and his men vanished, and despite our dire conclusions, we will continue to search for any clues that might reveal their fate to us."

"We'll issue the orders immediately, sir," Sue McKay promised for them all.

Ling Wu leaned back in his chair with a sigh and folded his hands in his lap. Long hours, overwork, and stress were taking a toll on him.

"Fleet Admirals, I fear this event may be the forerunner of the invasion we are expecting."

The four already believed that to be true, but it brought a chill to their hearts to hear Ling Wu come to the same conclusion.

"This intrusion comes far earlier than expected. Although we continue to receive thousands of volunteers worldwide, we still have more Dragons in our possession than we have people to fly them. You must all increase the number of training sessions, and we must strive to match the number of people who can pass training successfully to the number of incoming Dragons! Even though knowledge transfer via the Stickman devices works flawlessly, we must also look for ways to enhance the interaction between the pilots and their remarkable ships through more practice. It is the only way to ensure they can make of their newly acquired knowledge effectively."

"Fortunately, sir, thanks to the new screening methods we employ now, we've been able to reduce the washout rate," Sue McKay told Ling Wu.

"Even so, Sue, with the washout rate as low as it has become, I'm afraid sometimes the glamor of becoming an astro-aviator fighter pilot still bumps into hard reality when the volunteers find themselves in space for the first time. Accepting the possibility of being killed or disabled out there is not something a weak person can handle," Lee reminded her.

"Regardless," Pete Orsini countered with pride, "there are a lot of brave people in place already who are willing to remain out there regardless of the possible consequences. They are no different from the millions of soldiers who have been marching into battle for a couple of thousand years. To one degree or another, every member of the human race has warrior genes embedded within them."

"Studying how the human race has applied that characteristic over the centuries has been my life's work," Ling Wu agreed. "It is why I am sitting before you today."

"The men and women who are willing to brave the depths of space are truly remarkable people," Pete commented. Especially considering the mundane existence from which most of them come. Take Lieutenant Commander Murphy, for example. He told me once how isolated and routine his life used to be, yet he turned out to be an aerial combat genius! Paraplegic fighter pilots! How remarkable is that?"

"Even more extraordinary," Jackson Ruark added, "is that the people with the same disability are turning out to be the best of the volunteers. They have a gift for making their ships extensions of their bodies far beyond the abilities of the rest of us. It's incredible that out of all those volunteers with the same infirmity, not a single one has ever washed out."

Ling Wu raised an eyebrow in a rare expression of surprise. "Indeed? I must consider this as we continue to develop our strategies."

With an unsuccessfully veiled effort to hide his fatigue, he rose from his chair to take his leave. "For now, my friends, you must excuse me, for I have much to do. Before you go, though, I want to express my deepest regrets for the disappearance of our men. I know Colonel Duval became a friend to you all. I must stress, though, do not give up hope no matter what the facts seem to point to. We have seen many remarkable and unbelievable events take place these past months. Perhaps their absence is simply due to something remarkable we have yet to discover."

Chapter 5
Seeds

Duval slept for ten solid hours. He awoke and stared groggily at the dimly lit ceiling, wondering where he was, then sat bolt upright when he remembered. The light in the room immediately became brighter. Something in the room sensed his movement and automatically increased the light intensity. He looked at his watch and then shook his head, remembering whatever time it indicated didn't mean much of anything inside a spaceship having no perceivable day or night.

Knowing he and the others would soon be meeting with Ghost leaders, he went into his apartment's bathroom to clean himself up and examined the room with more interest than he felt when he used it the night before. It pleased him to find the toiletry products he required and a shower complete with hot water. After relieving himself, he stepped into the shower and turned on the water. There, he soaked himself in water as hot as he could stand for a full twenty minutes before reluctantly turning it off. At the sink, he found a can of shaving cream complete with the label of a popular brand. He squirted some into the palm of his hand and then spread it all over his stubble. However, he couldn't find one when he looked for the accompanying razor.

"Crap! The Ghosts must have thought I'd use it as a weapon somehow." Peeved, he bent down to the sink and washed off the shaving cream. He glanced at the mirror and did a double-take. Just as Jake discovered months earlier, he found that the stubble of his whiskers was gone!

"Just another damned thing human technology can't do either," he muttered to himself irritably.

He left the bathroom to get dressed, hating the thought of getting back into the unlaundered clothing he dumped on the floor before going to bed. It came as a pleasant surprise to find that not only were the garments gone from where he left them, they were folded and laid out neatly on the bedroom's dresser. Any annoyance he might have felt from the obvious conclusion that one of the Ghosts must have entered his room while he

25

slept failed to take root when he found that the uniform was clean and his boots polished without a speck of grime on them.

Noticing the dresser held several drawers, curiosity led him to find out what they contained. The top one had a set of underclothes and socks identical to the ones he wore the day before. The second drawer had three shirts and three flight suits also indistinguishable from the original, complete even to the detail of his name sewn on the pocket. He found the last drawer filled with several articles of civilian clothing. He recognized one of the shirts and a pair of pants as identical to what Jake wore the day before and wondered if they were Jake's size. He set that question aside for another time.

After dressing in a one-piece flight suit, he grabbed the boots and sat down on his bed's mattress to put them on. Lifting one from the floor, he noticed something different about them other than their being spotless. Examining them more closely, it dawned on him that they looked brand new, the wear and tear on their leather surfaces gone!

Just as he finished dressing, he heard the sound of a soft chime followed by Jake's voice coming from the translator disk around his neck, asking for permission to enter. Duval simply shouted, "Yes! Come on in!"

A portal in the wall opened up, and with a warm smile of greeting, Jake entered the room and shook Duval's hand.

"You have great timing. I just got dressed."

"Timing had nothing to do with it. The Ghosts informed me you were awake."

"Did they also tell you my stomach is screaming for food?"

"If you'll join me in my room, breakfast is ready. Captain Karlson is awake too now, and I invited him to join us too. Lieutenant Commander Murphy has been awake for hours and is eagerly awaiting us. He has something extraordinary he's bursting to show you."

Duval raised an eyebrow at that, wondering what Danny could have discovered already to get him so excited.

Duval's Ghost companion waited for him in the corridor outside his chamber, and the alien greeted them both. When the three of them entered Jake's room nearby, Danny sat at a table where platters of food awaited them. His Ghost companion stood nearby along with a third Ghost, presumably Jake's companion, Pat.

The table holding stacks of pancakes, hot coffee, fruit, eggs, and bacon drew Duval's immediate attention and made his stomach start to gurgle. Distracted, he paid no attention to Danny, already forgetting what Jake told him until Danny stood up without help and saluted Duval.

"Good morning, sir!"

Duval's raised his arm automatically to return the salute, "Good mor . . ." When he realized what he saw, he froze, his eyes going wide to stare in disbelief at the young man.

Grinning from ear to ear, Danny took an unsteady step in his direction, proud as he could be when he accomplished the feat without losing his balance.

"What the hell?" Karlson stood at the room's doorway, staring at Danny. Danny couldn't stop smiling, his assigned Ghost, Jacky, keeping close behind him presumably to help him maintain his balance if needed.

"They fixed my back, guys!" Danny told them with a cracking voice, unable to stop the tears from welling up again. "I woke up with pain in my legs last night. It was the first time in years I felt anything below the waist. The pain only lasted a few moments, but when it faded away, I could move my legs again. My companion Ghost, Jacky, came when I called and has been with me ever since. He wanted to know if I wanted them to reverse the repairs they made. Can you imagine that?" he chuckled. "Imagine asking me if I wanted to go back to being paralyzed?"

Karlson slapped him on the back, nearly knocking him off balance and having to grab him by the arms to help steady him again while offering an apology. Duval pumped Danny's hand and offered his sincere congratulations; both men thrilled to death for the young officer.

"How is this even possible? How did they do it?" Duval began to wonder if there would ever be an end to the technological miracles and wonders that kept popping up.

"Pat: We have been studying human culture and physiology since we discovered your planet. When Danny allowed us to examine him last night, our nanite scan indicated an unhealed severance of the main communication tissue in the segmented components that serve as a channel for that tissue."

"The communicative tissue is what we call the spinal cord, Pat, and we call the collection of the segmented components vertebrae that, together, form what we call our spines."

"Pat: Noted. Thank you, Jake. We have not yet determined why such a break in the spinal cord is not self-repairing, as are other components of your bodies, so we ordered the nanites to recreate the connection between the severed ends. A nanite support structure re-established the communications link, which transfers the electric pulses sent by Danny's brain. The nanites also physically repaired the damage to the segments of

Danny's spine, which we deduced coincided with the spinal cord damage."

"When they saw that I still couldn't walk after their repair, they wanted to know why, and I had to explain to them about muscle atrophy. Right now, the nanites are reinforcing my leg muscle's strength. My Ghost companion told me that, as my muscle density returns to normal, the nanite strengthening will diminish until my legs are strong enough to work unaided again! Best of all, they tell me the repairs to my spine can remain permanent!"

Duval shook his head in wonder. "You have no idea, Pat, how many humans suffer from such afflictions. Your technology could help tens of thousands of our people!"

"Pat: My people would gladly provide such help, but we may never have such an opportunity since the enemy you call Stickmen are joining together with your people to stop us from . . ." Pat stopped speaking and remained motionless for several seconds, a typical indication being in communication with others of his kind. The pause lasted several seconds.

"Pat: Our council is waiting to speak to you once you have consumed your meal. They are anxious to meet you, and they have many questions."

The four men needed no urging. Ravenous from not having eaten for more than a day, they all sat down together, with Duval first lending Danny a supportive hand to seat himself. Once they loaded their plates, they made a significant dent in the food on all the serving platters.

"Gentlemen, it's a certainty that the Ghosts are listening in on us," Duval told them, "so forget about the possibility of private conversations. However, I have to admit, from yesterday's revelations and from what the Ghosts did for Lieutenant Commander Murphy, I'm almost convinced that we can trust them.

"The evidence we've seen so far indicating that these creatures are on our side is inarguable. But keeping in mind how ingeniously the Stickmen misled us, I think we should reserve final judgment until after we talk to their council."

"I have to confess, Colonel," Karlson admitted with concern, "I'm struggling to accept all this. It's tough to believe that every bit of the information the Stickmen transferred into our minds about the Ghosts is turning out to be nothing but a pack of monstrous lies."

Jake glanced up sharply and put his coffee cup down. "Transferred into your minds? What do you mean?"

The three officers took the time to explain everything they knew about the Stickmen, the Earth Defense Force, and what the Stickman holograms taught the entire population of Earth about the Ghosts.

Jake, in turn, explained in detail how he came to be in the company of the Ghosts, their incredible talent for learning, and their inability to forget anything. He summarized everything he did with the Ghosts up to the point of capture of Duval and his men.

At the end of the meal, Duval took his napkin, dabbed at his mouth as he rose from the table, then tossed the napkin on top of his empty plate. Having lost track of which Ghost was which, he turned to the one Ghost he thought was Pat. "Please tell your leaders we're ready to meet them."

"I think you just did," Jake said, watching the opening begin to form on the chamber wall.

"Pat: Indeed, they heard your words as you spoke. However, we all have little understanding of them, and we are very much confused by most of your conversations. We have many questions to ask. Please come."

Following the Ghosts at a snail's pace to accommodate Danny, Duval advised his fighter pilots in a lowered voice, "The beings we are about to meet must be pretty damned important ones. I want you all to exercise formal military protocol."

He noted that even while Danny tried to listen, he also had to concentrate hard on each step he took. "Danny, do you want to use your chair for this?" he asked with fatherly concern. "We can still get it."

"No, Colonel. Thanks, but I never want to sit in another wheelchair again. I'd prefer to walk as long as you can put up with me being a little slow."

"No problem, son," Duval replied sympathetically.

They soon came to the chamber where the Ghost Council waited, not too far from their quarters. The Ghost leaders chose to come aboard this ship rather than transfer them to whatever ship or a planet served as their primary base.

Duval and Karlson kept close to Danny's side in case he needed help, but to Danny's delight, he made it to their destination unassisted. Another portal opened in the corridor wall, and Ghost companions of the four men led through it.

With the ingrained caution of soldiers, the EDF officers studied the chamber from the outside before stepping in. The room was large, about the size of a school gymnasium, its ceiling just as high. The lighting illuminated the chamber to the same extent as their shipboard apartments. Its gray, metallic walls were unadorned by any form of aesthetic features, but the men were pleasantly surprised to find a human-style table with chairs ready for them on one side of it; a courtesy provided by the Ghosts via an earlier suggestion by Jake.

The Ghosts made no use of furniture. Since the day he found himself aboard this ship, Jake never found anything remotely resembling furnishings of any kind that the Ghosts might use. Long ago, he concluded that every one of them remained upright throughout their entire lives.

In addition to their assigned Ghost companions, five other Ghost beings stood on the opposite side of the table. The four Ghost companions of the humans took their places behind their charges who had yet to seat themselves.

Duval ordered them to snap to attention, and his men did so in unison. He then took a step forward and gave the five Ghosts across the room a formal military salute.

"Colonel L. C. Duval, Captain Gunther Karlson, and Lieutenant Commander Daniel Murphy, Earth Defense Force, Northern Zone, reporting as requested along with civilian Jacob Bennings," Duval announced with a booming voice.

The pale, white bodies of the five Ghosts across the room rippled with the pink heat patterns of communication that the men recognized as such by now, and they could feel the pulses of heat coming from the bodies of their companion Ghosts responding behind them.

The translator disk Duval wore dangling from the cord around his neck said, "Pat: My companions and I wish to know the purpose of your hand movement to your head a moment ago and the reason for your accompanying rigid stance."

Duval didn't expect that to be the first question. The Ghosts' constant off-topic queries seemed to be endless. However, he considered how alien he and his men, themselves, must be to these creatures. They had no common frame of reference between Human and Ghost other than what little Jake and his Ghost companion already managed to establish.

"The hand movement is called a salute, and the rigid posture is called 'standing at attention.' Our warriors employ these actions as a sign of greeting and respect to our superior officers."

To let the Ghosts know that they still had a question of trust, he added, "A salute is also employed by captured military men when they must report to enemy officers in charge of their captivity. When such is the case, it is intended to show a lack of capitulation."

This explanation caused more untranslated conversations among the Ghosts laced with intermittent requests for definitions of some of Duval's words.

"Pat: My superiors are dismayed that you believe we could still be your enemies."

"Please extend my regrets to your superiors. You've provided us with quite a bit of evidence offering proof that you are indeed friends and not our enemies. However, there is so much at stake for our world and our people. For their benefit, we must reserve final judgment. My people have already been cleverly deceived by the Stickmen. For the sake of our entire world, we must make certain of your friendship. For now, please consider our salute as the same sign of respect we would present to a foreign dignitary of our planet."

"Pat: My associates understand your concern, and they are pleased by your gesture. They would also consider it an honor if you would provide them with human names as you have done for companions Jacky, Jan, Odin, and me.

"At ease, men," Duval ordered, bringing his men to a more comfortable stance before addressing the request.

Duval nodded to Jake and his people toward the available chairs, and they all took seats at the table. Duval noted Danny seemed to have less trouble sitting than he did earlier at the breakfast table, either gaining strength already or more likely adapting to the nanite reinforcement of his legs.

"Is there one here who leads the others gathered here, one who is of higher commanding rank?" he asked.

"Pat: There is." Pat sprouted a tentacle to point in the direction of one of the new Ghosts. "This Ghost is the one who leads all Ghosts everywhere. He has come far to meet with you, your men, and Jake in person. Such is the unprecedented importance of finding beings such as yourselves.

"The leader of *all* Ghosts?" Taken aback, Duval blinked in surprise and confusion. "Or do you mean the leader of the expeditionary ships already in our solar system?"

"Pat: He is the leader of all the Ghost people."

That revelation came as a shock to everyone. Distressed to find himself addressing such a powerful being, Duval knew whatever he said in this chamber today might affect not only the lives of his men but also the life of every human being in the solar system.

"I would be grateful if you would assign to me one of your human names," said the translator disk Duval had placed around his neck. The men noticed the voice came without a prefix name at the beginning of the sentence that would have identified the speaker.

Duval contemplated a new name for only a brief moment, a very proper choice for this being coming to him right away, given what he learned about the Ghost's desire to try to save the human race.

"One of the most famous leaders in the history of our world was a human named Moses. Moses saved many of his people from enemies, determined to destroy them. Do you find the name Moses to be acceptable to you?"

After another display of untranslated pink body patterns and heat waves between Pat and the Ghost leader, Duval's translator disc said, "Moses: Thank you. I would like very much for you to tell me one day about this human leader, Moses. For now, though, we have important matters to discuss once we acquire names for my four advisors."
Jake and the Earth pilots quickly came up with names for the remaining Ghosts, all of whom were part of the leader's advisory council."

"Humans who hold such high positions of authority, such as yours, are usually respectfully addressed by an honorific; a prefix to a name just like the words Colonel, Captain, or Lieutenant Commander precedes our names. By what title shall my men and I address you, Moses?"

"Simply by the name Moses as you address our scientist, Pat. We have no class and rank divisions among our race. We are all equal. I am the leader simply because I am the oldest among my people and have more experience in most endeavors. We appreciate your consideration, and we all thank you once more for the names you have given us. We welcome you! We have many urgent questions to ask, and we understand how you, too, must have many. We will try to answer them all.

"We did hear the words of your conversations before you came to us. We now understand why the Destroyers are providing your people with ships."

"Our common enemy you refer to as the Destroyers are the alien race that we humans refer to as the Stickmen," Duval explained. "They made contact with humans at a time in the past measured by approximately 150 rotations of our planet. They have been teaching the human race to believe, without a doubt, it is you, not they, who are the destroyers of civilizations, and that you Ghosts exist only to exterminate all civilized beings of the planets you encounter."

He paused and added. "I must tell you; my men and I held those same doubts about your Ghost people until you rescued us from destruction, and we learned it was Stickmen themselves who tried to destroy us. We are grateful to you for saving our lives."

Duval's words caused another frenzy of communication among the Ghosts in the chamber, enhanced by tentacles springing from various Ghost bodies to wave frantically. The waving of tentacles indicated a level of extreme agitation among the Ghosts that even Jake hadn't seen before.

When the frenzy died down, the Ghost leader moved closer to the humans. "Moses: As we informed you, Ghosts do not kill!" Duval's translator disc spoke in the usual monotone of Jake's voice, but no one doubted the adamancy behind Moses' statement.

"The Destroyers, the beings you call the Stickmen, are the killers. These Stickmen eradicate *all* life they purposely seek out, not just civilized beings. There were many, many worlds and many beings, great and small, who have fallen before them."

"We would like to believe what you are telling us," Duval responded. "You have all been very kind to us, and we no longer doubt that Stickmen are our enemies. Their attempt to kill us made that very clear. However, despite how well you've treated us all, we still have no evidence that you Ghosts are not deceiving us too.

"We believed what the Stickmen told us because they presented to the people of my planet images of your ships destroying the cities of other planets. We still do not know if those images were real or not, but since their ships tried to kill us, we certainly have grave doubts about everything they showed us."

"Moses: The Destroyers spread across space. Their hunger for new worlds and their thirst for eradicating all alien life forms cannot be quenched. We, the beings you call Ghosts, move across space before them, gathering seeds to save.

Duval began to comprehend that the constant reference to 'seeds' must be something more important than what he and his men concluded earlier. "We've heard the term 'seeds' mentioned many times. To us, seeds are from what Earth plant life grows. My men and I don't understand why seeds are so important. Please explain this to us."

"Moses: We understand the word, seeds, as you do, but we use the term metaphorically. We, too, record images for our records. We will present to you some images of our seed gathering efforts, so you will understand what we Ghosts mean by the term."

Seconds later, an image began to form on the chamber wall next to their table. Blurry at first with some dark areas where nothing appeared at all, a few answered questions asked by the Ghosts regarding how much of the image humans could see soon enabled the Ghosts to readjust the image. With the image colors still a bit out of skew and slightly blurry, they had no trouble making out the full images.

"Moses: This is how our Seed ships gather our seeds."

On the wall, a scene developed showing thousands of spherical ships descending into the atmosphere of an unknown world whose surface held three large continents surrounded and separated by emerald-green seas. The ships in the scene were identical to the ones shown in the Stickman holograms. Above the planet, a bluish-white moon resembling a massive frozen snowball orbited in the distance.

The image focused on the activity of one of the ships racing down through the planet's atmosphere and stopping just above an alien city of tall cylinders connected with filaments of magnificent crystal bridges.

A silvery dome of haze formed around the ship. It appeared to solidify and expand downward and outward in every direction, just like the Stickman holograms had displayed. As solid as the silvery wall seemed to be, as it made contact with the city's structures, it flowed around them to absorb them within.

When most of the city became enclosed, the dome stopped growing. Miles high and across, it concealed from view everything encased within it. Slowly it began to rise, revealing itself as a shell whose bottom half reached as deeply into the soil as its upper half rose into the sky, encasing not only the city but also the ground beneath it. As it ascended like an enormous elongated bubble, it left behind a smooth-walled crater where the city used to be.

The scene raised the hair on Duval's neck. Karlson and Murphy were equally affected. The recorded images were exactly like those the Stickmen revealed to the entire world. The Stickman holograms weren't lies after all!

"You're destroying them!" Karlson accused. "Our planet is nothing to you all but a prize to be won by whichever alien race proves to be strongest!"

He rose threateningly from his chair, fully intending to do as much bodily harm as he could to the Ghosts around him, but an abrupt increase in a gravity field imposed around him dragged him back into his seat.

Pat intervened. "Pat: As we have patiently tried to explain, Ghosts do not kill. These cities are the seeds we gather. Continue to observe and learn, Captain Karlson." A tentacle shot out of Pat's body to point in the direction of the images.

Aghast, the humans watched the image of the bubble rising above the planet, gathering speed as it left the atmosphere. The view panned back, and similar shells became visible, rising all over the planet. The scene continued to duplicate what the Stickman holograms showed them all along. Unlike the Stickman holograms, instead of flying sunward to hurtle the cities into the planet's star, one by one, each of the ships winked out of existence just outside the planet's atmosphere.

The scene changed to show the same ships popping back into existence on the outskirts of another solar system. Hundreds of ships advanced sunward toward the second world out from the sun. As the planet came closer, it became apparent that it was very similar to the Earth, this planet differing only by having more land than oceans. Ten green continents, unmarred by the scars of civilization, were scattered between the white ice caps at the planet's poles, all of them surrounded by green oceans indistinguishable in color from Earth's seas.

Again, the image focused on one of the spherical ships as it plunged into the atmosphere toward a pre-formed nesting crater on the surface. The silvery sphere identical to the ones created when the ships lifted the cities into the sky arrowed straight to the crater's center, on their homeworld. The surface of the silvery sphere fit into it perfectly.

Once settled, the sphere's shell receded back toward the ship that generated it to reveal the captured city once more, intact but transplanted without harm onto the new world. All over the planet, identical ships were depositing their cargoes of transplanted seeds of civilization.

"Fascinating," an awestruck Jake whispered to himself as he watched the image. "Now I know what they mean by 'seeds.' Those cities literally *are* seeds for that alien culture to grow from once again on another planet."

Karlson's anger changed to humiliation as he watched the image unfold. When it was over, he stammered out an apology. "I'm sorry, Moses. The first part of the scenes you presented matches exactly what the Stickmen have shown us. That's why I accused you all of lying to us. In the Stickman holograms, your ships ejected the captured cities into their planet's sun rather than taking them somewhere else to be transplanted." After Karlson's apology, the intensified gravity holding him to his chair vanished.

"We all owe the Ghost people an apology," Duval added. "But since we understand at last what you mean by 'seeds,' we would like to know why you and your people do this, especially when it takes such a terrible toll in Ghost lives to accomplish it?"

"Moses: Please continue to watch. What we are about to show you happened mere moments after the last of our Seed ships carried away their cargo. For this unfortunate world, we could not return in time to gather any more seeds."

The images on the wall formed again with more scenes of the planet. Even though the world appeared pocked with craters where hundreds of cities used to be, there were still hundreds of cities and outlying population centers all over this unnamed world.

Out of the planet's blue sky, thousands of swarms of Stickman fighter ships descended and began blasting apart structures and living things alike wherever they encountered them, concentrating most on anything that might possibly be defensive in nature. Then, in unison, all of the attacking fighter ships broke off their raid and soared back into space.

High above the planet's atmosphere, ten colossal, sickle-shaped dreadnoughts closed in, ships of a type the humans never observed before. Clouds of Stickman fighter ships preceded each dreadnought, forming vanguards of protective shields for their mother ships. Compared to the size of the smaller fighter ships, each dreadnought appeared to be at least ten miles wide and several miles deep, front to back.   As the attack swarms returned to the great ships after their devastating sweep of the planet, they sped past the guardian swarms and entered the dreadnoughts that also served as their base.

In unison, the colossal ships spread apart to create a ring formation wide enough to encircle the planet, the sickle blade side of their spacecraft pointing toward the center of the circle. The attack formation of the giant ships then advanced slowly forward, navigating so the world below would pass right through the ring's center. The blade edge of each vessel soon began to glow a brilliant white that faded to a barely visible violet color. With a purple flash, a curtain of ultra-hard radiation, thousands of miles in diameter, filled the center of the ring between the ships to link them all together with a wall of lethal energy.

When the ships advanced to where the wall of energy made first contact with the atmosphere, the upper clouds exploded into steam wherever the sheet of hard radiation met them. A supersonic tidal wave of superheated atmosphere advanced with a cyclonic force that demolished and flattened everything in its path. Close behind that devastating wavefront came a solid wall of superheated steam that mere moments before were part of the planet's oceans, lakes, and rivers.

By the time the doomed alien world passed entirely through the deadly ring, the planet's entire atmosphere turned into a pyroclastic cloud of steam and ashes that hid the planet's surface below. The four men watching the scene knew that nothing could have survived such an attack, even down to the smallest microbe. These final images faded from the wall. All four were staggered by the cold-blooded, merciless destruction they had just witnessed. Any doubts they had left about the Ghosts were gone.

"Moses: As you have seen, even though those ships exterminated the life left behind on this planet, we Ghosts prevented its native forms of life from becoming extinct. All of our seeds will grow somewhere further away than the Stickmen can ever find them again. This is why we do what we do."

"Good Lord!" Tears streamed down Jake's face. He felt like an icy hand gripped his heart. He rose to his feet and pleaded with Duval and his men, "We've got to find a way to stop this from happening to Earth! We have to do something!"

"What *can* we do?" Karlson asked. "With our technology, we're not much more than monkeys in the trees by comparison to either one of these alien races."

"Moses: Your technical intellect may be in its infancy, but your courage and lack of hesitation to endanger yourselves and even sacrifice your lives for others places your *moral* intellect on a level equal to ours. It is the force of that same morality that necessitates the Ghost people to preserve as many of your species as we can, no matter what the cost."

Duval remained silent for a moment as he contemplated the enormity of the danger the human race faced and their ignorance of it. "The Ghosts are right about one thing," he told his friends, unable to keep the frustration and anger from his voice. "With both the EDF and the Stickmen to oppose them, they'll be lucky if they can get a single Seed ship past our defenses to save even one of our cities. Ghost losses will be terrible.

"Once our people stop the Ghosts, what's to stop the Stickmen from turning on us. They've really stacked the deck against us. Humanity may very well be doomed if we do nothing. Our friends, our families, our homes; they'll all be gone."

He looked around at the anxious faces turned to him. "Jake's right! We can't let that happen. We have to figure out something!"

"How?" Karlson asked hopelessly. "If we try to warn anyone either by radio or by thought communications, the Stickmen will surely catch on. They can blow up every Dragon defender we have."

"And if we try to sneak back and they catch us, the same thing will happen," Danny reminded them.

"There has to be a solution!" Jake pleaded. "I have a family. My brother and my sisters have kids! I don't want them to die! I want to see my home again!"

"We all have families, Jake," Duval said sympathetically, "and we all want to go home again too."

"There is still something puzzling me, Moses," Karlson spoke up. "You believe the Stickmen have been in our solar system for many years lying in wait for you. How did you get a ship through to land on Earth and remain undetected long enough to grab Jake from the forest and pluck Colonel Duval out of the sky?"

"Moses: We captured and released Colonel Duval to demonstrate we mean no harm to your people, and we took Jake with us because he was injured and in need of care, but we did not go undetected. The Destroyers, the Stickmen as you call them, allowed us to land on your planet unmolested. This is not unprecedented. They have done this in the past to allow us to study the worlds of their intended victims."

"Why would they do such a thing?" Karlson asked, mystified by the revelation.

"Moses: Because they want to put an end to our opposition. They understand us well enough to know that when they reach a life-bearing star system before we do, the more they allow us to learn about the lifeforms on their targeted worlds, the greater our efforts will be to save at least some of them from extinction. They know we will have to send many of our Seed ships through the gauntlet of their opposing forces to make it possible for even a few of our surviving ships to take seeds."

"Concerning your world, they will undoubtedly want to lure as many of us into your solar system as possible. The Stickmen know that the number of our Seed ships they can destroy will be unprecedented, considering that your species will join them in their eradication.

"Even though their strategy is exposed, it makes no difference to us. We must still send our ships to rescue what we can of your species, no matter the cost. Your race must not become extinct." Moses stopped speaking as a burst of communicative heat came from another Ghost.

"Moses: Yes, as Pat has just explained one of your expressions to me, they are killing two birds with one stone by using your people against us."

Duval stood and addressed the Ghost across the table, whom he knew to be Moses. "Once again, my men and I apologize for doubting you. Until now, we had no way to see through the Stickmen's elaborate and very convincing deception."

Duval looked at the faces of Jake and his men; all turned expectantly to him. He knew they counted on him to do *something* but had no idea what that something could be. With a look of pure determination, he said to the Ghosts, "There once lived a very famous general who believed that, no matter how deadly a trap you fall into, if you keep your head, don't panic, and think things through carefully, there is always a means of escape. Together, we must find that means. There *has* to be one! Please work with us, Moses. The favorite expression of one of our fleet admirals is 'Never give up!'"

"Moses: We Ghosts are not warriors. We do not understand why you would not wish to keep your heads since your deaths would result otherwise, but we will gladly help you search for a solution any way we can. Tell us how you would like to proceed."

Chapter 6
Recovery

Duval, Karlson, and Murphy watched, fascinated, as the hull of the ship's hangar opened up to reveal bright clusters and groups of stars that were never seen before by human eyes. Wherever in the universe this place was, there were three or four times the stars out there that Earth's skies held. Brilliant stars scattered in clusters everywhere formed constellations that would never have names. A dozen galaxies appeared so close that the men, with unaided eyes, could make out their shapes.

Even though the hangar portal remained open to the vacuum of space, Ghost technology somehow managed to keep the chamber's atmosphere from escaping. The three men stood close to the opening, mesmerized by the glory of the stars outside as they waited.

"There they are!" Murphy said excitedly, the first to see the approach of the distant, tiny dots of three ships. The three men knew those ships were disabled thanks to whatever technological tricks the Ghosts managed to subject them to, but they didn't care; the three Dragons were a welcome sight. They approached in line as if their pilots controlled them, but some invisible force was actually towing them toward the Ghost ship. One by one, they passed through the opening just a few feet in front of the human observers, where they came in direct contact with the hangar deck just like the Dragons of the day before. Unlike the previous day's delayed events, holes began to form immediately on the hulls of the newly arrived ships.

Joshua Harkins appeared first, poking his head cautiously out of one of the openings. His face split into a huge grin of relief when he saw his fellow officers coming to greet him. Cries of joy and relief came from both Jethro Hawks and Homer Bigsby as they, too, emerged from their Dragons.

None of the three noticed that a ramp formed out of the hangar deck instead of their Dragons. All three strode joyfully down the ramps,

40

throwing formality to the wayside as they exchanged handshakes, and even hugs, with questions flying from everyone at the same time.

"One question at a time, boys, starting with mine!" Duval shouted. "First of all, are you men alright?"

"Yes, sir, but that was certainly no fun. Stickmen to the rescue, I take it?" Joshua Harkins asked as he took in the enormity of the hangar.

"Uh, not exactly," Karlson answered sheepishly, looking somewhat at a loss for how to provide an answer and passing that problem off to Duval with a deer-in-the-headlights look in his direction.

Puzzled by the response, Harkins raised one eyebrow questioningly and searched all of their faces as he waited for an explanation.

With a deep sigh, Duval simply told them, "Gentlemen, we have a lot of catching up to do."

With the search and rescue for the three lost Dragon fighters completed, the Ghosts kept out of sight, as requested, while Duval, Murphy, and Karlson took the three newcomers to the conference room where'd they'd met with the Ghosts a few hours earlier. There, they took the time they needed to break things as gently as possible as they updated the three new arrivals.

Harkins, Bigsby, and Hawks all went through the same difficulty accepting the fact that everything they believed about the Ghosts proved to be nothing but an enormous pack of lies. Even though they trusted the judgment of their commanding officer and friends, their doubt remained until Duval used his translator disk to make a remote request for the Ghosts to provide a replay of the images of the Ghost Seed ships rescuing alien cities.

Still keeping out of sight, the Ghosts complied with his wishes and, in moments, the scene of a Seed ship rescue played once more on the council chamber wall. When it ended, Danny Murphy learned even more imaginatively colorful phrases he'd never heard before from the three recovered fighter pilots, all as equally convinced and outraged of the Stickman deception as Duval, Karlson, and Murphy.

When the debriefing ended after the scenes of the Seed ship rescue, Duval knew Hawks, Bigsby, and Harkins must be exhausted from all they'd been through, including being lost in space and the shock of learning the truth about the Stickmen. Earlier, he and his men left Jake with the Ghosts to prepare new living quarters for recovered pilots, and he knew the rooms would be ready for them by now.

Duval, Karlson, and Murphy led their rescued friends back to those chambers next to the other living quarters. There, Duval introduced them to Jake, his presence a minor detail Duval neglected to mention during their initial debriefing. Even though the sight of a seventh human guest of the Ghosts came as a surprise, they were as happy to meet Jake as he was to meet them.

Introductions completed, the three new arrivals retreated to their new quarters to get some rest, having received enough shocks for one day. Tomorrow, they would meet their alien hosts for the first time.

~ ~ ~

The next 'morning,' humans and Ghosts gathered once more in the same conference chamber where they'd held their previous meetings. Duval, Danny, and Karlson, comfortable and familiar, at last, with the Ghosts, greeted Moses and his advisors no differently than they would have received old friends back on Earth. Jake, accepted now as one of the team, eagerly participated in the proceedings, hoping to contribute in whatever way he could. As before, the humans took seats on one side of the conference table while the Ghosts remained standing on the opposite side.

This meeting being the newcomers' first encounter with Ghosts, Bigsby blindly groped for his chair to take a seat, unable to quit staring stupidly up at the Ghost directly across from him. He had the same expression a person would have who just witnessed a third arm sprout from another man's forehead.

With pale faces, Harkins and Hawks appeared that they both wished they were still lost in space despite what Duval told them about the Ghosts. On the other hand, Duval was thrilled to death to have lived long enough to witness something finally managing to keep *both* Harkins' and Hawks' mouths shut. With the situation this grave, the time had finally come for both of them to grow up. Billions of lives depended on what strategies the few men in this room could devise to help the Ghosts with what they considered the most essential 'seed' gathering mission in their history. Jake handed out three more translator disks hanging on cords along with a brief explanation of their purpose.

The leader of all the Ghosts began the meeting. "Moses: We welcome all of you, and we are very pleased to meet three new humans." Moses' voice came from Duval's translator disk this time.

Duval responded, "I would like to introduce these three men who are also under my command. They are Lieutenant Commanders Joshua Harkins, Homer Bigsby, and Jethro Hawks," he said, pointing to each man as he stated their names. "They have already informed me of their desire to have the Ghosts to refer to them by their first names the same way Lieutenant Commander Murphy prefers. You may call them Joshua,

Homer, and Jethro." He pointed to each man as he spoke his name to clarify which name belonged to whom.

Harkins gave a barely perceptible wave as Jake named him. Hawks provided a nod, and Bigsby just stared, scarcely aware of the proceedings until Karlson sitting next to him jabbed an elbow in his ribs.

"Moses: We welcome our new friends, and we honor your selfless efforts to save your companions during the combat we witnessed, even though you must have known you could not possibly have survived the outcome. We will do everything we can to make your stay with us comfortable."

The praise Moses gave them took all three men by surprise and made them feel a bit more at ease among these hideous-looking beings.

"Colonel Duval, all Ghosts present in this chamber understand this will be a meeting to try to find a way to prevent the extinction of the people of your planet by the beings you call Stickmen. As I informed you yesterday, we Ghosts have never conducted offensive war in our entire history. We are ignorant of its ways other than to do what we can to defend ourselves in the manner you have already witnessed. Since we have no idea how to begin a meeting such as this one, may we yield the leadership of this meeting to you, Colonel Duval?"

"Of course, Moses, I would be happy to direct the proceedings of this council if you prefer. I've already given our problems a great deal of thought, and I think we all need to start from the very beginning. I'd like you to tell us everything you know about the Stickmen."

"Moses: That is simple enough, Duval. We Ghosts estimate that the Destroyers, those you call the Stickmen, have been devastating this arm of your galaxy for more than three thousand years in your measurement of time. With every star system they overrun, their numbers grow. The number of star systems the enemy envelops increases exponentially as they continue to expand outward simultaneously in all directions from each conquered world. They presently infest hundreds of solar systems where they eradicated every form of native life. Their homeworld is at the center of a vast, enemy-sterilized volume of space. Your world, Earth, is one of many worlds located directly in the path of their expansion.

"For the tens of thousands of your years that we have been a space-faring race. Since our beginnings of space exploration, our mission was always to send out research ships by the thousands to study and catalog the variety of life forms throughout the universe. By sheer chance, just over two thousand of your years ago, one of our research vessels uncovered one of the senseless acts of destruction and carnage conducted by the Destroyers, as we refer to them, as they consumed yet another solar system. When they detected our ship, it barely escaped destruction from an attack by thousands of their ships identical to yours.

"It took our people over thirty of your years just to uncover and map the magnitude of this plague. During this period, to our great sorrow and distress, we witnessed two more solar systems fall, the native lifeforms of both of those star systems lost forever.

"Afterward, we chose to dedicate ourselves to prevent this mindless obliteration of life that we, as a people, so revere. We began by bidding our Seed ships to move out in advance of this blight to harvest as many life forms as we could gather to prevent their total extinction.

"While we mourned the enormous loss of life extinguished by the Destroyers, we took comfort knowing the seeds we transplanted on other worlds would once again thrive someday far beyond the Destroyers' reach."

"But if your people can travel anywhere in the universe, and you so can so easily render their ships and weapons harmless as you did ours, your technology must be vastly superior to the technology of the Stickmen," Joshua Harkins reasoned. He found the Ghosts' story so fascinating, his uneasiness of them so near was almost forgotten. "Why haven't you been able to use your technology to stop them?"

"Moses: Although the technology of the Destroyers is indeed primitive compared to ours, our technological advantages are countered and negated by their vastly superior and overwhelming numbers. When we advance upon a solar system as a fleet, we exit our gateways at its outer reaches. As our Seed ships race across the distance to reach the Destroyer's targeted planets, they cluster tightly together for mutual defense. Regardless, vast numbers of the Destroyers' ships overwhelm and destroy many of us. While we send thousands of them elsewhere, there are still far too many of them for us to send all of them.

"Please do not think we regularly engage the Stickmen this way. We make these sacrifices only when we fail to arrive at a targeted solar system ahead of them. We accept and endure this conflict only when there is no other way to salvage the seeds of life-forms that are about to be eradicated forever."

Danny shook his head as if trying to clear it and looked questioningly at his friends to see if they too perceived something wrong with the picture Moses painted. Obviously, they didn't.

"When you say you send these ships elsewhere, how do you know the act doesn't result in the death of the Stickmen in the ships you send away?"

The question caused multiple untranslated pink patterns and accompanying bursts of body heat to form among all the Ghosts present, an indication of their agitation. It took several seconds to receive a response to the question.

"Moses: Although we strive not to kill directly, we concede delivering their ships 'elsewhere' may lead to the eventual death of those we send, but we have never known that to be a certainty. The difference may be insignificant to your species perhaps, but it makes a great deal of difference to us."

"What they don't know doesn't hurt them," Bigsby murmured to himself.

"Moses: To our sorrow, billions of life forms have died because of our inability to stop the Destroyers. If you humans, with your history of warfare, succeed in formulating a successful strategy capable of saving even one additional life, we Ghosts will be forever grateful."

Unable to see a solution, Jake despairingly told the Dragon pilots, "With the entire force of your EDF Dragon ships joining the Stickmen to destroy Ghost Seed ships, I don't see how any of them are going to reach Earth to save anyone. It's hopeless! They will slaughter the Ghosts!" He found himself on the verge of tears, fearing for his family and friends back home.

"As I mentioned earlier, our fleet admiral, Pete Orsini, is fond of saying, 'Never give up!'" Duval reminded Jake sharply. Duval and his men were far from the point of giving up themselves. On the contrary, they found everything Moses told them to be useful information. Their minds, filled with the tactics and experiences of the best fighter pilots on the planet, evaluated all the angles to find anything they could use to their advantage.

Duval turned to Murphy. "Danny, starting with you, you've turned out to be one of the best aerial combat tacticians we've ever seen. Does anything come to mind right out of the gate?"

Danny's eyes held a faraway look. Ignoring his commanding officer's question, he asked, "Moses, you say when you travel to another solar system, you emerge far at its edges as a group. Is there any way an individual ship can emerge more precise locations from these 'gateways,' as you call them?"

As the Ghost Chief Scientist, Pat answered this question. "Pat: In truth, our ships can all arrive at even the furthest destinations in the universe with great precision, but only if we have a ship or a device at the targeted location emitting what you would call a beacon signal. Via wormhole transmissions, these devices provide detectable target signals for our ships home in on, as you humans would say.

Suppose, for instance, that we wish to travel to distant star systems or galaxies where we have never explored before. In that case, we send unoccupied robotic beacon ships to our targeted destination to a point far from where large masses or debris might exist. From the data it sends to us, we correct the influences of gravitational forces affecting our exit points, thus avoiding the possibility of collision with resident planetary objects or other masses, great or small, when we emerge from our wormholes.

"Then why don't you deploy a beacon closer to your objective when you launch such a mission?"

"When we wish to enter an occupied solar system where we wish to gather seeds, our beacons are planted far outside the solar system to avoid their discovery which would provide the enemy with an advance warning of our pending arrival."

Now Karlson raised questions based on what Pat told them. "Once you arrive at the outskirts of a solar system, does your technology allow you to employ shorter wormhole jumps safely within a solar system?

"Pat: It does."

"Then why don't your fleets make short leaps toward your targets rather than speed through 'normal' space where the Stickman swarms can attack you?"

"Pat: Once our ships encapsulate themselves along with a population center, they can no longer send attacking Stickman ships elsewhere; they are defenseless. Even then, our Seed ships can absorb a great deal of the energy that the Destroyer's weapons direct against them, but there is a limit to that capability. The more enemy vessels that attack a single Seed ship, the sooner its protective shell fails, thus causing the destruction of the vessel and the lifeforms it carries.

"To our advantage, the Destroyers seem unable to resist being drawn to us, en masse. Luring them away from our targeted planet and allowing them to attack us enables us to greatly reduce the numbers of their ships that will ultimately prey on our Seed ships as they rise from a planet. We do lose Seed ships as we make our approach, but far less than we would if we jump, as you say, directly to the planet where they would be quickly overwhelmed as they rise with their captured population centers."

Jethro Hawks asked the following question, "Are you able to tell whether or not a human is flying a Stickman ship?"

"Pat: Quite easily. From our studies of life forms throughout the universe, we have developed a way to detect and measure biological signatures, radiations of life given off by every living creature, even if enclosed by a structure such as a ship. If we did not witness your ships engaged in combat with the larger vehicles, we would still have detected humans occupying them rather than the Destroyers."

"Auras," Jake told his new friends, happy to finally find something to contribute. "There have been reports of people being able to photograph what they called auras, which are supposed to be a kind of glow every living thing gives off. It's even speculated that a person's health can be determined by the color and radiance of their aura. It's a claim largely dismissed by the scientific community."

"Pat: Your scientific community has dismissed a fundamental, natural phenomenon, one we heavily make use of in our studies and research of life."

"Let's set aside the discussion about auras for later," Murphy suggested rather impatiently. He had another idea that relied heavily on the answer to his next question. "You sent my three friends here to a place where you could recover them. Did you have a beacon in place there?"

"Pat: We did not. We could not send them to the vicinity of one of our ships already serving as beacons since we believed, in all probability, your men would attack such a ship once they discovered it on their ship's sensors.

"Are you contemplating that such beacons might serve as a possible solution to saving some of your people? As I indicated, the warriors defending your world would surely attempt to destroy any beacon ships they find after our ships send them to another gathering point in the universe. With that destruction, we would lose our ability to send any more of your defending ships to that destination, would we not?"

"Not if one of the six of us were there to greet them," Danny answered with a sly grin.

"Damn! Murphy is as big a sneak as Harkins! He fits right into our little fraternity," an impressed Homer Bigsby told his companions.

"Thanks, Homer," Danny replied uncertainly. "I think."

Murphy's idea generated a frenzy of untranslated discussion among the Ghosts. Jake, long accustomed to dealing with the Ghosts and acquiring some insight into their body language, assured Duval and his men that, without a doubt, Murphy's solution excited them.

"Moses: Such a simple solution," Moses responded at last, "We can prepare for this immediately. We take great joy in this plan that will allow us to salvage the lives of many of your human warriors during the coming conflict.

"We can't go home, and we can't use the thought communications systems, but I have an idea of how to send a message home anyway," Duval said with a gleam in his eye.

In the hours of planning that followed, the Ghost Council found themselves awed by human military strategy as much as the humans were amazed by Ghost technology.

Chapter 7
First Intrusion

Forty-year-old Major Hans Schiller never grew weary of patrol duty. The beauty of the solar system and the vast emptiness of outer space filled with the colors of more stars than anyone could ever see through the thickness of Earth's atmosphere filled him with a deep, calming sense of reverence for it all.

Six months ago, in what seemed like another life, Hans served as a Captain in the German Luftwaffe's Tactical Training Group. Because of his skill and experience, Earth Defense Forces quickly snatched him up and trained him as an instructor, one of the very first.

At first, Schiller felt apprehensive about flying deep into outer space, but to his surprise, he took to space travel naturally. It thrilled him to find that the moons, the planets, the asteroid belt, and all the mysterious features of the solar system he'd been fascinated with since childhood were, incredibly, within his reach. From his patrol assignments, his dreams of seeing them for himself had already come true several times over. He felt an intoxicating feeling of freedom born from racing through the depths of outer space, and for him, the further out he traveled, the more he loved it.

The sensation of his ship becoming an extension of his body when he took mental control made it easy for him and thousands of others like him to adapt to outer space. When he soared out into the skies, his ship flawlessly responded instantly to every thought he directed to it.

Schiller found his initial duties as an EDF instructor kept him too close to Earth for his tastes, so he requested and was granted an appointment as a deep space scout leader in the Scouting Service of the EDF. The Scouting Service was a temporary branch of the EDF that would become disbanded when the solar system's defense grid became fully manned. Presently, EDF scouts were tasked with reconnoitering the solar system's outer reaches for the first signs of invaders to provide advance warning to

Earth. At this point in the incomplete development of the defense grid, they would be the first to deal with any detected intruders.

For the last two weeks, the orders given to the entire EDF Patrol Service emphasized being alert for any sign of the six missing Dragon ships. The mystery of their disappearance served as a chilling reminder to Schiller and all EDF Dragon pilots to be diligent at all times.

Schiller gazed out at the vista of stars through the viewing field and contemplated that enigmatic disappearance once again. The missing men were not only experienced and highly trained Astro-Aviators, but they were also key people in the EDF battle tactics unit, the last people anyone would expect to vanish without a trace. Given the instantaneous communication capability of all Dragon ships, a distress call should have come through from at least one of the missing ships, but such a call never came.

With a mentally commanded order to his tactical hologram, a three-dimensional view of the entire solar system filled the display. It revealed the power signatures of more than two million ships gleamed as pinpoints of green light. Together they formed a gridwork of concentric spheres expanding outward from the Earth, the outermost sphere achieving a radius well past Jupiter's orbit. If the grid had reached this level of expansion two weeks earlier, the six missing pilots might never have vanished.

A voice via the thought communications system broke Schiller's reverie. "Each day, they send us further and further out, Herr Major."

Schiller not only recognized the voice, but the thought communications system let him know it belonged to First Lieutenant Manfred Ludwig, one of the four other members of his scout team. Schiller readjusted his hologram to display a relatively local volume of nearby space and easily identified the location of Ludwig's Dragon ship a little more than a light-minute away. The other three ships of his team were also spread apart by the same distance. Chatter between pilots was never discouraged. It alleviated the boredom many Dragon ship scout and grid sentry pilots experienced during long missions.

"The further out they send us means, the stronger our defenses have become. Soon they will no longer need us as patrol scouts. We will be absorbed into the defense grid."

"Our days of spacefaring will be over when that time comes," came the voice of Second Lieutenant Hanna Mueller, one of the many thousands of recruited female Dragon fighter pilots and another member of Schiller's scout team. Communication links always remained public within scout teams.

"Once the EDF shifts us into the Sentry Corps, we will have to sit in this vast emptiness with our only movement limited to maintaining our grid position with respect to Earth as it moves around the sun." Hanna also shared Schiller's love of roaming the solar system. She, too, found the new assignment looming ahead too depressing to contemplate. "After so many free-flying scout missions, I fear we will feel like dogs chained to stakes in their backyards."

"There is an invasion coming," Schiller reminded her unnecessarily. "The boredom of such sentry duty will not last long. We must serve as ordered and be thankful for every day there is still peace. It will be we, the sentries, who will go to battle, and our casualties will be many."

He leaned back into the pilot seat as he spoke. The silvery mass reshaped and molded itself slightly to optimize his comfort. Schiller readjusted his tactical display to scan the outskirts of the solar system far beyond the orbits of the outer dwarf planets. His patrol's route sent them roaming to a distance out from the sun equal to that of the orbit of Neptune.

"The Major is quite right," said Second Lieutenant Friedrich Gudgast solemnly. The war, when it comes, will be a terrible one. Let us all wish for as much 'boredom' as God is willing to grant us."

"I, for one, will gladly accept the boredom of sentry duty while we wait," came the voice of the fourth member of Schiller's team, First Lieutenant Wolfgang Koenig.

Koenig barely finished his sentence when the tactical systems of the entire team came alive, mentally alerting them all to an anomaly. A bright red dot representing an unknown power signature popped in out of nowhere in their tactical holograms, its location far beyond Pluto.

Schiller's heart began to race as he studied the hologram carefully. His ship's sensors mentally fed him the statistics on the incoming object. They eliminated the possibility of the mystery object being an incoming Stickman ship or a rogue cadet on a joy ride. Whatever it was definitely did not exist out there moments earlier and could only have emerged from a wormhole. The mental alerts from his ship's sensors kicked up several notches as it analyzed more information and verified it to be an enemy ship.

With a simple mental command, he directed his thought communications to a general broadcast mode to all Earth Defense Force ships and all Fleet Headquarters.

This is Major Han's Schiller, Southern Defense Zone Patrol 482 reporting. We have detected an enemy spacecraft, inbound, originating in sector Charlie 104. Repeat, there is an enemy spacecraft, inbound, sector Charlie 104."

Schiller knew that, even though he spoke aloud, it was only his thoughts being transmitted instantaneously to the entire net of guardian sentries and scout Dragons throughout the solar system as well as back to Earth Command. He hoped his transmission didn't include his anxiety, apprehension, and excitement along with those thoughts.

"The intruder's present speed will have him crossing the outermost defense perimeter in 2 hours and 7 minutes."

Backup confirmations came pouring in from the other patrol ships.

"This is Captain Trami Sunan, Southern Defense Patrol 170, confirming Major Schiller's readings." Captain Sunan was eight light-minutes away.

"Hernandez, Eastern Defense Grid patrol 237, also confirming," came a report from the patrol leader in an adjacent sector.

With their primary duty of discovering and reporting the intruder's entry into the solar system completed, Schiller's duty shifted to the interception and destruction of the presumed enemy ship. Keeping a watchful eye on the incoming bogey, Schiller held his position while the nearest ninety-nine ships raced to his location, most of them scout teams, a few coming from the outermost limits of the defense grid. Because Schiller's squadron was closest to the inbound ship, he, as a squadron leader, automatically became responsible for commanding the Centurion squadron that would form around him soon.

∿ ∿ ∿

Fleet Admiral Pete Orsini sat in his headquarters command chair at the center of his vast, tactical hologram when Schiller's urgent message came in. Schiller and his scouts belonged to his command. A spherical tactical hologram enveloped him, representing the solar system, his half to defend displayed directly above him and surrounding him.

Since Orsini's zone represented the southern half of the solar system, the planets in his hologram orbited the sun in the reverse direction of how they would usually be depicted. Earth's South Pole would appear above him if Pete chose to superimpose the Earth's outline around him. Jackson Ruark and Susan both shared half of his hologram to provide reinforcements if necessary.

Schiller's alert was a redundant one. His headquarters' tactical system already alerted Pete of the intruder at the same instant Schiller's tactical system made Schiller aware of it. The scout commander's message simply verified the validity of the alarm. Orsini's tactical system told him the distance to the invading ship measured just over one light-hour solar south of Pluto's orbit.

The Dragon fleets Orsini commanded were the primary defenders of the solar system in the zone where the intruder arrived. Susan McKay and Jackson Ruark were responsible for providing support, if needed, to the halves of Pete's zone where their defense zones overlapped his, but their primary responsibilities were to defend Earth and the volume of space closest to it.

"We have multiple confirmations of the bogey, Pete. The first one is all yours!" Susan called out. "It's within my sector too, so I'll have reserve support readily available if you need it."

Orsini's hands shook from a rush of adrenalin, whether from fear or excitement, he didn't know or care. He was glad none of his friends could see it. "Yeah, this is just wonderful; the first contact we get is in *my* zone! These are the kind of lousy lotteries I always win."

"Everyone keep an eye out for more bogeys. That intruder could just be an advance scout for an invasion force close behind it!" Lee McKay warned.

"Cross your fingers, and let's hope not!" Jackson Ruark replied uneasily.

All four fleet admirals were worried and distressed to see an enemy ship appearing so soon. The Stickman holograms predicted Earth still had three months to go before the expected invasion, and the EDF needed every minute of those months to beef up the defense grid. Even with the hundreds of thousands of Dragon ship pilots trained, the EDF was far from ready to repulse the expected full-scale invasion.

Orsini found himself wishing he could go out and be a part of this first engagement rather than being stuck trying to orchestrate the interaction of other Sub-fleet Admirals from a safe distance behind the lines.

He made quick mental contact with all fifty of his sub-fleet admirals, their headquarters scattered all over the southern half of the planet. He found them all to be concentrating on monitoring their assigned sub-sectors, not one of them tempted by curiosity to shift their focus to the intruder's location. On the contrary, with one intruder detected, they all paid rapt on their defensive zones for any signs of more unwelcome visitors.

Only one of those subsector holograms contained the red dot representing the intruder. That subsector where interception of the intruder would occur belonged to sub-fleet admiral Alison Cain of Australia. She would be the one directing the Centurion Squadron's advance and the deployment of reinforcements, if need be, not Pete, which added to Orsini's frustration even more. Pete could only watch and focus on his primary job to orchestrate the efforts of all sub-fleet admirals in his command to make sure nothing got by them. Any attempt to micromanage them individually would defeat their purpose, half a solar system being too big a battlefield for any single fleet admiral to direct all the conflicts within it.

Pete magnified Cain's sector in his tactical hologram. Dozens of bright green pinpoints of light representing Dragon fighters converged on Schiller's position from all directions. His tactical system updated the status of the intruder and fed them mentally to both Orsini and sub-fleet admiral Cain. It told them that the ship traveled inbound at an unexpectedly slow pace. It either could not or would not accelerate to the speed Stickman holograms taught the EDF it was capable of achieving.

"It's odd that the bogey is coming in so slowly," Pete told his people. "They're supposed to be much faster than that."

"Roger that," Susan agreed.

"I'm betting it's just an advance scout feeling around to check us out," Ruark speculated.

"Could be. We'll find out soon enough. My troops are almost ready," Orsini informed them, observing Schiller's Centurion squadron to be nearly assembled.

He zoomed back out a little more, pleased to find that Admiral Cain, as a precaution, directed several hundred more of the patrol scouts and sentry ships nearest the bogey to form Centurion backup squadrons should Schiller's group fail to stop the intruder.

Remembering his responsibility, he rechecked his hologram and nodded with approval as other sentry ships in the grid moved forward to refill the few gaps in the outer defense grid created by the centurion ships. Ships from each grid level moved outward one level to refill empty positions. Dragon ships from Earth, in turn, launched to fill those new gaps created in the innermost grid sphere.

"Sue and Jackson, we need to make sure our sub-fleet commanders keep a close watch on the opposite side of our solar system in case this is just a diversion to sneak more ships through the back door," Lee McKay reminded his three counterparts unnecessarily. "So far, so good, nothing else has turned up yet."

"Roger that," Jackson replied. No surprises inside my part of the South Zone."

"Nothing on my side either," Sue added.

Everyone's training would soon be tested for the first time under actual combat conditions. So far, everything proceeded as planned and practiced, even though this was only a single invader. Someday soon, maybe even at any moment, there would be thousands more arriving simultaneously.

The last of the Dragons racing to be part of the Centurion squadron finally reached Schiller's location to take their place inside the Centurion formation. There they waited for the enemy ship to come closer to them.

After what seemed like hours, Sub-Fleet Admiral Cain gave the order to intercept the incoming bogey and give it a warm welcome. Her tactical system projected the intercept to occur ten minutes from now. As the minutes slowly ticked by, Orsini riveted his attention on the advance of Schiller's squadron closing the distance to the bogey.

"Well, here's an unexpected development," Pete proclaimed with some concern as he took note of unanticipated activity on his tactical hologram. "Stickman ships are racing to get out there too. It looks like they're converging into an attack swarm, and they're making a beeline for the invader. It looks like our allies intend to help out."

"That *is* peculiar," Jackson Ruark agreed. "They've never responded to our attempts to invite them to join in our battle drills!"

"Just one more friggin' thing for me to worry about." Orsini felt a knot growing in the middle of his gut from the suspense. From what they already learned from the Stickmen, he anticipated heavy losses to Schiller's Centurion. Grimly he watched as the Dragon fighters closed on the enemy ship.

~ ~ ~

When Hans Schiller received the order to advance upon the invader, he passed the command to his newly gathered Centurion squadron as they sped toward the invader. To Schiller's surprise, forty-four Stickmen fighter ships identical to his closed in on his formation and trailed behind.

"Centurion Dragons," he called through his ship's thought communications system, commanding it to send his thoughts only to the pilots of his ninety-nine squadron ships, "as you can see, we have company. You all know the Stickmen indicated to us from the very first that they would maintain a defensive presence on our behalf to fight the city killer ships when the time came. However, since they've never participated in our training maneuvers, we shall still attempt to take on the enemy ships as we've been trained to do, but watch out for our friends in case they get in the way."

Schiller ordered his communications system to switch to a general broadcast mode, which in theory should also be picked up by the Stickman swarm fighters.

"This is Major Hans Schiller of Earth Defense Force to the allied swarm group escorting our fighter squadron. We welcome your assistance. I recommend we agree on a plan of attack and coordinate our efforts. Please acknowledge." Schiller waited for a response from the stoic allies, and when none came, he repeated the message several times more before giving up.

"Perhaps they do not understand your German accent, Herr Major," someone quipped. Schiller begrudged himself a grim smile but didn't encourage additional comments by responding.

An unexpected, wordless implant of knowledge finally came into Schiller's mind. To his dismay, Schiller realized that the Stickmen intended to fight as they always did as an independent swarm unit.

"I have a response, Centurions," Schiller told his squadron. "Our allies will fight on their own. So be it! We must still strive to maintain our formation and adhere to our original plan of engagement."

This presented a potential problem. The uninhibited Stickmen could potentially screw up the finely synchronized tactical maneuvers programmed into their ships that the EDF Dragon pilots employed in practice to the point of being able to conduct them in their sleep.

For what little it was worth, Schiller sent out a request to the Stickman pilots to hang back and let the Centurion squadron handle the invader. Receiving no response at all, this time, he gave up any further attempts to communicate. By now, the Centurion squadron would intercept the enemy ship in less than two minutes.

"Fighters, you know what to do. Do not deviate from the plan. Schiller checked their positions on his tactical. "Excellent, people! Maintain the pocket formation until I give the order to contain the enemy ship! Begin rotation now!"

Unlike a Stickman attack swarm, the capture formation consisted of a deep bowl-shaped hemisphere with a standard eleven hundred miles across at the opening. The bowl's opening pointed to the oncoming invader like a baseball mitt turned toward a ball. Each ring began to rotate, with each succeeding ring rotating in the opposite direction of the one before it. Their Dragons' navigational systems interacted and synchronized with each other, while the Stickmen EVs maintained their standard swarm 'formation' of an undisciplined and chaotic cloud of ships. Despite their refusal to coordinate their attack with the Centurion, all of the swarm ships trailed slightly behind the revolving formation of Dragon ships leading the way.

Schiller forced the distraction of the Stickman swarm out of his mind and concentrated on the intruder. The invading ship had reached a point close enough to allow his ship's sensors to pick up detailed information about it. The system indicated it had a spherical shape with a diameter a large aircraft carrier could easily fit inside, but far too small to be one of the city killers they learned about from the Stickmen.

Having no previously imparted knowledge of this type of enemy ship, Schiller had no way of knowing how formidable its weaponry would be. He hoped its present speed was as fast as it could go. If so, his defending ships should have no trouble dealing with it.

Schiller could feel the tension building as the seconds ticked away. It would be within firing range in less than thirty seconds, but his squadron's Dragons were probably already within the superior weapons range of the enemy. Like a mother hen watching over its chicks, he couldn't resist checking the positions of his forces one more time. As expected, they maintained their Dragon's interacting navigational systems performed the Centurion formation flawlessly.

At last, the anticipated moment arrived without the loss of a single Dragon. Just like the simulations of countless practice drills, the enemy ship arrowed straight toward the concave, rotating shield of the Centurion formation like a speeding ball to a catcher's mitt. When it shot through the outermost ring, the Centurion ships forming the outer edge of the bowl collapsed behind it.

In perfect unison, the entire formation melded into a spherical cage that instantaneously reversed direction to match the invader's speed and direction to keep it trapped. It baffled Schiller why this bogey with a supposedly longer weapon range had yet to open fire, but he regarded their failure to do so as a welcome blessing.

"Orbit and open fire," he ordered, trying to sound calm.

Obeying Schiller's order, each Dragon pilot triggered their practiced and most difficult, preprogrammed battle maneuver. Their navigational systems still acting together, each Dragon ship initiated a high-speed orbit of the enemy invader to circle the invading ship in a random direction and distance while maintaining a blistering curtain of firepower. The maneuver was designed to make the Dragons extremely difficult targets for the enemy weaponry to lock onto with no two Dragons moving in the same direction simultaneously.

The Dragon ships contained built-in, automatic targeting and firing systems, but the EDF fighter pilots, without exception, shunned their use from the very beginning. The pilots learned early in their training that they could fire Dragon weapons much faster, target more accurately, and be far more effective via direct thought control. Their Dragon's slower automatic targeting system required two full seconds to lock onto a target. All a Dragon really needed was a simple mental command to focus its force weapon perpetually on whatever object its pilot focused upon within his tactical hologram. A practiced Dragon pilot could target and fire his weapon five or six times in two seconds.

To Schiller's surprise and disgust, before the encircling squadron could inflict any significant damage on the enemy ship, the Stickman EVs plowed through its rotating formation to attack the intruder like a cloud of bees.

In the process, the swarm wrecked the ability of the Dragon ships to maintain their precision attack pattern. Dozens of Dragon ships veered out of formation to avoid collision with the allied Stickman fighters, neutralizing and canceling the attack formation programming of their synchronized navigational systems.

With no other option left to him, Schiller ordered, "All Dragon ships, maintain the attack whatever way you can! Maneuver and fire at will, as you are able. Try not to hit any of our 'friends.'" His heavy sarcasm at the word friends came through loud and clear to his men.

Now, instead of a whirlwind of difficult targets pounding steadily away at the enemy, the barrage upon the invading ship became random and sporadic since the Dragon fighter pilots needed to pay most of their attention to avoiding collisions with both the Swarm ships and each other. The volume of space around the enemy ships became a spectacle of frantic maneuvering.

In the meantime, the invading bogey fearlessly ignored the firepower directed at it and contemptuously fought back without attempting to take evasive action. Maintaining its original course, it speared through the chaotic cloud of ships, its weaponry causing every fighter ship it targeted to disappear as if it never existed

Even though Schiller's hands were full in trying to fly his Dragon evasively and fire at the enemy at the same time, he still managed to check his tactical hologram every few seconds. His fury and horror grew as the number of defensive ships continued to dwindle, the fearsome weapon of the enemy ship not leaving the slightest trace of debris from its victims.

He knew that if the damned Stickman swarm hadn't interfered, the invading ship would have been dispatched by now with fewer casualties. Somehow, they needed to destroy this thing before too many more Dragons were lost.

Mercifully, despite the Stickman swarm interference, the battle lasted less than two and a half minutes, ending with the intruder ship exploding with a blinding and spectacular flash of light. Schiller blinked in surprise when he realized how short the battle proved to be. He would have sworn it lasted at least ten times longer.

"Good work Dragon Fighters!" he congratulated the survivors, relieved the battle was over, and no more of his men would have to sacrifice themselves in Earth's defense.

With a gnawing fear that made him feel nauseous, he ordered his tactical system to scan what was left of the defenders to assess his losses. Schiller was certain that the total number of his casualties must be far higher than it would have been if the Stickmen ships hadn't intervened. His system told him forty-four ships of the combined forces were missing. He dreaded learning whom among his original patrol squadron fell in battle, close friends all of them.

He ordered his thought communications system to identify the survivors of the Centurion squadron, and the list left him stunned! Confused and disbelieving, he rechecked the information to verify it and then checked it a third time, simply unable to accept it! Every Stickman Swarm ship was gone! Incredibly, not one human Dragon fighter pilot perished in the melee.

Chapter 8
Baffling Intrusions

Four weeks after the appearance of Schiller's intruder, Ling Wu sat in the conference room next to his office inside his newly completed headquarters. Carved out of a mountain outside the city of Hong Kong, its furnishings and décor were Spartan compared to the plush surroundings of his former temporary headquarters in the city itself. He preferred it this way. The room held only a bare, metal-framed, laminate-topped table and twelve barely comfortable metal chairs. A single bank of LED lights embedded in the ceiling provided the room's only light that automatically dimmed whenever the wall-mounted monitors were in use. Being underground, the room and the rest of the facility had no windows, the entire fortress designed to withstand anything but a direct nuclear explosion.

Ling Wu was alone but engaged in mid-conference. Four of the monitors on the conference room wall displayed the faces of his fleet admirals, each at their posts and making use of similar communications equipment based on human technology solely due to Ling Wu's refusal to use the Stickman thought communications devices.

"This morning's intruder was the fifty-second encounter since Major Schiller's squadron made the first interception a month ago, Doctor Ling," Lee McKay reported, the latest enemy intrusion having taken place in his defense zone. "We lost thirty-four more Dragons." Ling Wu knew that even though Fleet Admiral McKay tried not to let his distress show, he still knew that the losses affected him deeply. He knew that all of his fleet admirals took their losses to heart.

Ling Wu clasped his hands together and rested his chin on them, his expression grim. "These random probes are not what the Stickmen led us to expect, Fleet Admirals. Correct me if I am wrong, but does that not make fifteen hundred forty-four men and women killed in action?"

"That is pretty close to the correct number, sir. Four hundred seventy-seven of my people, five hundred forty-one of Pete's, three hundred twenty-three of Susan's, and two hundred three of Jackson's."

"That number would be a lot smaller if the Stickmen took on some of these intruders themselves," Orsini bitterly pointed out."

"They participated in the first nineteen skirmishes," Sue McKay reminded him. "Their losses were always ninety-five to one hundred percent, with ours only averaging about thirty percent."

"Well, the evidence would suggest that the enemy believes the Stickmen are commanding our people, and because of that, the enemy must be concentrating on eliminating the Stickman guidance over us; either that or they simply hate the Stickmen more than they hate us!"

"Either way, how the hell do they know which ships the Stickmen are flying?" Jackson interjected, exasperated by the number of questions having no answers.

"It doesn't matter!" Pete Orsini retorted in frustration. "The Stickmen are not joining us at all anymore! Hell, they never did take on any of those ships all by themselves. Instead, they just screwed up our maneuvers and caused more deaths among our people than would have occurred if they'd just stayed out of it! Good riddance to their so-called help!"

"We must keep in mind, Fleet Admiral Orsini, that it is the Stickmen who gave us the means to protect ourselves. Let us not be ungrateful."

Orsini mumbled something inaudible but undoubtedly better left unheard, his expression radiating the anger and outrage he felt.

"How much closer to Earth did this encounter take place, Fleet Admirals?"

"Like all the others, they never managed to get closer than the orbit of Pluto." Susan's brow creased with a frown. "It's as if they're not trying to penetrate any deeper. They seem to be testing the defenses and reaction times of our defending forces."

Ling Wu considered that possibility. "That is very unlikely. Any enemy trying to gauge our strength accurately would know that to do so, they would have to get closer to Earth where the main concentration of our forces would be."

"Well, the enemy is definitely gathering intelligence, regardless," Ruark pointed out. "They've figured out how much of a beating they can take while wreaking their havoc before jumping back to whatever hell they came from before our squadrons can destroy them. Out of all fifty-two interceptions, we've only destroyed eight of their intruders, including the first one Schiller's team intercepted. We destroyed the last one eighteen raids ago and haven't scored another kill since. All the other raiders escaped by using classic hit-and-run tactics."

"Once again, Fleet Admirals, they are employing tactics we were not led to expect."

"At least the casualty rate hasn't weakened the morale of our Dragon fighter pilots, nor has it slowed the number of volunteers trying to sign up. If anything, our losses just piss people off more and make them more determined than ever to get even!"

Pete Orsini suffered daily from a similar need for revenge. He longed to be out there drawing some blood himself. "All we can do for the moment . . . Crap! Here we go again! Another intruder is entering my defense zone now!"

All four fleet admirals received alerts from their thought communications systems calling them back to their command posts by their backup commanders.

"Sue and Jackson, be ready to back my guys up if we need you. Lee, keep an eye out on your side of the solar system." Orsini could feel the knot of tension beginning to squeeze his gut again. Every time one of these nuisance raids took place, they never knew if thousands more could be following right behind, and as always, they knew there would be another loss of good people.

"You'll have to excuse us, Dr. Ling," Lee McKay spoke for them all, the others having already gone for their posts. "Intrusion number fifty-three, coming up!"

Chapter 9
Graduation Day Pride

It was a proud day for the Ruark family. Jackson Ruark sat beside his wife, Karen, and their youngest son, Sean, among an audience of hundreds of other proud parents. Today Brian Ruark would be graduating from astro-aviator school, having completed his aerial combat training with top honors. He'd already received his orders assigning him to his first sentry duty post the following day out of his father's headquarters at the former Santa Cruz Air Force Base, now called the Santa Cruz EDF Spaceport.

With so many graduations taking place daily, Jackson seldom attended them, his duties rarely allowing him to leave his command center. However, for this graduation, he gladly made the time.

Ten sets of bleachers, filled with proud parents, friends, and relatives of the graduates, sat along the base parade grounds. The audiences rose from their seats and cheered as Earth's newest class of one thousand Dragon fighter pilots, Brian among them, marched onto the field. The ceremony would mark the completion of their successful training and their final induction into the Earth Defense Forces as commissioned officers.

Instead of a diploma, they would receive their silver astro-aviator pins depicting the EDF emblem of the winged dragon curled around the Earth. Jackson and Karen Ruark, together in person, would proudly present their son with his pin. Karen Ruark clung to her husband's arm as she tried to pick out her son among the one thousand newly trained recruits.

As the former students marched, they flawlessly divided themselves into ten separate teams of one hundred graduates each. When they marched past the bleachers, the last square formation of pilots halted, turned, and came to attention before the first set of bleachers while the rest marched on. Then, one by one, each trailing team of one hundred stopped before the next encountered audience in line until all ten groups stood before a prearranged seated assembly of families and friends.

The graduates stood at rigid attention as they faced the podiums, all of them dressed immaculately in their jet-black jumpsuits with a green and blue dragon patch on the sleeve of their right shoulders.

Ten training officers, one commander for each team, stood at a podium set on a raised stage between the audience and the graduates. There they would give a short speech, call out names of their former squadron of students, and hand out the coveted astro-aviator pins.

There were no microphones or blaring PA systems. A Stickman thought communications sphere sat on the top of each podium so that each commander could mentally direct a speech solely to his graduates and the audience seated in front of him. The new commanders would call each of the recruits in his group alphabetically to receive their Dragon pins.

Even though Brian Ruark stood near the end of the line, his parents and his younger brother Sean singled him out immediately.

"Look at him," Jackson said to his wife, beaming with pride. "It's hard to believe this is happening! He's barely nineteen, and he can put a Dragon through its paces with the best of them. He's already taken his ship out to the edge of the solar system for training maneuvers several times.

"It wasn't that long ago you played catch with him and Sean out in the backyard," Karen replied, tearing up and taking hold of his arm. "Now he's going out to fight alien monsters, and I'll have two of you to worry about!"

Jackson patted her hand in sympathy. Since he couldn't think of anything comforting to say that would make her feel better, he wisely thought it best to say nothing at all. He just put his right arm around her shoulder, gave her a gentle hug, and squeezed her hand three times, a Ruark family gesture of affection.

The graduation ceremonies followed a mercifully short format, the need to speedily deploy the new pilots far outweighing the need for elaboration. Each team training commander simultaneously gave three-minute designed-to-be-inspirational speeches to their former charges, followed by the most time-consuming part of the ceremony, handing out the Dragon insignias individually to their one hundred graduates.

When Brian Ruark's turn came, Jackson and Karen Ruark came out of the audience and stepped onto the stage to affix the Dragon pin on the breast of their son's jumpsuit. Jackson saluted his son, who beamed back at him, returned a proudly-given formal salute, and maintained it while his mother pinned his insignia on his breast pocket and kissed him on the cheek. Brian's cheeks flamed with embarrassment. He'd tried earlier to talk his parents out of doing anything that would make people think he'd received special treatment, but his mother wouldn't hear of it.

His fears turned out to be groundless, judging by the roar of approval and the applause from his classmates and the audience. It dawned on him his parents were showing the world that even a fleet admiral's son *wasn't* special or privileged. They did not use their influence to hold him back from putting his life on the line. They were just like several million other worried parents who allowed one or more of their children to endanger themselves in the depths of outer space.

When the last of Brian's class received their pins, instead of their commander dismissing them to active duty, Jackson Ruark walked over to the podium and, via the communications sphere, addressed the officer, the graduating pilots before him, and their audience.

"Commander Davis, I know you have one last session of battle formation practice scheduled immediately following the graduation ceremony. I would be honored if you would let me fly with you to observe."

The class of pilots sitting in front of Commander Davis stood and cheered their approval of the request. A fleet admiral never took the time to observe a training exercise among Dragon pilots.

Davis, already having pre-approved Ruark's request, acted as though it came as a surprise to him and simply replied, "The honor would be ours, Fleet Admiral Ruark." He shook Jackson's hand as a sign of agreement while the newly minted fighter pilots continued to applaud and whistle their approval.

He turned his attention back to his squadron and said, "Ladies and gentlemen, let's show Fleet Admiral Ruark what we can do!" Once again, the group enthusiastically roared their consent.

Davis nodded with a smile, pleased with his graduates' show of enthusiasm. "People, you have thirty minutes to prepare yourselves and board your ships. Fleet Admiral Ruark, please meet us on the North field at that time."

"I'll be there, Commander. Thank you once again for the privilege," He shook the commander's hand in parting.

Davis turned back to his new charges, saluted, and said, "Ladies and gentlemen, you are dismissed."

As one, the group of new graduates came to attention, saluted back, and then began to disperse, most of them in the direction of the buses waiting to take them to the Northern part of the base where their ships awaited them.

Jackson gathered his family to escort them back to their car. "You be careful out there," Karen admonished. "Don't be doing anything to show off!"

"I'll just be flying along behind to observe. It's perfectly safe. Besides, I've been stuck at headquarters so long. I'm thrilled just to get back to my Dragon and take it out there again. Since this is a special occasion, Ling Wu gave his blessing to the idea."

"I wish I could go too," Sean said with a sigh. "Two more years, and I can be a pilot too."

Karen rolled her eyes and glared at her son in mock disapproval, "And yet another one to give me gray hair before my time!"

"Let's just hope this war will be over by then, and the enemy will be gone forever." He gave her hand another three squeezes and held it as they walked.

An interesting thought occurred to him, and he stopped dead in his tracks. He turned to Karen and Sean and stared at them for a moment with a wry smile. Puzzled, they stared back, Karen raising one eyebrow in suspicion. She knew her husband well, and when she saw that look, she knew something outrageous was brewing.

"What do you to say to the idea of you both coming along with me," he asked them.

Karen's eyes went wide with horror. Do you mean on your *ship*? Out there? There are enemy raiders out there!"

"They've never made it yet to anywhere inside the orbit of Pluto. We're not going out that far. We'll all be fine. Besides, we'll be in the protection of Brian's entire graduating class and probably several more that are always out there practicing, not to mention we will be well within the established defense grid of sentries. The grid goes all the way out to Saturn now."

"Oh, Mom, could we?" Sean pleaded, clasping his hands together to beg.

"You'd be able to see for the first time what it's like and why I fell in love with this career," Jackson encouraged. "I promise we'll all be perfectly safe. My ship can seat three extra people, and we're only going to observe. I won't be participating in any fancy maneuvers."

Karen continued to stare at him, genuinely trying to determine if he'd lost his mind.

Come on," he urged, "let's all go together!"

"Please, Mom!" Sean pleaded once more, tugging at her hand.

Karen shook her head doubtfully with a stricken look on her face, but both Jackson and Sean knew from experience how to read her. They could see that, despite her fear, deep down, the idea thrilled her too. They knew she was going to cave.

Thirty minutes later, Jackson proudly ushered his wife and son into his personal Dragon, one of the first four ever given to the human race.

"It's so barren and sterile inside," Karen commented as she looked around the interior. The empty cabin added a slight echo to her voice.

"Oh, Mom," Sean said with exasperation, "haven't you followed the news? Everything changes once we're inside."

Taking his place in the command chair, Jackson mentally ordered two more seats to rise out of the deck. "Just walk around to the front of those seats and sit yourselves down," he directed.

Even though Sean followed the workings of the fighter ships on TV and the internet more times than he could count, watching the ship come alive left him in awe. Karen walked around to the front of one of the seats, gave it a doubtful assessment, then turned and gingerly sat down. A small squeak of surprise escaped her as the seat instantly began to mold itself behind her to fit her body perfectly.

"Oh, my! This is just wonderful!" The seat readjusted itself with her every movement, sensing the comfort level best suited to her. "Oh, my goodness," she said once more, her fingertips touching her chest in wonder as the ship's viewing field became active to make an entire section of the hull seem as if it no longer existed.

The inside of the ship lit up with the bright daylight from outside. Through the viewing field, they saw the Dragon ships of the graduates, one hundred of them as well as their commander's Dragon spread out on the airfield before them.

Ruark had just finished bringing up his tactical hologram in preparation for flight when he received word the squadron was ready to begin the exercise. There was no need to relay the information to his family since his ship's communication system mentally alerted Karen and Sean as well.

Karen found the view outside the hull mesmerizing as all of the ships rose into the sky in perfect unison. Within seconds, the blue sky around them became black, and the hundred and one ships ahead of them soared out in the direction of the moon in a V formation with Commander Davis' ship in the lead.

"Are we going to keep watching them on this video, or are we going to go along too?" Karen asked her husband.

"That's not a video. We are flying right behind them."

"What? How can that be?" she questioned in obvious disbelief. "I don't feel any movement, and I don't hear any engine noise."

Jackson explained how his Dragon's drive accelerated not only the body of the ship but every molecule within it so passengers couldn't feel movement even if the ship changed direction instantaneously.

Karen gulped, her face becoming quite pale. "You mean I'm in outer space right now?"

"And you're doing just fine too, aren't you?" Jackson pointed out.

"How far up are we now?" she asked in a strangled voice and not sure she truly wanted to know.

Jackson pointed at something in the tactical/navigational hologram surrounding him. "This group of green dots is the squadron ahead of us. We're just passing the moon, which is this huge white sphere. The moon itself should be right over there," he said, pointing off to her right and slightly behind her. The viewing field shifted in the direction of his gaze, revealing the moon in all its radiant glory from just a few thousand miles away. It quickly became visibly tiny in the distance as the squadron of ships gathered speed.

Karen teared up again, this time for at the beauty of it. "Oh, Jackson, it's incredible," she said softly, completely enchanted by the moon's beauty and the colors of the stars. "No wonder you love to be out here,"

"This is so cool, Dad! Where are we going?"

"Just to Jupiter's neighborhood."

"What!" Karen squealed. "You promised this would be a short ride!"

"We'll be reaching near light speed in a moment. That will enable us to cover the distance to get there in about thirty minutes. Commander Davis will race out ahead of us to play the role of an incoming invader.

"I think you'll find that the Centurion squadron maneuvers to intercept him are an amazing and beautiful thing to watch. The tricks these pilots can do with their ships by mentally synchronizing their maneuvers with each other via their navigational systems is beyond belief."

For the next half hour, Ruark's wife and son just sat in their passenger seats and stared out at the beauty and clarity of the stars outside the hull. In the deep space between planets, the colors of the stars, nebulae, and the magnificent view of the Milky Way became startlingly more well-defined and far more beautiful than what Karen and Sean ever imagined.

In deference to the Admiral Ruark's family, Davis chose a route that took them above the asteroid belt and, not too long afterward, close to the surface of Jupiter, for which Ruark sent the commander a silent, mentally driven "Thank you!"

The splendor of the gas giant and its multi-colored moons rendered his family speechless. It was also Jackson's first time traveling this close to the gas giant, and he, too, found the sight to be quite spectacular.

Just beyond Jupiter's orbit, the squadron began its drill. Ruark knew, by now, Davis should be several light-minutes somewhere ahead of the new group of pilots. To keep Davis' position unknown, he had their Dragons pre-programmed to prevent his ship's power signature from being displayed on their tactical holograms until he sent a signal to restore it. When he chose to reveal himself, he would be simulating an invading enemy ship popping out of a wormhole.

Jackson called Sean's attention to the tactical/navigational hologram and explained what the various colored lights meant. Some represented the nearest planets, some represented the moons, but all of the green dots represented the power sources of Dragon ships.

"When the squad commander decides to show his power signature again to simulate an incoming invader, a new red dot will show up, red indicating an unidentified power source presumed to be an enemy invader. Brian's squadron will maneuver into an attack formation called a Centurion and try to block its path to Earth while, at the same time, trying their best to 'destroy' him, so to speak, with extremely low blast settings from their ship's weapons. Commander Davis' ship will record which of the ships scored the most hits and will map the squad's maneuvers for replay and analysis back in the debriefing room later."

As he predicted, a bright red dot appeared on the hologram. "You see? There he is now," Jackson told Sean, pointing at the bright dot on the hologram. "Odd, though. He's pretty darn close, almost on top of us. I thought Davis would reappear several light-minutes further away."

Ruark's blood froze when he mentally heard Commander Davis' voice yell, "THAT'S NOT ME!"

A second dot appeared on the tactical hologram, representing Davis' Dragon. This time, the new dot appeared several light-minutes away, approximately where Ruark expected Davis to reappear in the first place.

Davis raced back toward his squadron at maximum speed. "Squadron, this is not a drill! Prepare for battle! Set your force weapons to full power! Fleet Admiral, get your family the hell out of there!"

Ruark needed no coaxing. As much as he wanted to join the fight, his need to get his family out of harm's way as fast as he possibly could was a far greater priority. He felt an icy grip of fear for the graduate squadron when he realized how close the intruder appeared to them.

The squadron itself had no time to react before the enemy ship plowed through its position. Ten graduate Dragons winked out of existence one after another. The new graduates, trained to approach an enemy ship from a distance within an offensive formation, were unprepared to deal with one materializing practically right in their midst.

The ninety surviving Dragon ships scrambled in an attempt to regroup to some semblance of an orderly battle formation. The enemy ship changed course to pass near the thickest part of the Dragon squadron. Seven more graduating class Dragons disappeared.

The remaining squadron pilots quickly relied on their training to work as a unit to fight back. Davis, still a light-minute away from his squadron, watched in horror as fifteen more ships disappeared in rapid succession over the next few seconds. Even in their disorganized state, nearly all the surviving squadron ships managed to pour on continuous force weapon blasts at the invader, scoring with almost every shot.

In a panic, Davis shouted uselessly for his men to take the enemy ship out, his heart sinking as the alien ship changed direction once more to race out of squadron weapon's range while heading directly toward Fleet Admiral Ruark's fleeing Dragon. With the intruder's superior weapon range, another five squadron Dragons giving chase winked out of existence even as the invader closed on Ruark's ship. Davis' tactical display showed Ruark's Dragon opening up on the intruder, and then the point of light on his tactical hologram representing Ruark's Dragon winked out.

Davis screamed in anguish. Fleet Admiral Jackson Ruark's ship ceased to exist. The invading ship, either no longer willing to fight or too damaged to continue, opened up a wormhole to escape before the surviving Dragons of the Centurion squadron could finish it off.

He wilted in his pilot's seat in complete despair at the enormity of the disaster. With this single chance encounter, that lone alien ship just destroyed one-quarter of the world's fleet admirals along with his family. His family! Davis did a quick mental status check on the ships that survived the encounter and moaned once again. The thirty-seven missing Dragons included Brian Ruark's. The enemy ship just wiped out Fleet Admiral Jackson Ruark's entire family!

∿ ∿ ∿

"Well, that worked rather well," Joshua Harkins told Jake and Jake's Ghost companion, Pat, inside the Ghost beacon ship far beyond the orbit of Pluto.

"Looks like we not only can jump ships with precision accuracy to a beacon ship, but a beacon ship can accurately map gravitational influences and feed them to our navigation systems. That eliminates the dangers of using mini jumps inside a solar system. As a result, our pilots no longer have to worry about solar system gravitational anomalies that would cause them to pop out of a wormhole somewhere unintended. We not only proved all of that but as a bonus, Hawks and Bigsby handling the wormhole weapons on that Ghost ship scooped up a whole bunch of new Dragons for us."

"Pat: Of course, the experiment succeeded, just as we assured you it would, Joshua. I recommend we return before your defensive network discovers our presence."

"I'm still not sure how we can put this short-distance wormhole accuracy to good use," Jake admitted.

"Don't worry, pal. It's going to be more useful than you can imagine."

Chapter 10
Casualties of War

Ruark pushed his Dragon to full acceleration away from the oncoming alien ship, beads of sweat forming on his brow.

"Jack, what's happening?" The pure fear in his wife's voice tore him up inside, and he cursed his stupidity for putting her and Sean in danger.

"That's a real enemy ship out there! I'm sorry. I never imagined this could happen. I'm going to try to get you and Sean away from here." He didn't reveal any trace of the fear and heartache he felt. From the mentally implanted tactical information his ship provided, he knew Brian's Dragon became one of the first ships winking out of existence when the alien plowed through the squadron's position. They would have to take the time to grieve for Brian later; that's *if* they survived.

"Mom, I know you're scared, but we have to let Dad concentrate!" Sean told his mother.

Jackson couldn't believe how well his son kept his calm, considering the danger they were all exposed to. He thought that his youngest son would make a great command-level officer someday if they ever got out of this alive.

Jackson watched, horrified, as the enemy changed direction unexpectedly. His tactical display indicated that it was speeding in *his* direction. The damned thing had already extracted a terrible toll. Five more Dragon ships winked out of existence on his hologram as he watched. In desperation, he set his ship's force weapon to maximum power then focused the force beam on the approaching invader to blast it with every bit of its available energy.

The remains of Brian's squadron continued to give chase, but the enemy ship was faster and was now beyond their weapon's range. It closed the distance to Ruark's ship so rapidly he could see it through his viewing field, its hull reflecting the light of Earth's distant sun. It bore down on him like a train ready to slam into a vehicle stalled on its railroad tracks.

He gritted his teeth and managed to fire one last salvo from his force weapon before everything went dark.

For the briefest moment, Ruark experienced a blackness and silence surrounding him so absolute that it seemed to have substance. A sensation of disorientation overwhelmed him to the point where he couldn't tell up from down, the feeling vanishing almost as quickly as it occurred. To his enormous relief, he realized his ship remained intact and miraculously undamaged.

"Jackson! What . . . just . . . happened?" Karen stammered, so terrified she could hardly speak.

"That's what I'm trying to figure out, Hon," he called back, trying not to let his fright show in his voice. His tactical hologram reappeared, and he whirled his seat trying to locate the enemy ship, ready to fight again. To his enormous relief, it was gone, probably having escaped back through a wormhole. The hologram displayed only the green dots of what he thought represented the Dragons that survived the attack.

He immediately turned his attention to his wife and son and felt so relieved to see them unharmed that tears welled in his eyes. "Karen! Sean! We are out of danger. Are you both alright?" He leaped from his seat, wrapped his arms around them, and hugged them with all his might. Both of them threw their arms around him and squeezed him back just as hard.

As he hugged them, he saw Sean's eyes go wide as saucers as they looked past his father. "Dad, look!"

Sean excitedly pointed toward the viewing field to Jackson's left at something out in the volume of space beyond. Ruark saw his wife's eyes go wide with shock as she too gawked where Sean indicated. Her mouth formed an unvoiced "oh," and she covered it with her hand, numbed by what she saw.

Ruark spun around, and his heart skipped a beat at what he saw outside the ship. The brilliant light of a spiral galaxy filled the view, spread so far across the blackness of space the viewing field couldn't contain it all. The galactic body appeared tilted and had four great arms forming a spectacular celestial pinwheel. Each arm curved back around the galactic center until it almost touched the center of the next arm. A thick dome bulged up out of the center of the galaxy, so densely packed with stars it was too bright to gaze upon for long. Sporadic bands and blotches of dark interstellar dust laced themselves throughout the galactic disk, blotting out some of its brilliance beyond.

As Ruark turned his head, the viewing field followed the direction of his gaze. They found that their Dragon sat within the outskirts of a second galaxy's tremendous disk of stars. From their perspective, it tilted upward at a forty-five-degree angle. It, too, had a dome of densely packed stars rising from its middle. Further to the right, the great plane of its stars thinned out to a not-so-distant galactic edge.

"Where are we?" Karen asked, her fear emphasized by her shaky voice.

"I don't know, Hon, but we're alive and in one piece. I still need time to figure this out." He pointed to his son, "Sean, stick with your mom. I'm going to be very busy for a few minutes."

He turned to look all around, the viewing field shifting with his gaze. Close enough to be seen, a dozen Dragon fighter ships peppering the nearby volume of space, remnants of the newly graduated squadron. Ruark sent out a thought-driven query to his tactical system and received back information that there were another twenty more of them scattered about in the vicinity, all of them too far away to see with the naked eye. To his enormous relief, the system identified one of the ships as to his son Brian's.

"Oh, thank God!" he whispered to himself, tears forming in the corner of his eyes. At least now, he didn't have to tell his wife that Brian was dead, as he'd believed him to be earlier.

He gladly put that thought aside. They were all still lost, without a clue how to return to Earth. To make matters worse, Ruark's tactical system sent him a mentally driven alarm indicating the approach of another enemy popping into nearby space practically right on top of his position.

Whipping his head toward the direction the system indicated, an icy hand closed over his heart as he recognized one of the city-destroying ships identical to the ones in the Stickman holograms. It was close enough to see through the viewing field. Incredibly, twenty unidentified Dragon-type fighter ships accompanied it, all twenty forming a circular shield formation between the enemy ship and the newly arrived Dragons as if protecting it.

"All Dragon Fighters, this is Fleet Admiral Ruark! We're about to have another fight on our hands. Lock on to this communications link and form up around me!" he ordered. "Battle formation! Prepare to . . ."

"EDF Dragon Fighters, stand down! You are in friendly space! Repeat, you are in friendly space! Please do not fire!" The plea came through the thought communications systems interrupting Ruark's battle orders.

"Stand down? This is Fleet Admiral Jackson Ruark! Who broadcast that stand-down order?" Ruark's tactical equipment already identified every ship except those positioned to shield the enemy vessel.

While speaking, Ruark kept a close eye on his tactical display, proud to find that, despite the shock of what just happened to them, Brian and his classmates not only obeyed his orders to join him, they rapidly formed a partial bowl-shaped battle formation. They positioned themselves between Ruark, the enemy ship, and its escort. The rings of the formation then began rotating in opposite directions to make themselves difficult targets.

"Fleet Admiral Ruark?" The voice sounded stunned. "Sir, I have no idea how we netted you, but welcome! And a warm welcome to everyone else! Please allow my ship to approach your position."

"Welcome to what? Who is this?" Ruark demanded furiously. With all that just happened to his family and the graduates, he felt a great need to lash out.

"This is Lieutenant Commander Daniel Murphy speaking, Earth Defense Force, formerly on the staff of Fleet Admiral McKay's Battle Tactics Unit. I don't know if you remember me, but we've met," Danny told him as his ship broke away from the center of the enemy ship's shield of Dragon ships. It cautiously approached the formation of newly arrived Dragons and came to a halt close to them.

Ruark couldn't believe what he was hearing! "Lieutenant Commander Murphy? You're still alive? We'd written your scout team off as the first KIA's of the war! What about Duval and the other four men who disappeared with you?"

"Alive and well, sir, and I'm sure they'll be anxious to talk to you."

Ruark found himself at a loss for words. Before he could reply, Murphy cut in again.

"Fleet Admiral, sir, it is imperative that you trust us and do what we ask. My people and I will lead you and your men back to where you can land your ships. We have to have them slightly overhauled.

"What do you mean, *your* people?" Ruark found himself shouting again. He found this all just too outrageous. "Where did you and these other Dragons come from?"

"We were already here, sir. Shouldn't you be asking where it is that *you've* all come to?"

"Don't get flippant with me, Murphy. I've got questions, and I want answers!"

"My apologies, sir. I meant no disrespect, and I mean no disrespect now when I tell you that you can ask all the questions you want shortly, and we'll gladly answer them. We have a long story that we are very anxious to tell you, but just not here and not now.

"Fleet Admiral, I have to make it abundantly clear that the ship behind me that I'm sure you all recognize is not the enemy you believe it to be. Please do not attempt to fire upon it. We're going to take you to a place that belongs to the folks who own that ship as well as the one you all fought a short while ago back in our home solar system. I repeat, you must not attack the alien ship! If you do, you'll end up somewhere else again, and it will be a while before we can locate you again."

"I have no idea what you mean by that, Lieutenant Commander Murphy, but considering our position . . . literally, I don't see where any of us have a choice. Very well, you have my word we will not attack! When we get to wherever you are taking us, you are going to have one hell of a lot of explaining to do, Lieutenant Commander!"

Murphy let out a deep sigh. "More than you can possibly imagine, sir. May we lead the way for you?"

"You may, but I warn you, my people and I are pissed, ready, and anxious to kick someone's ass after what we've all that's already happened to us. Be well aware yourself that we're all feeling very trigger happy, so don't do anything that might make us more upset than we already are!"

"Understood, Fleet Admiral."

"Squadron, when I give my word, I give it for all of us! Honor it, or else! Do I make myself clear?" He received instant and unanimous acknowledgments from all of his misplaced Dragon fighters.

Ruark then set his Dragon's thought communications system to a general broadcast mode so Karen, Sean, and all the other ships out there could hear the conversation between him and Murphy. Questions came flooding in now, the communications system also relaying the feelings of confusion, fear, and anxiety among his group of graduates.

"Quiet everyone! They gave us a promise that we'll have answers to all of our questions later. I have several million of them, and Lord knows, I don't have answers to any of them any more than you all do. Maintain formation, and let's see where Lieutenant Commander Murphy takes us. Stay vigilant! Watch your tacticals for any sign of funny business!"

One more anxious question came through. "Dad, are Mom and Sean okay?" It was his son Brian asking via private communication.

Karen answered him herself. "We're fine, Brian," she tried to assure him even though it couldn't be further from the truth. She didn't know that the ship's communications system also transmitted her feelings to reveal the lie.

"Mrs. Ruark?" a baffled Danny Murphy asked over the communications system. "How did you ever end up in a combat zone?"

Ruark was glad no one could see his flush of embarrassment, knowing poor judgment on his part dumped his entire family into this situation. "Never mind that now, Lieutenant Commander, just lead the way!"

As the lost ships followed Murphy, Ruark used the time to study the surrounding volume of space via the ship's tactical hologram. The display revealed his location to be on the outskirts of a solar system with twelve planets and a yellow star similar but smaller than Earth's sun. Only one of the planets had no moons. Three of the planets had Saturn-like rings encircling them.

From the trajectory they followed, Ruark guessed that the vicinity of this solar system's fourth planet must be their destination, about two hours distant at maximum Dragon speed. As his tactical system continued to map this solar system, it identified the world ahead to be a gas giant with a dozen moons in orbit. Hundreds of power signatures dotted one of the moons that measured about half the diameter of the Earth. Without a doubt, Danny Murphy was leading them there.

This is so cool," Sean muttered under his breath to no one in particular. His eyes became as wide as saucers as he watched Danny Murphy's group of ships lead them deeper into the solar system with an entire galaxy forming a brilliant ceiling of stars above them. The vast disk of its stars seemed so close that Sean imagined he could almost touch them.

Karen longed for the comfort of her husband's arm around her but knew he needed to stay alert and focus his attention on his tactical hologram. Instead, she slowly walked to where her son stood and took comfort by putting her arm around him instead and joining him in his awe of the wonders the viewing field presented.

Chapter 11
Among the "KIAs"

Karen and Sean stood close to Jackson as he piloted his Dragon; his command chair raised a few feet above them to the ship's center. All of them gazed in wonder at the splendor of the blue, green, and purple atmospheric bands of the enormous planet dominating the view outside the ship, with thousands of streaks of lightning flashes appearing all over the swirling cloud structure to colorfully illuminate them.

As much as Ruark wanted to gawk at the sight with them, he focused his attention on following Murphy's ship as it guided him and his squadron remnant around to the far side of the planet, where three more of the planet's twelve moons came into view, one of them their destination.

The viewing field shifted, tracking the direction of Ruark's gaze as he turned his head. Even though it was nearly the size of the red planet Mars, the moon they approached seemed tiny compared to the Goliath of the planet it orbited, passing to their rear. Wispy white clouds in its upper atmosphere cast shadows on small purple-colored continents and deep green seas covered with thousands of islands, large and small. Though his tactical hologram showed his people trailing close behind his Dragon, he still felt compelled to glance back for a visual check since most of them were close enough to see. When he did, he heard the "Ohhh" of appreciation from his wife. The pearly line of ships strung out behind them, their mirrored hulls shimmering with the reflected but distorted images of the spectacular galaxies above them and the colors of the nearby giant planet.

Entering the atmosphere of the destination moon below them, Murphy's ship shot straight down toward the edge of one of the larger continents to a place near the moon's equator. The distant outline of a spaceport soon came into view.

Ruark's tactical system indicated power signatures of what could only be hundreds of Dragons parked in the purple lawn of a central field surrounded by clusters of buildings. The tactical system gave him a count of more than fifteen hundred Dragons parked down there; almost exactly the number of ships presumed destroyed from all the individual enemy raids of the last month that took place back inside Earth's solar system.

As they drew closer, he could see a jungle of squat, black-trunked trees surrounding the clearing the base occupied. Dark purple fronds serving as leaves cascaded down from the tree limbs to blanket the ground around them. The perfectly level landscape displayed a lawn of something violet-colored that would later prove to be a fine moss carpeting the grounds.

The small fleet of ships passed over the base perimeter and glided toward the central airfield where the hundreds of Dragon ships sat in orderly rows, all of them floating three feet off the ground in standard park positions. Everywhere the Ruark family looked, the astro-aviators who flew those ships poured out of the buildings and parked Dragon ships to watch the approach of the newcomers, many of them waving a welcome.

Word spread over the base that none other than Fleet Admiral Ruark had been captured. Every single person on the base rushed toward the center of the tarmac where they knew he'd be landing.

Ruark paled, a chill racing up his spine when he saw dozens of towering white beings he recognized as enemy aliens moving freely among the humans. He knew the graduates saw the same thing, and he feared that any nervousness among them might lead to trouble.

Ordering his communications system to tie only to them, he rebroadcasted his orders. "Dragon Fighters, remember to hold your fire. No matter what, do *not* open fire on anything you see below unless I give the order, and do *not* hesitate to obey any order I may give! Don't descend until I give the word, and be ready to run like hell if I say so." He felt foolish giving that last order, wishing he could take it back. After all, where could they go?

Murphy's annoyingly cheerful voice sounded in their minds, "Newcomers, we cleared a place for you to land. I'll lead you there. Just park your ships near mine.

Ruark led his people as he followed Murphy's ship, his nerves on edge as his ship fed his mind with tactical information that would instantly alert him to any potential danger. Instead of landing as Murphy instructed, he and his people came to a halt to hover fifty feet over the field while Murphy parked his ship below. Ruark saw the portal of Murphy's Dragon open, its ramp extend, and Danny Murphy coming out of his ship. Even though Danny couldn't see Ruark, he knew the fleet admiral must be watching him, and he beckoned encouragingly to the admiral to park his ship.

Seeing no sign of danger and receiving no alerts from the tactical system, Ruark lowered his ship next to Murphy's. As he did so, the line of thirty-seven newly captured Dragon ships gracefully moved together to form a protective hovering circle of potential firepower above this inexplicable airbase. There, they remained on guard as ordered.

After Ruark settled his Dragon to a park position, he ordered his ship to extend the ramp and open the hull portal. "People," he told his collection of kidnapped pilots, "I'm going out. Stay put until I tell you otherwise and, I repeat, don't get trigger happy!"

"Jack, be careful!" Karen pleaded, the fear in her eyes tearing at her husband's heart once again.

"I think I'll be safe, Love. There are a lot of our people out there," he told her, pointing out through the viewing field. Crowds rushed toward the ship from all directions. Even though she could see them for herself, the number of friendly faces out there did nothing to ease her anxiety.

With so many people out there gathering, he set his ship's thought communications system to a general broadcast mode so everyone could mentally hear him and then stepped out onto the ramp.

A pleasant warm fragrant breeze brushed his face as he stepped through the opening to stand at the top of the ramp. The applause, cheers, and whistles of the many people before him became thunderous. Looking over all the exuberant faces, he felt so grateful and relieved to find so many people, thought to be killed in battle all still alive that a lump formed in his throat. However, not knowing how all of these people, including his own family, were plucked out of one solar system and dumped in an altogether unknown galaxy frustrated and infuriated him. He wanted answers!

Danny Murphy crossed the few feet separating their ships and snapped to attention. Scowling, Ruark was in no mood to concern himself with military protocol but, regardless, found himself automatically returning the salute.

"Lieutenant Commander Daniel Murphy, do you mind telling me where we are?"

"We're in another galaxy, Fleet Admiral!"

Ruark's lips compressed, and his temper rose several notches higher. He looked pointedly up at the sky filled with the stars of two colliding galaxies and then glared back at Danny with a 'no shit' expression on his face.

Danny's smile faded. He coughed into his fist and stood up straighter. "Uh, from what we've learned, we're about seven million, four hundred thousand light-years from our galaxy, give or take a few thousand light-years, sir."

"Seven mil . . ." Ruark was staggered.

"Are you alright, sir? You don't look so well."

"I've had better days, son," Ruark growled. Off to his left, another voice called out, and he saw a familiar figure approaching.

"Nice to see you again, Fleet Admiral Ruark!" L.C. Duval shouted above the cheers and unending applause of the still-growing crowd. He gave a quick salute and then offered his hand in greeting. "Welcome to Ares, Sir. That's what we call this moon."

"Another one," Ruark muttered irritably to himself. Unsure and wary of the entire situation, he grudgingly took Duval's hand to shake it.

"You look awfully good for a dead man," Jackson growled, eyeing him up and down suspiciously.

"My Daddy always said, 'Live fast, die young, and make a good-looking corpse,'" Duval replied quite seriously.

"I said you looked good for a dead man. No one said you were good-looking," Jackson returned just as seriously. "While I am delighted and somewhat astonished to find you and Lieutenant Commander Murphy unharmed, not to mention these hundreds of others, I want to know right now, and no bullshit, are we in trouble here or not?

"Believe me, Fleet Admiral, you are all perfectly safe now, more so than you can imagine."

Ruark raised one eyebrow at that peculiar comment but did not question it. Instead, he observed the vast collection of faces surrounding him, all smiling and cheering for him. "I presume all these people are also some of our KIA's?"

"That's correct, Fleet Admiral. They are, in fact, the entire collection of all your battle casualties. You'll find us all very healthy for a bunch of killed-in-action zombies."

Ruark raised one eyebrow at that astonishing claim. Knowing the EDF casualty count so far, he rubbed his chin as he looked over the surrounding crowd, making a rough estimate of the crowd numbers, finding Duval's statement to be true.

"I don't mind saying I'm mystified, Colonel. You have a lot of explaining to do, and I assure you that you have my undivided attention. Can I safely presume we've just become prisoners of war and that this place is a POW camp of sorts?" he asked, glancing about the compound at the revolting, white gelatinous bodies of the aliens mixed among the crowd of Dragon fighter pilots. He reached the most obvious conclusion that the beings within the compound must be the alien equivalent of prison camp guards.

"Uh, not exactly, Fleet Admiral. Not even close."

Ruark's brow furrowed again, and he glared menacingly at Duval, his blood starting to boil once more. "If you are not prisoners, why then are you all consorting with the enemy?" he demanded icily.

Karen and Sean Ruark, just then, poked their heads out of the ship's portal, the ongoing sound of all the applause having drawn them out. Duval, momentarily distracted by the movement at the opening of the Dragon behind Ruark, glanced up and did a double-take. His eyes went wide, and his normal imperturbability became visibly jarred when he recognized Jackson Ruark's wife and his young son. They were the last people he expected to see emerging from an EDF Dragon ship recently engaged in battle.

He looked questioningly at Ruark, then to Karen and Sean, then back again to Ruark. Finding it unnerving that his fleet admiral's face turned a brilliant shade of red, accompanied by a murderous glare daring him to say anything about it, he wisely chose not to ask about their presence.

"I'd be more than happy to explain shortly, Fleet Admiral, but first . . ." he held up his hand toward the crowd to draw their attention to him as he turned to face them.

"People, let's all welcome Fleet Admiral Jackson Ruark . . . and his family!" The thought communications systems of Ruark's ship sent Duval's thoughts out to everyone. The cheering crowd broke into a deafening ovation of welcome that couldn't be subdued for a full five minutes. The applause finally did subside when Ruark, himself, raised his arms and motioned them to stop so he could address them.

"People," he began, "while I appreciate the warm welcome, at the moment, I don't know where we are or why we are here. I want you all to know, though, how very grateful and relieved I am to see you all alive and well." Once again, the crowd burst into lingering applause.

"There are thirty-seven more brave men and women hovering their Dragons above us, all brand-new graduates who found themselves transported here with me. They're waiting above for my approval to land," he said, pointing to the motionless formation floating above their heads.

"Forgive my caution, but I see there are members of our alien enemies among you, and I'm going to need a very remarkable explanation before I order those people to land. I've been told that I erroneously concluded we are all prisoners of war. I need to know then exactly what this is all about!"

The crowd became quiet, realizing that Ruark doubted their loyalty in his ignorance of the situation.

"I've got this covered," said another new voice mentally coming through, loud and clear. Ruark could also hear him aurally, the shout coming from someone close pushing his way through the crowd. Ruark searched for the source of the voice and recognized Gunther Karlson weaving his way through the crowd toward him. Karlson pushed through to the front and joined Duval, Murphy, and the fleet admiral.

"Welcome, Sir!" he said with a quick salute that Ruark found lacking in every possible way. Without waiting for a reply, the fingers of Karlson's left hand unfolded to expose what looked like a Stickman sphere of some kind, only a much smaller version of what he was used to seeing. Ruark immediately felt information start to flow into his mind. In seconds, he knew the entire story; the capture of Duval and his men, the truth about the Stickmen, and why the raids were being conducted back into Earth's solar system.

The newly acquired, appalling information chilled him to the core, and he shot a glance in the direction of the portal of his ship where Sean and Karen stood. From their pale faces and frightened looks, he knew they mentally received the same information.

Without another word, he mentally accessed his ship's thought communications system. "This is Fleet Admiral Ruark," he sent to the formation of Dragons above and to the surrounding crowd of captured Dragon fighter pilots. "Land your ships. We're among friends."

Chapter 12
Deceit Revealed

Ruark realized how badly upset Sean and Karen had to be over the revelations of the knowledge transfer. He could see the tears rolling down Karen's cheeks and Sean's hands trembling, so he asked Gunther Karlson to gather up the thirty-seven new refugee pilots who just landed while he spent a few moments with his family, taking them back inside his Dragon.

"Five minutes ago, I was mortified and angry that my stupidity pulled you both into this fiasco. Now, I thank God you're here with me. Given what we've just learned, this is the safest place you two could be, Brian too. It's the ones back home whom we have to worry about now."

"I know that," Karen admonished. "I'm not crying for myself. I'm crying for the millions and perhaps billions back home who might not be able to be saved. We have friends and family back there, our parents, brothers, sisters, and their families, Pete and his family, Lee and Susan. None of them have the faintest clue of the danger they are in and the magnitude of the Stickmen's deceit!"

"Dad, isn't there anything we can do to warn them?

"I don't know, son, but we're going to try. We know now that Colonel Duval and his men are behind all the intrusions into our solar system. They've been doing it to gather in as many of our Dragon fighters as they can. Take an important lesson from them, son, that even against impossible odds, they simply refused to give up. They found a way to fight back. We have to adopt that same admirable attitude and never, ever give up! We'll figure out a way to do something. For now, the kidnapping tactics these people have employed are ingenious, and I intend to help them keep it up."

He glanced up and saw hundreds of expectant faces waiting for him to address them. "Right now, they are waiting for me to say something. I'm the one they're going to be counting on to lead them now. Can you help me do that? I don't think I can lead anything without you two backing me up."

Karen wiped the tears away with the back of her hands and took her husband's hand. "Of course, we will. We have faith in you." She stood on tiptoe to kiss him on the cheek.

"I want to fight too!" Sean begged.

"You're still a bit young to fight yet, but I'm going to need your help here on this base. There are so few of us here that we're all going to need to work hard; your mom too. Can I count on you?"

"You can count on me," Sean told his father earnestly. He held out his hand to shake, and his father took it feeling enormously proud of his son.

"As you said, they're waiting for you," Karen told him. "Go!"

Ruark walked back out to the top of the ramp of his Dragon to overlook the crowd so they could see him. He saw anxious faces out there with the light of new hope shining in their eyes. Still, alarmed and sickened by what he learned, he wasn't sure what to say to them, especially since the hideous beings among them would be listening, beings whom he believed, moments ago, to be enemies of the entire human race.

The crowd became silent as they gave him their undivided attention. Ruark knew not all of the people out there spoke English, so he ordered his ship's thought communication system to transfer his thoughts to them once again as he spoke. "You all know me, but to all the Ghost people out there among you who don't, I'm Fleet Admiral Jackson Ruark, one of four primary commanders of our planet's defense force, which is an organization formed, quite frankly, to protect our world from you, I now regret to say."

He knew from the knowledge transfer spheres that the Ghost translation disks, like the ones Duval and Murphy wore, would pick up his words for the Ghosts.

Ruark paused for a moment as he searched for the right words to express what he felt. "First, I want to say to all of you brave men and women that you are the first group of warriors in the history of our world who literally made the ultimate sacrifice for the people of your world and yet lived to talk about it!" Ripples of laughter ran through the crowd.

"I didn't intend that to be a joke," he told them seriously. Knowing the risks, you all willingly went up against those whom we thought were our enemies. While carrying out your duty, you all fell in battle. The fact you are all still alive doesn't diminish your acts of selflessness, heroism, and courage. I can't even begin to express what an honor it is to stand here before you."

Ruark choked up as he told them, "I salute you all."

Ruark did just that and snapped to attention. His audience of warriors, much moved by his tribute, remained quiet for a moment, and then someone began to clap. Others joined in, and the applause and cheers grew to a thunderous roar. It lasted a long time before it died down enough for Ruark to speak to them again.

"To our Ghost benefactors, in whom we've found true friends and allies, it is with our greatest esteem and admiration that we honor you too for the sacrifices your people have already made for us and the many civilizations of other worlds. Whether we succeed or fail in our joint venture to save our world, we will never forget you for it. Win or lose, you will always have our deepest gratitude. For those you've already standing among you on this moon, we are already forever in your debt.

"Ladies and gentlemen, all of us here understand how the Stickmen misled us. To counter their treachery, the plan Colonel Duval and his men devised to bring you all here is an ingenious one. They did it to get you to safety and to save you from the self-destruct devices embedded in your Dragon fighters. I understand you are all acutely aware that if any of us go home, then the lives of millions of your fellow warriors could be extinguished in a heartbeat the moment any one of your Dragons is detected.

"I know the anguish you must be feeling for those loved ones who are still back there on Earth and knowing they are still at the mercy of the Stickmen. My family and I are also deeply concerned for the family and friends we, too, left behind.

"I tell you now, do not believe for one instant that we are all going to sit here in exile, safe but helpless to do anything to save our people. Moreover, Ghost friends, do not believe for one second that we are going to simply sit back and allow you to sacrifice yourselves by the thousands to save a small handful of our people.

"I have an idea of how to expand upon the strategy you've already adopted, but that idea alone won't be enough. We must first take the time to plan carefully, and when we finish that plan, I promise you that you will all return to fight alongside the Ghost people and not only help them gather the seeds of our world but to do our best to drive the Stickmen away from our world forever."

Once again, the crowd roared their approval, and through the thought communications system, Ruark felt their emotional determination to win. He began to believe that there couldn't be any way they could lose.

Chapter 13
Ruark Meets the Ghosts

As the crowd dispersed from around Ruark's ship, dozens of thought-directed messages sent his way were filled with assurances of full support and expressions of joy that he'd arrived among them. He mentally thanked everyone, waving to several he knew who served under his defense zone command back on Earth. He took a long look around at this base, knowing this would be his new command post for some time to come.

With a deep sigh, he could almost physically feel the weight of new responsibility bearing down on his shoulders. "I thought Orsini swore he was the only one who always won these kinds of lotteries," he muttered to himself as he walked back down the ramp to where his family, Duval, and Murphy waited.

Karen and Sean's anxious faces were towards him. They knew Jackson held their future in his hands, and he knew how much they depended on him. *Hell*, he thought, *everyone is depending on me! Even those still back on Earth, though they don't know it.*

He managed to give them both a smile that displayed a state of confidence he didn't really feel and stepped between them to put a great arm around each of them to give them a comforting squeeze.

"Fleet Admiral, one of the Ghosts who has been helping us would like to meet you," Duval informed Ruark.

Upon hearing that, Karen's heart beat a little faster. She found even the thought of coming in close contact with one of those repulsive beings to be unnerving, but she wisely refrained from saying anything. She didn't want to add to her husband's troubles. He had his hands full, trying to figure out what he should do without adding her fear of the aliens as a distraction.

On the other hand, Sean felt excited about the chance to meet one of the Ghost people for his first encounter with a real live alien.

Karen's anxiety rose sharply when she heard her husband reply, "And I would like to meet one of them myself, Colonel. After the Stickman holograms, I would like to form my own opinions and judgments."

"Understood, Fleet Admiral."

Duval turned, surveyed the crowd for a moment, and beckoned to a young man he spotted in the crowd. Ruark noticed him standing out among the rest earlier, the only one among the gathering who had a nine-foot-tall Ghost constantly by his side. If that wasn't enough to draw his attention, the young man wore the only khaki civilian clothing among a sea of black EDF jumpsuits.

Ruark saw the young man acknowledge Duval's summons with a huge grin and watched as he approached with the tall, pale-white Ghost trailing closely behind. For the first time, Ruark witnessed in person how the Ghost seemed to glide across the ground, its means of locomotion hidden by the outward flair of its lower body.

Jake Bennings, about to meet the person Duval and the others told him was one of the five most important people on Earth before his arrival on this moon, felt nervous and tongue-tied.

"Fleet Admiral Ruark, I'm . . ."

"Jake Bennings," Ruark finished for him, managing a grim smile and shaking Jake's extended hand. The knowledge transfer made him aware of exactly how Jake became mixed up in Duval's grand scheme.

Jake's eyes went wide with surprise, and his cheeks flushed. "H-How did you know my name, sir?"

"The knowledge transfer information we just received included everything Colonel Duval and his people knew about you. That, plus I met your friend Richard Caldwell, and he told us all about you long before we ever left Earth."

" Richard made it out of the forest?" Jake's face positively lit up. "He's alive! That's wonderful!" Jake was so happy to hear that piece of news he grabbed Ruark's hand and pumped it again, his exuberance giving Ruark cause to smile despite the fact a nine-foot-tall alien stood closely behind the young man.

Duval glanced around with a puzzled expression. "Jake, where's Josh Harkins and the other two? Didn't they come with you?"

Jake's face flushed pink. He sheepishly told Duval, "Uh, I'm sorry, Colonel Duval and Fleet Admiral Ruark. When they found out they captured a fleet admiral, they told me to go on ahead and join the welcoming party without them. They said they were going to lay low and make themselves scarce for a while. I don't think they're even on this moon at the moment."

"What's this?" Ruark demanded in surprise.

Duval shrugged apologetically. "If you search your newly downloaded knowledge, sir, you'll see that your capture was the outcome of a couple of our experiments. What causes the disappearance of our ships engaging a Ghost ship is a wormhole generator the Ghosts use to defend their ships simply by sending their attackers somewhere else in the universe. It's not a weapon. That type of generator is no different than the one that brought you all here today.

"The Ghosts use ships that employ what we would call a beacon that other ships can lock onto via their wormhole technology navigate themselves accurately across virtually the entire universe. They can cross that vast distance with a single wormhole jump if they choose to.

"When we found that out, we began to experiment with the beacons. Our findings indicated our Dragons could easily be adapted to use Ghost beacons to safely make shorter jumps inside a solar system with extreme precision ranging from a few hundred yards to half the length of the solar system! Given that, we can improve our zigzag tactics by magnitudes by popping in and out of nearby space via wormhole rather than physically crossing the distances in real space! We tried it, and that's how you and your family ended up here."

"I can tell you, first-hand, that will be an astounding advantage to us that the Stickmen don't have!" Ruark exclaimed. "We know the Stickmen are afraid of making min-jumps within a solar system!"

Duval continued. "During that same experiment back home, we wanted to determine if humans could direct and operate the Ghost ship wormhole generators in battle better than the Ghosts could. So we sent two Ghost ships, one with a beacon, to the outskirts of Earth's solar system. Their orders were to locate a group of EDF Dragon ships deep inside the solar system and have a second ship accurately jump to their location close enough to pull off a successful ambush.

"I assigned Jake and Lieutenant Commander Bigsby to locate and target a group of Dragons from the beacon ship, and I assigned Lieutenant Commanders Hawks and Harkins to man the wormhole weapon on the ship sent to attack them. The entire ambush worked exceptionally well."

To Hawks' and Harkins' defense, Jake added, "It was just pure good luck on our part your ship just happened to be among the ones we ambushed, sir."

Duval winced at Jake's choice of the words 'good luck.'

Ruark's brow wrinkled as he searched his memory, "Harkins, Bigsby, and Hawks; they were among the six of you who disappeared, were they not?"

"Indeed, they were, Fleet Admiral, and also part of my intercept flight the time the alien ship kidnapped me at the Cape."

Ruark made a huffing sound, not sure whether to be angry or not. The alien behind Jake drifted a bit closer, and Ruark became mortified to realize he'd rudely ignored the Ghost, who requested to meet him, Duval's revelation about his family's capture having distracted him.

"Jake, I am so sorry. Please extend my apologies to your Ghost companion. I didn't mean to ignore him."

"He understands your words, Fleet Admiral Ruark." Jake reached out and touched the thick bulge around the alien's body. "This is my friend Pat, one of the Ghost Chief Scientists whom I've worked with ever since I left Earth."

"Pat: I am pleased to meet you, Fleet Admiral Ruark," came Jake Bennings' voice from the translator disk Jake wore around his neck, "and I am not offended."

Ruark's brow wrinkled in confusion. "Pat? You're telling me your name is Pat?" Duval and his people neglected to include that particular piece of information within the knowledge transfer data.

Karen Ruark, up until now, remained standing fearfully behind her husband, gawking apprehensively at the ghost and keeping him as a protective barrier between her and the frightful looking thing towering above the nice young man. However, when she heard the being's name was Pat, she began to giggle. The giggle turned into a snort, and she began to laugh uncontrollably.

Of course, this drew the attention and some puzzled looks from the men around her. Jackson stared at her, frowning as if she'd abruptly lapsed into insanity to be laughing with such an utter lack of diplomacy right in the middle of his first introduction to a new alien race.

At last, she managed to regain control of herself and looked around at the staring faces around her, her eyes watery from the laughter and her ears pink with embarrassment.

"Oh dear, I'm so sorry," she said between gasps for air. "It's just that . . ." she began to lose it again, "an alien whom, a short time ago, we believed to be a monster, and a killer is named Pat!" She laughed so hard again that tears began to stream down her face. Duval and Murphy readily perceived the humor of the situation, but they also could not help but notice that

Fleet Admiral Ruark was not amused. It became a royal struggle for them to keep from showing even the slightest trace of a smile.

Embarrassed by his wife's behavior, Ruark coughed and made a lame attempt to salvage what he could of the moment. "I'm very pleased to meet you . . . Pat." Ruark knew from the knowledge transfer that the Ghosts understood certain human gestures, so he touched Karen on the shoulder, and through gritted teeth, he said, "This is my wife, Karen."

"I truly *am* pleased to meet you, Pat." She barely managed to croak out the alien's name without losing control again.

Ruark stood stiffly with his arms behind his back, and he rocked on the balls of his feet, his lips tightly compressed with annoyance. One eyebrow raised, he gave his wife a warning look that conveyed, *try to be quiet now*!

Being a wife, she ignored him, of course. Then, seeing the Ghost in an entirely new light and finding herself no longer afraid, she stepped past her husband to get a closer look at the tall alien named Pat.

"Pat, I'm so sorry I laughed when I heard your name, but for months, the Stickmen taught us to fear you and your people as frightful monsters coming to annihilate us all. When I heard your name was Pat, all of my fear and anxiety the Stickmen indoctrinated us to feel just melted away from me. As I said, the thought that one of the dreaded alien killers who were supposed to be coming to kill us had the very human name of Pat made the entire concept of monsters just absurd. That's what made me laugh."

Pat's body generated a brief ripple of pink patterns along with a burst of heat that radiated from it.

Jake's translation disk said, "Pat: I am pleased to meet you, Karen Ruark. This is an extraordinary moment for me. Karen Ruark, you are the first of all the humans whom we've met so far who has so easily and readily cast aside the prejudicial suspicion and distrust of my species so deeply ingrained within you all. We are gratified by the unique path you took to arrive at your acceptance of us, despite how mystified we are by it."

"Again, I do apologize. And please just call me Karen."

"Pat: I understand that your son came with you to Ares. Is he the young human standing behind Fleet Admiral Ruark?"

Sean, unable to take his eyes off the massive alien since he first laid eyes on him, found it fascinating beyond words to be this close to a real live alien. He gulped when the alien asked about him. Karen reached for his arm and tugged him closer to introduce him.

"You are correct, Pat. This is our son Sean. Our other son Brian is also among the other Dragon fighter pilots brought here today."

"Pat: I would like very much to have a conversation with you soon, Sean. May we do that? There is much I would like to learn about young humans."

"S-Sure," Sean stammered. "That would be so cool!"

"Pat: I fear you are under a misconception, Sean. Your body temperature and those of our surroundings will not be affected."

Jake covered his mouth to hide a snicker, while Karen barely managed to keep from laughing again.

"Oh, I uh, I just meant . . . I mean."

"It's yet another one of our expressions, Pat," Jake interrupted, coming to Sean's rescue. "I'll explain later," he promised with a sigh as yet another future explanation became added to the never-ending list.

Sean knew as much about the Ghosts as everyone else, thanks to the knowledge transfer they'd all just received, but there was still something else he wanted to know.

"Mr. Pat, there's something I've been curious about. We've learned the truth that your people actually carry cities from other planets to save the beings who live in them. Why? What do you get out of it?"

"Sean means what benefit do the Ghost people receive in return for doing this," Jake clarified.

"Pat: We do this simply because we revere life. We believe there is no higher purpose we can pursue greater than preserving life. Every form of life is a marvel to us. Every living thing serves as a wondrous example of the artful creativity and biological engineering skills of the being who created us all. His work must be preserved, not destroyed, and we believe those of us whom he made capable must do all in our power to protect his creations."

Karen Ruark's eyes went wide, and she looked up at her husband, who locked eyes with her, equally astonished. Duval and Murphy were also surprised.

"Are you telling us, Pat, that your people also believe in God?" she asked.

"Pat: Jake, what is God?"

Jake was as stunned and moved as everyone else by this unexpected revelation. He smiled at Karen as he answered his alien companion. "God is what we call the being who created us all, Pat."

"Pat: Humans, too, are aware of the creator?"

Jake shook his head in amazement that such a vast topic to discuss between Pat and himself never occurred to him until now.

"Among all the many, many conversations I've had with you, Pat, the subject just never came up. Yes, we are aware of the creator, and most of us revere him as you revere his creations."

"This is incredible," Danny Murphy whispered to Duval. "We're not the only ones who believe in the concept of God."

Pat's body emanated ripples of color in and bursts of untranslated heat communications.

"What's happening?" Sean whispered to Jake, afraid that something was wrong.

"Pat is having a discussion with all the nearby Ghosts who are within his range of communication," Jake told him. "We've seen this many times before. Often something new they learn about us gets them excited. This time, I think the feeling is mutual."

The humans waited for Pat's activity to die down again. Before long, the rippling colors of his body and heat bursts ceased. "Pat: We will speak of this again soon," he said simply.

Karen smiled and found her husband's hand. Her eyes were moist from the revelation she'd just heard, and there was a look of wonder and relief on her face.

Jackson squeezed her hand three times.

Chapter 14
Honoring the Fallen

Susan McKay and Melissa Orsini held an arm around each other's waist. Their tears flowed freely as the Santa Cruz EDF Senior Chaplain, Captain Gwendolyn De Silva, delivered the eulogy for the Ruark family, and the graduate pilots lost along with them. The world watched the solemn service through the eyes of television cameras.

Susan McKay was the only fleet admiral present. Though he understood the deep friendship among the four fleet admirals, a more-cautious-than-ever Ling Wu ordered her husband, Lee, and Pete Orsini to remain at their posts, allowing only Susan to represent them. Fleet Admiral Svetlana Ivanovna, Ruark's former backup and now permanent replacement, was also absent from the ceremony to stand watch at Jackson Ruark's former post.

While personally distraught over Fleet Admiral Ruark's death, Ling Wu also felt furious over Jackson Ruark's poor judgment by taking his family into space with him, even though the attack unexpectedly occurred at a point deeper inside the solar system than ever before.

He believed that the deep penetration of that enemy ship might be the herald of new enemy tactics. So, as a precaution, he placed all EDF forces permanently on high alert while keeping three fleet admirals and Susan's backup in place at their stations.

De Silva finished the service with an 'Amen' echoed by all present. Only Susan heard the 'Amen' accompanying her own, spoken by her husband and Peter Orsini, all three listening to the service from their headquarters through the thought communications devices.

From somewhere, a bugler played the somber notes of Taps. As the last mournful note faded, the mourners present on the base became aware of the roaring sound of jets approaching. A formation of Navy F-43 Copperheads flew overhead in memory of Jackson Ruark. One ship broke away as they passed over the mourners to create the missing man formation.

Fifteen seconds behind the F-43's, a square formation of 100 Dragons silently passed overhead, the standard number of ships of a Centurion Squadron. But, this time, thirty-seven of the ships veered away, representing the Dragons of the graduating class lost in action along with the Ruark family.

With that, the service ended. The McKay's and Orsini's knew they and the world would continue to mourn the loss of Jackson Ruark, his absence forever leaving a painful hole in their hearts.

Chapter 15
New Friends Far from Home

"This will be your new quarters," Duval told Ruark and his family after he and Danny led them to a very normal-looking house. Much to the family's surprise, it was a rectangular, single-story dwelling about forty feet long and twenty-five feet deep with a peaked roof and Earth-style windows and doors. Its solid outer wall consisted of a light tan material as hard as stone with a texture similar to stucco.

"This house is so close to Jackson's ship," Karen observed. "You didn't chase someone out of their quarters just for us, did you, Colonel Duval?"

"Not at all, Ma'am. This house didn't exist an hour ago. We located it near the ship for the fleet admiral's convenience."

By the doubtful expression on Karen's face, it was obvious she thought the Colonel must have misspoken.

"It's true, Mrs. Ruark," Murphy told her, reading her disbelief accurately. "The Ghost's use . . ."

"Nanites!" Karen Ruark finished, surprised that she already knew that from the knowledge transfer. "The Ghost people use them to build everything!"

"That's right, Ma'am," Danny replied. "When we used the knowledge transfer on all you newcomers, we gave you nearly everything we've learned and experienced so far. The part that's hard to get used to is that there is such a massive amount of information upstairs," he said, tapping his head, "sometimes you don't know what you've learned until you need the information, and then it just pops out of your memory."

A faraway look came to her eyes as she focused her thoughts on the subject of nanites. They grew wide as she realized the enormity of what they did for Danny.

"Oh, my goodness! Lieutenant Commander Murphy! You were paralyzed, and the Ghosts repaired your spinal cord!"

Ruark's eyes darted Danny's direction, a shocked expression on his face too. "Good lord, you and I met only once back on Earth, and while I remembered that something seemed different about you, I couldn't quite put my finger on what it could be!'

Even though grinning from ear to ear, Danny was taken aback and at a loss for words when Karen went to him and gave him a big hug, the first he'd had in a very long time.

"I'm so happy for you!" Her gesture made his eyes well up. "Thank you, Mrs. Ruark," he managed to say, his voice cracking. He coughed in a lame attempt to try to cover the change in his voice. It didn't work, but they all pretended it did.

Duval and Murphy escorted the family into the house and, with a sweeping gesture of his hand, said, "This is it! I hope it suits you. If it lacks anything, I can assure you the Ghost people will remedy that for you."

Karen led the group to begin exploring the inside. The home had a central great room containing the kitchen and main living area. The ceilings and doorframes were unusually high, but she guessed correctly that the height was meant to accommodate any tall Ghost visitors. Entrances to two bedrooms opened along the far wall with the doorway to a very human-style bathroom between them. Every room held large curtainless windows to let the daylight brighten the interior. The walls were barren of paintings or adornment of any kind. The furnishings of the great room were Spartan, too, with only four chairs placed around a table in the center of the room and a single couch along one wall.

"I know everything looks pretty barren right now, Mrs. Ruark," Jake told her, but rather than guess what you might like, we thought you'd like to direct the Ghosts yourself about what you'd like to add how you would like to decorate the rooms."

Karen nodded her head and smiled at him, relieved to hear that bit of news, then she walked over to the part of the great room set up as the kitchen. It held a large sink with a double-handled faucet, a stove with an oven and four burners, and a large refrigerator not quite like the ones back home, but close enough. Above the sink, she peeked into several hanging cabinets containing dishes and glasses. Two of the cabinets, as well as the refrigerator, were well stocked with familiar-looking food items.

Karen found pots, pans, and utensils in the cabinets and drawers below the kitchen countertop. Exploring further, Karen was thrilled to find a large, deep bathtub in the bathroom."

"Oh, Jackson! There's a big tub and a shower in here!" she informed her husband.

"I can assure you that it comes with a never-ending abundance of hot water," Duval informed her.

Jackson spotted something that interested him and walked over to the kitchen counter, where he pointed to an ordinary coffee pot. It was filled with steaming coffee and sat on a ceramic-looking base with clean coffee mugs and cups sitting to one side of it. Ruark pointed to it, giving Duval a questioning look.

"A great feature, Fleet Admiral. It's always full, it's always hot, and it's always good. Don't ask me how they do it."

"This home is truly an unexpected and welcome surprise. I expected my family and I would be stuck living in the cramped confinement of my ship's quarters regardless of the fact how much I know my wife has had quite enough of spaceships for a while." Karen rolled her eyes at that understatement.

"I'm glad you approve, sir. I know it's late, but if any of you are hungry and you don't feel like preparing anything for yourselves, we have a twenty-four-hour cafeteria open. Actually, on this world, it's a twenty-hours-eleven-minutes cafeteria."

Too exhausted and emotionally drained to go out and find some dinner, Ruark urged his wife and son to go on ahead with Duval and Murphy to get something to eat, failing to note Karen's hesitation to leave.

Karen knew, though, her son had to be hungry and went along to keep him company. She also wanted to find their son Brian to reassure herself of his welfare. Danny Murphy escorted them both.

Ruark went into one of the two identical rooms and, without undressing, just dropped onto one of the two beds and immediately fell asleep.

～ ～ ～

Hours later, Ruark awakened to the distant sound of Sean's snoring in the other bedroom and found Karen sitting at the bedroom window just staring at the beauty of the sky above. The planet that Ares orbited still lit up the night sky, a giant pale blue-green lantern touching the horizon.

She heard Jackson stir and gave him a sad smile. He rose out of bed and stretched as he crossed the room to look out the window with her. The great planet was starting to set behind the indigo silhouettes of mountains in the distance. Now just at the beginning of its multi-million-year collision with its neighbor, the galaxy's main body stood high in the sky, a breathtakingly beautiful display. It lit up the landscape like a great night light, many times more so than a full moon would light the night back on Earth. Ruark judged from the night/day borderline on the sinking planet that, given its present position in its orbit around the planet, this solar system's sun would soon rise on this moon.

"It's magnificent, isn't it?" he said to his wife.

"Yes, everything here is beautiful, but it's not home," she told him sadly. Her voice broke, and tears welled in her eyes. "It's hard to accept that we're probably never going to see home again."

He put an arm around her shoulder and hugged her. "The odds are certainly against it," he told her with brutal honesty. "What's more important, though, is that by some miracle, we're all together here and safe. But," he said with feigned optimism, "that doesn't mean we give up hope! On the contrary, as I told Sean last night, we will never give up until we've made every effort to save our world!"

He kissed her on a cheek dampened by her tears and gave her another squeeze. It was all the comfort he could offer for now.

She nodded her head in the direction of Sean's room. "Sean is trying not to show it, but I know he is worried about everyone left behind back home as much as we are. He's afraid he'll never see his girlfriend or his other friends again. It's hitting him pretty hard, Brian too. Brian chose to stay in a barracks with his squadron mates. I spoke to him last night."

Now Jackson felt guilty about sleeping when his entire family needed him to draw some comfort, so he reached out and took his wife's hand.

Karen pulled herself from her doldrums with a shake of her head, and with a deep sigh, she smiled lovingly at her husband and drew him closer. Her nose wrinkled, and she quickly pushed him away again. "You need a shower and a change of clothes, now! You're not leaving this house until you take one!"

"Everyone thinks I'm the highest authority on this world, but you're the only person who can give *me* orders!" he quipped.

She pointed to the table where there were stacks of neatly folded clothes. "These are fresh clothes. Somehow, our hosts managed to duplicate our clothing. I changed earlier and look," she said, pointing at a button on her blouse, "this button is a clone. It's so identical to the one I wore yesterday and even has the same chip on its edge as the original."

"Our new friends have demonstrated some surprising talents," he agreed as he spotted a large ham and cheese sandwich wrapped in plastic wrap sitting on the table next to his pile of clothes. The perpetual pot of steaming hot coffee still sat on the counter, waiting for him too.

Karen saw his eyes light up at the sight of food, and he gave her a pleading look. She smiled again and caved. "Ok, food first, then the shower!"

She made him sit down at the table, poured him a cup of coffee, and watched as he sipped at it gratefully. "We brought the sandwich back for you last night, but you were out cold."

Jackson took a sip of the surprisingly good coffee and then a bite of the sandwich. As he chewed, a thought came to him, and puzzled, he stared at his sandwich and asked rhetorically, "If the Ghosts never kill, how did they come up with ham?"

"It's not ham."

Ruark stopped chewing and looked suspiciously at his sandwich again, and then at his wife, one eyebrow raised questioningly.

"We asked the same question last night. Jake told us the Ghosts duplicated the variety of food supplies his archeological expedition carried as well as the variety of food the EDF stocks within its Dragon ship quarters, all reproduced out of heaven knows what.

"As far as that ham goes, we can't tell the difference from real ham even though we know it didn't come from a living animal. The variety of supplies we have that the Ghosts copied may still be somewhat limited. However, they supplemented the food at the base cafeteria with some delicious edible fruits and vegetables from the surrounding fields and forest."

After Ruark wolfed down the rest of his sandwich, he went straight into the bathroom to get cleaned up. He found some shaving cream and became just as surprised as Jake and Duval had been when he discovered his whiskers gone when he, too, failed to find a razor and needed to wipe the cream from his face. He felt his cheek and chin and judged the results to be as close a shave as he ever had.

By the time he showered and put on a fresh uniform, the distant sun began to peek above the horizon, opposite the direction of where the giant planet set. He emerged from the bathroom to find Jake Bennings and Colonel Duval already waiting in the home's great room. Four Ghost people also stood near Jake, the high ceiling just inches above their heads.

Sean, awake now, shuffled out of his room, stood at its doorway, and just stared at the alien beings with an expression that suggested he thought he might still be asleep and dreaming.

Duval saluted his superior officer, who immediately told him to be at ease. "Sir, we've made the arrangements for a conference, and we came to escort you there. All of the MIA pilots will be attending.

"Who are these Ghost visitors?" Ruark asked, crossing the room to meet them.

Jake smiled and said, "These Ghosts have volunteered to be your guides and, hopefully, your companions if you would be willing to accept them as such. You will find yours, sir, to be an exceptional friend. I suspect you both will have a lot to learn from each other."

Ruark readily nodded his acceptance. He had a great need to know much more about these alien beings and could think of no better way of learning.

While Duval handed out translator disks to all the Ruarks, Jake made the introductions. "Ladies first, Mrs. Ruark."

Apparently, from his time spent among them, Jake developed a limited ability to tell the Ghosts apart. He gestured in the direction of the Ghost nearest him. "This is the Ghost being who would like to be your companion, Mrs. Ruark, if not a friend to you too. If you choose to accept, it's become customary for their human counterparts to provide them with a name."

Karen Ruark stepped closer to the alien, but not too close. It wasn't because she feared the Ghost; on the contrary, she just needed the distance to enable her to look up at the Ghost without straining her neck too much.

"Hello. I'm Karen Ruark, but you can call me Karen. I appreciate and welcome your kind offer of friendship, and I thank you for it. Would the name Kelly be acceptable for you?"

A ripple of pink patterns crisscrossed the being's body, and the translator Karen placed around her neck said in Jake's voice, "Kelly: I accept the name Kelly with pleasure. I am very pleased to have you accept me as your companion."

Karen introduced her husband and son to her new companion.

This time, Jackson's translator disk spoke, "Kelly: I am very pleased to meet you, Fleet Admiral Ruark, and you too Sean," this last greeting came through Sean's translator disk, and he almost dropped it out of surprise.

"Hello, Kelly, how are you?" Ruark found the introduction to be somewhat awkward. "Normally, we humans shake hands upon meeting, but please consider my hand extended in friendship to you."

"Kelly: I am well, and I am pleased to accept your friendship, too, Fleet Admiral Ruark."

Jake gestured toward a second Ghost and said, "Fleet Admiral, this is the Ghost being, who specifically requested to be your companion. I'm told this Ghost would consider it a great honor to be given a name by you."

The translator disk dangling from the cord around Ruark's neck began to speak, but without the usual preamble of the name of the Ghost speaking.

"I would indeed be honored, Fleet Admiral Ruark. I, too, have a similar rank as yours, except my area of expertise comes from leading our Seed ships to rescue planetary life forms. Primarily, my current duty is to guide our Seed ship fleets through the waves of enemy ships to snatch what seeds we can from the Stickmen's grasp. I hope to learn much from you. We Ghosts know very little of the skills related to offensive combat."

Ruark felt surprised and pleased that a Ghost of such rank would have the time to become his companion, however upon reflection, the match made a lot of sense.

"I am greatly honored to have a Ghost of your rank who would want to take the time to be my companion. As for a name . . ." Ruark thought for a moment, and inspiration came to him. "Our planet's history has a famous ship's captain tasked by our Creator to save as many species of creatures of the Earth as he could from a great flood soon to come. His name was Noah. Would the name Noah suit you?"

There came a few moments of silence as the bodies of all four Ghosts rippled with untranslated color and gave off heat. While the Ghosts communicated among themselves, Jake leaned toward the admiral and whispered. "I think you've surprised them once again with the mention of a human who did the same thing they do. It's a topic, like religion in general, that has never come up in all the months I've been with them."

After another moment, Ruark's companion Ghost broke the silence. "Noah: I am proud to be named after such a human. Thank you, Fleet Admiral Ruark. I must know more about this human when we have a better opportunity to speak of him."

"If you're to be my companion, Noah, then we must also be friends. Since we are of the same rank, please address me as Jackson rather than Fleet Admiral Ruark."

"Noah: Friends - I have never had a friend before, as I understand the term. We Ghosts have very few activities that you humans would call social. Once again, I must tell you what a privilege it is to acquire your friendship."

Ruark couldn't help but take an immediate liking to the giant repulsive-looking creature standing before him. Even though the translator disk spoke in monotones and all of them in Jake's voice, he could sense that the Ghost's words were sincere.

"Do I get a companion too?" Sean asked hopefully from the doorway of his bedroom.

"Pat: Sean, this associate of ours," a black tentacle shot out from the middle of Pat's body, pointing in the direction of the single, yet unintroduced Ghost remaining, "is to be your companion if you wish one."

This was the first time the Ruark family witnessed a tentacle emerge from a Ghost being, and it startled them all, even though they knew from their knowledge transfers that the beings sprouted tentacles as needed.

"I, too, am pleased to meet you, Sean," Sean's translator disk said.

Excited now, Sean told the Ghost," I am so looking forward to talking to you. I have a million questions to ask you."

Immediately Sean's companion Ghost's body rippled with pink color and radiated more bursts of heat generated without the usual accompanying translation from Sean's translation disk.

"Pat: Your new companion does not wish to offend you at this, your first meeting Sean, but he is concerned about the time it will take to answer one million of your questions."

All of the humans in the room burst out laughing. Still chuckling, Jake took it upon himself to explain. "Again, Pat, it's another one of our figures of speech that we've often discussed. You should know enough about those, by now, to be able to explain them to Sean's new companion."

"Pat: Oh! Indeed. It should have been obvious to me, but such expressions are very confusing to us. It has always been our way to interpret things literally." Pat emitted a burst of heat and ripples of color meant for Sean's new companion.

"I am so sorry, Sean. I misunderstood," the translator disk Sean's now wore too stated.

Jake explained, "The Ghost people, until they met me, always communicated in absolute, literal terms. Unfortunately, even after quite a bit of exposure to the idiomatic ways of our language, they still have trouble understanding what we mean. Don't worry, though. Before too long, you'll get the hang of speaking to them to avoid confusion on their part."

"Sorry. My bad, I think," Sean said, somewhat embarrassed. He took a moment to consider a name for his companion and asked, "Can I name you Stevie?"

"Stevie: I am pleased with the human name Stevie. Thank you, Sean. We have much to learn from each other. You are the youngest human residing on this world. My people are anxious to learn about you through me, and I will teach you about them. I, too, have a 'million' questions for you."

Ruark watched the exchange with the Ghost and his son approvingly. However, despite the friendly atmosphere, he still felt apprehensive about leaving Sean and his wife alone with the aliens, especially when he failed them the previous night by not being with them when they needed him.

He turned to Duval and, in a low voice, asked, "Are you certain it's safe enough on this planet to leave my wife and son with these . . . these people?"

"Quite safe, Fleet Admiral," he whispered back, then, wrinkling his brow in thought, he began to ask, "By the way, about your wife and son being here Admiral . . ."

"You will find it very unwise on your part, Colonel Duval, to finish that question."

"Uh, yes, sir."

Sean and Karen were already so engrossed in conversations with their new companions that Ruark decided that they wouldn't miss him at all; in fact, they barely noticed his departure even when he called goodbye to them. He felt more at ease to see that Jake Bennings chose to stay behind with them too, Jake's companion, the Ghost scientist Pat, still at his side.

Chapter 16
A Plea for Help

With the great conference still more than forty-five minutes away, Colonel Duval and Ruark's new companion, Noah, gave him a short tour of the rather Spartan base. This was Ruark's first opportunity to get an in-depth look at his new base of operations.

The base consisted of dozens of human-style buildings, mostly barracks, with a few large hangars lining one side of the grounds. A very alien landscape surrounded the acres of the base's purple, mossy tarmac. Tiny, penny-sized, scarlet blossoms, similar in shape to microwave dishes, dotted the tarmac individually and in small clusters, all of them pointing toward the distant sun. Bordering the entire base, a jungle of squat, dark purple growths grew, apparently this world's version of trees but shorter and much broader than those back on Earth. Some of the trees had black trunks with a texture similar to a petrified sponge. Just like Earth-born trees, their branches extended from the trunks in all directions, but the resemblance ended with feathery fronds hanging down from them instead of leaves. Where the fronds touched the ground, they continued to spread out to form a blanketing skirt around the tree. Small, immature bright yellow pods sprouted along the inner branches, all of them growing progressively larger from the trunk outward as if parts of an assembly line. The further their progression outward onto the limbs, the deeper yellow they became. Noah informed Ruark that the fruit traveled slowly outward along the branches as it ripened, and when the ripe, deep yellow fruit reached the end of the branch, it dropped to the ground, the limbs never ceasing to produce new fruit.

Turning his attention to the sky, Ruark admired its alien beauty once again. The sky had a hue more violet than blue on this world; the darker color contrasted by the wispy clouds above contrasted its sky far more than the clouds back on Earth. The great planet Ares orbited presented a breathtaking view as it finished sinking below the horizon while, at the same time, the sun of this solar system rose slowly on the opposite horizon.

"This is an astonishingly beautiful place," Ruark said, in awe of the extraterrestrial landscape. "How I wish this war would go away so we could spend the time just exploring and studying this world.

"When the Ghosts brought us here many weeks ago, this base was nothing but a wilderness," Duval explained. There are some harmless animal life forms here, but no indigenous sentient species. The Ghost people built this base in less than two days with just the rough instructions we gave them to go by."

Ruark found the information doubtful, but he'd come to accept whatever Duval told him as truth.

"Noah: These nanites, as you call them, are our primary tools, Fleet Admiral Ruark," his Ghost companion offered. "We've used them for countless of your millennia. We control them perfectly to perform nearly all our engineering functions and scientific analyses. For example, we used them to disable the destruct mechanisms of all the Dragon ships we managed to collect here. We also created more efficient, portable knowledge transfer and thought communications devices modeled after those within your vessels.

"With the nanites, we analyzed, down to the last molecule, every detail of the ships you fly. We also used them, with Lieutenant Murphy's permission, to analyze and repair the damage to his body."

Ruark shook his head at the enormity of it all. "First the Stickmen and their technology, and now this! We humans must seem intellectually inferior to an extreme to you all."

"Noah: Your lack of technological knowledge does not make you inferior, Fleet Admiral Ruark. You are merely in the infancy of your technological and scientific explorations as we once were."

"The Ghosts have emphasized to us that, even though we barely rate as a technical species in their eyes, they judge us by more than just our technology," Duval informed the fleet admiral.

"Noah: Undoubtedly, Fleet Admiral Ruark. You are the only species we have ever encountered who not only would risk their lives to save a fellow human but also the life of a being of another species altogether. It astonished us to discover this human trait when Jacob Bennings became seriously injured when he exposed himself to obvious peril to save the life of one of my fellow Ghosts, a being not even of your world. Yet, paradoxically, your species are equally willing to take a life as you are to save one.

"Fleet Admiral Ruark, I have chosen to become your companion because I am intrigued by these traits of your species, and because of them, there is something urgent I must ask you on behalf of the Ghost people."

Ruark stopped strolling again and turned to face the Ghost. "What is it you need to ask me, Noah? I'll do my best to answer."

"Noah: As we indicated, my race reveres life. We have learned from our observations of your people that though you are capable of killing, your fundamental nature is opposed to it. As I have said, you are even willing to sacrifice yourselves to save others. That characteristic binds our species together in spirit as equals; however, my people are incapable of taking a life directly without extreme anguish, no matter how evil or deserving of extinction we may find a life form to be.

"We do recognize, though, a great and sadly irrevocable and unavoidable need; these Stickmen, as you call them, have exterminated uncountable billions of lives, innocent life forms ranging from sentient beings to microbes. My people perpetually grieve over their tragic and needless passing. Our enemy, whom you call the Stickmen, wants to exterminate all life everywhere alien to them.

"As they spread their race across your galaxy, the toll of lives they take grows exponentially and will continue to grow. Until now, all that my people are able to do in the way of intervention is to move ahead of the Stickmen to gather our seeds of life with our ships and transplant them across the universe. We place our seeds far from where these Stickmen can reach with their primitive technology so that these life forms will at least not become extinct.

"Unfortunately, we Ghosts can only rescue small samples; just enough for the perpetuation of species. In the process, we were forced to abandon countless billions of their former populations, precious lives lost forever."

"If you are unable to kill, what happens to . . ." Ruark saw Duval shake his head and mouth the words "Don't go there." Ruark took the hint. From the knowledge transfer he received earlier, he belatedly realized the need not to broach the subject.

"These Stickmen have often taken a great toll of my people in our efforts to save samples of the life forms they would exterminate. If we continue as we have done, there will soon come a time when the Stickman numbers will be too great and too far-reaching for even my people to save anything. Our numbers will continue to decay while the enemy population continues to explode. We dread the day when they develop the technology to bridge the galaxies as we have done."

"I understand your dilemma, Noah. It's our problem too now. Whatever it is you need to ask, I will try to answer."

"Noah: We have come to recognize, to our endless pain and shame, that these Stickmen must be the ones who must become extinct. With our deepest sorrow and regret for the need, we wish to know if you humans will help us make this happen."

Duval gave a low whistle and said, "Déjà vu."

"Noah: Déjà vu. What do these words mean?"

"The words refer to an overwhelming feeling that we are reliving something exactly as we lived it once before," Ruark explained. "The reason Colonel Duval said that is because your request is exactly what the Stickmen asked the human race to do to help them destroy you."

Hearing Noah's request, Ruark felt a great weight lifted from his shoulders. "Noah, I understand how your request must pain you, but I am greatly relieved to hear you ask it. I am relieved because I've been trying to figure out how to make the same request of your people to help *mine* eradicate the Stickmen. I presumed that your reverence for life would cause your people to deny us their help."

Noah's body rippled with color and heat. Ruark didn't see any others of the Ghost race nearby, but he felt sure Noah was announcing Ruark's answer to others of his kind.

"Noah: We are grateful to you, Jackson," the Ghost said simply, "but our shame is great to make such a request of your people, to ask for a deed we, ourselves, are not capable of performing."

"Your people should feel no shame from your request, Noah. You have a noble goal to stop a senseless wave of death that's been going on for far too long. I believe if we work together in cooperation, then we have a chance to stop the Stickmen, but only if we succeed in saving the people of my planet."

"Noah: That problem may be insurmountable. We Ghosts have no concept of military strategy, especially not to the vast degree that seems to come so naturally to your race. Given the forces against us now, including those humans who will attack us on sight, we cannot perceive a successful outcome, but we will do everything in our power to save as many humans as we can."

Ruark smiled grimly to himself. "Noah, as I told my wife a little while ago, we must never give up! Allow my people and me to search for the best possible path to take. With your help, it will be a far better path than either of our species would ever be able to take independently."

Chapter 17
Birth of the Ghost Force

As the time drew near for the meeting, Ruark and his companions drifted toward the hangar where people gathered for the conference. At present, every EDF warrior present on this world gravitated in that direction, all of them anxious for Ruark to give them a sense of purpose and hope, along with a plan to help them save their planet and the people they left behind.

Duval spotted three figures slinking toward one of the entrances. He caught the eye of one of them and pointed to the ground in front of him. The man's shoulders sag as he muttered something to the other two, which resulted in two more anxious gawks in Duval's direction. Duval pointed to the ground again, more adamantly this time, the attention of all three upon him now.

Like men walking to their firing squad, the three reluctantly shuffled toward him. Two were good-looking young men in their early twenties. The third, slightly older, had a homely countenance contrasted by the more attractive features of the other two. As they came closer, Ruark couldn't help but note their worried expressions and that their faces seemed drained of blood.

"Fleet Admiral Ruark, may I present Lieutenant Commanders Joshua Harkins, Homer Bigsby, and Jethro Hawks," he said sternly. The three men snapped to attention, none of them too happy to be there.

Ruark, his face expressionless, took a moment to look them over. "Gentlemen," Ruark replied at last in a none-too-pleased tone. "I understand you are the three responsible for bringing us all here yesterday and scaring the living shit out of my family and me, not to mention a full class of graduating cadets?"

The three men fidgeted nervously. "Fleet Admiral," Joshua Harkins began to whine, "we were framed, sir," he said lamely as he cast a glance at Duval that begged for rescue.

109

"That's right, sir," agreed Jethro Hawks speaking up quickly in support without thinking, "We were . . . *We were what?*" he yelped, casting a horrified and venomous glare at Harkins spawned by the pitiful excuse.

"Framed, sir . . . sort of," Joshua repeated as his mind raced to provide a foundation for the pretext that he'd just committed himself to.

Homer Bigsby's shoulders slumped. He knew Harkins just doomed them all and wondered if Ghost nanites could restore hanged men.

"You see, sir . . ."

"Silence," Ruark ordered calmly.

Unhappily, Harkins complied, but to his credit, he defiantly kept his chin up to look Ruark squarely in the eye as he bravely awaited his sentencing. Ruark studied each pale face before him then held out his hand.

"Thank you, gentlemen." Speechless, the three dumbfounded men, in turn, numbly shook their fleet admiral's hand.

"Colonel Duval, my family and I would be very pleased if you, your five men, and Jake Bennings would join us for dinner tonight. I'm sure my wife and son would like to thank you all in person too for saving us from what the Stickmen still have in store for the rest of our unsuspecting comrades and families back home."

When Ruark and company entered the hangar moments later, someone called out "Ten-Hut!" which caused a small thunder from everyone coming to their feet to salute their fleet admiral.

Ruark proudly returned the salute. "Ladies and Gentlemen, as you were."

Eleven hundred and twenty-two men and four hundred sixty-five women sat on benches before the raised platform where Fleet Admiral Ruark took his place to address them. His Ghost companion Noah and L.C. Duval joined him to stand at his side. Danny Murphy, Gunther Karlson, Josh Harkins, Jethro Hawks, and Homer Bigsby chose to find seats among the last rows.

The conference participants ranged in age from eighteen to sixty-five, all of them were pilots who recently 'ceased to exist' from engaging in battle with invading Ghost ships, the people of Earth believing all of them killed in action.

The people in the audience consisted of many races and spoke many languages. Inside the building, none of them came within line-of-sight of any Dragon ship's thought transfer systems; however, a Ghost-made, new-and-improved thought communications sphere hung from the hangar ceiling that would enable everyone to understand what he had to say.

Unfortunately, no sphere worked with the Ghosts, but the translator disks every human wore made it possible for the Ghosts to participate fully in the conference.

Anxious fighter pilots waiting to hear Ruark speak sat in rows of benches in front of the platform. All wore black EDF flight jumpsuits, the emblem of a dragon-wrapped Earth showing prominently on the shoulder of their sleeves. Hundreds of Ghost beings, incapable of sitting, filled the surrounding aisles and the open space at the rear of the hangar.

"Dragon Warriors and Ghost allies, we have a lot of work to do," Ruark began simply. He turned to face Noah. "First, let me assure our Ghost friends, once again, that I can speak for all of us present here and for the rest of the human race whom we've left behind when I say we offer you the gratitude of our race for the selfless and courageous efforts you are making to save us. Our one great regret is that you must unavoidably face a host of our brothers and sisters in battle who are unaware of your true mission. Please forgive them for their ignorance.

"The people of Earth have been horribly and cleverly deceived to a point where they are unknowingly contributing to the demise of their own planet."

Ruark turned to Duval. "Colonel Duval, I commend you, your five men, and Jake Bennings, for starting this resistance movement of yours.

"The methods the seven of you devised together for gathering and, in effect, rescuing so many of us are ingenious. You've saved us not only from unwittingly participating in the destruction of the selfless Ghost people but also from certain death by the eventual detonation of the self-destruct mechanisms built into our ships."

Almost as one, the audience rose to their feet and applauded the six men present of the seven Ruark lauded, Jake being absent. Though they would have preferred to avoid the spotlight, the thought communications system revealed to everyone where Duval's men sat, and the entire assembly turned in their direction. Ruark grinned broadly and joined in, letting the ovation go on as long as the audience wanted.

When it quieted down again, Ruark continued. "People, right now, back on Earth, there are several million more of our EDF astro-aviators, deadly fighter pilots all, who are unwittingly ready and anxious to defend their ho7mes against our new friends here. They are still as convinced as we once were that the Ghost people are the deadliest enemies humanity has ever faced in all of our history. Thousands more are joining the Earth Defense Forces every day all over our planet to join the ranks of Dragon fighters.

"Our problem is to find a way to help the Ghosts defeat both Earth's forces and those of the Stickmen and still have the capability to save the people we love back on our homeworld. The few of us gathered here are not enough to wage this battle by ourselves. Together, with the Ghosts, we need to devise a way to succeed with as little loss of life as possible."

He saw the doubt on many of the faces before him. "Yes, it's a tall order, but we absolutely must believe that no goal, however lofty, is unachievable. We *will* find a way!"

Again, the audience came to their feet with thunderous applause. When it subsided, Ruark continued, "Our new friends, the Ghosts, have dedicated themselves throughout the centuries to plant the 'seeds,' as they call them, of hundreds of civilizations and lifeforms somewhere in the universe where they will flourish outside the reach of the Stickmen. When they brought us to this planet, they planted another kind of seed. Those of us gathered on this world, with the help of our new allies, will become the new seed of a deadly force that will not only rescue our people but will someday wipe from the universe the cancerous scourge we call the Stickmen! At this moment, I freely admit that I don't know any better than you do how we'll accomplish that, but we *will* succeed, I promise you!"

The audience went wild. People cheered, whistled, and applauded. Someone started to chant 'Ghost Force,' and the cry spread over the entire crowd show shouted it repeatedly at the top of their lungs, all of them ignoring Ruark's best efforts to quiet them down again. It went on so long that even Karen, Sean, Jake, and their Ghost companions came to one of the entrances to see what was causing all the commotion.

When the din subsided, the gathering of pilots retook their seats, all of them excited to have a purpose again to which they could dedicate themselves.

"Well then," Ruark said, grinning broadly, "I don't know which one of you said it first, but I guess we've just rechristened our band of exiles as the Ghost Force. When the deadly seed of warriors the Ghosts planted on this world takes root, the Stickmen are going to get a great taste of the same lack of mercy that they, themselves, have always dealt!" He quickly held up his arms and gestured for quiet to forestall another outburst of applause.

"People, we have to begin working together now! Today! I intend to use the same methods that our EDF leader, Ling Wu, conceptualized to create the strategies we've all learned to implement. You all received transplanted knowledge from some of the best strategists and commanders on Earth. Let's see if we can generate feasible battle plans that we can use by tapping into that great pool of knowledge.

"I told you all yesterday that I had an idea. It starts with massively expanding the plans of Colonel Duval and his team to bring as many EDF Dragons as we can back here to us. Here's how I intend to do that."

Ruark laid out the foundation of a strategy. The conference lasted several hours, with the audience breaking up into dozens of groups, each tasked with finding possible solutions to the tactical and logistic problems assigned to them.

The giant planet that Ares belonged to was rising again when the last conference participants left. With daylight replacing the glow of the planet's brightness, Duval walked alongside Ruark back to his home, Noah accompanying them.

"You certainly succeeded in raising their spirits, Fleet Admiral. You gave them a huge dose of hope and a goal to reach. Up until now, I could see their morale declining day by day before you arrived."

"Maybe I did raise their spirits, Colonel, but now I have to deliver."

Chapter 18
Obstacles

Inside the building, Ruark's new command referred to as 'the skunkworks hangar,' Jackson Ruark sat at a long conference table with L.C. Duval, his five men, and Jake Bennings. With them seated at the table were representatives of the various groups tasked with identifying every potential problem that needed resolution to make possible the seemingly impossible feat of destroying the Stickmen. They'd been at it for two days.

For this assembly, Ruark reminded all of the participants to speak aloud, despite the presence of a thought communications sphere, so that the Ghosts could follow the proceedings through translation discs. Among the Ghosts present were Noah, Pat, the companions of Duval's team, a dozen Ghost Scientists, Nanite Engineers, and Seed ship Commanders.

"Ladies, gentlemen, and Ghost allies," Ruark called out after several hours of reviewing the work done. "Thank you for your efforts. I believe we've captured every conceivable obstacle and problem that we have to find solutions to before we can even begin to fight back. I'm giving you the list of these problems starting with the worst at the top of the list."

Ruark waited while aides passed out copies printed on good old-fashioned paper, or rather an indistinguishable, Ghost-produced facsimile of it. This way, the Ghosts could also study the written reports the same way they first learned to communicate with Jake.

As the Ghosts received their copies, multiple thin black tentacles protruded from their bodies and deftly manipulated several pages simultaneously. The heat they radiated from their bodies made the dark ink characters visible to them. Their ability to read several pages simultaneously gave them an advantage over the humans.

"You've all done a fine job, and even though you'll find the challenge intimidating, we *will* find a way to defeat our real enemies."

Ruark reviewed a copy of the issues they had to address. They included:

114

- The potential of the self-destructs of the Dragons still in Earth's solar system being triggered by any attempt to alert the Earth
- The certainty of a vast number of Stickman forces from across their hundreds of solar systems
- The unknown number of the masked reserves of Swarm ships already in Earth's solar system that remained undetected by the EDF forces, such as the Stickman base on Mars Duval and his men stumbled upon
- The destructive power and might of the colossal Stickman dreadnoughts described in detail by the Ghosts
- The great and urgent need of those present to at least rescue and protect their families still back on Earth, no matter what
- Transferring to safety as much of the human population as possible by Seed ships simultaneously engaging in battle against overwhelming odds
- The sheer impossibility of rescuing all humans from Earth
- The Stickman ship's masking devices rendering their ships undetectable to EDF Dragon ship tactical systems
- The Ghost inability to take a life of any kind
- The Ghost total ignorance of the concepts of military tactics and strategy
- The inability of the Seed ships to protect themselves once they've encased a population center for rescue
- The already effective Stickman indoctrination of the human population causing them to believe the Ghosts were the true enemy

The list went on for several pages, Ruark finding the reading horrifyingly fascinating. The weight of solving these problems fell directly on Ruark's shoulders as the leader of this small band of humans. Though he found the burden almost unbearable, he refused to let that show to anyone, especially his family.

When he finished reading the list, Ruark stood and looked over the faces in the assembly. He saw many worried looks out there but no despair at all. Taking courage from that, he told everyone, "Now that we know what problems we have to fix, let's figure out ways to fix them."

Over the next several days, the weight on his shoulders began to lighten as both he and the Ghosts marveled at the ingenious, outside-the-box thinking that enabled them to generate realistic approaches to all of the problems on the list! Working with the Ghosts to get a better idea of what their science was capable of, the group melded human military talent with Ghost super-technology. When the great assembly finished their work, Ruark not only felt they could save a large part of the human race, he believed they might buy enough time to save all of it!

Chapter 19
Embracing Ghost Technology

"Well, today's the big day where we find out if the innovative ideas the think-tank teams came up with will work," Jackson Ruark said optimistically to L.C. Duval as they strolled toward the base tarmac.

"We must have given the Ghosts some real technological challenges, even for them, since it took them over two days to incorporate our most promising concepts into a Dragon," Duval remarked.

"We'll be putting them to the test shortly. I hope the prototype of the modified Dragon doesn't disappoint us."

"Looks like just about everyone is here," Duval observed as he looked out where every soul on the base, human and Ghost alike, gathered around the tarmac to watch the coming test exercises.

"If everything works, there's no reason why we can't begin the Ghost invasion of Seed ships back to Earth's solar system at last," Ruark replied determinedly. He allowed himself a half-smile and thought to himself, *When Pete Orsini sees how the invasion starts, I hope for his sake that he'll be wearing a diaper.*

∾ ∾ ∾

Danny Murphy leaned back in the command chair of his newly modified Dragon. He couldn't wait to begin the tests he would be performing, starting moments from now. He felt as excited as if the Ghosts had given him a brand-new ship, which in essence, was precisely what he did have.

"Damn, even the seat is better than it used to be," he muttered to himself as his seat adjusted itself to his body.

His Dragon was the prototype, the one that Ghost-directed nanites reworked so thoroughly that very little remained of the original Stickman construction except for the framework and the hull, and even those had been strengthened and reinforced several times over. The Ghost nanites had integrated into the ship nearly every enhancement that both the Ghosts and the humans concocted.

117

"Everyone and everything is ready," came Fleet Admiral Ruark's voice through the thought communications system. "You're cleared to proceed, Lieutenant Commander Murphy."

"Yes, sir!" Murphy replied enthusiastically. It thrilled him to be the first one to test the new changes, some of which he conceived himself.

Murphy ordered his ship to rise to a point several hundred feet off the ground where everyone on the base could see it.

"I'm activating the new masking system now."

"Brian," Ruark sent a thought message to his son Brian's whose Dragon ship sat parked nearby, "what is your tactical display showing?"

"My tactical hologram displayed Lieutenant Commander Murphy's Dragon ship right above us a second ago. Now it's gone."

"Well, it's definitely *still* right there above us; we can see it. Brian, activate the new tactical enhancement module on your ship that the Ghosts installed."

"Roger that, Da . . . Roger that, Fleet Admiral!" Brian sent a thought command to his ship, his Dragon still unaltered save for the nullified self-destruct and a power signature detection enhancement the Ghost nanites added that he was ready to put to the test. Activating the new device, he nodded with approval when Danny's ship reappeared in the hologram.

"Success! I have his ship back on my holographic display again!"

On the ground, every soul, Ghost and human alike, were following the progress of the tests. The human contingent of the observers 'listening' in on the thought-driven message applauded and cheered the achievement.

The Ghost observers felt the tests to be a waste of time. Even though they knew their technological marvels never failed, they patiently indulged the humans in their need to prove the modifications' operability to their satisfaction.

Ruark and Duval smiled broadly at each other and shook hands over the accomplishment of that significant improvement to Brian's ship, undoubtedly the most critical modification of all. The nanite-embedded module enabled Brian's tactical system to reveal all masked ships, Stickman and friendly ships alike, including the Seed ships already employing the Ghost-enhanced masking systems. Moreover, once all of Ruark's Shanghaied collection of Dragon ships became similarly upgraded, their reworked masking systems would blind the Stickmen to their presence, thereby turning the Stickmen's former invisibility advantage back against them.

By their standards, the Ghosts found the masking system of the captured five-warrior ship primitive, so they re-invented and installed vastly superior systems into their Dragons.

"Lieutenant Commander Murphy, proceed with phase two of the testing."

"Yes, sir, Fleet Admiral."

Murphy watched through the viewing field and sent his Dragon streaking into the sky. As his ship speared through the thin wisps of clouds, the violet sky quickly turned black in the short seconds it took him to clear Ares' atmosphere. His tactical system located two unmanned objects, the same size as Dragons, orbiting Ares a few miles apart, both sent out there as targets ten thousand miles out above the atmosphere. Murphy closed on them in seconds, and, controlling his Dragon's new wormhole weapon with his thoughts, he fired twice in less than a second. Both satellites vanished from the sky.

"Satellite one just popped through," came a thought-directed confirmation of success coming from Josh Harkins, watching' for its appearance aboard a Ghost beacon ship on the outskirts of the nearest solar system six light-years away. The beacon ship served as a reference point for Danny's wormhole weapon to focus on. The other satellite would never be found again; Danny had directed his weapon to send that one randomly elsewhere.

"Phase two is a success," Ruark announced, causing the cheers of the crowd to erupt once more. "Commence the next run for phase three, Lieutenant Commander Murphy."

"Commencing phase three, sir."

Murphy turned his Dragon back toward his adopted world and re-entered the atmosphere to race at maximum atmospheric speed over the modest spaceport. From the hull of his ship, dozens of nanite splinter projectiles shot out, one for each of more recently captured Dragon ships that still retained self-destructs. With ships deliberately parked in a random pattern all around the base, the experiment's purpose was to test the projectiles' abilities to nanite-infect both incoming Dragons during the coming battle as well as ships still parked on the surface of a world. If successful, the nanites would not only spread to nullify Dragon self-destructs, they would simultaneously modify Dragon tactical systems to locate and display the power signatures of all masked allied and enemy ships alike, as the earlier experiment illustrated. The results of this particular test would come later, the nanites requiring time to do their job.

His test run completed, Murphy maneuvered his ship to land in the same place his Dragon sat before the test began and remained aboard his Dragon for the final experiment to come.

Three Ghost Seed ships waited one light-minute out from Ares for the final test. Danny's prototype Dragon with its enhanced tactical system was vital in determining whether or not the new devices about to be deployed would perform the functions the Ghosts designed them to accomplish.

Using the captured Stickman Eradicator ship, an observation team activated its tactical system, which was presumed to be identical to or better than the Swarm ships used. When the team reported that they had their tactical systems showing the positions of the Seed ships, Ruark ordered the test last to proceed.

Out in space, the three Seed ships each deployed a drone the size of a basketball with outer shells hardened to prolong resistance to the blasts of Stickman force weapons. The drones immediately generated and surrounded themselves with perfect holographic images of the Seed ships that deployed them. Then, with perfectly synchronized timing, the drones created the identical power signatures of the Ghost ships that ejected them while, simultaneously, the Seed ships themselves used the new masking technology to hide their original power signatures from the Stickman Eradicator ship. The Seed ships themselves then wormhole jumped to the other side of the solar system.

"We still see the seed ships still in place," the commander of the Eradicator team reported. "Did the decoys work or not?"

"My new tactical is still showing that the three seed ships haven't moved, Fleet Admiral, but it's also showing three new identical power signatures eight light-hours away. The decoys work perfectly, sir!" Danny proclaimed, his ship the only one capable of detecting the Seed ships' new locations with their new masking systems engaged.

Elated by the success, Ruark breathed a great sigh of relief. These technological achievements were vital to the success of the coming battle back in Earth's solar system. He leaned back in his command chair, the seat readjusting itself to his new position, and took a moment to enjoy the feeling of a large part of his stress draining away. He knew that with these new tactical devices and weapons, the well-laid plans he and his people took pains to formulate had a great chance to succeed!

"Well, you all heard Lieutenant Commander Murphy's final report, everyone!" he called out over the communications system. "Congratulations to us all! By putting our heads together to make use of the Ghosts' extraordinary technological abilities, we've created some fantastic tactical devices and weapons. When the time comes for the Ghost Seed ships to perform their rescue work on Earth, we will make the Stickmen wish they'd never heard of the human race! We have only to wait for the outcome of Lieutenant Commander Murphy's earlier projectile test flyover, but given what we've seen so far, I have no doubt what the results will be!

Chapter 20
Battle Plans

The testing completed, Ruark, Duval, and their strategists gathered in the hangar they usually used for gatherings and conferences to wait for its results. Also present were the Ghosts Noah, Pat, and the recently arrived Ghost leader, Moses, to witness the tests of the devices they conceived and discuss the plans of their new human allies.

Forty minutes after Murphy's flyover of the base, the Ghosts were ready to report results of the nanite projectiles fired at the parked Dragons on the ground from Danny's revamped ship

"Pat: As you wished for us to prove, our nanite projectiles worked perfectly." Even though translator devices spoke in a monotone of Jake's voice, the Ghost managed to convey an element of his disdain for human doubt that required the Ghosts to validate the functionality of Danny's re-engineered Dragon, an effort Pat considered a precious waste of time.

"Our readings indicate that every recently captured Dragon on the base received a direct hit from one of the nanite projectiles as Lieutenant Commander Murphy's Dragon passed overhead at full atmospheric speed. None of the pilots aboard those ships detected the impact of the nanite projectiles striking them, nor did their tactical systems detect Lieutenant Commander Murphy's presence."

"How long did it take the nanites to spread enough to be able to dismantle their self-destruct mechanisms?" Ruark asked anxiously.

"Pat: An average of thirty-three of your planet's minutes, but it took only between ten and eleven minutes for the nanites to construct and implant the tactical receiver modules needed to enable Dragon tactical systems to detect masked Stickman ships. Also, with that change, their tactical systems will be able to make use of the beacon ship signals to safely make precise mini-jumps within a solar system without the previous dangers of gravitational influence affecting their exit points."

"I guess that cements it," Ruark said, looking around at the faces of his staff as he sat at the head of the conference table. "I'm beginning to wonder if there's anything in the realm of technology the Ghost people *can't* create.

"The next step, Moses, is to upgrade all of our Dragon ships identically to Lieutenant Commander Murphy's . . . Super Dragon, I guess would be the appropriate description. Pat, how long will it take for your nanites to convert the rest of the ships on the base to duplicate all the upgrades of Lieutenant Commander Murphy's prototype?"

"Pat: The identical time it took to convert Lieutenant Commander Murphy's Dragon; twenty-seven hours, fifty-seven minutes, twenty-three seconds of your time units for each one, all of which we can convert simultaneously.

Pleased with that estimate, Ruark nodded his approval. "Then the launch of the Seed ship invasion into our home solar system merely awaits the completion of three final elements. The first is completing the construction of your artificially intelligent robot Seed ships. The second is the need to use our superior new masking systems to reconnoiter our home system to determine the Stickman forces' true size. The third is the construction of the remaining decoy pods we will need," he said, gesturing toward one of the prototype decoys floating nearby four feet above the ground, a unit placed there by Moses for all to examine. In addition to the decoys' ability to mimic power signatures, their holographic projections of Seed ships would be indistinguishable from solid ships.

"Who would have thought that saving the human race would depend on such a small device?" Ruark asked rhetorically with a wave of his hand toward the decoy. He was exceptionally proud of it, the concept solely his. He and his people had grand plans for the decoys in the coming battle.

"Noah: There are already many aboard each of our Seed ships," Noah informed him. "Each ship can easily produce these units."

"Pat: Robot Seed ships are in production as we speak. They will be externally identical to the Seed ships operated by Ghost crews. Internally, they will be empty, hollow shells with only weapons, navigation, and targeting systems, all controlled through artificial intelligence."

"Why haven't you used robot ships in the past to capture cities?" Murphy asked.

As Commander of the Ghost Seed ship fleet, Noah answered this time.

"Noah: The taking of a city is a complex procedure involving evasive action, defense against attackers, and the rapid determination of the most lifeform-rich target locations on any given world. We cannot trust this to an artificially intelligent ship; too many lives are at stake. However, these new automated ships will be more than adequate for the ruse they were created for. They will be quite capable of directing their wormhole weapons on attacking ships, but unlike the crewed Seed ships, they will continue to fight until they are destroyed. In essence, they will provide the illusion to the Stickmen that the defending human forces are effectively resisting our invasion by destroying a large number of our Seed ships."

"If that impression is not successful, the Stickmen might find little reason to keep their human 'allies' alive. Are you sure they will be indistinguishable from the Seed ships," Duval asked with genuine concern?

"Noah: Based on our analysis of their primitive tactical systems and the successful test we made using their ship that we captured, the Stickmen will be unable to detect the difference between our Seed ships, our robotic ships, and our decoy pods. Our primary delay in the robot ship construction is from gathering and processing the mineral resources needed to construct the thousands of robot ships we plan to have. We Ghosts have never tried to construct so many ships before in such a short time."

Duval turned back to Pat. "How long will it take to complete the ships, Pat?"

"Pat: Eight of your planet's days and ten more of its hours. We are manufacturing these ships in hundreds of places across the universe at locations rich with the resources needed. However, no matter the distance, our wormhole drives can, of course, send them to your solar system within moments of their completion."

Ruark could not cease marveling at the technological achievements enabling the Ghosts to do the many wondrous things they seemed to take for granted.

"I'm glad you Ghosts are on my side," he told the Ghost leader, Moses.

"Moses: I am standing before you, not by your side." Moses corrected.

"I meant . . . Oh, never mind!" Ruark said in exasperation. He hadn't quite mastered the art of conversation with beings who always interpreted the literal meaning of everything said.

"Commander Noah, during those eight days, I would like to take advantage of every possible moment to instruct and drill your Seed ship commanders in new tactics which will significantly reduce your Seed ship casualties."

He caught himself, this time, looking up at Noah and adding quickly, "By drill, I mean the engagement of practice maneuvers, not creating a hole in something."

"Noah: Noted. Our commanders are anxious to learn these tactics from your Dragon fighters. They will be ready. Since we've learned how the Stickmen detect our Seed ships, they are undergoing improvements to incorporate the superior masking devices so they too can become invisible to Stickman tactical systems. This change alone will undoubtedly help more of our ships survive long enough to rescue many of your population centers. The Stickmen will have no means of detection left to them except visibly detecting us through their viewing fields. Of course, we will delay the use of those masking systems as long as possible to lure as many human defenders into battle with us as we can."

"Moses, do you have an estimate of how many of your new robot ships will be available?"

"Moses: Nine thousand ships; a number almost equal to the number of crewed Seed ships we will also have available."

"Your people are going to complete nine thousand ships in just eight days?" Ruark's stared at Moses in disbelief. "Christ!"

"Moses: You are mistaken, Fleet Admiral Ruark. I am Moses."

Gunther Karlson snorted, unable to prevent the beginning of a burst of laughter from escaping. Ruark shot him a menacing glare. Karlson's facial muscles strained, and his face became beet red as he struggled to contain himself.

Ruark's eyes darted menacingly about the room, his expression daring anyone else to be amused. Jethro Hawks struggled to suppress a coincidental coughing fit, and there were some barely suppressed smiles around the table, but no one else dared to make a sound. Genuinely annoyed, Ruark didn't bother explaining his irreverent human expression to Moses.

Returning his attention to the original subject, he asked, "Commander Noah, how many of your Seed ships will be involved in our final invasion?"

"Noah: All the ships we presently have experienced commanders for, nine thousand, four hundred twelve."

The numbers of Seed ships stunned Ruark, but this time he refrained from exclamation, unwilling to provide Captain Karlson yet another moment of entertainment.

"From our increased ongoing raids back into our solar system, we've gathered over twenty-four hundred additional Dragon fighter pilots, with more being captured every day. With your nine thousand Seed ships arriving, I will need every one of those Dragon fighter pilots to help instruct your Seed ship commanders in new defensive and offensive tactics. Right now, that's about four Seed ship crews apiece for each of those people to train. It's not a bad ratio. Noah, I hope your people are fast learners."

"Noah: You need to show us only once, Fleet Admiral Ruark."

"Being shown is one thing, but developing the skill through practice to make the tactics work is another. We humans have an expression, 'practice makes perfect.' We will be drilling your people with as much practice as we can give them over those next few days. I believe that with the use of our counter-tactics applied against the EDF battle maneuvers that we already know they will use against you, we can dare to hope for victory at the end of this battle.

"Noah: We are grateful and most anxious to learn, Fleet Admiral."

"Excellent! We need to start today! Immediately!"

He hooked a thumb in Gunther Karlson's direction. "It seems Captain Karlson has just volunteered to take the lead for the task of overseeing the training exercises for all of your ships."

"Noah: Thank you for that information, Fleet Admiral Ruark. That sound Captain Karlson made earlier was not in our translation vocabulary as a word for volunteering for a yet unnamed task."

"Well, I can assure you that it is *exactly* the correct translation," Ruark told the Ghost with conviction, observing with satisfaction Karlson no longer seemed to be entertained. "How soon can your commanders be ready?"

"Noah: We have summoned them. Captain Karlson needs only to direct them to the location where he desires them to arrive."

"Captain Karlson, you are well familiar with the new tactics we want our forces to learn. You have a local day and a half to formulate a training schedule and prepare everyone on base while their ships undergo reconstruction. You then have at least seven days more to train and drill the Ghost commanders before the robot ships are completed."

"But sir," Karlson protested, the knowledge transfers don't work on the Ghosts!"

"You have all two thousand combat pilots to give you a han . . . to give you help," he corrected himself before the need came to explain yet another expression. "Handle it! And take your merry buddy Hawks with you!"

Jethro Hawk's smile also faded away.

"Yes, sir," Karlson replied gloomily. "I'll get started right away."

"See that you do," Ruark replied testily, still annoyed with the both of them. He turned his attention back to both Noah and Moses.

126

"The test runs we made with Lieutenant Commander Murphy's ship have not only met our expectations but exceeded them. We still need to conduct a reconnaissance mission before we can finalize our invasion plans. Noah, are your preparations complete so you can conduct that mission with Colonel Duval and Lieutenant Commander Murphy?"

"Noah: My Seed ship and crew are ready and at your disposal."

"I have to tell you, Noah, I'm very uncomfortable with your participation in this operation. There's still an element of risk involved, however small, and I would hate to lose you."

"Noah: A minuscule risk indeed, Fleet Admiral Ruark, although I do appreciate your concern."

Ruark looked up at the giant Ghost at his side, unable to think of any argument that would convince Noah to change his mind. "Very well then, proceed with the mission, but be extremely cautious."

Chapter 21
Reconnaissance

Noah's Seed ship popped into space just beyond the edge of Earth's solar system and began traveling slowly sunward. Not only would it perform surveillance of Earth's entire solar system using its new tactical system, it would also make sure its new masking system successfully prevented the enemy from detecting its presence. There was also a third goal of the mission . . .

～ ～ ～

On what would be the equivalent of a bridge on Noah's ship, L.C. Duval sat in a Dragon-style seat next to where Noah stood, both of them observing the images on the ship's new tactical hologram system. The bridge chamber was a colorless, spherical room with a band of control consoles embedded in the surrounding wall, all of them sprouting Ghost-style control levers. The ring of a deck formed a platform around the center of the bridge where a tactical hologram floated.

Duval already knew the walls above the consoles gave off varying patterns of heat only the Ghosts could see, but to him, they remained nothing but bare metal walls. To the Ghosts, the heat patterns on their surface displayed a multitude of indicators and monitors. Tall, white columns of the Ghost bridge crew stationed themselves around the consoles, all monitoring and reacting to the variety of information their devices provided.

Noah and Duval both focused their attention on the holographic image. It currently displayed a spherical view of Earth's solar system enhanced to reveal masked Stickman ships and hidden installations. It also allowed the Ghosts to see what the humans saw by duplicating and overlaying the holographic images with the infrared wavelengths of light that Ghost vision was sensitive to.

What the hologram revealed to Duval made him nauseous. Appalled, he almost cried out, "Son of a bitch!" but caught himself, not wishing to explain why that wasn't an intentional insult to Noah.

All Stickman ships and bases hidden within Earth's solar system became exposed for the first time, their locations no longer a secret. Masked Stickman bases peppered planets and moons throughout the solar system. The number of power signatures representing Stickman ships lighting up the hologram horrified him.

Duval mentally ordered the tactical system to return the number of Stickman ships it identified. He vigorously cursed again as it reported more than eighteen million Stickman ships scattered throughout the solar system, all but a million and a half of them masked and hidden from EDF tactical systems.

"Noah: This is most distressing, Colonel Duval. Never have our Seed ship rescue attempts encountered as many enemy ships as we are presently detecting."

"I guess these Stickmen want to make certain they can exterminate the entire human race if we humans turn out to be a disappointment to them. This single revelation makes this entire mission worthwhile."

"Noah: It was indeed a wise move for Fleet Admiral Ruark to send us back to reconnoiter the magnitude of their forces here."

"I've ordered the tactical system to record all of the power signature locations. Fleet Admiral Ruark and his strategists can figure out what to do about them later. To be thorough, let's see what else is out here."

Duval extended the range of the detection system and found yet another unpleasant surprise. Outside the solar system and well beyond the range of a standard EDF unenhanced tactical system, ten more ships lurked, enormous ones judging by the power signatures on the hologram.

Duval magnified that hologram segment and found that each of those ships' signatures also included one hundred thousand smaller ones, the latter being of Swarm ship size or larger. All by themselves, the smaller ships represented almost a third of the present size of the entire EDF Dragon fleet.

"Dammit! Commander Noah, do you see the group of huge ships way out there beyond the solar system?"

"Noah: Of course, Colonel Duval. Those are the great ships we described to you that ultimately destroy targeted planets. They also serve as a Stickman version of Seed ships to spread their empire. Many of the occupants of those ships become colonists of the solar systems they sterilize. They have the skills to transform planets and moons to the conditions and environments that will enable their race to thrive.

"They're colonization ships as well as planet slayers? Your people never mentioned *that* particular bit of information to us before, Commander."

"Noah: You have never asked us that question."

Speechless, Duval stared stupidly at the Ghost for the moment. Then, shaking his head in disbelief, he turned his attention back to the hologram. "We're going to have our hands and tentacles full when the time comes for us to try to stop them all," he muttered.

"Noah: I must tell you this hologram, as you call it, is a remarkable tool. Such a simple concept, yet it provides a greater concentration of information at a glance than what we used previously.

"What did you use previously?" Duval asked distractedly, more out of politeness than interest as he endeavored to perceive anything else the hologram exposed for the first time.

"Noah: It is difficult to describe our senses to you. Let us just say that because we see things all around us simultaneously, our navigation and tactical systems give us a sense of being located at a central point where we can visualize a limited part of the volume of space around us. That is why this control room is spherical. We display stars, planets, and ships on the hull walls. The brightness of an enemy ship tells us precisely how distant they are from us. It never occurred to us to create an accurate presentation of a large volume of space in miniature to observe."

"As you know, Noah, what you described as your primary viewing system isn't very different from the way we use our Dragon's tactical holograms. We, too, sit at their centers to view the volume of space around us in every direction. If you find the additional functionality of this new system useful, you may want to provide all of your ships with it."

"Noah: We have already done so, Colonel Duval. Why would we not? We have made this new tactical system a standard unit for all Ghost ships. However, we can only control ours by an auxiliary bank of levers since we cannot yet control them mentally as you humans do."

"Perhaps someday, if we ever survive all of this, you Ghosts can use humans as part of your crew to mentally manipulate Stickman technology for you," Duval suggested.

"Noah: That is an interesting suggestion. However, we too are studying the Stickman telepathic units, and we expect to understand this intriguing technology soon. I believe we will soon be able to adapt them include our transmissions too rather than just copy them for human use alone."

"Well, let's make the best of what we already have and hope your new masking system works as well as we think it does, Commander. We are going to need it more than ever now. Keep your tentacles crossed."

"Noah: We've already proved the masking system operates perfectly," he said with unmistakable indignation woven in the reply. "And what conceivable purpose does it serve to cross our tentacles?"

Duval ignored the question. "I apologize for being doubtful, but like Fleet Admiral Ruark, I'm a bit paranoid, especially when we're the ones who are the guinea pigs in enemy territory. We are engaged in a test that could prove fatal to us all if the system fails us. It's our nature to be nervous. I certainly meant no offense."

"Noah: We do not take offense from your words, Colonel Duval, but why is it you believe we have become pigs?"

∿ ∿ ∿

Noah's ship took an hour of advancing slowly inward toward the sun. Even though fully exposed to possible detection, they saw no sign of any ship, human or Stickman, coming out to intercept them. The masking system continued to prove itself as the Ghosts insisted it would.

"I think we can proceed to the next phase of the mission, Commander Noah. Millions of Stickman and EDF tactical systems have failed to detect us since there are no Dragons or Stickman swarms coming out to intercept us. We couldn't have a better test than that! Let's pick up some speed so we can get on with the next phase of our mission."

"Noah: As you wish. We will choose a path to avoid Stickman patrols and your people's sentry positions to reduce any chances of being observed visually."

Noah's ship proceeded to make its way past the orbit of Jupiter to the asteroid belt without a single Centurion squadron or Stickman swarm coming out to bestow upon them their usual unsociable greetings.

Choosing a particularly dense cluster of asteroid debris in the belt, Noah guided his ship deep inside it where no Stickman EV or EDF Dragon would be able to spot them visually.

"Noah: We're ready to proceed with the last phase of this mission, Colonel Duval. We are activating the beacon signal and sending the target locations."

∿ ∿ ∿

"We have incoming in sector Romeo 5, Fleet Admiral McKay," Sub-fleet Admiral Kapus announced from his Pittsburgh headquarters, as he sent out the alert for a bogey popping into his sector of the defense zone.

The EDF still maintained the old army alphabet standard to indicate sector locations.

McKay snapped his attention instantly to the volume of his tactical hologram encompassing that sector, and he mentally ordered the display to zoom in on it. Again, a single intruder was working its way into the solar system; this one disturbingly popped out of a wormhole well within the orbit of Saturn.

"He's all yours, Sub-Fleet Admiral Kapus. Heads-up, Sue! We have one inbound in our shared space. We haven't seen one of them penetrate this deep into the solar system since we lost Jackson."

"Here comes another one just as close, only South of the sun in sector Uniform 13," Pete Orsini added. "It's just outside of Jupiter's orbit."

They all watched their tacticals with rapt attention as sentry ships, directed by Sub-Fleet Admiral Kapus, left their sentry grid positions, and joined up to form a standard Centurion formation. The first intruding ship popped into the solar system so close to the nearly complete defense grid that it took only eight minutes for the first Centurion squadron to reach it, a record interception time. Using the magnification functions of their tactical holograms, the fleet admirals watched the first interception unfold as if viewing the event from just a few dozen miles behind the defenders.

The Centurion gracefully slid into its bowl-shaped formation, eleven hundred miles across the rim, and reversed course instantly when the intruder passed inside the bowl perimeter. Then, as the Admirals witnessed dozens of times in the past, the squadron enclosed the intruder, matched its direction and speed, and began blasting away. Also, as usual, Dragon ships began vanishing as if they'd never existed.   One   after another, they disappeared while the surviving defenders kept up a heavy barrage from their force weapons.

This time, the squadron was lucky. Not only did the intruder explode before it could escape through a wormhole, but they lost only nineteen of their one hundred ship formation, an exceptionally low casualty rate. To each fleet admiral, even one lost person was one too many. Now, another nineteen families would have to be told their loved ones died in battle defending the planet.

As the survivors turned back toward home, the second Centurion squadron caught up with the next invader. But before the next fight began, Svetlana called out, "We have a third intruder in Sector Alpha 33!"

"And yet another one coming in again at the exact place the first one appeared!" Susan McKay announced. "This is just not right! They're not supposed to be able to jump to the inside of the solar system at all, let alone this deep! What kind of game are they playing now?"

"They're making themselves a royal pain in the ass!" Orsini commented.

"It is still better than hundreds or thousands of them showing up at once, Fleet Admiral Orsini," Svetlana Ivanovna admonished, addressing him formally as she maintained her ever-present sense of formality with her counterparts whenever she was on duty. "The longer they wait to launch a full invasion, the stronger we become to resist them."

"Amen to that, Fleet Admiral," Orsini responded with equal formality, knowing it would irritate her if he did otherwise.

"This is bizarre behavior," Sue commented. "They must be trying to figure out if the first ship weakened the defense grid enough for them to get through to the next layer."

"Well then, they're going to find out the answer the hard way," Lee responded without sympathy.

In moments, his prediction came true. EDF Dragons rapidly intercepted all three of the intruders, but this time the invaders all managed to escape through wormholes before the defending Centurion squadrons could damage them enough to be destroyed. Unfortunately, the EDF casualty count for this strange raid came to ninety-three Dragons from the four intrusions.

"With all of these random forays, they must know already that they have more on their hands to deal with than just the Stickmen. They must be trying to figure out all the angles before coming in at full force. Maybe that's why they're daring to make these deeper inbound jumps," an aggravated Orsini speculated.

"That or they're trying to figure out how many of us there are to contend . . ."

"Incoming again in sector Kappa 9," Sue interrupted her husband. They all watched as another Centurion formed and caught up with the bogey in only six minutes. This interception squadron succeeded in destroying the ship with just sixteen losses, another previously unheard-of success.

All four fleet admirals remained on edge, waiting for one of their tactical systems to detect additional invaders. Minutes went by without any new arrivals.

"Well, I'm baffled," Orsini mused. "They've never done anything like that before.

"Who knows how the heck they think," Susan replied. "They're aliens. Their idea of reconnaissance is probably incomprehensible to us. What's important, though, it looks like the main invasion isn't coming today."

"This is true," Svetlana agreed. "We must be thankful we have yet another day to grow stronger."

The four fleet admirals returned to the routine of command, the unpredictability of the enemy keeping them all on edge.

∿ ∿ ∿

A short while later, Ling Wu's headquarters received the daily report of any incidents involving the deep insertion of the intruding ships that Ling Wu always reviewed. Even though Dr. Ling found the baffling pattern of attacks disturbing, it pleased him to see the defense network proving itself capable of dealing with the random deep penetrations of invaders just as it was designed to do.

∿ ∿ ∿

Noah's Seed ship slipped back out of the asteroid belt and went straight through a wormhole back to their distant base solar system. Duval felt thoroughly pleased with the performance of the two experimental robot Seed ships they let the Centurions destroy during their first test ever. Without a doubt, the Centurion squadrons that attacked them couldn't tell the difference, even though the robots sent fewer ships back through wormholes than a crewed ship normally would have.

Duval hated leaving Earth's solar system without knowing whether Ruark's message idea worked. As a wormhole doorway opened to take them back to their base, he felt as if he'd just put a note in a bottle and threw it into the ocean. They might never know if the EDF command figured out the message. He had no way of knowing Ruark's attempt to communicate with Earth's command already failed. No one in any of the command headquarters caught it. The letters of the sectors in which the invading Seed ships appeared, in order, spelled RUARK.

Chapter 22
Plan Adjustments

Jackson Ruark grimly studied the hologram of Earth's solar system that revealed the Stickmen's true strength as recorded by Noah's ship. The hologram floated above them circular where he and a small group of his best planners and strategists analyzed it. Ghost beings were also present to observe and learn what they could from the Earthmen since their own strategic talents were dismally underdeveloped. Duval, sitting next to Ruark, completed his reconnaissance report for the group. He used a thought communications sphere to relay his thoughts clearly for the English and non-English speaking humans in the room while his translator disc communicated his spoken words to the Ghosts.

" . . . as you can see, everyone, just as we anticipated, there are Stickman hidden bases scattered throughout the solar system, but far more of them than we ever expected. In my opinion, I believe we can assume the majority of swarm fighters will remain hidden as our people and the known Stickman swarms resist the incoming Seed ships. The odds against us just when way up!

"If the Stickmen decide to trigger the self-destructs in the EDF Dragons, that's when all those masked Swarm ships will likely come in to try to finish off the Seed ships along with the rest of the human race. They'll be coming from planets and moons all over the solar system from multiple directions all at once, not to mention those dreadnoughts outside the solar system which will be joining them along with their dedicated escort of Swarm ships."

"Noah: As I informed Colonel Duval at the time of this holographic recording, we Ghosts have never encountered such a sizable military presence in our past efforts to gather our seeds."

Jackson Ruark hoped the Ghosts couldn't tell how deeply shocked he, himself, felt from Duval's unwelcome revelation. Even if his Ghost Force acquired the strength of numbers of every EDF ship in existence, they would still be outnumbered more than six to one against the now-exposed

Swarm ships without including the colossal dreadnoughts and their ship-based collections of Swarms. To anyone else, it would appear their chance of defeating the Stickmen looked like it just went from remote to nearly hopeless.

"Even with this new information, we still have to have faith in our plan," Ruark insisted. "Our plan is a good one! However, more than ever, we need every ship that we can gather from Earth's solar system to defend the Seed ships and help them get through to Earth. Our foremost objective during the battle *must* be to continue, as planned, to capture as many of Earth's defending forces as possible on a massive scale. The way I see it, we can only achieve this by using the full-blown Seed ship invasion to gather in EDF Dragons in one grand sweep.

As this is happening, we won't be able to send back our Super Dragons until we've rounded up every newly captured Dragon we possibly can. There will be so many captures flooding into this solar system that we'll need every one of our Super Dragons to serve as beacons at widely scattered collection points for the Seed ships sending them here. The newcomers simply *must* be met only by humans and quickly convinced to change sides as we have already been doing so successfully thus far."

"But, sir," one of Ruark's strategists argued, "once we diminish the EDF defenders to the point where it becomes obvious that they've lost the battle, how do we know the Stickmen won't see the Dragons as useless failures and trigger their self-destructs anyway? They'll be wiping out not only our people doing battle in space but all the reserves on the ground! We can't possibly save enough of them!"

"We *can't* know that, but if you were the enemy deliberately expending the EDF Dragons as a means of preserving your forces, wouldn't it be more to your benefit just to let every last one of them continue to fight until there were none left?" Duval argued.

"Of course, that's what we *humans* would do, but the Stickmen may have a whole different way of reacting. We know nothing about them except for the fact they are devious and ruthless killers," the strategist argued.

"Fleet Admiral Ruark, we know that with our improvements, our Dragons can effectively mask themselves to the Stickman tactical systems," Danny Murphy spoke up. "Using that advantage along with the nanite projectile systems, I propose we risk sneaking a few Super Dragon back to Earth to infect ground-based Dragons with nanites just as we plan to do with incoming captured ships. We'd be able to disarm the destruct systems of thousands of those ships, and the nanites will modify their tactical systems to enable them to detect Stickman masked ships! We could save several hundred thousand ships without having to engage them in combat!"

"Are you out of your mind?" Karlson protested. "What if, against all odds, they discover us visually anyway?"

"Wait a second," Ruark interjected. "Lieutenant Commander Murphy has an interesting idea. You know as well as I do that when it becomes evident to our people that they can't win, they aren't going to commit suicide by fighting to the last man out there in space. They *will* retreat to make a run for Earth and rally there to defend their homes and families. When that happens, that will undoubtedly be the point where the Stickman will trigger their Dragon's self-destructs. Earth will be left defenseless!

"Considering Lieutenant Commander Murphy's idea, though, the risk of sending back masked Dragons undetected would be enormously reduced when the Seed ships are engaged in battle all over the solar system with hundreds of thousands of EDF and Stickman ships scattered everywhere. Then we can sneak a team back to Earth in the chaos of battle.

"I think Lieutenant Commander Murphy's idea is brilliant! No one will be looking for masked Dragons returning from the grave." Ruark turned to the Ghost Commander. "Noah, I'd like to hear your opinion."

"Noah: Given the enormous number of masked Stickman ships hidden inside your solar system, they don't need you humans at all. Knowing that they live to kill, then clearly, this is an experiment on their part to see if they can weaponize your people's talents to their benefit. I agree that if they determine your people cannot win, they will take great pleasure in destroying with a single blow all of your fighters that we have not captured by then."

Ruark and his officers sat in silence, weighing their limited options. "We have to succeed in getting Seed ships to Earth no matter what. Helping the Ghosts fight this battle against EDF defending Dragons is the only way to accomplish that, and we need to preserve every Dragon we can. People, I believe we have no choice but to take the risk and adopt Lieutenant Commander Murphy's infiltration ruse. The Ghosts have a limited number of Seed ships. The longer we wait, the more Dragons the EDF will have to resist them, thus making it harder for the Seed ships to reach Earth."

"Noah: You must all realize no matter what the outcome, given the size of the Stickman forces in your solar system, the opportunities for our Seed ships to rescue even a small number of your race will be limited."

"While the number of enemy ships against us is truly an unpleasant and difficult problem, Commander Noah, theoretically no problem is without a solution," Ruark replied with more confidence than he possessed, a level very close to zero. For the sake of the morale of everyone under his command, Ghost and human alike, he dared not display anything except confidence, no matter what misgivings he felt.

Ruark remembered something from Earth's history he hoped would provide a bit of inspiration. "There was once a similar military problem from Earth's history. A group of three hundred warriors called Spartans, leading an additional six thousand warriors, held off more than one hundred fifty thousand invading warriors for seven days at a place called Thermopylae. Their success came from an ingenious strategy they developed to accomplish that incredible feat. People, this is our present-day Thermopylae. Let's get started! We have a Spartan style strategy of our own to develop."

As the group began to discuss matters among themselves, Duval leaned over and whispered to Ruark, "Sir, the Spartans were all killed by the enemy."

Ruark shot him an angry and exasperated look. "Do you want me to tell them what happened at the Alamo too, Mr. Sunshine?"

Chapter 23
The Eve of Battle

"Captain Karlson, please give us your report."

This meeting was the final debriefing before Ghosts and humans alike committed themselves to the final invasion back to the home solar system. The Ares night sky held thousands of glittering new 'stars;' the thousands of gathered Seed and robot decoy ships reflecting the light of this solar system's sun. With the arrival of the last autonomous robot ships the previous evening, the wait to return was over.

Even though the collection of Ruark's Ghost Force Dragons remained pitifully small compared to the combined EDF forces and Stickman swarms, their new integrated technology made them vastly superior to anything the Stickmen could ever produce. Once the invasion began, the success of Ruark's plan depended on the number of Dragons the Seed ships could capture during the coming battle, adding them to Ruark's Ghost force. With the growing number of new Dragons the EDF placed into service every day, Ruark couldn't afford to wait any longer to launch the invasion. The more newly commissioned Dragons adding to Earth's defense, the greater the chance of more Seed ships being destroyed in the battle to come, and the greater the number of EDF defenders who would die if the Stickmen triggered the Dragons' self-destructs.

Gunther Karlson rose from his seat. Seated around the table in the conference room were those in charge of mission-critical assignments. Their Ghost counterparts, as always, stood around the table, having taken places behind those seated.

"Sir, as ordered, we worked intensively with the Ghosts for the last eight days. When I 'volunteered' for this assignment," several at the table chuckled at this, "I figured that without the use of knowledge transfer systems to help us, the task was going to be impossible. To the credit of the Ghost people, I couldn't have been more mistaken.

"As ordered, all of our available people helped to put the Ghost commanders through the new drills and tactics we devised to maximize

139

the number of Dragons we capture while, at the same time, minimizing Ghost casualties. At first, things began even worse than I expected. We found the Ghosts to be as militarily inferior to us as we are technologically inferior to them, and I assure you that is no exaggeration.

"The one single tactic the Ghosts have employed for centuries is to race like madmen as hard and fast as they could, as a unified group, through a gauntlet of Stickmen swarms in their effort to get to their target planet. It's very similar to a school of Salmon trying to reach their spawning ground in a river lined with grizzlies, only much worse. Some Seed ships make it, and too many do not."

Karlson paused to let the analogy sink in before he continued. "What came as a surprise, though, even without the advantage of being able to use the knowledge transfer spheres for teaching, these Ghosts never forget anything they've been told or shown! We only needed to demonstrate a tactic once, and they could repeat it flawlessly time after time.

"Commander Noah, no matter how you and your people manage to accomplish that, it worked to our advantage. We completed the training two days early and spent the rest of the time just practicing our drills. The Ghosts are as ready as they can be, Fleet Admiral Ruark. Mission accomplished if I do say so myself."

"Noah: I must tell you the martial talents you humans have revealed to us are nothing less than astonishing to us. The lessons you taught us will preserve many Ghost lives in this coming conflict and undoubtedly in future conflicts to come."

"The Ghosts may not have the natural instincts and reflexes humans have to react in a fight," Karlson said, "but from the EDF training that we all received, we gave them the full variety of Earth's defensive strategies we know they will have to deal with in battle. We've prepared them to react instantly and properly to counter them."

"Excellent work, Captain! Colonel Duval, you're up next. Make your report, please."

Gunther Karlson took his seat, and L.C. Duval stood up. "Sir, while Captain Karlson vacationed with the Ghosts," Karlson scowled while others around the table chuckled once more, "we were able to send another seventy-eight Seed ship forays back into the home system. Two-thirds of the ships we sent were the first of the new autonomous robot ships. Just as the Ghosts assured us, the robot ships fought indistinguishably from Seed ships having crews. The robots sent a large share of captured Dragons back to this solar system right up to the moment our forces back home destroyed them. I'm confident they successfully provided the illusion to the Stickmen that EDF Dragon ship fighters are as deadly as they hoped them to be.

"The crewed Ghost ships we sent took a bashing too, but all managed to escape back to this solar system before we lost any of them. Personally, I believe the Ghosts will voluntarily wait far too long and take too much punishment when they're capturing our Dragons before they jump back to safety. Regardless, we successfully captured another twenty-eight hundred ten Dragon ships in the course of it all. We are now almost five thousand strong, and the last of those captured ships will be fully modified before the day is out."

"Commander Noah," Ruark said, turning to the being he now considered a good friend as well as an ally, "Please express to the crews of your ships how grateful we all are for the risks they take on behalf of our people. We will never forget it."

A burst of undeciphered heat and ripples of color played across Commander Noah's body. "Noah: It is done, Fleet Admiral Ruark."

"Thank you, Commander Noah. Our appreciation is heartfelt." He turned his attention back to Duval. "Colonel Duval, how much difficulty did you have bringing the newcomers around to believing the truth once they arrived? We're going to have the same problem tens of thousands of times over during the coming battle."

"Persuasion would have been a bitch without knowledge transfer systems. Persuasion was no longer a problem once they learned the Stickmen rigged their Dragon ships to blow. They were all one hundred percent thoroughly pissed and extremely anxious to send the Stickmen straight to hell when they get back home."

"Twenty-seven hundred ships is a damned good haul! When the Seed ships begin the invasion, we'll need every one of them to help with the roundup of incoming captured Dragons."

"There is no question though that we'll have our hands full infecting incoming Dragons with nanites and convincing their pilots of the truth before they get feisty with us, Fleet Admiral."

"I know our people are all anxious to go back to kick some Stickman ass," Ruark told everyone present, "but I need everyone to remain here in this solar system until that terrible moment finally comes when Stickmen figure out what's going on. Let's just hope that discovery is a long time in coming. The longer we can avoid it, the more Dragons we can capture to save them from their self-destructs.

"The one comfort our small band of Ghost Force fighters can take from their delayed return is that, when I do turn them loose with their modified ships, they'll be the deadliest force the Stickmen could ever have imagined!"

The meeting lasted for several more hours as others at the table presented the status of their part of the preparations and, most importantly, the strategies they developed for dealing with the unexpected size of the Stickman forces.

At the end of the meeting, Ruark stood and looked at the faces around the room. "Well done, everyone. We will never be more ready than we are now. If we wait any longer, the numbers stacked against us back home will grow, and the loss of life will be all the greater when the Stickmen universally trigger the self-destructs.

"Tomorrow, we launch! I want everyone gathered on the field and ready to begin one hour after dawn tomorrow. All of our people better get a good night's rest tonight. There's no telling when they'll get a chance to rest again."

∾ ∾ ∾

Early the next morning, almost the entire collection of fully enhanced Dragon ships hovered three feet above the tarmac, awaiting their human pilots. At the edge of the field, Jackson Ruark stood to address nearly five thousand humans and three thousand Ghosts one last time. His wife, Karen, and his son, Sean, stood at the front of the crowd.

Ruark saw thousands of eager expressions out there, their long wait over. The weeks of working and drilling together made the small force of warriors more of a closely-knit family rather than a group of brothers-in-arms.

Over nine thousand Ghost commanders and their crews were already aboard their Seed ships waiting for Ruark's command to begin the operation. Noah assured Ruark that they, too, would hear his address.

Now more than ever, Ruark knew he needed to present an air of total confidence and hide the almost overpowering sense of anxiety he really felt. The coming battle would be for all or nothing, and he was painfully aware that if it failed, the failure would be on his shoulders alone.

He took a deep breath and, not wanting his audience to know how nervous he was, mentally ordered the communications system of his nearby ship to turn off the function that transmitted his sense of emotion. He looked out over the thousands of upturned faces waiting to hear him speak, and he felt a massive swell of pride for them all.

"People," he began, "the moment we've waited so long for has finally arrived. Today the Ghost Seed ships will return to our solar system with the most extraordinary mission in humanity's history, to save the human race from annihilation. One hour from now, the first wave of Ghost seed and robot ships will jump through to our system to pave the way for the rescue of our people back on Earth.

"This will be our only battle, as well as our only chance. There will be no opportunities to try again. Have faith, though, my friends, that we won't need another chance because we absolutely will succeed!" The humans among the gathering cheered and applauded their agreement, forcing him to pause until the commotion died down.

"The Stickmen expect thousands of Seed ships massed together to run through their gauntlet of Swarms as they've always done in the past. That is not going to happen this time. The tactics we've taught to our friends no longer require them to seek safety in numbers like a school of fish or a flock of birds. Instead, what we have in store will undoubtedly come as an unpleasant surprise to the Stickmen.

"Unfortunately, as you already know from your EDF training, Ling Wu and his strategists have prepared the EDF Dragon forces for every conceivable mode of attack from the Seed ships, including the one we've planned. The change from the Ghost's traditional tactic of grouping together will NOT affect the EDF's capability to defend the solar system. To save them all from their ship's self-destruct devices, we *must* defeat them in battle. It's a tall order, I know, but we can do it! The more of our brothers and sister warriors that we can bring back here to safety, the more of them we can send back again against the Stickmen.

"Pray for our success and say an extra prayer for the success of the twelve brave men I'm sending back to Earth to try to save the Dragon reserve ships still on the ground. Their covert mission is as critical as the invasion of Seed ships.

"I want you all to know I have the utmost confidence in you all, humans and Ghosts alike. I am so very proud and honored to serve with you all." He snapped to attention and saluted them all. Five thousand people saluted back.

Before he could dismiss them, a mental request came through from one of the combat pilots in the assembly who asked him to lead a prayer for the mission's success. Everyone heard the request except the Ghosts, whom the communications spheres could not reach, but Jake passed on the request for Pat's benefit, murmuring a quick explanation of what prayer was. His enlightenment caused the Ghosts to become excited once more.

"People," Ruark said, "you all heard that request. If you don't mind, I'd like to step aside and pass that privilege on to someone who is far better

143

suited to lead us in prayer than I will ever be." He gave his wife a loving smile and said, "Karen, would you come and stand by me, please."

Surprised and pleased by her husband's request, Karen crossed the short distance and took her husband's hand. She paused to consider what to say, trying to find words she thought would be appropriate for all of the many religions represented by the people standing solemnly before her. The assembly became silent, most of the audience bowing their heads.

"Creator of us all, please bless our Human and Ghost warriors who are selflessly placing themselves in harm's way to rescue our loved ones and all of the people still left behind. Grant them your protection and success in the coming conflict and bring them all safely back to us. Amen."

"Amen," echoed thousands of voices.

PART TWO
Invasion

Chapter 24
It Begins

One hundred thousand miles out from Ares, Jackson Ruark, aboard his ship, concentrated his attention on his tactical hologram as he orchestrated the widely scattered positioning of his small fleet of Super Dragons. With Noah's help, the preparation of over nine thousand Seed ships and another eight thousand combative robot ships also neared completion.

"Colonel Duval, I see you and your infiltration team are already in position. Do *not* be impatient! It shouldn't be too long before things get hot and heavy enough back home for you and your boys to sneak back. Keep yourself and your crazies under control until then."

"Fleet Admiral Ruark," Karlson objected, "speaking for the team, we resent being called crazies."

"If you weren't crazy, you wouldn't have all volunteered without coercion this time," Ruark replied, cutting communications with them to move on to matters more important.

"Commander Noah, do you have the first wave ready for injection?" Noah's massive armada of seed and robot ships sat positioned beyond the far side of the giant planet Ares orbited. Hundreds of masked beacon ships were already in place on the far outskirts of Earth's solar system to provide return wormhole navigational reference points.

The translation disk around Ruark's neck gave him a quick reply. "Noah: my people are ready. Five hundred of my crewed Seed ships and autonomous robot ships await your command to begin the first wave of our invasion. A total of over seventeen thousand ships of both types are ready for the additional waves to follow. We also have eight masked beacon ships equally spaced around the outskirts of your entire solar system. Those beacons will allow us to jump anywhere within your solar system accurately. Our initial arrival points will be close to the edge of your people's defense grid so that engagement with the defending ships will occur shortly after our arrival.

"We are all anxious to make use of the training you have given us. With it, we will effectively send back to this solar system the Dragon ship defenders who attack us, and we will send the Stickmen ships elsewhere."

"From what Captain Karlson reported to me about their training, I have every confidence in your people."

"Noah: Thank you, Jackson. That means a great deal to us."

"Dragon ships, what's the holdup? Get to your positions and turn your beacons on! Get it done!" he ordered. His display glittered with moving dots of light, indications of all of several thousand Super Dragons taking their places throughout this solar system at designated collection points for captured EDF ships. Over the past few days, the Ghosts managed to reconstruct them all with the identical functionality of Danny Murphy's prototype ship. The Ghosts could have provided hundreds of beacon ships to take their place, but it was imperative human-occupied Dragons meet them instead of Ghost ships.

"People, anywhere from half an hour to forty-five minutes after Commander Noah's first wave goes back to our solar system, the defending forces back there will begin to intercept and attack them. The Dragons the Seed ships send back to us will come in at a trickle at first, but it's going to turn into a flood as more as more Seed ships and robots engage the EDF defenders and start pushing Dragons back through to this solar system. Keep them under control! You know what to do! Round them up, infect their Dragon ships with nanites, and use the knowledge transfer devices to pump the truth into them. They have to be convinced to change over to our side as quickly as possible. We're going to need every one of them to join us when the time finally comes for us to return.

"The invading Seed ships have already divided your Dragon's beacon signals among themselves so that the ships that we capture are equally distributed among you when we send them here to this solar system. Gather every one of them!"

"What do you want us to do when we're not busy, Fleet Admiral?" replied some clown who wisely set his communication system to keep himself anonymous. Ruark smiled and hoped the sarcasm would ease some of the tension and anxiety among the troops, but he officially ignored the remark.

With the last of the ships in position, at last, there was no reason to delay any longer.

～ ～ ～

The McKays, Pete Orsini, and Svetlana Ivanovna, Ruark's successor, were all at their headquarters' command stations in a teleconference with each other via the Stickman thought communications spheres. As they talked remotely, their eyes never left the massive tactical holograms surrounding each of them, displaying the individual zone they were responsible for defending. A faint line bisected each defense zone to indicate the overlapping volumes of space that two other fleet admirals shared with them to provide support resources if needed.

At present, they were all attempting to analyze the recent increase in enemy intrusions into the solar system, trying to determine a discernible pattern that they could take advantage of to predict a subsequent intrusion.

"I don't get it," Pete Orsini complained as he studied tiny bright blue dots of light imposed within the three-dimensional holographic displays signifying all of the locations where unwelcome deadly visitors entered the solar system in recent weeks. "The entry points seemed to be randomly scattered throughout the volume of space, but with few exceptions, all the intrusions are just inside the orbit of Pluto when we know from sad experience that they can jump to places well inside the solar system."

Within Orsini's hologram, power source lights depicted lone Dragon ships in their assigned sentry positions, all forming layers of concentric defense grid spheres throughout the entire volume of space well beyond Saturn. Like tree rings, the gridded pattern of spheres was dense close to the Earth but grew farther apart as they spread outward to nearly the orbit of Uranus.

"It would be nice if the Stickmen gave us their ideas of what the purpose of the enemy could be for these distant raids," Sue McKay added to the complaint.

Unorganized dots of lights in the tactical hologram revealed Swarm ships either nested in their lunar base hangars or grouped in patrol swarms scattered randomly throughout the solar system even though many weeks had passed since any of the Stickmen responded to an intruder.

"I don't see anything that makes sense as far as predictable entry patterns go," Lee muttered distractedly to his associates as much as to himself as he studied the intruder pattern.

"I, too, see nothing," Svetlana added, "but I also observe no significant gaps in our layers of defense. If the enemy attempted to discern any weakness of our defenses by testing us with their forays, then they must certainly be frustrated by their efforts."

"Reconnaissance seems to be the most logical explanation for their forays," Susan agreed, "but as Pete pointed out, why so distant when we know they can jump in closer and jump back out again before they have to engage any of our Dragons? Surely they'd accumulate more information that way."

"I'm not so certain," Orsini replied doubtfully. "Surely their technology is at least as developed as the Stickman technology. If so, one intrusion into our solar system would be all they need to get a snapshot of our defenses throughout the entire . . . Whoa! An incoming raider just jumped into our territory Susan!" he warned unnecessarily. Their tactical systems simultaneously gave them instantaneous mental warnings, and their holograms provided an accompanying bright flashing red dot of light to show where the intruder emerged from its wormhole.

"Looks like you got your wish, Pete. This one's close in, just twenty light-minutes from the outermost sphere of our defense grid. It's close to the centerline of where Sue and Svetlana's defensive hemispheres overlap in your Southern Defense Zone."

A second dot appeared at an equal distance from the sun but in another direction high above the planets' orbital plane.

"Make that two of them!"

In a heartbeat, dozens of additional invading ships popped into the solar system, followed seconds later by cascades of hundreds more, all scattered randomly but equally close to the defense grid outer perimeters of all four fleet admiral's defense zones. Power signatures of arriving invaders continued to populate the edges of their holograms as the solar system blossomed with enemy ships scattered in every direction. Their tactical systems reported an ongoing count of the invaders whose number rapidly approached five hundred.

"This is it! The invasion is here!" Sue McKay warned unnecessarily, glad the thought communications system could not reveal the shakiness of her voice as she said it."

"Good luck, everyone," Pete Orsini replied grimly.

Without another word, all four fleet admirals took action, first by satisfying themselves that their sub-fleet admirals were already directing sentry ships, then by carefully evaluating the overall picture their holograms gave them. Next, each of them made sure none of their sub-fleet admirals had overlooked anything in the surprise of the moment.

The incoming invaders permeated every subsector of every defense quadrant. The time had come at last where they would need to exercise the entire spectrum of their training.

Chapter 25
The Weight of Command

Taking an opportunity to nap on a couch inside his office as he'd become accustomed to doing in his underground headquarters, Ling Wu became startled awake by a visibly agitated officer who burst unexpectedly into the room. The officer practically babbled in his anxiety and excitement as he reported that the alien invasion had begun.

Ling Wu's anxiety rose, and his heart began to beat faster. He spent his entire career studying and writing about great military strategies and leaders, but the outcome of this campaign, the greatest one in humanity's history, depended upon how great a strategist he, himself, would prove to be. Shirt wrinkled, his necktie askew, he rushed out the office door directly into the heart of his headquarters, a ready room of his design where his staff constantly monitored a tactical hologram of the solar system.

From the very beginning, Ling Wu adamantly resisted the notion of keeping all of his command eggs in one Stickman technological basket, however advanced it proved to be. It would have been poor judgment, in his opinion, to have his entire defense system reliant on Stickman technology alone.

Unlike the Stickman holograms his fleet admirals viewed, the best human-produced technology available on the planet generated this hologram. Even though its display did not have the clarity and solidity of the images produced by Stickman technology, it created an excellent substitute. Unfortunately, as much as Ling Wu wanted a backup system that relied entirely on human technology, his hologram still had to depend on the images of a Stickman tactical hologram remotely located on another base altogether. Unavoidably, no other source existed with the capability of providing instantaneous, real-time events taking place throughout the entire solar system.

As Ling Wu took a moment to examine the display to evaluate the situation, his is brow became wrinkled with concern. Already thousands of dots of light identifying the positions of both friends and foe alike filled the entire volume of the hologram. Without a doubt, the long-awaited invasion had truly arrived.

Surprisingly, the enemy ships didn't emerge as the single, massed armada the Stickmen led the EDF to expect. These several hundred invaders appeared individually in every conceivable direction.

Ling Wu immediately opened a communications channel to General Hiro Kumitsu, a former Japanese logistics expert and currently the head of the EDF civil defense. The general's face appeared on the monitor in front of him.

"General Kumitsu."

"Sir!"

"Make a public announcement immediately that the invasion has begun. There will be the expected panic and spontaneous mass evacuations in the cities, but it is the right of the people to know. We must hide nothing from them. Activate your entire civil defense force and deploy them all to minimize the inevitable chaos as much as possible. Ensure all the refugee centers are ready for an inrush of people fleeing the cities.

"The centers are ready, Dr. Ling, and I have already given the instructions to my men to stand by for additional orders." The face on the monitor vanished as the monitor went black again.

Ling Wu ordered his external security people to fall back into the compound and secure its blast doors. Next, he gave his undivided attention to the hologram, studying it intensively to determine an attack pattern. He and his strategists had planned for every scenario they could imagine, and he was relieved to find one of them envisioned this very same scattered, random entry of invading ships. However, of all the possible invasion scenarios they perceived, *this* one was the worst one of them all. This type of attack by the enemy would stress the defense grid to its maximum capability.

Now, instead of his defense squadrons flowing smoothly outward in a single direction to meet a single giant group of enemy ships, as the Stickman holograms predicted, the EDF Dragons would be forced to intercept invaders coming from every direction simultaneously. This not only taxed the ability of the defending sub-fleet commanders to assign targets to their forces effectively, but it also challenged the ability of the reserve elements to fill in the empty grid gaps as the sentries moved out to form intercepting Centurion squadrons.

Most alarming of all, not one single Stickman combat swarm moved out from their bases to help the EDF forces engage the enemy. Eyes narrowed,

Ling Wu nodded grimly to himself as if an unanswered question resolved itself.

He settled in his command chair and leaned forward to watch his holographic display as it came alive with ever-shifting light patterns of maneuvering ships. From all over the solar system's defensive grid, fifty thousand Dragon ships coalesced to form five hundred Centurion interception squadrons at the edge of the defensive grid. Layer by layer back to Earth, thousands more Dragons moved outward to refill the constantly shifting gaps in all sentry grid layers.

At this point, Ling Wu could only watch, the actual command of the conflict finally placed entirely in the hands of his fleet admirals and their sub-fleet commanders. With the calm concentration of a chess master, he gave his undivided attention to the moves playing out before him.

∿ ∿ ∿

It didn't take long for the announcement to go out to the media, who, in turn, rapidly spread the alarm to the civilian population that the long-feared, city-destroying aliens were on their way. The seeds of panic became firmly planted, and fear spread like wildfire. In cities worldwide, frightened people herded their families into their cars with whatever food and possessions they could swiftly gather up, then took to the highways.

In past months, those who held little faith in governments to protect them and survivalist types alike were already long gone having no desire to be waiting in the middle of what would be primary targets of a coming invasion. However, even with the forehand knowledge of an imminent attack, most of the city populations remained in place, most having nowhere else to go or being without the funds to go anywhere. With the enemy at Earth's doorstep, the spontaneous need of the masses to escape the cities swept all former concerns aside.

Worldwide, without exception, the thoroughfares of every city and town on every continent quickly became clogged with vehicles and people on foot, traffic everywhere coming to a standstill as all major highways became severely overloaded. Hundreds of thousands of EDF ground troops and civil defense personnel spread out to do what they could to ease traffic congestion and aid the exodus of panicked populations.

Ling Wu's emergency response organization had long since set up evacuation areas that were ready to receive fleeing populations well outside of every city in anticipation of this event. But even by their most optimistic calculations, it would take several days for most of the refugees to reach those areas, given the expected chaos of the exodus. Depending on the outcome of the battle soon to begin, they might not have days.

～ ～ ～

Inside her headquarters in Baikonur, Susan McKay managed to take the briefest of moments to mentally send her love to Lee with an appeal for him to take care of himself. She then quickly broke communications with him to avoid distracting him further, but not before she heard him return the same plea from him echoed back to her.

～ ～ ～

Pete Orsini felt the hair rise on the back of his neck as hundreds of invading ships popped into the outer edges of his hologram. Despite the numbers, he kept calm, took a deep breath, and muttered under his breath to the spirit of his good friend Jackson Ruark, "Wish us well, Jackson old buddy!"

Unintentionally, his thought went out to all the sub-fleet admirals at their command posts. The fifty "Amens" mentally echoed back startled him.

～ ～ ～

Lee McKay felt a chill creep down his spine when he saw the invading enemy ships appear like malevolent spirits materializing out of the dark. To him, it seemed as if a giant cage was forming around the entire solar system to keep anything from escaping. He knew it would continue to shrink until the Dragon ships decimated it, or it squeezed the whole planet to death.

Despite his anxiety, he refused to allow the thought to break his concentration or determination. He had great faith in his command staff, his tens of thousands of Dragon fighters, and in the skills of his counterpart fleet admirals. He knew their superb training made them the greatest and deadliest commanders and warriors in the history of the planet.

Lee's sub-fleet admirals busily directed their forces with little need for his supervision from their headquarters. He heard his wife's brief message of love, and he sent one back to her. They all had their hands full now.

～ ～ ～

Now, in her late thirties, Svetlana Ivanovna always presented a cool, self-confident, and professional image her entire life. Orphaned as a child, the government placed her in a state-run school where she excelled in every phase of her education. Her grades were so impressive that her government entered her into the Zhukovsky-Gagarin Air Force Academy at eighteen. By the time she turned twenty-five, she had fulfilled her dream of being selected for the Cosmonaut Corps.

Consistently demonstrating a professional demeanor backed by real substance, talent, and integrity, Svetlana rapidly advanced through leadership ranks within the Corps. Several weeks ago, serving as Jackson Ruark's second in command, she never dreamed there would be a need to take his place completely. Despite her portrayal of a hard, professional exterior, she was frightened now. She prayed that her knowledge and skills would not fail the millions of people counting on her for their survival.

Chapter 26
Anticipating the Slaughter

Monitoring the defense activities of the humans from his command ship hidden under the surface of the moon, the Stickman hive master felt mystified by the unprecedented manner in which he considered a handful of enemy ships appeared. Fascinated, he watched the systematic, structured maneuvering of the human-piloted ships as the Earth's Sentry Dragons throughout the solar system began to form orderly, one hundred ship interception swarms waiting to intercept each enemy ship.

From the humans' planet to the outermost layer of their defense grid, human-piloted sentry ships moved outward, layer by layer, to fill the shifting gaps left behind by others flowing outward toward combat. The hive master found the humans' efficient response to the invasion thoroughly impressive.

Most of the hundreds of the humans' interception squadrons had already locked themselves into their bowl-shaped formations that raced toward the incoming intruders, the hive master recognizing this as the standard attack formation the Earthmen devised and practiced endlessly to engage the enemy. He did not doubt their methods would be far more effective than the swarm tactics Hive forces employed unfailingly.

Before coming to this system, these elaborate maneuvers the Earth people exercised were unheard of by the Hive race. The Hive always chose to destroy enemy ships by the sheer force of overwhelming numbers. The hive master's people never imagined a concept of tactics that might preserve the lives of swarm warriors during battle. The race of Stickmen always maintained an endless, disposable, and easily replaced horde of swarm warriors to draw from among their vast populations all over their sterilized colony systems.

Despite the hive master's disdain for humans, it pleased him to see the organized and evenly distributed network of defenders reacting with machine-like efficiency to deal with the torrent of invading ships. Even though the invasion began only a short while ago, the humans were

156

already racing to meet the incoming enemy ships. The Hive race would have taken much longer to organize and distribute their swarms to deal with threats coming from so many directions.

As gratified as he felt to see the human's efficient reaction, the hive master found this invasion alarmingly out of character compared to any encounter the Hive race ever experienced in their entire history of dealing with this enemy. Not only were the enemy ships approaching from every direction, but the total number of incoming enemy ships represented only a fraction of the multiple thousands that, in past encounters, always arrived in one massive self-protecting cluster.

Equally baffling, his tactical hologram revealed yet another anomaly; the incoming invaders traveled toward Earth at a relative crawl compared to what past Hive experiences led him to expect. The hive master perceived their inexplicable behavior to be a foolish tactical error on their part, and it delighted him to see it. He believed these lone unprotected ships, behaving like animals separated from a herd, could be easily overwhelmed and slaughtered by his swarms if the humans' defensive efforts failed.

The first clash of opposing forces would occur in a matter of minutes. The hive master eagerly waited for the slaughter to begin and did not care which side suffered the most.

Chapter 27
An Unpleasant Surprise

The combination of expletives coming out of Pete Orsini's mouth were not ones even he normally allowed himself to say, let alone broadcast to everyone via the communications network. Even if he had been consciously aware of doing it, he was far too busy to have cared about it.

"So much for the Stickman preview holograms of coming attractions!" he barked angrily as he needlessly pointed out the obvious to his three counterparts. "What happened to the one giant armada the Stickmen told us to expect?"

"It was supposed to be like a D-Day massed landing, not hundreds of individual commando raids," a frustrated Sue McKay added furiously to the growing list of complaints.

"We'll handle it!" her husband replied with more confidence than he felt. "It may even work to our advantage. Remember the old divide and conquer rule? They've divided themselves for us and are making it easier for us to engage more of them without our Dragons getting in each other's way."

"Always the friggin' optimist," Orsini muttered to himself.

"They've all emerged from their wormholes deep inside our solar system at equal distances from our defense perimeter everywhere." Svetlana pointed out needlessly. Their wormhole technology must be exceptionally advanced.

"Not to mention their reconnaissance capability. Even so, it won't make a difference," Lee replied. "It will only speed up the start of the battles to come. Sue and Svetlana, keep your people ready just in case the invading ships begin to make near-Earth jumps and be prepared if Pete and I need to draw reinforcements from your zones.

"Our Centurions are ready, but where the hell are the Stickmen?" Outraged, Lee McKay scanned his tactical hologram to find every visible fleet of Stickmen ships holding themselves back from battle and leaving the Dragon ships to fight alone. "What the hell are they waiting for?"

158

"Maybe this change of attack comes as a surprise to our allies too," Svetlana suggested. Her counterparts were not as willing to give the Stickmen the benefit of the doubt as she was, but this was no time for further speculation and debate. Lee and Pete's Dragons, responsible for the defense of the outer solar system, were already forming interception Centurion squadrons.

Lee announced several minutes later, "Our first Centurion interception just occurred at nineteen minutes after the enemy's appearance. A good bit faster than our people managed from any of the earlier raids, but back then, the invaders were farther out." Moments later, he grimly added, "The first attacking squadron lost only eight ships before they could come within their Dragon's weapons range."

"We already know those enemy ships all have longer-ranged weapons. All of our Centurions are going to lose ships that way. There's nothing we can do about it," Orsini responded bleakly.

"The good thing is that the rotating formation approach must be working. The Stickman holograms showed us that their swarms lost far more ships than we're losing before their attack groups could get within range of their target. What's left of our squadrons should be able to take out the enemy ships before their losses get out of hand, just like they've done with the raiders they've dealt with over the last few weeks."

"I'm sure everything else will go just as the Stickmen told us to expect!" came Susan's worried and bitterly sarcastic reply.

Susan and Svetlana held back their forces, waiting for the fighting to reach the inner solar system. Until that time came, their duty was to refill any critical grid shortages only if needed. Just as the first Centurion squadron engaged its targeted invader, Susan warned anxiously, "We've got more incoming! I see close to three hundred new bogies on my half of the solar system!"

"I, too, have over two hundred new invaders on my half," Svetlana added.

Even though squeezing the hologram of half a solar system into a room-sized arca made judging distances difficult, Svetlana was sharp-eyed enough to notice that the second wave emerged from o their wormholes closer than the first wave did. The mental query she sent to her tactical system confirmed it.

"This second wave of invaders entered the solar system five light-minutes closer to Earth than the first wave. I believe they are initiating a leapfrog tactic, as you Americans would call it."

"If they did it once, they'll do it again," Lee speculated. "Pete, advise all of your sub-fleet admirals."

~ ~ ~

Twenty-six minutes after the invader's first appearance, five hundred Centurion squadrons, a total of fifty thousand Dragons, had all five hundred Ghost seed and robot ships engaged in battle. At their headquarters, the fleet admirals' tactical holograms were chaotic with the movements of hundreds of thousands of repositioning ships within the defense grid layers, those going out to intercept enemy ships, and those moving outward from Earth to refill the vacated sentry positions.

"Our counterattack against the first wave is only minutes old, and we've already lost over sixteen thousand Dragon ships. We've managed to destroy only one hundred ninety-five enemy ships in return!" Lee McKay announced grimly, "The rest of the invaders vanished, all of them ducking back into wormholes to keep our people from destroying them. That hit-and-run tactic has me worried."

"No time to worry about it now," Orsini replied. "Our next groups of Centurions are closing on the second wave of incoming ships."

The fleet admirals watched the advancing Centurions as the Dragon survivors of the first engagement returned to Earth. With their previous sentry positions already filled with replacements, the survivors would remain ground-based until their turn came to move outward again.

Once again, squadron Dragons began disappearing before their chosen targets came within weapon range. As Centurions began to engage their chosen targets, a third wave of five hundred more enemy ships appeared. Just as Svetlana predicted, the third wave emerged from their wormholes, yet another five light-minutes closer to Earth than the previous wave.

"Looks like you were right, Fleet Admiral Ivanovna," Sue McKay said. "It seems the invaders intend to continue with their leapfrog tactic, but I don't understand though why they are making such short leaps."

"I'm sure we'll figure out why sooner or later," Lee replied to his wife. "Right now, we should expect a fourth wave to jump in on us soon!"

Chapter 28
Infiltration

"How long do you think it will be before it's our turn, Hammer?" Jethro Hawks asked Duval, resorting back to callsigns now made obsolete by the instant identification provided by the thought communications system.

"However long it takes, Gator. Back home, the Dragon ships surviving their battles with the Seed ships are rotating back to Earth in exchange for fresh replacements moving out. Those returning are the ones we have to blend in with. The more there are, the less chance the Stickmen will have to visually spot us sneaking back.

"Right now, our Ghost friends are taking their time advancing so they can suck in more of Earth's Dragon ships into our capture nets." The remnant of a smile formed on his lips. "You boys aren't worried about going back home, are you?"

"Damned straight, I am!" Gator responded without hesitation.

"Roger that!" Karlson agreed.

"That makes three of us!" Joshua Harkins chimed in, "All of these new gizmos the Ghosts gave our Dragons had better work, or we'll all be screwed!"

"At the risk of sounding insubordinate, Hammer, that was kind of a dumb-ass question to ask us!" Bigsby retorted.

"Relax, guys," Danny Murphy comforted. "The one thing we can be certain of is that we can trust Ghost technology, and no one can vouch for that better than I can. I'm able to walk again, thanks to them."

Their nervous chatter continued, Duval listening but not joining in. They had a right to be worried. They were all painfully aware of the pressure put upon them as part of the twelve members of his reinsertion team. The lives of many thousands of Dragon Fighter Pilots still on the ground waiting for deployment depended on the success of their mission.

"The plan will work," he heard Danny reassure them all with conviction. "And then we'll finally be able to kick some Stickman ass!"

"Do Stickmen even have an ass?" Joshua Harkins asked speculatively.

∾ ∾ ∾

Ruark became infuriated when he'd first learned from the reports coming from captured Dragon pilots that the Stickmen were not joining in the battle as they'd promised. However, even that unexpected news contained a positive aspect. Even though the team he sent back to Earth would have far fewer reserve Dragons on the ground to infect with nanite projectiles than anticipated, every defending ship would have a human pilot. That meant the Seed ships would be sending through far more Dragons than they would have been able to if Stickman swarms were participating in the defense.

Ruark followed the battle's progress by absorbing every bit of information he could from returning damaged Seed ships and captured Dragons. Two hours after the first wave of Seed ships returned from battle, he knew from the massive loss of Dragons that the defense grid had collapsed inward in every direction to a distance equivalent to that of Saturn's orbit. He also knew that with the chaos of Dragons returning from battle and sentry Dragons moving outward from the defense grid, this would be the perfect opportunity for Duval and his team to sneak back to Earth by blending in with returning Dragons.

"Ghost team, it's your turn up at-bat. Get going!" he ordered.

Duval's ships winked immediately out of existence within Ruark's tactical hologram. Even though Duval's team consisted of only a dozen Dragons, their mission was the most dangerous, risk-filled mission of all. If the Stickmen discovered them, all would be lost. To add to Ruark's anxiety, his son Brian was one of Duval's team.

∾ ∾ ∾

In the chaos of battle, Duval's technologically advanced and masked team of Super Dragons emerged from wormholes right at the battlefront. Just like the Seed ships, they all came emerged scattered throughout the solar system in places where the greatest concentration of battles was taking place; the team Dragons widely separated from each other by light-hours. Their Super Dragons were invisible to Stickman and EDF tactical displays alike. Keeping to the rear of the retreating packs, they successfully mixed themselves, unnoticed, among battle survivors returning to Earth while.

"Ghost team report," Duval ordered. Now that his ships arrived back in the home solar system, he knew his team remained undetected by the simple fact that the Stickmen didn't detonate the self-destructs of all the defending EDF ships.

Duval and his team used their undetectable Ghost communication medallions to speak to each other to eliminate any additional risk of discovery via the use of their thought communications systems,

Once the last member of his team reported a safe arrival, Duval told them, "All of you have the locations of your assigned base and headquarter targets programmed into your navigation system. Get your butts back to Earth fast and infect as many ships as you can before the ground command launches too many more reinforcements! Time is of the essence, people! The nanites need thirty-three minutes to nullify the self-destructs on the ships we infect, so get moving!"

Even though the teams' modified dragons had the ability to jump closer to Earth accurately, Ruark's strategist agreed that there would be less risk of visual discovery if Duval's Dragons simply blended in with returning Dragons. However, given their various distances to Earth from their insertion point, it would still take them all between twenty and forty minutes at near light speed to reach home, depending on whether or not they were on the same side of the sun as the Earth.

Everywhere Duval's team emerged from wormholes, EDF Dragons were returning from battle. However, it would have taken an alert and observant pilot to notice that Duval's masked Dragons didn't belong with them, let alone that their power signatures were missing from tactical displays. Nevertheless, Duval knew he would breathe a lot easier when the last of his team reached Earth's atmosphere without discovery.

By the time Duval entered Earth's atmosphere thirty-six minutes later, more than half of his men who arrived ahead of him were already racing between spaceports to nanite-infect parked reserve Dragons.

"Ghost team, I've arrived over Canada. I'm heading to Lee McKay's headquarters as planned. Since I was part of his staff, I should have no trouble convincing him that the Stickmen are the real enemies. Just in case you don't hear from me an hour after I land, I want Karlson, Harkins, and Bigsby each to pick another fleet admiral to try to warn. Harkins, if Karlson drops out of sight, you try next, then Bigsby. We can't afford more than one of us on the ground at a time until we defuse every Dragon self-destruct mechanism on this planet! Got that?" Eleven 'affirmatives' came back. "Karlson, you're in command of the team as of right now."

∿ ∿ ∿

Duval had fifteen hundred miles to cover to reach McKay's Hill EDF Spaceport. Shooting straight down to within a few hundred feet above the ground, Duval ordered his navigation system to set the zigzag course he needed to pass over all six additional spaceports before arriving at

McKay's headquarters in Utah. It would take a little bit of extra time, but in doing so, he would be able to infect the thousands of parked ships at those spaceports on the way to his destination.

Chapter 29
Battle Status

For nearly three hours, invading ships continued to repeat their leapfrog strategy as Centurion squadrons continued to fight off unending waves of incoming invaders. To the fleet admirals' frustration, far more enemy ships escaped through wormholes than were destroyed, and the new invading waves appeared at an ever-increasing rate to put a terrible strain on the defense grid.

Even with over three thousand enemy ships scattered throughout the solar system, Pete and Lee still maintained more than enough EDF defenders to keep the enemy at bay, but Dragon losses continuously depleted the number of their reserve forces.

"The enemy strategy is an effective one," a vexed Svetlana called out to her counterparts. "Our fighters are doing all they can, but the enemy line continues to advance steadily."

"There's no question that we're hurting them, but we're certainly not beating the hell out of them," Pete Orsini sent his thoughts in reply. "Their advance may be steady, but they still don't seem to be in a hurry to reach the Earth. Their leapfrog jumps are still short compared to what we know they are capable of making. I think it's becoming obvious they want to kill as many of us as they can before they rush the planet."

"Makes sense they'd want to do that to thin us out," Lee McKay agreed. "That's what we'd probably do if we were in their place. What worries me is that when our Dragons pound them, most of the enemy ships keep jumping back to wherever they came from before we can finish them off, and we haven't a clue how many ships, total, they still have to throw at us."

"We've destroyed more than eleven hundred of their ships," Orsini responded, "but it took over six thousand engagements to do it. In the meantime, we've lost over two hundred eighty-five thousand of our Dragons, and the number keeps climbing. To make matters worse, our casualty rate is so high that some of our people are beginning to lose their nerve, causing our desertion rate to climb. We may soon have to begin drawing reserves from Sue and Svetlana."

"We wouldn't have so many friggin' casualties if those damned, son-of-a-bitchin' Stickmen would join in and help us!" an angry and frustrated Susan McKay added, uncharacteristically employing words she normally wouldn't approve of hearing from anyone.

"They would not have given us the means to defend ourselves if they did not want us to succeed," Svetlana Ivanovna speculated logically. "For whatever reason that they make us fight alone, let us hope they still intend to join us."

"Another friggin' optimist," Orsini muttered again.

"We're still holding up without them," Lee McKay responded irritably. "As you said, we're hurting them, and that's despite our desertion rate."

"With this damned leapfrog tactic of theirs, they've progressed to just beyond the distance to Jupiter in all directions. If those asshole Stickmen haven't joined the party by now, I don't think they're ever going to," Susan growled, her language continuing to suffer a steady decline since the battle began.

Her attention was still focused on her tactical hologram when something changed that left her feeling gut-punched.

Ohhh, shit!" she exclaimed.

Chapter 30
Ambushed

Captain Seamus O'Malley kept an eye on the Centurion squadron's formation as they rapidly approached the enemy ship they were assigned to intercept. Seconds away from the enemy, one of his ships vanished, then another; that was to be expected. They knew from the Stickman holograms that the invading ships used weapons with an effective range much greater than the Dragon ship force weapons.

One of O'Malley's Dragon pilots lost his nerve and broke formation to run for home. It didn't save him; his ship vanished next. Seconds later, the squadron came within Dragon weapons range of the enemy, and Seamus' team began to blast the enemy ship as hard and as fast as they could. When the invader finally passed within the bowl of the formation, the remaining Dragons of the squadron shifted their positions to surround it.

"Close in on him, lads!" O'Malley shouted excitedly. The Dragons instantaneously reversed direction to match the speed and direction of the invader, and the outer edges of the bowl formation folded inward to enclose their prey in a giant spherical cage.

With the enclosing formation complete, every Dragon shifted into high-velocity, randomly-directed orbits around the invader, each orbit a different radius from their target, making collisions among themselves impossible.

Nine more ships vanished as they orbited the enemy. However, enemy targeting of the Dragons became more difficult, and the casualty rate diminished as the squadron pounded the invader with their force weapons from all directions.

Seamus, himself, sent salvo after salvo of force blasts into the massive enemy vessel, his tactical system mentally feeding him the status of his squadron so that he didn't have to watch his tactical display. A pang of anguish squeezed his heart with each loss of a squadron ship. He desperately needed to see this vile thing killed before too many more people ceased to exist. With so many of his men dying around him,

O'Malley developed an overwhelming need for his Dragon to be the one to deliver the final vengeful blast that would send this bastard enemy invader to hell.

"We have him, mates," Seamus encouraged the remnants of his squadron. "I can feel it," he called out excitedly as the surviving ships of his command pounded their target mercilessly. "We just . . . Mother of God!" he cried out.

Their targeted ship vanished, escaping through a wormhole before the Dragons could finish the kill. At that exact moment, two more enemy ships came out of nowhere, catching the remains of O'Malley's squadron directly between them.

The two ambushers opened fire on O'Malley's people from opposite directions, and his Centurion's ships popped out of existence at a horrifying rate.

The sphere formation, rendered useless without their prey caged within, tried desperately to defend themselves. With the two enemy ships devastating their ranks from opposite sides, panic reigned among his team, preventing a cohesive counter-attack. Thirty-three additional Dragons vanished in less than ten seconds.

"Evasive maneuvers and retreat!" a horror-struck O'Malley screeched as five more squadron ships disappeared. Twenty-six surviving vessels, including his, raced to get away from the ambush, but within seconds only three of O'Malley's original Centurion squadron still existed, including O'Malley himself. Suddenly O'Malley experienced a sense of disembodiment. Everything went black, and he knew he must be dead.

Chapter 31
Unpleasant Surprise

"What the hell?" Lee McKay shouted.

Without warning, where every Centurion squadron held an enemy ship under siege, two more enemy invaders appeared nearby to flank them from two sides. At the same time, their originally besieged targets ducked back into wormholes to escape. To his shock, over fourteen hundred Centurion squadrons were ambushed simultaneously within his defense zone alone, and he knew there must be that many or more in Pete's zone. To his horror, groups of lights in his tactical hologram representing entire Centurion squadrons began to disappear.

White with shock, McKay barely managed to keep his wits about him. "Sub-Fleet Admirals, order all ships to withdraw immediately! Lift all Western Zone ground reserves. Prepare for an inrush of enemy ships!"

He mentally 'heard' Orsini give the same orders. Their sub-fleet admirals instantly obeyed, and the advancing Centurions, as well as those already engaged in battle, retreated from the front lines at maximum speed.

Unfortunately, the damage was done. The tactical system mentally informed him that the surprise enemy ambush took a devastating toll of over three hundred thousand Dragons in a single blow.

"Dammit! Dammit! Dammit! Where the hell did they all come from?" Orsini raged. He couldn't believe what had just happened. At every point where an enemy ship was under attack, the ambushing ships wiped out nearly one hundred percent of every attacking Centurion squadron. Even those squadrons in the process of enclosing their targets lost dozens of Dragons each to the combined and unexpected firepower of two counter-attacking enemy ships.

"This is a catastrophe!" a horrorstruck Svetlana shouted. "We just lost nearly ten percent of our in one disastrous blow!

"More than that, their little trick surely dealt a huge blow to the morale of our fighters. The number of dragons deserting the defense grid just went way up," Sue reported.

"That trick also explains why there were fewer intruders than we expected up front! They allowed us to get used to the pattern of their wave attacks, and then they swatted us down!" Susan replied bitterly.

"Well, we fell for it, but let's learn from it," a furious Lee McKay said. "We still have almost two and a half million fighters left among us, but Pete and I are going to need you both to transfer a quarter of your forces to our command, and quickly! We need them right now! An enemy surge is surely going to rush in on us!"

McKay sent them an idea for a counter plan to triple each interception force from one to three Centurions, a strategy that the others gladly agreed to and immediately adopted even though it would leave the defense grid temporarily in tatters.

To the astonishment of the fleet admirals, the enemy ships made no effort at all to exploit their success to rush in closer to Earth.

"This is not logical! The invaders are not taking advantage of our retreat to close the ground between us," a bewildered Svetlana Ivanovna observed with amazement. "What can they be possibly be thinking?"

"What gentlemen these clowns are. They knocked the sword out of our hand, and they're allowing us to pick it up again," Pete responded bitterly.

"They must still want to draw us out to thin our ranks even more," Susan speculated.

"Well, let's see how much they like our new triple welcoming committees. Sub-fleet admirals, refill the desertion gaps in your parts of the defense grid, and initiate three-Centurion interceptions for all incoming bogeys!" Orsini ordered.

Lee McKay repeated the same command to his admirals.

Moments went by as several hundred thousand Dragon ships shifted positions to form new centurions and restore the dilapidated defense grid.

"Perhaps they are taking the time to revise their tactics based on how we've resisted them so far," Svetlana hypothesized. "Perhaps we hurt them in a way they were not expecting."

"I'm hoping that ambush was their best shot . . . and it *was* a good one," Lee said grudgingly, "but despite all of our losses, we still have over two-thirds of our original forces left."

"Let's hope anyone prone to desertion has done it by now. Anyone with half a brain knows that there will be simply no place anywhere to hide if we lose this. We've got no choice but to keep on fighting with everything we've got."

"I think the bad apples are mostly gone now," Pete told everyone. "Tune in to your thought communications systems. The majority of emotions it's conveying are telling me that rather than being scared, most of my fighters are more pissed off and determined than ever! Nearly all of them want another crack at getting even."

"Recess is over, kids," Sue announced. "Our Dragons are beginning to re-engage!"

Four thousand enemy ships remained within the solar system after their devastating ambush. The fleet admirals concentrated on their tactical holograms as sub-fleet admirals deployed more than four hundred thousand Dragons to resist them.

Chapter 32
Friendly Space

The penetrating darkness lasted only an instant and then vanished again as if someone flicked a light switch off and then back on again. When Seamus O'Malley's Dragon emerged on the other side of the wormhole, his eyes went wide from the unexpected view his transparency field revealed. Not only did a myriad of gorgeous stars pepper the sky, but two vast colliding galaxies hung above him out there in the depths of space, seemingly so near they presented the illusion of being close enough to touch.

"Jesus, Mary, and Joseph, what the devil just happened?" he muttered to himself as he stared in wonder at the glorious display. "Is this heaven?"

Believing he suffered from hallucinations, he shook his head to try to clear the image of vistas that could not possibly be there. Bewildered, Seamus glanced around in other directions, his viewing field moving with his gaze, and he spotted several dozen Dragons floating in space nearby, his tactical system identifying them all of them as belonging to his squadron mates.

Encouraged by their company, he scanned the volume of space around him with his tactical system. It not only identified the rest of his recently demolished Centurion squadron but indicated they were among a massive collection of Dragons all within light-minutes of his position! He felt a tremendous sense of relief to find he had the company of friendly forces no matter where they were now.

Still baffled, though, he couldn't understand why they were all here and where all these other Dragons came from. He remembered two enemy ships flanking his entire squadron in an ambush that placed them in the center of a devastating crossfire. He also recalled being one of the last three survivors of his team trying to escape the deadly trap.

A voice sounding in his mind startled him, his thought communications system providing him with a general broadcast. "Dragon combat ships, welcome! You are in friendly space. Please stand down."

The message seemed authentic, but the image of the two galaxies still refused to go away. Gathering his wits about him, Seamus responded to the stand-down request. "And who might this be ordering us to stand down?" he demanded back to the source of the voice.

Jackson Ruark happened to be listening in and chose to respond. "This is Fleet Admiral Jackson Ruark. Stand down! Welcome to your new base of operations."

"Fleet Admiral Ruark? Fleet Admiral Ruark is dead!" Seamus replied contemptuously. "Do you think us fools to believe such a tale?"

From his ship a half a solar system away, Ruark drew Seamus' identity from the communications system. "Captain O'Malley," he replied with a grim smile. "If I'm dead, then so are all of you! I know you all have a lot of questions, so stand down as ordered, and we'll give you all some answers."

Immediately Seamus felt the familiar sensation of information filling his mind from his ship's knowledge transfer system. He concentrated on what the information contained and paled at the enormity of revelations it held. After the information stopped flowing, Seamus understood everything at last. He shook with fury over the Stickman deceit the knowledge transfer revealed. He also knew the details of Fleet Admiral Ruark's battle plan, and he understood what the admiral needed from him and his captured team.

Taking the initiative, he sent out a mental command to his squadron. "You heard the fleet admiral, Mates. Form up around me, and we'll head for the beacon ship so we can get our ships repaired. We'll be needed before too long, lads and lasses!"

~ ~ ~

"Keep gathering them in," Ruark ordered his people at the collection points. "We have to get them ready to go back into battle."

Ruark's Super Dragons proved to be very effective at gathering and assimilating incoming captured ships. At each collection point, infecting nanite projectiles began the cleansing process for those ships that would rid them of their self-destructs and enhance their tactical systems.

The vast majority of captured fighters looked anxiously forward to a chance to get back into the fight, this time against the Stickmen. However, a small percentage of the newcomers, badly unnerved by their own combat 'deaths,' was sent back to Ruark's new base of operations, all of them excused from further conflict without prejudice. After all, they already faced the enemy once before, only to be 'killed in action.' No one would doubt their courage.

~ ~ ~

The hive master was furious. With the surprise appearance of the reinforcing enemy ships, the invaders just butchered an enormous number of the Earth forces engaged in battle with them. Once again, he failed to understand where and when the enemy could have developed these inexplicable and maddening new ploys. In the Hive's entire history of war, enemy ships never once engaged in such tactics! Even the invading ships' demonstration of precise wormhole navigation was unheard of!

Just as unexpectedly, the humans changed their tactics too. Despite his anger and frustration, the hive master marveled at the ease with which the Earth forces adjusted to this surprising innovation of enemy tactics and the consequent disaster they spawned. While the Hive race would have considered this unpleasant surprise a major setback, the humans seemed to regard the flanking tactics as only a minor nuisance. Their defending forces reacted as if they knew all along that such a counter-attack would eventually happen, even though it caused their spherical defense perimeters to shrink significantly back toward their planet.

With only the briefest respite to regroup and repopulate their defense grid, the humans began to send three of their swarms to join together to pursue and intercept each enemy intrusion. One group engaged an approaching invader, and two more guarded it against enemy reinforcements. Perhaps these Earth warriors could indeed become marvelous, permanent weapons for the Hive race after all! On the other hand, maybe they were too good, something the hive master would have to consider.

The hive master made note of yet another perplexing anomaly. Even though the enemy ships took several hours to advance against heavy resistance, they illogically ignored the advantage the human retreat provided, an opportunity that would have allowed them to penetrate much deeper into the solar system and closer to the human home planet. For the moment, though, he needed to give his full attention to the battle and record any further anomalies for Hive tactical systems to resolve. He could decide the future role of humans later.

Chapter 33
Cold Reception

The EDF utilized hundreds of spaceports all over the planet, widely scattered and deliberately so. Any large, invading force would have to divide itself many times over to attack them simultaneously, but that also made it more time-consuming for Duval's Ghost team to reach each one. The zigzag course each infiltrator needed to make to pass over their assigned target spaceports would take time, even at top speed. Racing against the clock, they didn't know how much time they had left to work. The Stickmen might figure out the human involvement with the Ghosts any second, or they might not figure it out for many hours, but without a doubt, something would eventually let the cat out of the bag.

Gunther Karlson felt like a swimming man trying to beat a shark to shore as he raced from base to base, the pressure on him terrible.

He only had just enough time to fly over twenty-two EDF bases when, to his horror, a surge of thousands of Dragons lifted off from his next targeted base ahead. Even worse, his tactical system indicated similar Dragon surges were occurring all over the planet, not just this one base. Massive reinforcements rose to take their places to help refill the defense grid. He heard several violent fits of cursing coming from most of his team who were witnessing the same thing.

"Friggin, friggin hell! Ruark must have called for the double ambush ploy too early! What was he thinking?" he cried out to his team with a sinking heart.

"Now what?" Gator asked. "Should a few of us try to chase after some of them?"

"Absolutely not!" Karlson ordered. "They can't know we're here or what we're doing. Look at the power signatures on your tactical hologram! There is still twenty times the number of Dragons that just left that are still on the ground. Stick to the plan, everyone!"

Karlson didn't need to point out that, except for the ships his team already infected with nanites, most of those newly deployed Dragons were doomed unless they became lucky enough for a Seed ship to send them back to Ruark's base during battle. The self-destruct devices in their ships would remain unaltered, and the team had no way to warn any of them without tipping off the Stickmen. Presently only half the reserve ships Ruark and his planners expected Duval and his team to find remained on the ground.

~ ~ ~

Duval reached Hill Spaceport in minutes. Even though sickened by the unexpected lift off of Dragon reinforcements, he couldn't afford to take command of the team back from Karlson. He needed to complete a far more important mission, and he had every confidence in Karlson to make the right decisions for the team.

Duval passed over the Hill Spaceport without reducing speed as his ship discharged nanites at thousands of reserve ships still parked in orderly groups all over the tarmac. The nanite projectiles even managed to tag a few hundred Dragons within range in the sky above just as they launched themselves from the base.

From full in-atmosphere speed, he came to an instantaneous stop forty feet off the ground directly in front of the main entrance to Lee McKay's command center. Ten seconds later, his ship parked itself three feet above the ground, and Duval leaped through the portal even before it finished opening all the way.

Special Forces guards materialized from every direction before he could take ten steps. "Stay where you are!" one of them shouted out a warning to him.

Duval froze in mid-stride, seeing half a dozen automatic weapons pointed at him. "I'm Colonel L. C . . ." That was all that he managed to say before a guard tackled him hard from behind, knocking the wind out of him and taking him down to the ground. His right cheekbone would have fractured if his face had hit the concrete sidewalk instead of the lawn.

Duval's vision went dark around the edges, but he didn't quite pass out. Though dazed, he could still hear the blare of sirens in the distance of approaching Military Police vehicles. As he shook his head to clear it, his captors yanked his arms behind his back and tied his hands with self-zipping ties before pulling him none too gently to his feet.

"I'm Colonel L.C. Duval," he croaked painfully. "I have to get an urgent message to Fleet Admiral McKay right now!"

In his woozy state, he mistakenly imagined the announcement of his name alone would be enough to make the security guards back off, so he tried to jerk himself free of their grip. He realized the attempt wasn't one of his brightest moves when he found himself back on the ground spitting out grass again.

As his dizziness subsided, unbridled fury and frustration took its place. "I'm giving you an order!" he bellowed uselessly as he struggled to raise himself back up. "Take me to see Fleet Admiral McKay now! I'm Colonel L.C. Duval, and McKay knows me! He'll want . . . No, he'll *demand* to see me!"

He cried out in pain as a knee slammed down on his back to pin him to the ground yet again. He still struggled as the MPs searched him for ID. Finding none, two of the soldiers yanked him roughly to his feet again. His nose bled profusely, but with his hands bound, he couldn't wipe the blood and snot from his face. One of the soldiers unzipped the top of Duval's flight suit to look for the dog tag chain around his neck. Finding it, he yanked on it, snapping the chain apart to pull the dog tags free, the chain leaving friction burns on the sides of Duval's neck.

Three Humvees filled with security forces came screeching to a halt to disgorge another dozen troops around him, several of them charging up the ramp of his ship, weapons ready, to check for more occupants.

Satisfied that he came alone, the soldiers half pulled and half dragged Duval toward the back open door of one of the vehicles.

"Listen to me!" he pleaded, "It's imperative to the success of the war that I see Lee McKay right now! The lives of millions of people are at stake!" His plea fell on deaf ears. The military police officers shoved him roughly into the back seat of a vehicle with two beefy soldiers sliding in next to him, one on each side. The driver climbed into the front seat, and the vehicle doors slammed shut. The engine already running, the driver hit the gas to whisk Duval away to security headquarters.

~ ~ ~

Leaning forward in his command chair and concentrating on the swirling movement of ships within the tactical hologram spread before him, Lee McKay worked feverishly to order the orchestrated deployment of reinforcement Dragons from spaceports all over his defense zone. Now that he and Pete Orsini were committing three Centurion squadrons for each new invader, they effectively neutralized the enemy's flanking tactic. However, since there were three times more individual conflicts between Centurions and invading ships than before, the casualty count rose three times faster.

To make matters worse, the strain of committing three hundred ships to engage each new invader forced the fleet admirals to pull the severely weakened defense grid perimeter back by several layers. They also required triple the ground reserves to refill empty grid spaces. Sue and Svetlana automatically ordered a full third of their reserve ships within their zones to help replenish the grid.

McKay's orchestration of his sub-flee admirals became interrupted by a thought-driven message from the spaceport's head of security, General Bruner.

"Fleet Admiral McKay, my apologies for interrupting, but a serious issue has occurred warranting the need."

"The entire solar system is one gigantic battleground, General Bruner! What could possibly be more important than that?" McKay snarled back.

"A Dragon ship landed right outside your headquarters entrance ten minutes ago. Its pilot demanded to see you immediately and attempted to dash to the entrance to your command center. We have him in custody. He claims he's Colonel L.C. Duval."

"Duval has been MIA and been presumed dead for several months, General!"

"I know, sir, but the officer's face matches the photo of Duval that we have registered in the system. I ran the fingerprints too, Fleet Admiral, and we do indeed have Colonel L.C. Duval in custody. He is howling like a demon demanding to see you."

McKay didn't think anything more could surprise him today; he was wrong. Stunned to the core, he shook his head in denial and disbelief. "General Bruner, that just can't be possible!"

"I assure you, sir, there's no mistake."

"Bring him to my headquarters immediately! I want him here as fast as you can get him here!"

"Yes, sir, he's on the way."

"Admiral Delaney," he called to his backup commander, "take over!" His second in command, Sub-Fleet Admiral Delaney, who monitored the battle next to McKay to step in in case of an emergency, did not receive an explanation, nor did the man ask for one.

McKay raced for his headquarters entrance, too impatient to wait for this person claiming to be Duval to be brought to him. Outside he noted the Dragon parked on the lawn near the entrance where a ship shouldn't be, but he couldn't identify who owned this one since all Dragons were identical.

With the security holding area a quarter-mile away, to the impatient McKay, the two-minute wait for the Humvee to bring the prisoner to him seemed like two hours. With lights flashing and siren sounding, a security vehicle finally raced into view and skidded to a stop on the road in front of the building.

McKay couldn't yet make out the prisoner's identity inside the vehicle, but he saw that the handcuffed prisoner was so anxious to get out of the back seat that he tried to climb over the guard sitting beside him. None too gently, the guard shoved him back down again.

"Let me out, you moron!" the prisoner bellowed. McKay was stunned to hear what he recognized immediately as L.C. Duval's voice threatening and cursing his captors. McKay roughly pushed past the ring of security officers surrounding the thoroughly pissed-off Duval to rescue his officer and friend.

"Back off! Back off, that's an order!" he shouted, shoving the nearest guard away from the long-lost Dragon pilot and protectively pulling Duval away from the band of now confused and doubtful soldiers.

"Get those cuffs off him," McKay commanded angrily.

Even as the guards removed handcuffs, Duval forgot all about the manhandling he'd received the moment he recognized McKay.

"Fleet Admiral McKay!" he pleaded urgently, "This is going to sound crazy, but those incoming ships are here to save us! It's the Stickmen who are the enemy!"

"Where the hell did you come from, what the hell are you talking about, and why aren't you dead?"

Chapter 34
Duval's Tale

Lee McKay glared at his resurrected friend as he waited for an answer to his question.

"My scouts and I were captured by the other team, the aliens sending in those invading ships you're fighting, after our own Stickmen allies tried to kill us! The Ghosts brought us back to warn you."

"You're not making any sense, Duval. Ghosts? Dead people? Do you have any idea how crazy you sound?"

Despite the desperate circumstances, Duval had enough presence of mind left to realize how crazy he did sound and what McKay must be thinking of him. He took a moment to compose himself and took a few breaths to calm himself down. Then, as calmly and as rationally as he could, he explained what happened to him and his squad during their scouting mission so many weeks earlier.

A cold knot formed in McKay's gut as he listened to Duval's story. The more Duval explained, the tighter the knot became.

"Enough!" McKay ordered with exasperation. "I can't deal with this by myself. Save your story until we put you through to Ling Wu's headquarters.

"Don't use the thought communications spheres!" Duval warned him. "We believe the Stickmen can eavesdrop when you use them!"

McKay motioned for Duval to follow him, and he hurriedly led him back inside the command center. Four of the security force soldiers followed in case Duval made any threatening moves.

The command center, building 238, a massive structure a couple of hundred yards in length and about a hundred yards wide, was a former aircraft repair facility just months before. Despite its size, McKay and Duval didn't have too far to go. Inside the South entrance doorway and to the right was a row of administrative offices, with the base communications station placed right in the middle of them.

180

McKay, Duval, and the small troop of soldiers burst into the comm center, startling the officer in charge and the technicians there, all of whom turned and stared wide-eyed at the unexpected intruders. That the room existed at all, despite the vastly superior thought communications devices of the Stickmen, was due to Ling Wu's order for all EDF bases to maintain a human-technology-based communications center. The technicians always kept the communications links open between Hong Kong and the fleet admiral headquarters.

"Get Dr. Ling on a landline communications monitor!" McKay shouted at the surprised officer in charge, a young lady with lieutenant's bars on the shoulders of her officer's tunic. "Move it, and link in Fleet Admirals McKay, Orsini, and Ivanovna on their lines!"

"Yes, sir," the Lieutenant gulped.

"I want them all to hear this story of yours, Duval!"

As the comm techs went to work setting up the connections, McKay glanced around the room at equipment spectacularly primitive compared to the communication abilities of the Stickman spheres. Nevertheless, McKay thought to himself; *Now I understand why Ling Wu ordered all this stuff put in place!*

"The Stickmen could be monitoring landlines and radio," Duval warned.

"If what you've told me is even half true, then we have no choice. We have to risk it. More than likely, they're not listening in on human communications technology since the military is using Stickman thought communications spheres exclusively to direct our battle forces."

Dr. Ling's face appeared on one of the monitors above the main communications control board, a severe look of concern on his face. "Fleet Admiral McKay, what has caused the need for you to leave your command station and employ this form of communication?" It was evident Dr. Ling could see Lee McKay too via his monitor.

"This happened, sir," he told Ling Wu, pulling Duval by the arm into the field of view of the camera.

Dr. Ling was visibly taken aback. "Is that man not the presumed-deceased Colonel Duval?"

"It is, sir, but if you give us a few more seconds, I'm linking in the other fleet admirals too."

One by one, three other monitors came alive as the remaining fleet admirals came online. All of them appeared to be deeply concerned, knowing it must be a great emergency indeed to warrant a need for them to be called from their stations in the midst of ongoing battles and take communiqués directly from land-based lines. All of them began asking questions at the same time but stopped when they recognized Duval's face on the monitors."

"What the hell?" a dumbfounded Orsini asked.

"Colonel Duval has an incredible and horrifying story you all need to hear. You'd better start at the very beginning for all of our sakes, Colonel!"

Dr. Ling and all of the fleet admirals listened intently. Their expressions became grim as Duval laid out the details of his training team's capture and the events that followed. Then Duval described what the Ghosts told him of the cancerous and deadly spread of the Stickman infestation across the galaxy.

"We discovered that we are just an experiment to the Stickmen to determine if they can use the human race as a weapon against the Ghosts. If our forces are whittled down to a point where they are no longer effective, the Stickmen will begin to believe they won't be able to use us as the tool they intended us to be.

"Even if we prove to be successful in stopping the Ghosts, years from now, we would still eventually be exterminated once the job is done. The Stickmen want all life forms alien to their homeworld wiped from the galaxy! All forms! From their point of view, every time they see a Dragon ship vanish or an invading ship explode without taking casualties, then they've gained a victory.

"If this is true . . ." Svetlana began.

"It *is* true!" Duval shouted impatiently. "You've got to believe me!"

Ling Wu interrupted. "Colonel Duval, your tale offers answers to questions that have disturbed me from the beginning. The behavior of the two Stickman liaisons since their arrival on Earth has always seemed questionable to me. However, my staff and I chose to overlook it as a peculiarity of an alien culture. What you have revealed explains their failure to aid us in this conflict so far, that and much more."

"The Stickmen have behaved rather strangely, but it may still indeed be a peculiarity of their alien culture," Svetlana spoke up in accented English. Without the mental communications devices, she was self-conscious of her command of English and her ability to communicate effectively. Her fears were groundless; her English, though accented, was excellent.

"That is still a possibility, Fleet Admiral Ivanovna," Dr. Ling responded. "Consider, though, that even though the Stickmen have, in the past, provided us with enormous amounts of convincing evidence that diametrically opposes Colonel Duval's testimony, it isn't hard to deduce, given their technological abilities, that their fabrication of holographic evidence would be child's play to them."

"That's still just speculation," Pete Orsini chimed in.

"I agree," Susan McKay added. "With all due respect to Colonel Duval, even if what he says is true, these Ghost aliens of his could be using him the same way he claims the Stickmen are using us!"

"Colonel Duval, Fleet Admiral McKay is correct," Dr. Ling conceded. "You are here advocating a reversal of our alliance and our trust in the Stickmen. Instead, you want us to believe in the assurances of yet another self-declared ally of the human race, an ally whom the rest of us know nothing about and whom the Stickmen have effectively convinced us to be our deadly enemy."

Lee McKay supported Ling Wu. "These Ghosts of yours, Colonel, have destroyed well over one million of our ships!" he growled. "Even if they claim the need to kill our people is justifiable to defend themselves, or that they do so for the loftier purpose of saving more lives than they take, why should we believe they are any better than the Stickmen?"

"Agreed," Pete Orsini chimed in. "How do we know we are not just trading one enemy for another?

"Because those Dragon ships you lost today and during the past weeks *aren't* destroyed, not a single one! There are *no* casualties in this war so far, except for the Stickmen and the Ghosts killed in battle today and during early raids!" an increasingly frustrated Duval declared impatiently. He mentally berated himself for not explaining that sooner.

"Do I look dead to you? All of those pilots are still alive, all of them, just like I am!"

He defiantly glared at every face on the monitors, expecting to hear additional doubt about his claims. "The Ghosts don't destroy our Dragons; they capture them! We just didn't have an opportunity to come back to tell you all this until now. We knew the Stickmen could listen in on any warnings we might try to give you!"

"With so many EDF Dragons that we could use to turn back against the Stickmen, why would that even matter?" Susan McKay demanded.

"Because the ships the Stickmen gave us are rigged with self-destructs!"

"They're what?" Orsini bellowed; his friends equally rocked by this horrifying new revelation.

"All of the ships have self-destructs built into them! When the Ghosts examined our ships after they captured us, they found them rigged to overload their power sources and explode upon receiving a single, remotely sent thought command! That's why we've all kept our distance until now. We were afraid that if the Stickmen discovered any of us who returned, they'd destroy all of our forces in one single blow!"

Duval's bombshell of an announcement left them all stunned. Even the comm room personnel, who couldn't help but hear the exchange, looked pale and shaken by the news.

"Right now, the Ghosts are trying to save as many of our people as they can. Their weapons aren't weapons at all. They are wormhole generators that push our ships through to a rendezvous destination somewhere else in the universe far out of range of any Stickman destruct signal. That's why you never see any explosions or debris from the Dragons you thought were destroyed!

"To accomplish the capture of our Dragons, the Ghost people have been sacrificing themselves. They've been willingly taking on casualties to save the very people who are attacking them!"

"Dear Lord!" a horrified Sue McKay said. "I think I believe him!"

"I too," Svetlana agreed, equally sickened, all of Duval's arguments making sense now.

"And that means Jackson Ruark is still alive out there somewhere?" Susan asked, almost afraid to hear the answer.

"Damned straight! He's the one coordinating this battle for the Ghost team. His wife and boys are alive too!" He grimaced, disgusted with himself, as he remembered something else significant that he should have recalled earlier. "Look at this."

He reached into a pocket of his flight suit and pulled out a charm bracelet that Lee and Susan bought Karen Ruark for her last birthday. He handed it to Lee to examine. "Karen Ruark thought this might help to convince you. She wore it to her son's graduation."

Lee took the bracelet from Duval's hand and examined it carefully, impressed Duval knew about the Ruark family's disappearance after the graduation ceremony.

"It's Karen's alright."

"Oh, Lee! They're alive!" Susan McKay said, her eyes brimming with tears of joy.

"Damn! Our old buddy's still alive!" Orsini added happily.

"Dr. Ling," McKay said smiling for the first time, "incredible as it seems, this does belong to Karen Ruark!" He clutched the bracelet with a triumphant grin.

"Jackson and his family must indeed be alive!"

Despite the relief Duval's news gave them, Lee's smile faded, and he looked up at Ling Wu's face on the monitor. "This still doesn't mean Duval and Ruark weren't duped by these Ghosts."

Disheartened by Lee's remark, Duval's shoulders slumped, and he said, "I'm not sure what else I can say to convince you. All I can add is that the Ruark and the Ghosts staged all of those raids you've experienced for the past few weeks. They did it for the sole purpose of collecting as many of our people as possible without arousing the Stickmen's suspicion.

"Thanks to those raids, there are almost five thousand of us. By now, they've rounded up; how many did you say? Over a million of our forces alone today, and I assure you that there hasn't been a single human death among them!

"As for Fleet Admiral Ruark, I talked to him myself two hours ago! He's coordinating the efforts to collect all of those incoming EDF Dragons at the gathering points where Ghosts are sending them. I'm sure he has his hands full trying to convince *them* to switch sides too. Look at all the trouble I'm having convincing just the five of you! He has hundreds of thousands to deal with!"

"Why didn't Jackson come back himself?" Lee demanded.

"He stayed behind to coordinate the invasion, and because he's someone who all the incoming Dragon ship warriors can recognize and trust as a leader. Thank goodness he is out there with us! We'd have nothing but chaos without him.

"He's personally working with the Ghosts to try to build your supposed KIAs into an entirely new defensive force to send back to help you. He's using all five thousand of our original captures to help gather and organize the tens of thousands of Dragons being pushed through to them from this solar system to theirs so humans and not Ghosts can greet them."

"And just how can Fleet Admiral Ruark even hope to send this reserve force of our people back when you, yourself, just indicated that the Stickmen could destroy them with a single command the moment they reappear?" Ling Wu demanded.

"When our ships pop out of the wormholes into our rendezvous area, the Ghosts are using their technology to disable our Dragon ships' self-destructs. The process takes thirty-three minutes. For the five thousand of us who were already out there before the battle began today, the Ghosts not only disarmed the destructs, they added improvements to our Dragons that you wouldn't believe.

"To provide you with evidence, let me point out that my Dragon has some of those modifications, and neither your tacticals nor the Stickmen's, detected my return until I landed my ship literally on your front doorstep! For the Dragons we captured today, there's not enough time to fully modify them to the full level that my team's Dragons are modified; it takes too long. The one thing the Ghost technology can do quickly, though, is disable Dragon self-destructs fast enough to allow us to put captured ships back into action."

"That's well and good for the ships you've captured, but what about our ships here?" Susan demanded.

"I've already started the disarming process for all the ships on this base and several other spaceports I passed over on the way here."

"You've done what!" Lee McKay bellowed, horrified by this bit of news. Bristling, he shouted, "Are you out of your mind? Did you ever stop to think you may have been fooled by the Ghosts as much as you claim we all were by the Stickmen? Do you realize if you've been misled, then you may have just lost this entire war for us?"

Ling Wu silenced McKay's outburst. "No, Admiral McKay, Colonel Duval has just provided many missing pieces of a puzzle I've been trying to solve from the very beginning. They all lend foundation to Colonel Duval's claim.

"Consider the supporting evidence; in the very first encounters with raiding enemy ships, only Stickman Swarm ships suffered casualties until the Stickmen no longer joined in our forays against these raiders. There was undoubtedly a message there for us."

"My idea," Duval interrupted with a tinge of pride. "We needed to do something to get you to start thinking."

"It did cause me to do that," Ling Wu conceded, "but unfortunately, the act in itself did not present strong enough evidence for me from which to draw conclusions. In support of Colonel Duval's claims, Fleet Admirals, please also consider the Stickmen's self-isolation, which has prevented any substantive communication with them. The world has only seen two members of their race. These supposed 'allies' of ours have avoided all direct, personal communications with us, preferring instead to communicate indirectly through holograms and knowledge transfers.

"They have also resisted all of our attempts to gain information about their technology, which would allow us to duplicate it for ourselves. However, Fleet Admiral McKay, what has troubled me most since the arrival of the Stickmen are the holograms they first brought to us to reveal their plan to enlist our cooperation. They displayed perfectly presented scenes of you, scenes indistinguishable from reality. In these scenes, you piloted one of the Stickman ships, and with it, you destroyed an invading ship. These scenes were perfectly presented and indistinguishable from an actual event, yet they never happened!

"With that level of advanced holographic technology, the Stickmen can exercise an ability to fabricate and present to us any event they wish along with a claim of its reality! Indeed, Fleet Admiral McKay, too many things support Commander Duval's story. Most telling of all is that our forces have been in battle for almost five hours, and our so-called allies have not yet committed a single ship to battle."

"Let me add one more piece of evidence," Duval interjected. A few days ago, you reacted to a raid of five incoming Ghost ships, each invading a different sector of the defense zone. That little raid captured a nice chunk of the Dragons that chased them down, but their primary purpose was to deliver the clue Fleet Admiral Ruark tried to give you. If you check the alphabetic characters of the sector designations in the same order the intruders arrived, you'll see that, together, they spell 'Ruark.'"

Lee McKay stared, unseeing, at some distant point as he searched his memory. "Romeo, Uniform, Alpha, Romeo, Kappa," he muttered to himself as he pulled the characters from memory. "Damn! How the hell did we miss that?"

"It's so obvious that it's embarrassing," Orsini added, somewhat chagrined.

"In hindsight, everything becomes obvious in all cases," Dr. Ling chided sympathetically. He paused and stared at some point below the monitor in contemplation of everything he'd just heard.

"Colonel Duval, I am convinced of the legitimacy of your story." Ling Wu paused again, mentally considering the scanty options left to them all.

"But sir," Pete Orsini objected, "we can't even scratch the surface of the hull on a Stickman ship. How are we supposed to believe Duval is capable of deactivating thousands of ships at a time without our even knowing it?"

Before Ling Wu could respond, Duval interrupted and explained to them the nanotechnology skills of the Ghosts and how they used the nanites to neutralize the self-destructs.

"My team has been here for almost an hour now, spreading the nanites to every base they can reach. I told you, I did several spaceports on the way here myself and this one too, of course.

"There's one other thing I need to mention; I told you the Stickman ships that chased my boys and me back on Mars were masked and invisible to our tacticals along with their base of operations. When the Stickmen finally decide to turn on us, they'll mask all of their ships, just like those of our pursuer's ships. Unimproved Dragon ships would normally be blind to them, but the nanites we infected your ships with will correct that problem too. Fleet Admiral Ruark sends his urgent request that you all turn the Stickman masked ship exposure into a very unpleasant surprise for our so-called friends."

"Colonel Duval, "Svetlana interrupted, "can you and your team do anything to alter the self-destructs of the ships presently engaged in combat?" she asked hopefully.

Duval's face fell, and his shoulders sagged. He shook his head sadly, "Not effectively and not without unacceptable risk. They are all too scattered all over the solar system and moving too fast. We really can't do it safely or effectively without sending them through wormholes to our rendezvous point. That is why the present advance of Ghost ships into our solar system is moving at a snail's pace. It's deliberately slow! The longer the Ghosts can engage in combat with our Dragons, the more of our people they can save by sending them through the wormholes and out of range of the destruct signal.

"The Stickmen are undoubtedly monitoring the battle just as we are. If we recalled our Dragons back to Earth to deactivate their self-destructs, the Stickmen would immediately become suspicious of our motive.

Duval turned his head to look up at the monitor displaying Dr. Ling's face. "Dr. Ling, Fleet Admiral Ruark plans to let our forces continue to engage the Ghosts for as long as possible, even to the point where the EDF is on the brink of defeat. Every ship the Ghosts snatch is another pilot saved who will return to fight again against the real enemy. You need to stop sending reinforcements off-planet, though, until we know the self-destructs of our Earth-based ships have been neutralized."

"But if we don't recall our ships, our forces will continue to destroy the people who are trying to save us. Every Ghost ship they destroy is another city and its entire population that won't be rescued," Susan McKay argued.

"We have no choice," Dr. Ling concluded.

"That's not entirely true," Duval interrupted. "We too were aware of that problem and took care of it as best we could. Yes, the Ghosts are taking some casualties, but I assure you they are minimal. The Ghosts are putting on a good show for everyone."

Duval told them about the thousands of robot ships built for the sole purpose of letting EDF defenders destroy them to create the illusion that EDF forces were far more effective in battle than they really were.

"The Seed ships crewed by Ghost people are ducking back through wormholes before they become too damaged to continue. We've managed to cut the Ghost losses to next to nothing!"

"Ingenious," Ling Wu nodded with approval. "Fleet Admiral Ruark and his people have planned well, but my strategists and I also established a contingency plan to order our Dragons to turn their attacks on the Stickmen spacecraft if need be. Unhappily, that plan is obviously rendered useless by the implanted self-destruct mechanisms."

"They would be destroyed the moment they turned on the Stickmen," Duval assured the doctor.

"I do not see any path we can take to save our deployed ships, no matter what we do, other than what the Ghosts are already doing," Ling Wu said grimly.

"Dr. Ling," Lee McKay interjected, "our losses are rapidly increasing at a rate where the Stickmen could conceivably conclude that our fighters are no longer effective. That could happen soon and cause them to trigger the self-destructs anyway. We may not have long."

"We came to the same conclusion this could happen," Duval informed them, "but we speculated the Stickmen would probably prefer to use us to the last man to preserve their own forces."

"That is very likely," agreed Ling Wu, "but there is another reason to doubt that will happen. The Ghost ships are currently employing tactics that are not the same as those demonstrated by the Stickman during past conflicts. Those earlier holograms the Stickmen gave us served as the foundation from which we modeled most of our defense strategies and training. However, I still believe those holograms accurately portrayed the only tactics these Ghost aliens have ever employed against the Stickmen.

"It is only through Colonel Duval and Fleet Admiral Ruark's influence their strategies have changed. Because of those changes, the Stickmen may want to study those new Ghost tactics as long as possible to use them for themselves at a later time. We must hope either one of these reasons will be enough to delay the destruction of our Dragon ships.

"Fleet Admirals, I want you all to order your reserve fighters still on the ground to remain there. You also need to communicate these disturbing revelations to all spaceports under your command. Emphasize that it is essential for all future communications between our EDF bases to be made strictly through the land-based, fiber optic communications links. We must buy Colonel Duval and his men as much time as we can to allow them to defuse as many of our ships as possible."

"Yes, sir," All of the fleet admirals responded automatically.

"I need to get back out there now," Duval told them all. "It's imperative for my men and me to cover as much ground as we can. Remember, the nanites will need about half an hour to disarm the Dragon self-destructs."

Duval turned on his heel without waiting for dismissal and left them in his urgent need to get back to his ship.

McKay pointed to two of the four MPs who followed Duval and McKay into the comm room. "You two, make sure he gets back to his ship and that no one tries to stop him this time!"

Without saluting, the two guards raced to catch up to Duval, one of them rushing past him to make sure the way was clear.

As Duval took his leave, Ling Wu's eyes went wide with alarm, his characteristic imperturbability visibly shaken as another possibility occurred to him.

"Fleet Admirals, if the spacecraft the Stickmen gave to us truly have destructive devices embedded in them, then in all probability, the thought communications and knowledge transfer spheres they gave us have them too!"

In stunned silence, the four fleet admirals considered the ramifications.

"Oh, shit," Orsini said with his usual signature flair of eloquence. He sagged in his seat, looking deathly ill. "They're spread throughout most of our EDF spaceports except the ones designed solely with human technology."

Susan McKay and Svetlana Ivanovna felt just as stricken. Lee McKay swore under his breath, his face turning scarlet with anger and frustration.

"All of you must order the immediate evacuation of all of your non-essential personnel!" Ling Wu turned his head momentarily to give an order to someone off-screen and then turned back to the camera. "My people have been told to pass that same order to our bases all over the planet."

Chapter 35
Evacuate!

"The evacuation of our spaceports and command headquarters may tip our hand all by itself," McKay advised Ling Wu.

"We must pray the Stickmen's focus is completely on the battle itself," Ling Wu replied.

"Dr. Ling, the majority of our fighters are heavily engaged in battle and require our continued guidance. We *must* remain at our stations and provide that guidance," Svetlana told him and the others. "We cannot abandon our commands."

"She's right," Pete Orsini agreed grimly.

"A noble gesture, Fleet Admirals Ivanovna and Orsini, but not an optional one. Your forces would lose their guidance anyway, would they not, if you are destroyed along with your headquarters? All of you, including your sub-fleet admirals, can still monitor and command your forces from your Dragons via your onboard tactical systems. If what Colonel Duval told us is accurate, you will need to do so anyway since your ships can now reveal masked enemy positions that your headquarters systems cannot detect.

"My planners and I considered the flexibility of airborne commands over land-based headquarters. However, we chose in favor of the ground-based system we have now. There is no other option but for you all to take your commands airborne.

"What we don't know is whether Duval's people have finished cleansing the Dragons at your remaining three headquarters as he did at the Layton base. Your ships may be nanite-infected, as Colonel Duval put it, but these nanites may not have had time yet to complete their function. That is the one great risk remaining. Once your ships are airborne, there is no chance Colonel Duval's team can approach them."

"It's a risk, but it's one we have to live with, Dr. Ling," Susan McKay replied determinedly. If Pete, Svetlana, and I don't survive, we at least know that Lee will be safe if he can get to his ship in time. From there, he'll be able to rally all of our survivors to help Jackson and his Ghost allies."

Lee's face turned pale, and he gave his wife a stricken look, but for the sake of the planet, he couldn't object.

"Sue is right," Orsini agreed. "We can't leave the battle unattended until our airborne commands are operational. In the meantime, we have to order the evacuation of all EDF spaceports, and we have to do it right now!"

"Go then, and good luck to us all," Ling Wu finished. His screen went blank.

"Let's get to work," Lee ordered. He looked up at his wife's face on the monitor and added, "Sue, I love you. We *will* get through this."

Susan's eyes welled up again. "I love you too, Lee."

With that, her monitor went blank, too, as did Pete's and Svetlana's. Lee forced himself not to dwell on the thought he might never see her face again.

Determined not to fail them, Lee turned to the communications officer in charge. Having heard the entire high command's exchange, the young lieutenant and the four other technicians were obviously frightened by it. Lee observed the name "Bryant" stitched into the breast pocket of the Lieutenant's black EDF tunic.

"Lieutenant Bryant, get me General Bruner at security headquarters on the line."

The Lieutenant grabbed a phone, punched in five numbers, and handed it to McKay. Bruner, who'd been expecting further orders from McKay, answered instantly.

"General Bruner, this is Fleet Admiral McKay. I'm ordering a total evacuation of the base. I'll be issuing the order myself in a few moments. Our people will need to hear it from me!

"Make sure my order is carried out! When the evacuation is complete, I want all of your security people to report to the Layton ground force commander, General Helfrich, and place yourselves under his command. Afterward, I want you both to coordinate and execute a full-scale evacuation of Layton."

"Layton is already nearly a ghost town, Fleet Admiral. Most of the residents left in droves when they received word that the invasion had begun, but now the roads to the mountains are clogged everywhere with refugees trying to escape their cities from Provo to Ogden."

"Then do whatever you can to help those left by any means necessary, General. I'll make sure our base personnel are taken care of." With that, McKay threw down the phone then turned his attention back to Lieutenant

Bryant. "Lieutenant, point out the public address microphone and turn it on for me. Then I want you to get your people out of here."

"Yes, sir!" The young woman stepped past McKay, took a handset off its cradle, and gave it to him. Having just heard McKay's conversation with General Bruner, she had it ready in anticipation of the need.

McKay raised it to his face. "This is Fleet Admiral McKay! This is not a drill! I am ordering an immediate evacuation of the entire base! Do *not* report to the emergency evacuation staging areas. I repeat, do *not* go there. Go, instead, to the airfields.

"To all trainee Dragon pilots, your orders are to pack your Dragons with as many of our base personnel as you can carry and take them to Croydon, east of here. I want mountains between our people and this base. After everyone has evacuated, you are to return and place yourselves under the command of Generals Helfrich and Bruner to help them evacuate any citizens left in the Layton area.

"To all reserve Dragon fighters, take your Dragons to the edge of the atmosphere above us and continue to follow deployment orders from there. Again, this is not a drill! Follow my orders exactly and immediately!"

With his base evacuation order given, McKay turned his attention back to the communications room team.

"You communications people, thank you for your help, but get the hell out of here, *now!*" he bellowed with a jerk of his thumb toward the door. "Head for the airfield!"

He waited while the technicians rushed past, all of them happy to obey. McKay headed for the door too, but he saw Lieutenant Bryant still seated at a communications console when he glanced back.

"What are you waiting for, Lieutenant?" he shouted in exasperation. "Get out of here! That's a direct order!"

Unintimidated by the Admiral's tone, she replied stubbornly, "Not until you do, sir. You might still need to contact the other Fleet Admirals again. I'm staying."

McKay could tell by the determined look in her eyes that arguing with her would be a waste of time. He'd seen that same stubborn look before in his wife's eyes too many times. Besides, the young lady was right; he still might need her to connect to the other headquarters via landlines. He reluctantly nodded acceptance of the Lieutenant's insubordination.

"What's your first name, Lieutenant?" he asked.

"Megan, sir."

"I won't forget your help, Megan. I also won't forget that I owe you a week in the brig for disobeying a direct order."

"Just doing my job the same as you are, sir."

McKay nodded grudgingly. "Carry on then, Captain Bryant."

"It's Lieutenant Bryant, sir."

"Not anymore," he called over his shoulder as he sped from the room.

McKay rushed back to his tactical center and took his place again in his command chair. He wasn't the least bit surprised to see his backup, Admiral Delaney, still directing Dragon forces, seemingly as unconcerned as if he never heard the evacuation order at all.

"Admiral Delaney, I want you to get moving and coordinate all of our sub-fleet admirals together to form an airborne command under your direct supervision. I'll take over when I get up there myself." He paused then added, "If I don't make it out of here, I'm counting on you to do us proud."

"Sir, I respectfully insist that you be the one to go topside and establish the command," Delaney replied. "You are too valuable an asset to risk."

"No," McKay said flatly. "I will continue to orchestrate our forces myself from here until you get a command structure effectively operational. I want no further argument! The faster you get out there, the sooner I can get out of here too. Move!" he barked.

Delaney hesitated briefly with a pained expression but nodded grudgingly and took off at a jog.

McKay ordered his sub-fleet admirals to take to the sky to reestablish an airborne command to continue to direct the Dragons against the invading ships. He trusted Ling Wu, by now, alerted all of the EDF spaceports to the alien deceit and its likely catastrophic consequences.

Ready to try to keep coordinating and directing his defending Dragons himself, he found he didn't have to. It filled him with pride to find not one of his sub-fleet admirals at any of their headquarters had obeyed his order to leave their command post to take their Dragons airborne. Like McKay, they all chose to send their backup sub-fleet admirals aloft as they continued to direct their forces until their airborne commands could take over.

McKay mentally queried the communications system and tactical systems and learned that his wife, Pete, and Svetlana remained at their posts too. He sank into his command chair, ignoring the risk and the potential danger of staying behind.

Mentally he ordered his tactical system to update him with the current battle status and found that, under his command alone, another seventy-five thousand ships disappeared since he left his post to find Duval. The irony did not escape him that it pleased him now to see how high the casualty count had climbed in that short period of time and found himself wishing it was higher.

McKay studied his hologram and found hundreds of battles taking place between EDF forces and the Ghost ships, the spherical battlefront having advanced throughout the solar system to less than the distance to Jupiter. He knew without a doubt that the Ghost ships could easily have reached Earth by now and that the invading ships continued to create the illusion of being held back by the might of the EDF Dragons for the sole purpose of 'harvesting' as many of the Dragon defenders as they could.

McKay calmly waited out twelve long minutes more, occasionally giving orders to sub-fleet admirals and watching the reserve ships from his base leave Earth's vicinity a few at a time to fill newly emptied grid positions. He observed that the Dragon ships belonging to the trainees headed overland to the east with base personnel rather than outer space. There were so many Dragons that they efficiently managed to transport all of the base evacuees in a single trip.

At the end of the twelve minutes, most of the Dragons conducting the evacuation of base personnel had returned from Croydon, then scattered themselves all across Layton and the nearby highways to round up what few civilians remained behind along with those stranded by gridlocked traffic.

McKay knew that if the communications and knowledge transfer spheres scattered all over his base were rigged to detonate, the effective blast range could not be predicted. He prayed Croydon was far enough away to keep his evacuees safe.

At last, the message he had been waiting for came that his airborne command group was ready to take over the direction of the battle forces.

"Alright, people, move it!" McKay mentally ordered his distant sub-fleet admirals. "Our airborne command is in control now. Get to your Dragons now!"

Instead of racing to his Dragon, McKay took another direction, heading for the communications room. He burst through the door and shouted, "Captain Bryant, we're done here! Come with me on the double!" The young lady didn't argue with him this time.

∾ ∾ ∾

"What the hell?" Homer Bigsby exclaimed to his teammates through his thought communications system. "It's happening again! My tactical is showing nearly every reserve ship on the planet is lifting off!"

The rest of the team didn't need to be told. They could see it for themselves on their tactical displays.

"What the hell do we do now, Viking?" Jethro Hawks questioned anxiously as he watched several thousand ships rise from his next targeted base.

Gunther Karlson felt as shocked as the rest of his team, and as the team commander, he needed to make a decision quickly! As his Dragon raced across the Amazon rainforest, he mentally ordered his hologram to view the entire South American continent to try to assess the situation. His display only added to his confusion. All EDF bases everywhere across the continent were sending their reserve forces aloft. However, to his relief, nearly all of those Dragons took stationary positions above the atmosphere. Inexplicably, at least a thousand others from each base remained behind. Karlson focused on the ships from one base and saw Dragons racing along the ground away from their headquarters.

"Don't panic, guys," Karlson ordered. "I don't know what's going on, but the ones that just lifted are still grouped together above their bases at the edge of space. We can still sweep over them, just at a higher altitude!"

"Viking, I think they're all evacuating their bases!" Danny Murphy called out after watching his display for a moment. I think the Dragons still close to the ground must be evacuating people. Something terrible must be happening!"

"Yeah, maybe so, but no Dragons have blown up yet, so keep going! Everyone, chase after the groups in the sky."

"What about the ones still zipping around below?" Bigsby asked.

"They're too scattered. We can't do anything for them. We can save more Dragons by moving on rather than wasting time chasing the mavericks. When we're done up above, we'll come back down for them."

"But Viking…"

"That's an order, Homerun! Do as I say!"

Chapter 36
The Signal

From his command ship under the moon's surface, the hive master studied the ongoing battle intensely. Without a doubt, with their clever defense tactics, the Earth people held back the enemy ships, but not without their casualty rate climbing rapidly. It would be hours yet, but his ship's artificially intelligent tactical system predicted that the number of human defenders would eventually dwindle to the point of ineffectiveness. He was both mildly disappointed that the years of planning would not bear the fruit the Hive hoped for and angered because, undoubtedly, the failure resulted from the unheard-of tactics the enemy ships had adopted.

Despite the unpleasant surprises of the day, the hive master felt no concern about the inevitable fate of this solar system. He had over seventeen million swarm fighter ships at his command, with five hundred thousand on his lunar base alone. The remainder was masked and hidden within underground Hive bases throughout this solar system. Besides, just outside the human's solar system, a dozen Hive dreadnoughts waited, each carrying one hundred thousand more Swarm ships and five thousand Eradicators apiece.

Unlike humans, all of his reserve fighters were bred for battle in space and genetically engineered with a fanatical need to destroy all forms of life that greatly exceeded their natural instinct for self-preservation. At his command, the multitude of Hive ships virtually assured the outcome of this conflict no matter what maddening tactics the enemy employed if the humans failed to defeat them.

Given the enemy's disturbing new battle strategies, the hive master chose to continue to hold back his swarms to study and analyze the battle while allowing the human forces to fight until they were either victorious or completely wiped out. This would preserve his Hive ships while harvesting the maximum amount of information about these new tactics that he could pass on to the Hive home planet for further study. If the enemy defeated the humans, the hive master would simply release all of his forces to continue exterminating the enemy ships and then deal with whatever was left of the humans within this star system.

To his annoyance, his tactical system sent him an alert that broke his concentration as it forced him to become mentally aware of it. His ship's self-aware, artificially intelligent sensor arrays discovered something they categorized as urgent enough to require his immediate attention.

Three anomalies appeared on the tactical hologram at three widely separated positions throughout the solar system, each generating a conflict of information his monitoring system could not resolve. The hive master directed his tactical hologram to zoom in on a sector where one anomaly occurred. His hologram generated a spherical indicator around that volume of space then zoomed in on it until it filled the entire viewing chamber.

Data transferred to the hive master's mind indicated that the timeline on the image referred to a recent period occurring about one hundred twenty-five minutes earlier. From there, the timeline of the scene played forward.

Despite careful examination, the hive master saw nothing unusual about the fragment of the battle unfolding. This tiny segment of the conflict that played out before him took place on the outskirts of the most active combat area and seemed nothing more than an overall view of the new, three-ship attack tactic that the enemy adopted.

He dismissed the alert as a belated warning of the new tactic when the monitoring system called for his attention once again, this time changing the hologram from a power signature view to a visual one displaying the ships involved. This time the hologram concentrated on a single human-piloted ship. It indicated that it popped into space very close to two enemy ambush ships that had just wreaked havoc on a formation of defenders. Incredibly, that ship clearly employed a wormhole jump within the confines of a solar system, a jump impossible to control accurately because of the gravitational influence of planets and moons.

He watched the newly arrived ship pass by the invaders unmolested and blend in with the retreating ships heading back toward their planet. The hologram flashed to a power signature overlay to provide the hive master with the visual images of the retreating ships overlayed with their power signatures. Impossibly, his tactical system did not find any sign of the mystery ship's power signature! The swarm ships given to the humans did not have the masking systems that Hive swarms had, and Swarm ships having such systems could *always* detect each other. The power signature of the ship in question did not exist at all on any Hive tactical system, and it sent a chill through the hive master's body. He knew the random visual samples his monitoring system collected had detected this anomaly and the other two only by sheer chance. With three such anomalies discovered, his monitoring system informed the hive master of a high probability of the presence of an additional number of undetectable ships!

Rage swept over the hive master. The source of the unheard-of tactics he'd witnessed today became crystal clear; the humans were working with the enemy! Without the need for further analysis or investigation, the hive master unhesitantly sent out a deadly, mentally directed signal.

Chapter 37
Mass Murder

McKay delayed vacating his base only long enough to collect Captain Bryant and bring her along. As they raced out to his Dragon, he felt gratified to see the tarmac empty of every other Dragon and his base as empty of personnel as a ghost town. His ship's boarding ramp came down in response to his mentally directed order and closed again as soon as he and Captain Bryant were safely aboard.

Captain Bryant had never personally been inside one of the Dragon ships before, and the bare metallic floor came as a surprise to her and left her at a loss for where she was supposed to sit or stand until two seats raised themselves from the deck.

"Just plop down on that thing over there, Captain," McKay waved distractedly in the general direction of the second chair as he took his seat, which then formed around him, adjusted itself to the shape of his body, and raised him to the center of the ship.

Megan became surprised once again when the oddly shaped floating stool shifted and formed around her the moment she lowered herself onto it.

As McKay's tactical hologram encased him, Lee wasted no time sending out orders through his ship's thought communications system. "Primary Sub-fleet Admirals, be ready to take over command again from our backups when we get past the atmosphere. Reestablish your sector holograms on your tactical displays, maintain your communications with my ship, and resume communications with your sector fleets. We will all have smaller holograms to work with, but they'll be revealing things to us our headquarters systems were not capable of displaying."

By the time Megan settled herself, the scene outside the ship had changed from a sunny day on the base tarmac to a view of the stars from above the atmosphere. Since she never felt the slightest bit of motion or acceleration, she had difficulty convincing herself that what she saw was the actual view outside the ship. Earth's horizon filled half the viewport, and brilliant stars of all colors contrasting themselves against the blackness filled the other half. She touched her fingertips to her chest and stared in awe of it all.

McKay, too, was distracted, but not by the beauty of the universe. He knew from what Duval told him that the functionality of his ship's tactical system should already be enhanced far beyond its previous capability, and he anxiously scanned his hologram to see what it would reveal to him for the first time.

He ordered the hologram to focus on the volume of space around Mars and magnified the planet in his hologram. To his anger and dismay, the power signatures of dozens of Stickman bases materialized where none ever appeared before.

He readjusted his tactical display again to cover the entire volume of the solar system. "Dammit to hell!" McKay roared, his voice snapping Captain Bryant's attention back to him and away from the magnificent view outside the ship. His upgraded tactical system uncovered hundreds more Stickman bases scattered throughout the solar system than the EDF command ever knew about and, along with them, the power signatures of uncountable Stickman Swarm ships. The fact that the Ghost enhancements successfully negated the Stickman masking systems gave him little or no comfort.

In McKay's estimation, the Stickman forces included several times the almost three million ships the EDF forces possessed at the start of the day's conflict. The number of Swarm ships his hologram revealed could have easily repelled the entire Seed ship invasion without human help. He regretted ever having doubted the truth of Duval's tales.

"Fleet Admiral McKay, what's wrong?" Bryant asked, fearful of whatever was upsetting him.

Hearing her voice, he turned from his tactical display with a surprised expression as though he'd forgotten her presence. "I'm sorry, Captain Bryant, you're going to be stuck with me for a while, maybe a long while. We seem to have a lot more to deal with than what we planned for."

"Is there something I can do to help?"

He pondered the question for a moment and said, "As a matter of fact, you can," he replied. "Do you know how the thought communications systems work?"

"I guess I'm one of those who never had the chance to use one yet. Human communications technology is my area of expertise."

"Well, hang on a second." He sent his ship a mentally directed command, and Captain Bryant felt her mind filling with information. In less than two minutes, she not only knew about the communications systems, she knew everything McKay himself knew about the entire ship.

Wide-eyed and speechless from the experience, she raised her hand to her chest in awe for the second time. She stared, unfocused, at some point on the ship's deck, seeing but not seeing as she tried to assess the information she'd just received. She couldn't believe the depth and detail of it all. She felt as if she'd studied the ship and its systems for her entire life.

"Captain Bryant!" McKay barked, startling her out of her trance.

She snapped her attention back to him. "Yes, Fleet Admiral? Sorry, sir."

"Captain, I want you to help me establish selective communications to my sub-fleet admirals so we can . . ."

He didn't get to finish the sentence. The inside of the ship lit up as thousands of Dragons in near-Earth sentry positions exploded simultaneously with colossal flashes of light. Thousands of equally bright flashes peppered the Earth's surface and upper atmosphere. Those were the reserve and evacuation ships Duval's team either could not reach in time or did not have enough time for the nanites to repair.

"Dear God!" McKay cried out in anguish. He felt as if an icy hand squeezed his heart when he saw that hundreds of thousands of Dragon power signatures simultaneously vanished from his tactical hologram. He stared at his Dragon's viewing field in disbelief as flashes of uncountable explosions continued to blossom in every direction further and further out in the darkness of space like an expanding balloon as the delayed light from the more distant explosions reached his ship. The Stickmen just obliterated the Dragon ship sentries of the entire defense grid and all of those engaged in battle with the Ghost ships!

～ ～ ～

Ling Wu had guessed correctly about the gift spheres the Stickmen provided. Containing no explosives in the conventional sense, each sphere responded to the hive master's mentally directed destruct signal by generating a force field around it that rapidly expanded to over a quarter-mile in diameter. As the field walls ballooned outward, they pushed the atmosphere away to create immense hemispheres of perfect vacuum within. The fields abruptly vanished when they reached full expansion to generate massive atmospheric implosions. As the voids refilled, cyclonic winds scoured the earth as they swept anything and everything, large and small, back toward the source of the vacuum. Within seconds, the inrushing walls of air crashed back together, creating thunderclaps more deafening than any before. The colliding pressure waves then radiated back outward again as atmospheric tidal waves flattened everything for miles beyond the original quarter-mile radii of the force fields. Thousands of EDF spaceports worldwide and most of the surrounding countrysides became flattened wastelands.

From Lee McKay's headquarters in Layton, the area of devastation stretched from South Ogden north of the base to Kaysville south out it. Only his trainee's group of Dragon ships caught within it survived within that area. The shockwaves passed around the Dragons, deflected by the same fields that pushed the atmosphere aside when they flew at maximum atmospheric speed. Those deflecting fields along with the Dragons' impregnable hulls fully protected their pilots and any civilians lucky enough to be aboard, thanks to Lee McKay's orders. Even though the trainees saved the lives of nearly twenty-five thousand Layton citizens and highway refugees, the blasts killed eleven thousand more.

~ ~ ~

If the hive master could smile, he would have. In a single stroke, he annihilated the human's entire command structure and the cream of the human warriors of this planet who hadn't already been destroyed in combat. He effectively erased any potential threat these fearsome beings could ever present to the Hive.

In a way, it was regrettable. Even though they were filthy forms of alien life, their skills held great potential for helping the Hive wipe out the enemy once and for all. The additional bonus of the thousands of Hive warriors' lives already preserved by their absence from combat didn't even occur to him. Hive warriors, bred in abundance, could easily be replaced.

The hive master sent yet another signal where, far beyond the solar system, twelve Stickman Sterilizer dreadnoughts received his command and prepared to jump. The time had come to cleanse the humans' planet of all forms of life.

~ ~ ~

A small moan of anguish escaped the lips of the usually imperturbable Dr. Ling when sensors registered the instantaneous disappearance of tens of thousands of EDF ships from the skies just above the Earth's atmosphere. Seconds ago, his satellite-based radar, made obsolete by Stickman technology, displayed the locations of thousands of sentry ships within their limited range of coverage just above the Earth. Now those radar screens showed nothing but chaff, the effect of radar signals bouncing off uncountable billions of pieces of Dragon ship debris.

To add to the catastrophe, one of his communications officers began calling out multiple lost contacts with EDF spaceports worldwide. The list included the four headquarters of his fleet admirals. Colonel Duval's revelations about the Stickmen could not possibly have been confirmed in a more horrifying manner. However, like the hive master, Ling Wu also did not hesitate. Upon hearing Duval's account earlier, he had prepared himself emotionally and mentally for this inevitable, horrific outcome.

Grimly, he walked to a secured command panel, one locked and guarded against everyone's access except his. The secret, sole purpose for its existence was to provide a means of response to the remote chance of a future need, a moment that, until today, no one believed would actually happen.

Short seconds after the hive master sent out his destruct command, Ling Wu touched a tiny fingerprint scanner on the panel without the faintest trace of doubt or indecision. Upon recognizing Ling Wu's fingerprint, a protective cover popped open, and the button it protected immediately began to flash a glaring red warning light. With a great need for vengeance uncharacteristically filling his heart, Ling Wu pressed the button.

～ ～ ～

At the abandoned site of the lunar base Lee McKay and his team partially constructed months ago, the three miniature nuclear power units built into the supply ships responded to Ling Wu's signal and awakened from their dormant mode. Delivered to the moon to provide power to the fledgling base and for its later expansion, the three units held another secret function buried in their design in case of need, given the secondary nature of the mission. The internal software of the three power units interpreted the incoming coded signal and triggered a mode that forced their plutonium cores to go to critical mass.

NASA picked the location of the lunar base the astronauts built because of the preponderance of UFO activity observed at that location over the years. Ling Wu had no way of knowing how close the Stickman underground base might be to the landing sites of the lunar supply ships, but the power supplies built into them were the only retaliatory weapons he had at his disposal. The process took just three seconds from the instant Ling Wu pressed his flashing button; a second and a half for the signal to reach the moon and another second and a half for the three nuclear devices to detonate simultaneously.

Three spectacular nuclear explosions combined to rip through the lunar surface with a destructive force that would forever alter the moon's face, the mighty blasts carving out a new, enormous crater. The explosions sent incandescent debris of former lunar landscape soaring out into space, their devastating energy ravaging the nearby hangar where the Stickmen first gave the four astronauts their ships.

Although the ships within that hangar had hulls virtually indestructible against all of the tools available to human technology, they could not withstand the nuclear hellfire pouring into the vast hangar cavity. In an instant, over fifty thousand alien spacecraft, all of them also serving as quarters for their Stickman pilots, were vaporized or half-melted.

When the nuclear blast speared through the lunar rock into two adjacent hangar chambers, it destroyed twenty-three thousand additional Swarm ships. Over six thousand more were smashed against the hangar walls or buried as the lunar surface above them caved in.

The hangar chamber became exposed to the hard vacuum of space, resulting in explosive decompression that swept through the adjoining tunnels and quarters, wiping out most of the base's worker caste support personnel. Those who still survived in sealed-off areas did not have the benefit of the hull shielding that protected the surviving Swarm ship occupants. Most of them would die shortly from the lethal radiation waves generated by the blasts. They would have died anyway since they were about to be abandoned.

In the aftermath, any attempt to search for and rescue survivors would be unimportant to the hive master. As he reflected earlier, the Hive could easily replace its losses.

Three more hangar chambers beyond those destroyed by the nuclear explosions remained unscathed, their Swarm ships undamaged. Their hulls, designed to protect their pilots from the intense radiations encountered as they passed through interstellar space, efficiently protected their occupants from the blast radiation as well.

Tens of thousands of the hive master's Swarms survived, ready for combat despite the devastation. As destructive as Ling Wu's counter-strike proved to be, it made an insignificant impact on the total number of Swarm ships all over the solar system that would soon be heading to Earth.

Chapter 38
Make a Stand!

Megan Bryant rose from her seat to stare out at the lights that Lee McKay knew would continue to flash for another hour and a half until the furthest light from the most distant Dragon ship explosions reached Earth. She felt as if they were witnessing fireworks explosions from the inside of a burst, except that the sparkling lights kept getting further and further away and seemed never-ending. As they watched in horror, another brilliant flash erupted on the moon to one side of their viewing field.

Captain Bryant's voice was tremulous with fear. "Sir, what just happened?"

McKay had trouble finding his voice. He stared in disbelief at the constant flashes, each series more distant than the last, and each flash representing the death of a Dragon ship combat pilot.

"The Stickmen just turned on us," he choked out despairingly. "We just didn't have enough time. I'm not sure how many of our Dragons survived, but I am sure that the Stickmen just obliterated most of our remaining Dragon ship forces that were still manning the defense grid."

"What? How is that possible?" She stared at McKay in horror, then back at the viewing field. Realizing what those flashes of light out in space represented, she sank back into her seat in disbelief, the blood draining from her face.

Pure fear gripped McKay's heart like an icy fist as he thought about his wife. In a panic, he said aloud to himself, "I've got to find out if my wife . . ."

Without warning, his head felt as if it would explode, the pain cutting off his ability to think clearly. He gasped, his body stiffening as his mind flooded with thousands of simultaneous, thought-transferred questions and demands for answers. Adding to his agony were the corresponding emotions transmitted by the multitude of surviving Dragon pilots sending those questions from the ships Duval and his team managed to save.

He could feel their confusion, anxiety, fear, hate, and rage all blended into one unbearable blast of mental energy. Never before had so many tried to communicate with him simultaneously. He squeezed the side of his head against the pressure of it all jamming into his mind. Sensing McKay's spasms, his command chair lowered itself back to the deck where he tumbled out of it onto the floor.

In a panic, Captain Bryant rushed to his side. "Fleet Admiral McKay! Sir, what's wrong?" When he couldn't answer, she gripped his hand tightly and urgently shook him by the shoulder. "Are you alright, sir? Please answer me!"

Oblivious of Bryant's attention, McKay groaned and gripped his head in both hands as if he were trying to keep it from bursting. Through sheer willpower, he fought to clear his mind enough to order his communications system to halt all incoming messages. On the brink of passing out, he barely managed to succeed. The pain vanished in an instant, but tears from the intensity of it all still streamed down his cheeks. He realized he could still hear one voice calling to him, a nearby one this time, not a mentally directed one.

"Fleet Admiral McKay!"

"I'm okay, Captain," he replied weakly but breathing heavily. He looked up at her, unable to focus at first.

Greatly concerned, Captain Bryant continued to squeeze his hand in both of hers, watching him closely as he recovered from the unexpected seizure.

"I just received thought-driven questions being directed at me by thousands of Dragon survivors all at the same time," he told her hoarsely. "It hurt like hell."

As Captain Bryant helped lift him to his feet and back into his chair, he frantically called out to Sue.

"Susan! Sue! Are you out there? Are you alright? Answer me!"

"I'm here, Lee! Oh, my head!"

"Are you injured?"

"Ohhh," he heard her say as she recovered from the pain from a similar flood of incoming mental contacts she received. It took a moment for her to respond. "I'm okay, Love; I think. My head felt like it was going to shatter. Thousands of people tried to communicate with me all at the same time."

"Thank God you're safe!" His body wilted with the relief he felt from knowing his wife survived the destruct signal.

"Lee, they're gone. All of our ships out there are gone! Only the ones Duval and his team managed to save are left."

"I know, Sue. There was nothing else we could do. Pete? Svetlana? Are you out there? Are you alright?" Lee called out anxiously to his friends.

"I too have survived along with my command staff and ground reserves," Svetlana answered, "but my near-Earth sentries above the planet have been obliterated." Lee and Susan could feel the radiated grief, anger, and hatred she now bore toward the Stickmen, all of those emotions conveyed by the communications systems along with her thoughts.

"Pete!"

"I'm here, Lee," came Peter Orsini's worried response. "We just lost all of our near-Earth, and deep space sentries," Pete informed his friends bitterly. "Hundreds of thousands of brave men and women have just been mass-murdered!"

Sue frantically examined her tactical display and reported, "Nearly all of my defense zone spaceports are gone too, but their reserve ships are still intact above the atmosphere. The survivors are terrified and frantic to know what just happened! I'm getting reports from my sub-fleet command. Panic is running rampant among all of our surviving forces. We've got fighters breaking ranks to land their ships to get away from them for fear of being blown up too."

"I, too, am receiving similar reports," Svetlana advised. "We must do something quickly!"

"We've got to bring them back around before things get worse," Lee told his friends. "I'm going to link my communications and knowledge transfer system to all of the surviving ships. I'll be the one to talk to them."

"Do it, and do it fast!" Pete urged. The approval of Sue and Svetlana was unspoken, but Lee knew he had that too. He sent a mentally directed command to his communications system to broadcast his message to everyone who survived.

"This is Fleet Admiral McKay to all forces; activate your ship knowledge transfer systems immediately. In a moment, you will know everything that has occurred and what will soon happen! Afterward, I want all of you to hear what I have to say. Stand by." He waited several seconds to allow them to access their knowledge transfer units. Without trying to hide anything, he gave all of the surviving forces every bit of the information he had. When the knowledge transfer finished, Lee addressed them again.

"Now you know the entire extent of everything we fleet admirals know. We are facing a vast number of Stickman forces who are coming to destroy us. I know all of you are concerned about your families and friends back home, but even if you desert your duty to go back to them, where can you hide? Where can you go? There is no place to run. The only chance your families have is the one you alone can give them by not panicking and by maintaining the order and discipline essential to our ability to fight back effectively!

"We've learned the invading aliens we were fighting are really here to help us and to save the human race from extinction. It's true that they are coming to take as many of our cities and population centers away as they can and, as hard as that is to accept, we *must* let them! They are trying to save as much of our population as they can. Protect those incoming Ghost ships! They will be taking our people to safety and out of harm's way, some of your families among them.

I'm not going to try to sugarcoat our situation. If we win, our people can be returned later. If we lose, we will go down fighting, knowing that the human race will survive somewhere else in the universe, and you all know as well as I do, someday they *will* avenge us.

"We owe our survival to the efforts of an infiltration team sent back to Earth by Fleet Admiral Ruark. You are alive because your ships' self-destructs were successfully neutralized thanks to the technological abilities of these Ghost aliens coming to take our cities. Our new allies also upgraded your tactical and communications systems. If you examine your tactical holograms, you'll find they've been modified to enable you to see the massive number of enemy forces that were hidden from us throughout the solar system. Last but not least, they've made our ships capable of making short, precision jumps inside the solar system that will give us a tremendous advantage over the Stickman Swarm ships. Your knowledge transfer systems have already given you the information you need to use these new abilities. Just concentrate on that knowledge for a few moments to accustom yourselves to it.

"Though the Stickmen Swarm ships vastly outnumber us, we have another huge advantage. Every Dragon fighter that we believed lost to us in battle, over a million of them, are still alive and coming back under the leadership of Fleet Admiral Ruark. We also know our enemy knows only one way to fight, by ganging up on their targets with overwhelming numbers. You all have skills they simply do not possess. With those skills, we can teach the Stickmen that coming here will prove to be the greatest mistake in the history of their race.

"You all have a patch on the sleeves of your uniform of a Dragon wrapped protectively around our planet. Fighting as a unit, we must all literally become that Dragon. Protect our world and the people on it. No one will survive without your willingness and determination to fight back!

"Soon, our new allies will be arriving at Earth. Remember, no matter what the Stickmen tried to tell us before, those people are our friends. Let them pass and, as they take our cities, above all protect their ships from the Stickman swarms."

He did a quick check of his tactical display. He saw that an unbelievable number of Stickman Swarm ships from previously hidden bases all over the solar system were already racing to converge on the Ghost Seed ships, all of which were free at last of EDF Dragon attacks. For the time being, the Stickmen were ignoring the surviving Earth forces in favor of chasing after the Ghost Seed ships.

"People, our Stickman pals seem to believe the Ghost ships are more of a threat than we are for the moment. That buys us some time. I want each of you to reposition yourselves around your hometowns so you can personally defend your homes and families. Take your commands from the sub-fleet admiral responsible for the sectors where you choose to make your stand. For those of you who have no families, reposition yourselves to fill in any weak spots. Do it now and remain on guard to await further orders! Do not hesitate to carry those orders out when you receive them. For now, Fleet Admiral McKay out."

"I can't think of anything better you could have told them," Sue told her husband. "That was brilliant. They'll fight like demons to protect their homes and families."

"They're going to have to."

"Bozhe moi!" Svetlana's thought interrupted. "There are so many Swarm ships out there! I pray Fleet Admiral Ruark arrives soon."

"We need to reorganize our survivors. I'll try to find out what I can about Ruark's plans," Lee told them. He turned to his passenger, the unanticipated addition to his ship's crew. "Captain Bryant, I can really use your help right now. Do you think you're up to it?"

Tears streaming down her face and, still trembling from the catastrophe that happened, she looked up at him and nodded weakly.

"Good! I'm going to be extremely busy in a moment, but I want you to contact all of Colonel Duval's team and put them through to us."

"You can count on me, sir."

"You've already more than proved that to me, Captain."

Chapter 39
Retaliation!

For the first time in his very long life, the hive master felt fear. Fortunately for him, the hangar where his command ship hovered, parked underground, was not as close to the nuclear blasts as the chambers just destroyed by them. Nevertheless, the edge of the explosions still ripped through the far end of it, demolishing several hundred Swarm ships and rocking his command ship with a force that injured some of its crew.

The hive master's ship was huge and heavy compared to the fighter ships in the hangar. Its hull held up to the massive shock of the explosion and easily protected the hive master and his crew from the blast radiation. However, the attack left the hive master badly shaken and experiencing the first taste of terror he had ever known.

The entire chain of events was beyond his ability to comprehend. The vermin of the planet below could not possibly possess the technology to deliver such a devastating blow to his base of operations! His tactical displays never triggered a single warning of attacking ships or any incoming projectile weapons these humans were so fond of, yet the strike happened! He jumped to the erroneous conclusion that their ancient enemy had provided the humans of Earth with a new and deadly masked weapon previously unknown to the Hive.

In a panic, he ordered his crew to launch his ship away from the moon before he could fall victim to another such attack. In response, his command ship effortlessly broke through the blast debris that partially covered his ship. Forty-one intact and functional Swarm ships formed a personal escort for him in a protective vanguard to lead the way. With the humans' moon no longer a safe haven, he chose to direct his Hive forces from his masked ship in the safety of deep space.

As his ship and escort soared away from the moon, the hive master's anxiety began to subside when the additional attacks he expected failed to materialize. A sense of security gradually returned to him, and he began to regain some of his composure.

As his fear subsided, his outrage intensified. An attack against the Hive people was unprecedented, let alone an attack on a hive master! That the enemy and their human turncoats would dare to launch a direct attack upon his person was inconceivable, yet they succeeded! His only comfort came from the knowledge he would soon take great pleasure in eradicating every trace of the humans from this galaxy. Perhaps he would participate personally in the final destruction of their planet when his Sterilizer fleet arrived.

Right now, he considered the humans on the planet as unimportant. Their final extermination was secondary to keeping the enemy ships from reaching the planet's population centers to save any of these dangerous humans. He ordered his millions of remaining Swarm ships hidden in hangars inside the moon and his Hive bases all over the solar system to intercept Earth-bound Seed ships and complete their destruction that the human warriors were no longer alive to carry out.

From the dark side of the moon, tens of thousands of Swarm ships burst from concealment to carry out his order. Throughout the solar system, more than seventeen million more rose to join them.

Chapter 40
Defenseless

Noah's command ship, masked since the beginning of the battle, sat hidden in the asteroid belt as a precaution since enemy ships could still identify it visually. There Noah monitored the status of his Seed ship fleet much the same way as the human fleet admirals had monitored the battle.

Jake Bennings and his Ghost scientist companion, Pat, were at the ship's bridge with Noah monitoring the battle's progress via their new Stickman version of a tactical hologram.

Jake was the only one of Ruark's collection of displaced humans, other than Karen and Sean Ruark, who didn't possess a Dragon to fly. However, the Ghosts and their human allies asked him to serve as the primary communications liaison between their fleets. From a small chain around Jake's neck, there hung a Ghost-improved thought communication sphere the size of a grape. All in one unit, it combined a Ghost translator with a thought communications system that they back-engineered and improved from a Dragon ship system.

The holographic display that Jake gave unwavering attention to changed unexpectedly, most of the pinpoints of light within it winking out all at once. For a moment, he thought the tactical display malfunctioned, then he saw an unusual and extended rippling of pinkish color among Noah, Pat, and the few Ghosts present with them on the bridge, and he could feel bursts of their body heat that went untranslated. A knot formed in the pit of his stomach. He knew something terrible must have happened.

Noah himself 'flowed' toward him and stopped directly before him.

"Noah: Jacob Bennings, I am greatly saddened to report you're your enemy has just slain many hundreds of thousands of your people's defenders. Our Seed ships are no longer under siege from their attacks."

Jake became quite pale and felt his knees go weak. He sank into a Stickman version of a command chair the Ghosts kept on the bridge for him.

213

"Then it's happened. We knew it would come, but we never thought it would come so soon," Jake said dejectedly, primarily to himself. He felt his eyes well up, the pain of the disaster squeezing his heart.

Pat flowed closer to express his sorrow. "Pat: You must believe that we Ghosts mourn the loss of those warriors just as you do."

As shaken as Jake felt, he tearfully looked up at the two Ghosts and said in a choked voice, "We have to set aside our grief for later, my friends. Right now, we have to get ready to proceed with the next phase of Fleet Admiral Ruark's plan, or many more humans will die soon."

"Noah: It will be done the moment Fleet Admiral Ruark's masked Dragons arrive." That said, he left Jake with his companion, Pat, and returned to his station.

"Pat: Are you emotionally capable of conducting your duties, Jake Bennings?"

Jake felt nauseous, badly shaken, and full of dark hate for these sick, demented Stickmen. Despite his feelings, he answered, "I am!"

∿ ∿ ∿

Debris pinged off the impenetrable hull of Danny Murphy's Dragon just as he reached the edge of his next targeted gathering of Dragons high above a French spaceport. Every Dragon below him simultaneously detonated in blinding flashes of light so intense the viewing field of Danny's ship automatically filtered the radiant light to keep him from being flash blinded.

Far below, a series of secondary explosions rippled across the base as the thought communications and knowledge transfer spheres detonated their vacuum bombs. What used to be an EDF spaceport seconds earlier lay under a mushroom cloud surrounded by a landscape scrubbed for miles around of every structure that once stood within the blast zones.

Danny screamed in rage and horror, not only from what he'd just witnessed but also from the uncountable points of light within his tactical hologram that also winked out, every vanishing light representing a Dragon ship that no longer existed.

His voice heavy with emotion, Danny called out to his teammates, "Those Stickman bastards went ahead and did it! They wiped out everyone!" Through the thought communications system, he could sense the pain of his companions too. It made the twisted feeling in his gut even worse.

"I'm over Australia," Karlson reported gravely. "The ships above my target base up ahead are gone too, along with the spaceport below! Ships, buildings, everything; they're all destroyed! There's what's left of a mushroom cloud over the base with debris still raining down from the sky! Something far worse happened here than just Dragons detonating. It looks like a huge shockwave spread out from the base and flattened the countryside around it. All of that certainly didn't just come from exploding Dragons!"

"I'm between targets," Bigsby reported solemnly, "but the horizon ahead of me just lit up with the biggest lightning flashes I've ever seen. It looks like the EDF spaceport up ahead at Yokota just disappeared too."

"I just doubled back toward my last target base to assess the damage. There's silvery debris everywhere!" Josh Harkins called out. "I can see meteor streaks below me as dense as raindrops! The upper atmosphere and space beyond are filled with silvery pieces of Dragon debris."

"That's what's left of our defensive guardian sentry force," Gator declared grimly.

"Ghost team, get it together!" Duval's voice ordered inside their minds. "We knew this would happen sooner or later. The Stickmen finally caught on to us, but if you expand your holograms, you'll see, thanks to you, that our fleet admirals and several hundred thousaıd others have survived! Keep your heads clear, and go to Phase 2 right now! Your liaison with the high command is Captain Megan Bryant onboard Fleet Admiral McKay's ship. Go through her to speak to the Admiral. I repeat, go to Phase 2 now! My part of this infiltration mission is over. Captain Karlson, take command! I'm jumping back to Ruark's base solar system."

Despite their grief, anger, and shock, all eleven team members obeyed. Their ships shot deeper into space to points where they could safely jump. One by one, they vanished briefly only to reappear in predetermined locations one hundred thousand miles above the Earth, positions that, together, distantly surrounded the entire planet. Once they arrived, each Dragon activated beacon signals for the Seed ships waiting to zero in on them.

Chapter 41
Mankind's Second D-Day

Jackson Ruark leaned forward in the command chair of his Dragon, anxiously studying his tactical hologram, his ship floating in space several hundred miles above Ares. He'd been monitoring the incoming flow of Dragons from there since the Seed ships launched the invasion back to Earth hours earlier. Scrutinizing the number of captured Dragons growing on his tactical display like a miser eagerly counting his pennies, Ruark treasured every captured EDF fighter ship that poured in through wormholes into this new solar system. As he watched, he listened in on the chatter of his people trying to soothe and re-educate the disoriented newcomers, sometimes joining in to help convince those more reluctant to believe the truth.

Every single minute he sat there waiting, he prayed for yet another minute. The longer he could just sit watching, the more lives of the EDF forces would be saved by Seed the ships pushing them through to this solar system. If they could keep up this capture rate for a few hours longer, then the Seed ships could reduce the defending Dragons in Earth's solar system to the point of defeat.

Forty-nine hundred of Ruark's completely rebuilt Dragons remained staged throughout this new solar system. They would all serve as beacons for the invading Ghost ships to pinpoint destination locations as they pushed captured Dragons through to them. The distant separation the receiving Dragons kept from each other gave the massive number of incoming ships plenty of room to spread out. Using the nanite projectile systems embedded in their hulls, Ruark's Ghost-improved Dragons infected every incoming ship almost as quickly as they arrived.

The gathering of the incoming Dragons proved to be more chaotic than Ruark would have preferred. The fighter ships kept popping into the solar system at a much greater rate than he and his people anticipated; a good problem to have, though, not a bad one. For that, he knew they could give credit to the Stickmen's failure to participate in the battle for the

216

unanticipated bounty of Dragons. Since the humans carried the fight alone, the EDF had no choice but to commit more fighters into the conflict than expected. For once, the Stickman treachery worked in everyone's favor except theirs.

Through knowledge transfers, the newly acquired fighter pilots became rapidly re-educated. For the thousandth time, Ruark thanked God for the knowledge transfer systems; otherwise, making these newcomers aware of the truth would have been impossible in the short time available to convince them. With their self-destructs nullified, their newly acquired mini-jump capability, and their tactical systems restructured, the repaired Dragons would provide a very unpleasant surprise for the Stickmen when the time came for them to return to Earth.

So far, Ruark's plan was working to perfection. The invading Ghost Seed and robot ships already managed to transfer over one million Dragon ships into this solar system, nearly one-third of all of the EDF forces in existence.

Ruark knew that the chances for the Seed ships to reach Earth and take some of its cities improved with every single Dragon the Ghosts could capture. Even so, no matter how many Dragons he had available to return to Earth's solar system when the massive Stickman forces finally decided to turn on the human race, there would be virtually no chance for the Seed ships to save everyone on the planet. That realization gnawed painfully at Ruark's gut.

Returning altered Dragons to Earth's solar system would be easy since they no longer needed to be captured in battle to accomplish the transfer. Five thousand Ghost scout ships equipped with wormhole generators waited to push the Dragon ships back; only this time, the Dragons would voluntarily fly en-mass through the wormhole openings. Thoroughly educated with the battle plan, all of the Dragon ship warriors would know what to do the very second they arrived back inside Earth's solar system.

"Fleet Admiral Ruark," came a grim-sounding voice from one of his people, "a mass of debris just came through a wormhole."

Jackson abruptly felt as if his heart froze in his chest. He knew the dreaded end of his long vigil had come far sooner than he expected. The shock of it left him nauseous. For whatever reason why the Stickmen triggered the destructs, he knew that he and his people couldn't have captured nearly enough of the EDF forces they'd hoped to catch.

Eighty-nine similar reports of debris came in one after another, the wreckage all that remained of Dragons self-destructing at the very moment the Seed ships sent them through wormholes. The flow of incoming captured Dragons ceased altogether at all the collection points. Without a doubt, hundreds of thousands of Earth's Dragon fighters had just been massacred. Every captured Dragon pilot throughout this new solar system knew it now too. Through his Dragon's communications system, Ruark could sense their grief and rage.

Even though he knew the despicable act was inevitable, his mind could never quite believe that the Stickmen would go through with it. The depth and barbarity of the Stickman betrayal left him dazed. He pressed his face against clasped hands to gather his courage, and he uttered a short prayer for Divine help.

Over a million of his captured Dragon fighters awaited his orders. The survival of the human race depended upon how well he would direct them. It took him a moment to summon the ability to keep the fear out of his voice as he addressed his people.

"Friends," he called gently to his forces, Ghost and human alike, "the moment we all dreaded has arrived. Take a moment to offer a prayer for our brother and sister warriors who just perished at the hands of the Stickmen." He gave them some time to do just that, tears rolling down his cheeks as he, too, paid homage to the dead.

When he spoke again, he told them, "The time has come for us to begin the first stage of our return. I want you all to remember every one of our lost heroes as you prepare yourselves to fight for everything we hold dear back home! Let our memory of them fuel the fires of our need for revenge. As planned, only our Super Dragons will return to Earth's solar system first. The rest of you stay ready. Your time will come too before too long."

Ruark mentally asked his tactical system for a ship count and received back a total of over one million one hundred thousand captured Dragons collected this day. At the time he and his family were captured, he knew the EDF forces numbered nearly three million Dragons, and he took some comfort from the count, knowing that the Ghost Seed ships managed to capture a good third of the EDF forces during the battle. Ruark prayed Colonel Duval's infiltration team succeeded in saving many more of them back home. He would soon find out upon Duval's expected return.

As Ruark made final checks on his Super Dragons before ordering them to make the jump back to Earth's solar system, his tactical system alerted him to a ship popping into space near his. Duval's returned Dragon moved closer after using Ruark's ship as a target beacon to make his return as planned.

"It's happened," Duval reported grimly inside Ruark's mind.

"We already know," Ruark responded, having difficulty keeping his voice from cracking even though he knew Duval couldn't hear him that way. "A lot of wreckage came through a while ago, and the inflow of Dragons ceased altogether. We are ready to make the jump back with our Super Dragons as soon as you make your report. Use your knowledge transfer system to send out a general broadcast. I want everyone to know what happened."

Ruark set his Dragon's thought communications system to a general broadcast mode. "People, Colonel Duval has just returned. He is going to brief us on what happened back home. Go ahead and make your report, Colonel."

Duval obeyed, starting with a simple, directed command to his knowledge transfer system to impart his recent experiences to all of Ruark's forces. Grief and rage engulfed Ruark as he learned the details of the simultaneous destruction of the EDF forces. The story became even more painful upon hearing that so many ground reserve Dragons took to flight before Duval's team had a chance to disinfect any of their self-destructs. His only consolation came from the fact that Duval's team at least managed to disinfect over seven hundred thousand ships parked both on the ground as well as those gathered at the edge of space. Between the Dragons Duval's team saved and the Ghost ships sending Dragons to this solar system, nearly two-thirds of Earth's original forces remained intact and ready for battle once again, this time all of them prepared to fight on the right side of the war.

Another shock came when Duval told everyone that the Stickmen also rigged all thought communications and knowledge transfer spheres that destroyed most of Earth's EDF spaceport headquarters. The fact that Ling Wu somehow managed, just in time, to deduce those devices must also be booby-trapped came as no comfort.

Ruark gave his people a moment to let the information Duval sent to them sink in before he addressed them again. "People," he said gravely, "You know the whole story now. The Stickmen used us, betrayed us, and murdered hundreds of thousands of us who accepted their hand in friendship. When we go back after those bastards, I expect every one of you to teach them to fear the human race forevermore!

"Group leaders, you have your orders. You all know the plan. Let me remind you all, the enemy has no concept of what a real dogfight is among their equals, let alone their betters. It's a certainty the Stickmen will outnumber us all many times over, but they don't know how to fight without ganging up on their victims, and we all know that, unlike us, they depend almost completely, if not totally, on their automatic targeting systems. They have never known an enemy the likes of you or the depths of hell to which you will all send them."

He paused again to let his words sink in. "In the entire history of humanity, no battle has ever had so much at stake as this coming one. I wish you good hunting, and I pray for your safe delivery from this evil we are about to face."

"I'm placing Colonel Duval is in command of all newly arrived Dragons in this solar system. He'll be leading you all back to Earth's solar system when my Super Dragons send the beacon signals. Be ready to go through your jump points as fast as possible and come out on the other side fighting. This will be mankind's second D-Day, only this time the D stands for Dragons. All Super Dragons, prepare to jump."

Chapter 42
Countermeasures Begin

Now that the destroyed EDF Dragon ships attacking his Seed ships were gone, Noah's forces numbered over six thousand one hundred unscathed Seed ships speeding unopposed toward Earth, thanks to the battle tactics Karlson taught his Seed ship commanders. There were also still twelve hundred surviving robot ships quite capable of putting up a fight with the Swarm ships already on the way to hunt them down.

Watching the tactical hologram on the bridge of Noah's ship, Jake Bennings observed nearly five thousand new points of light appear all over the solar system. Each light represented a Super Dragon emerging near one of Noah's Seed ships, all of them invisible to the Stickmen's tactical systems.

"Commander Noah! If I read this tactical display correctly, Fleet Admiral Ruark has arrived."

The Ghost, Noah, moved closer to the tactical system and paused before it.

"Noah: Indeed, he has." Noah sent out a greeting. "Noah: Fleet Admiral Ruark, welcome back to your home solar system. I must tell you how deeply my people regret the loss of Earth's warriors. As we feared, their destruction came far too early. The hordes of Stickman ships hidden within your solar system have divided themselves into thousands of attack swarms. As I speak, they are racing toward my Seed ships. What are your orders?"

Ruark heard his call through the tiny translation and communications device he wore around his neck.

"We will proceed as planned, my friend, even though we are short, by far, the number of fighters we hoped to gather."

Via his tactical hologram, Ruark made a quick evaluation of the enemy ships speeding toward Noah's Seed ships, all of them intent on destroying Noah's fleet before it could reach Earth.

"The first of the swarm fighters will be hitting your Seed ship positions in moments, Commander Noah. Begin the simultaneous activation of your decoys in tandem with your Seed ship masking systems. Send the decoys and robot ships toward Earth and jump your ships to our beacon points close to Earth before the swarms reach your positions. Good luck to us all, and please keep yourselves safe."

Noah sent out a command to his armada to jump to Earth's vicinity just as Ruark directed. Each of his thousands of crewed Seed ships ejected one of the newly conceived decoys upon receiving Noah's order. As they did so, they activated its new masking system, which simultaneously triggered the small decoy spheres to generate a power signature identical to the one its parent ship just masked.

Each decoy module encased itself within a full-scale holographic image of a Ghost Seed ship to serve as bait for drawing in the enemy swarms. The deployed decoy modules and what remained of the robot ships continued to speed toward the Earth just as the Stickmen would expect Seed ships to do. The ruse worked. The Hive tactical systems identified and targeted the decoys as Seed ships, the real Seed ships now invisible to them. With doppelganger decoys successfully deployed, Noah's masked Seed ships jumped far ahead to the near-Earth beacon points provided by Duval's infiltration team.

Ruark's masked Dragons, monitoring the incoming Swarm ships, quickly determined the most massive swarms pursuing the decoys. With their presence invisible to the Swarm ships, they scattered themselves among the decoys to await those swarms.

∽ ∽ ∽

"Several thousand ships just arrived at the battlefront," Sue McKay apprised the other fleet admirals excitedly. They have the identical power signatures as Duval's infiltrator Dragons!"

"Those would be me and my beefed-up fleet of Super Dragons," Jackson Ruark interjected, having set his thought communications system to the same private mode the fleet admirals used among themselves.

"Jackson! Thank God you're alive, old buddy!" an overjoyed Orsini welcomed.

"Welcome back, Jackson! We can sure use your help," Lee McKay told him happily.

"Welcome, Fleet Admiral Ruark," Svetlana greeted simply.

"Jackson Ruark, if and when the time comes when we have a whole lot less to worry about, I'm going to give you the biggest hug you've ever had, and then I'm going to slap you silly for what you put us through!" Sue

McKay promised with a vengeance. Then, bursting into tears, she added, "We're so glad you're alive and back with us!"

"Love you guys too. It's great to be out of hiding and back among the living again. As much as my troops and I are relieved to be back, we don't have time for happy reunions. We will shortly have a host of unwelcome guests to deal with. My people and I have a few tricks up our sleeves that we're bringing to the party as an unpleasant surprise for our former allies."

"Jackson, do those tricks you mentioned have anything to do with the fact hundreds of new Seed ships are arriving above the Earth near Duval's team right now?

"Those aren't new ships. They're the same ones that were just out here with us. Activate your knowledge transfer systems and stand by."

The four fleet admirals followed his instruction, and Ruark transferred his entire battle strategy.

"Decoys!" Pete Orsini said approvingly. "That will buy us some time."

"And we can expect over a million of our MIA's coming back soon too," Susan stated rhetorically. "Fantastic! You can see we have close to eighteen million enemy Swarm ships out there to deal with. Even with all of your MIA Dragons coming back, we're still going to need some major miracles."

"Then we'll just have to make miracles happen! As for the Stickman forces, my people already know how many enemy ships are out there. We scouted the solar system a couple of days ago. Have you dreamed up any countermeasures to deal with this mess?"

"Countermeasures? We have nothing! Of all the possible events Ling Wu and his people made contingency plans for, the instantaneous loss of most of our Dragon ships sure as hell wasn't one of them!"

~ ~ ~

Noah's masked fleet of ships popped into near-Earth space at points all around the Dragons of Duval's insertion team, now serving as beacon ships. However, rather than begin their harvest of population centers, they remained in place above the planet to give Ruark's Super Dragons time to wreak havoc on the Swarms attacking the decoys. The more Swarm ships they sent 'elsewhere,' the less there would be that would eventually attack seed ships taking their harvests. If the decoy ruse remained undetected, at the velocity the decoys traveled, Ruark's Dragons would have more than an hour to decimate and diminish the number of Swarm ships attacking the decoys before Noah's seed ships could receive the order to start harvesting cites.

~ ~ ~

After Noah gave his Seed ships the order to jump, he held his command ship back while monitoring their transfer. He refused to let his command ship make the jump until he became certain that his entire fleet reached Earth's vicinity safely. His attentiveness would soon reap an unexpected reward.

Chapter 43
The Flight of the Hive Master

Now that the hive master's ship cleared of the vicinity of Earth's moon, and he no longer feared another attack that could endanger him, he turned his full attention back to his ship's tactical system. Its sensors sent him the knowledge of how many of his lunar-based Swarm ships survived and how many more thousands remained hopelessly trapped, buried in the rubble of the destroyed hangars below.

That particular bit of information was unimportant to him. The Hive had millions more to replace them throughout its ever-expanding empire.

He called for his tactical hologram to display the entire solar system to check the progress of his swarm fleets racing to intercept the enemy ships before they had a chance to save any of Earth's vermin. Scrutinizing the hologram with a practiced eye, the human's planet immediately drew his attention.

Ordering the hologram to zoom in on the vicinity of Earth, the hive master stared at the image in disbelief. The hologram revealed several hundred thousand power signatures of ships that should no longer exist!

Though the beings of the Hive race rarely made a sound, he hissed in shock. His destruct signal should have wiped the human warriors from the entire volume of this solar system. However, his ship's tactical system and sensors undeniably verified that the nearby human world remained infested with human-piloted ships still intact and fully functional!

The hive master failed to comprehend how any could possibly have survived his destruct signal! No longer confident of anything, he scanned the entire volume of the solar system and anxiously studied the results with care. To his relief, except for ships immediately within Earth's vicinity, the rest of the solar system held nothing but the debris from destroyed ships. He verified that his destruct signal worked after all, but it was unfathomable how so many of the humans' ships escaped the carnage of its deadly command.

Those surviving humans represented a new and significant danger to him. Unlike the Swarm warriors of his race, his personal sense of self-preservation still dominated his being. It drove him with an urgent need to get as far away from those surviving warriors as possible. The safest place of all to be would be among the incoming Sterilizer ships.

He ordered his ship's crew and his escort to set an evasive course at maximum speed through the net of incoming enemy ships to the location where the Sterilizer ships would soon arrive at the edge of the solar system. He had no fear of discovery; the solar system was vast, and his masked ship could easily outrun and outmaneuver larger enemy ships, given the remote possibility his masked ship and its escorts would be discovered visually. Besides, his swarm guardians should be more than adequate to eliminate any threatening enemy vessels that might try to prevent his escape. Confident of a successful retreat, he continued to put distance between himself and the vile humans whom he could never again regard without fear.

Chapter 44
The Jump to Earth

The beacon signals Duval's infiltrator team of Dragons transmitted provided with pinpoint accuracy the jump locations the Ghost Seed ships needed to get close as possible to Earth. Seed ships by the hundreds began to scatter themselves safely into the volume of space above the planet to serve as additional beacons for more Seed ships to find. Soon the volume of space between the Earth and the moon became packed with Noah's entire armada. Jake's Ghost companion, Pat, kept Jake informed of the activities around the command bridge as Noah directed his forces remotely.

"Pat: All of our surviving Seed ships have successfully reached your planet, Jake Bennings. It is time for us to join them. Swarm ships, many millions of them coming from their hidden places all over your solar system, are pursuing our decoys and are rapidly closing on them. There is no longer a need to remain here. Commander Noah is preparing to jump to near-Earth space to direct his forces from there."

Jake waited for the familiar but momentary feeling of disorientation and distorted time that came with wormhole travel, but nothing happened. Glancing questioningly about the bridge, it became apparent to Jake something unexpected drew the attention of Noah's bridge crew to the ship's new Stickman-style tactical system. Familiar with the infrared patterns rippling across their bodies, Jake could tell that these patterns indicated excitement. Noah himself glided toward it and paused before it to observe for himself.

"What is it, Pat? What's happening?" Jake asked, looking at the huge hologram floating above the bridge floor. He examined it intently, trying to glean from it what, specifically, the Ghosts were studying.

"Pat: The new tactical system has detected a single group of Swarm ships and one larger ship moving away from Earth instead of toward it, and curiously, it seems to be avoiding the paths of our incoming decoy ships. The group's point of origin has been traced back to your planet's moon, and they are leading a larger ship. There is only one conclusion we can draw from this information, and Commander Noah has given orders to deal with it."

Chapter 45
Elsewhere

As the hive master fled away from the human's planet, it pleased him to see that his tactical system indicated his planet-cleansing Sterilizer ships were about to arrive at the outer reaches of the solar system. The hive master's command ship and its escort would soon be safe aboard one of the giant sterilizer dreadnoughts coming in to deal with this hateful planet full of humans. Their arrival guaranteed this solar system's cleansing would soon begin. With his ship's course already set to the dreadnoughts' arrival point, he settled back to savor the holographic images of his swarm forces converging on enemy ships.

The hive master's peace of mind lasted only moments. Once again, his tactical system flashed him a mental warning of the highest alarm level. One of his escort ships had just vanished! He watched his tactical display in horror as, one by one, more of his escorts began to disappear.

He hissed in pure terror. There was no reason for this to be happening! His tactical display revealed no possible threats anywhere within many light-minutes, and the only Earth ships that could pose a threat were left far behind.

In desperation, he turned his attention to his ship's viewing field. Whatever served him as blood froze when he saw the distant silvery light of an enemy ship bearing down on his position. Before he could give the command to flee, he felt the familiar sensation of vertigo that always accompanied long wormhole jumps, and the viewing field turned black.

Despite the command ship still being within a solar system, his ship's crew must have taken the risk to activate the jump drives just in time to escape the oncoming enemy vessel. The timely jump eased the crushing terror he felt a moment earlier, not only from the imminent threat of death but also from his proximity to the filthy life forms the enemy ship contained.

The feeling of vertigo faded again, and he knew his ship managed to exit the wormhole safely. However, another frightening thought occurred to him to reignite his fear. He hastily turned his attention back to his tactical display to see if the enemy followed his ship through the jump. To his great relief, the hologram showed no sign of any ships' power signatures anywhere within its vast scanning range.

Something still felt wrong, though, and it dawned on him that the hologram seemed to be too empty. Even though his ship must have jumped clear of the solar system, his tactical system should still display the now-distant planetary bodies, yet nothing was visible at all out there, nothing anywhere! Undoubtedly, the tactical hologram must have suffered a massive failure, likely due to the battering his ship received during the attack on his hidden lunar base.

He turned to his viewing field to find it, revealing nothing but a deep blackness outside his ship without even a single star visible. Confused, he turned his head, searching in all directions, the viewing field following his gaze until finally, towards the lower rear of his ship, he glimpsed the faintest patches of light. He mentally ordered the viewing field to enlarge the external view to its maximum capability. Even at that magnification, he could just barely discern that the light came from a distant, broad scattering of thousands of galaxies.

The hive master had no way of knowing that those star clusters were the forward edge of a wavefront of galaxies still expanding outward toward him from the creation of the universe. His ship's sensors would soon inform him that, even with his ship's wormhole drives working at maximum jump distance and frequency, the ship could not possibly reach the closest one of those galaxies in less than nine hundred and forty-two years.

Chapter 46
The Arrival of the Sterilizer Fleet

One by one, twelve planet-killing dreadnoughts appeared at the border of Earth's solar system just seconds apart. Shaped much like the blade of a scythe, the Hive race called them Sterilizers. Twelve miles long, the back side of the 'blade' exceeded a mile in thickness. Its three-mile slope down to its front edge measured just a few hundred yards thick by comparison. Each vessel also served as a space-born, independent Hive city, as well as a leviathan capable of unimaginable destruction.

Like spiders transporting their young on their backs, the backside hull of each Sterilizer carried dense clusters of over one hundred thousand anchored swarm ships and another thousand five-warrior Eradicator ships. The twelve Sterilizers, linking their weapon systems together, could create a curtain of intense radiation capable of cremating everything on the surface of a planet. In a matter of hours, Earth would fall prey to them.

Now that the dreadnoughts completed their final jump to the outskirts of Earth's solar system, the ships came together into a C formation with one lone Fleet Command ship centered between the trailing ends of the configuration. Within that ship, the commanding fleet master sat in the dark chamber of his bridge and, with an experienced eye, concentrated on his tactical hologram as images of this next vermin-ridden solar system came online. What the display revealed left him baffled and confused.

His tactical system indicated that, while the solar system held the scattered debris of hundreds of thousands of human-piloted swarm ships, close to three-quarters of a million ships remained intact when there shouldn't have been any!

The culture of the Hive race consisted of levels of casts where those of high caste did not lower themselves to communicate directly with subservient castes any more than they would converse with a human other than through indirect knowledge transfer, and even then, only when necessary. The hive master of this solar system, the fleet master's superior and therefore of a higher cast, should have indirectly sent him his orders

231

through a knowledge transfer upon his arrival along with an explanation of the presence of the intact human-piloted ships.

The fleet master ordered his artificially intelligent tactical system to request an information transfer to acquire the hive master's orders. Much to the fleet master's dismay, the system failed to make contact after several attempts.

Baffled, the fleet master ordered his tactical system to locate the hive master's command ship. He became even more perplexed and alarmed when his tactical system indicated that the hive master's ship could not be located within this solar system even though he'd received commands directly from it a short while earlier, ordering his fleet to make their final wormhole jumps.

His last orders for his fleets to jump to this solar system implied, without a doubt, that the Sterilizers should direct themselves to the human's planet and initiate its destruction. To his inherent Hive arrogance, it was a foregone conclusion that the Hive would eventually eradicate all humans from this system whether the Hive successfully made use of them as warriors or not.

The surprising absence of this system's hive master puzzled and disturbed him. The undetected demise of the hive master came so swiftly that the fleet master and the hive master's subordinate Hive bases throughout the system remained in ignorance of the discovered alliance between the humans and the enemy of the Hive race.

Just as unsettling as the absence of the hive master and the unexpected survival of human-piloted Swarm ships, the display on the fleet master's tactical hologram revealed that the invading enemy ships did not cluster together as they'd always done in the past. Instead, they were scattered individually throughout the entire outer volume of the solar system to create a vast sphere formation that slowly squeezed itself closer to the human's world.

In the absence of the hive master's directives, the fleet master ordered his artificial intelligence system to transfer to him all the records of the events of the last several hours automatically recorded by every Hive base scattered throughout this solar system. What he learned from them troubled him deeply, the information making no sense to him.

From the data gathered, he verified that, for some unknown reason, the solar system's hive master decided that the plan to use the humans as Hive warriors had failed. With that always a likely possibility, the original plan included allowing their ancient enemy and the humans to keep fighting until one side destroyed the other. The reason why the hive master chose to destroy the humans' ships before that happened remained a mystery.

Records also indicated that moments after the destruction of the humans' Swarm ships, an attack of unknown origin destroyed a large part of the hive master's main base on the moon orbiting the humans' planet. Undoubtedly, the hive master survived the attack, but the level of destruction it caused mandated the abandonment of the base.

The last commands sent by the hive master summoned the Sterilizer fleet from its remote location. They ordered all Swarm fighters in the solar system to concentrate their attacks on the enemy ships still advancing toward the third planet to begin their collection of humans and other filthy lifeforms. Shortly after the hive master sent out those commands, the tactical systems of every Hive base in the solar system recorded the hive master's ship vanishing from the solar system just seconds before the arrival of the Sterilizer fleet.

With no enemy ships near the last recorded location of the hive master's command ship, the only conclusion he could reach was that the hive master ordered a wormhole jump for a reason yet to be determined. However, given that to be true, the hive master's command ship should still be within the detection range of the dreadnoughts' powerful tactical systems, yet it was nowhere to be found. The perplexed fleet master failed to find a logical explanation for any of these inexplicable events.

The fleet master found it chilling that either the humans or the enemy managed to carry out a successful devastating attack against the hive master's base by using an undetectable destructive weapon. No enemy the Hive encountered in its history of Hive expansion ever displayed the audacity, let alone the technical capability to attempt a retaliatory counterattack.

Because of that attack, while the fleet master would typically have released most of his onboard forces to join in the pursuit of enemy ships, he sided with caution for the sake of his fleet's protection. He directed his flotilla of Sterilizer ships to dispatch their entire armadas of swarm fighters and Eradicators to precede their mother ships in a dense shield formation to lead the great ships slowly and cautiously toward the human planet.

With the entire collection of Hive forces inside the solar system left leaderless by the disappearance of their hive master, the fleet master, as the highest-ranking representative of the Hive race, automatically became commander of all of the Hive forces. Given that authority, he saw no reason to countermand the missing hive master's last orders to his swarms to locate and destroy enemy ships.

While waiting for the myriad of swarm fleets to engage the enemy, he focused his attention back on the human planet. The fact any human fighter ships still existed at all mystified him. Hive technology never failed to operate to perfection; therefore, the self-destruct signals sent out to the humans' ships should have destroyed all of them.

Unaware of the human alliance with the Hive enemy, the fleet master concluded that the surviving humans would believe the invading enemy caused the mass destruction of their forces. Under that assumption, they would have no other choice left but to continue resisting the invaders, much to the benefit of the Hive.

Seeing no flaws in his deductions, the fleet master sat back in his command chair to observe and direct his swarms toward enemy ships and whatever remnants remained of the human-piloted Swarm ships. Afterward, he would take pleasure in sanitizing this solar system of all its life forms, once and for all, in preparation for its addition to the Hive empire.

Chapter 47
McKay Meets the Ghosts

The four fleet admirals watched their tactical holograms in awe as hundreds of Seed ships continued to pop into space all around the points of light representing the Dragons of Duval's infiltration team. It was hard to accept that these ships they'd dreaded for months were arriving here as saviors, not enemies. However, instead of heading immediately down to the planet through a newly established but vastly diminished defense grid of Dragons just above the Earth, the Seed ships remained in the places where they arrived. One last Seed ship appeared a few moments later, popping into space several thousand miles above the Earth's north polar axis. Moments later, Megan Bryant received her first incoming message aboard Lee McKay's Dragon.

"Captain Bryant, this is Captain Gunther Karlson reporting. I'm presently in command of Colonel Duval's infiltration team. I need to speak to the fleet admirals immediately!"

Megan Bryant used the thought communications system to connect all the fleet admirals to Karlson, including Lee McKay, who sat in the Dragon's command chair only a few feet away.

"Fleet Admirals, sirs, I have one of Colonel Duval's team in contact with us, a Captain Karlson who is in command of the infiltration team now. He urgently wishes to speak to you all."

"Thank you, Captain Bryant." Lee McKay answered for them all, mentally adjusting his thought communications system to allow Karlson to talk to him.

"Captain Karlson, this is Fleet Admiral Lee McKay. Fleet admirals Orsini, Ivanovna, and Susan McKay, are also listening. We want you and your infiltration team to know how deeply indebted to you we all are."

"Unfortunately, we didn't do nearly enough," Karlson replied sorrowfully, still distraught over the loss of so many combat pilots. "Fleet Admirals, are you making use of the enhancements to your tactical displays yet?"

"Roger that, Captain. What they uncovered for us came as a very unpleasant surprise."

"Unpleasant to all of us, sir. Unfortunately, Fleet Admirals, while the Ghost nanites used to infect Dragons were able to defuse the self-destructs and construct the small changes we devised, they could not provide the ability to mask Dragon ships from the Stickmen. That modification takes too much time. The Stickmen can still see your power signatures, and they know where all of you are! What they don't know is you can see them too, even though they think they've masked themselves from you! They still believe you're blind to them."

"Thank you, Captain Karlson. We know that, and we plan to put that bit of information to very good use."

"Damned straight, we are!" Pete Orsini chimed in.

"Excellent! Fleet Admirals, as you can see, the Ghost Seed ships here are ready to go down to gather our cities. Their command ship just arrived under the leadership of a Ghost whom we have named Commander Noah. We need to establish permanent communications between Commander Noah and all of you immediately."

"What do you want us to do?"

"Sir, aboard Noah's ship is one human civilian who has volunteered to act as an interface between the four of you and the Ghosts since the thought communications spheres don't work at all with the Ghost beings. He, too, has a thought communications device to establish contact with you all. My men and I have those devices too that we use to communicate with the Ghost Commander directly, but we are going to have our hands too full to be relaying messages for you all."

"One person is serving as the only channel we have to communicate with all of those ships? And a civilian to boot? Where the hell did he come from?"

"Sir, his name is Jake Bennings. I believe you are already aware of Mr. Bennings' disappearance from Peru."

"Indeed, we are," McKay replied, "Colonel Duval told us his story. We were gratified to learn Jake is alive and well."

"Fleet Admiral Ruark needed every Dragon pilot at our disposal for the coming fight. Other than Karen and Sean Ruark, Jake was the only one left among us who we could count on to station himself aboard Noah's command ship. Let me establish contact between you."

Without waiting for permission, Karlson linked their communications systems with the communications device in Jake's possession.

"Jake, this is Gunther Karlson. I've connected Commander Noah's ship to all four of Earth's fleet admirals. They can now communicate with Noah through you."

"Fleet Admirals, I'm Jake Bennings. I'm at the side of Noah, the commander of the Ghost Seed ship fleet."

"Please convey our warmest welcome and our deepest gratitude for his help and the help of his people." There was a pause as Jake did as requested.

"Commander Noah expresses his thanks for the training he and his people received from us, training that undoubtedly saved a lot of Ghost lives today too, sir."

"Mr. Bennings, no offense, but we have an enormous number of enemy ships attacking the decoys ships, and they will soon be heading our way. While we deeply appreciate your assistance that I suspect you volunteered to provide, you are untrained for the complex communication duties you have are required to handle."

He glanced up at Captain Bryant, who stared back, her eyes going wide. She bore the expression of someone stuck on railroad tracks watching a train bearing down on her.

"I'd like to present you with some help." He cocked his head and looked pointedly at Captain Bryant, one eyebrow raised in question. Bryant became quite pale but slowly nodded her acceptance.

"Sir, you have no idea how wonderful your offer sounds to me."

"With Commander Noah's permission, I'd like to make a delivery to his ship."

There was another pause. "Commander Noah grants permission and welcomes the opportunity to discuss matters of great importance personally with you, matters he would rather prefer not to address with the complication of trying to talk through me."

"If Commander Noah's ship was the last one that came through, I have his position."

"That's the one, Fleet Admiral."

"I can be there in . . . two minutes," McKay replied, receiving the information from his tactical. "I presume you have a place for me to land?"

"You only need to get close, and we'll pull you in," Jake replied.

~ ~ ~

Jake Bennings came alone to greet the fleet admiral and Captain Bryant as they emerged from McKay's Dragon presently parked inside the Seed ship hangar bay. The young man, dressed in wrinkled Khaki's and sporting a day-old beard, had a haggard look about him, the day's events having taken their toll upon him as much as it did everyone else who survived the Stickmen's betrayal so far.

The unexpected sight of an attractive young woman dressed in the crisp black jumpsuit of an EDF officer came as a surprise to Jake.

"Fleet Admiral, I'm Jake Bennings," he said, extending his hand to McKay.

"I'm pleased to meet you, Mr. Bennings. We know quite a bit about you."

"Call me Jake, please, Fleet Admiral."

"Very well, Jake, this is Captain Bryant, my communications officer."

Turning to Captain Bryant, Jake extended his hand once more. "Hi," he told her, trying not to stare.

"Hello, Mr. Bennings," she said simply with a brief, limp handshake. She seemed much more interested in taking in her surroundings than meeting Jake.

With the introductions completed, Jake held out a necklace to McKay with a small, marble-sized sphere attached. "The Ghosts created this device both to duplicate the functions of a Stickman communication sphere and to serve as a translation device to enable you to talk to Commander Noah directly or to anyone wearing one." He looked apologetically at Captain Bryant. "I'm sorry, Captain, I don't have one for you too yet. We weren't expecting two of you."

Bryant gave him her full attention for the first time. From her expression, she didn't seem impressed, "I'll get over it, sir."

Jake stared for a moment, not knowing what else to say. It suddenly became very important for him to make a good impression. A thought came to him, and he fumbled with removing his translation device from around his neck.

"H-Here, take mine. You certainly need it more than I do right now, and I can easily get another one." Bryant skeptically examined the sphere and chain he held out to her and then accepted it without thanks.

"Commander Noah will be joining us in a moment. A human's first contact with a Ghost being has often proved to be an unsettling experience in the past. We felt that I should come out and prepare you first with the assurance that, despite their appearance, these beings, for the lack of a better way of saying it, are good people and good friends. For those of us who work with them, we know they value our friendship as much as we value theirs."

"Believe me, Jake," McKay replied, "if Jackson Ruark trusts these people, then we do too without question."

As much of a jolt that it was for McKay to see Noah flowing toward him from a newly formed opening to the hangar wall, it was even more traumatic for Captain Bryant. The captain's face turned as white as the Ghosts themselves, but she showed no other signs of fear or revulsion. Lee, too, hid his discomfort well as the towering white Ghost approached them. Even though he'd seen images of the Ghosts many times from viewing the Stickman holograms, he found them even more repugnant seeing them up close.

"Noah: I am Noah, Commander of this Seed ship rescue mission, Fleet Admiral Ruark," came Jake's voice from the translation necklace McKay had placed around his neck.

"I forgot to mention that the voices coming out of translator devices all sound like me. They also always begin by announcing the name of the Ghost who is speaking since it's impossible to tell which of them is speaking when more than one of them is present," Jake said apologetically.

"I am Fleet Admiral Lee McKay, Commander of the Earth's Northern Defense Zone, and this is Captain Megan Bryant, as of this moment, my Senior Communications Officer and appointed liaison between our commands. I am honored to meet you, Commander Noah."

"Noah: Your offer of providing us with Captain Bryant's help is greatly appreciated."

"Commander Noah, I speak for our people all in conveying our deepest regrets for the harm we've already caused the Ghost people. We ask that you forgive us for our ignorance. We will do everything in our power to protect your ships from this moment forward."

Noah's body rippled briefly with untranslated pink patterns and small bursts of heat. "Noah: We understand how and why you were misled. However, we want you to know that the tactics and strategies Fleet Admiral Ruark and his people taught us have already saved many Ghost lives this day and undoubtedly will continue to do so in any future engagements with our enemy. We are grateful to have found your people.

"My entire fleet of Seed ships are ready to descend upon your planet to locate and position themselves above your largest population centers. But before they do, we must let Fleet Admiral Ruark work undetected among our decoys to advance the illusion of Seed ship heavy resistance to the swarms of attacking enemy ships and reduce their numbers as much as possible."

"Shouldn't we take advantage of that time to begin the rescue of some of our population?" McKay asked.

"As difficult it is to refrain from doing so, you must understand that the moment our ships begin to excavate those populated areas to transfer them to safety, our enemy that you refer to as the Stickmen will undoubtedly detect our efforts. They will immediately withdraw from the decoys to race straight to your planet. The fewer enemy ships that arrive, the better the chances for our seed ships to escape with their precious cargoes. That is why we must let Fleet Admiral Ruark work as long as possible before we begin our efforts.

"Fleet Admiral McKay, there is one more thing that is essential for you all to understand. We Ghosts have little more than six thousand Seed ships left to rescue your population centers, all that remains of our entire fleet. Our scans have located over four hundred thousand cities, towns, and large population centers on your planet. Do you understand the implication?"

McKay's heart sank. "I do," he replied grimly.

"Noah: We wish we could do more but, with our deepest regret and frustration, we know that our efforts will certainly be cut short. For now, I must return to my command duties, Fleet Admiral. My people will do their best to preserve as many human lives as possible. I wish you success in the coming conflict."

"Good luck to you and your forces too, Commander Noah. Captain Bryant, you have your orders."

"Yes, sir, Fleet Admiral."

McKay returned to his ship, leaving Captain Bryant to fend for herself aboard the Ghost ship. With Jake there to advise her and keep her company, he had no concerns about her ability to perform her assigned task.

Since McKay's ship couldn't mask itself from the Stickman tactical systems, he navigated his Dragon far from Noah's Seed ship so its power signature wouldn't draw Swarm ships to Noah's masked position when they arrived. He used the knowledge transfer system to update Pete, Susan, and Svetlana on the details of his meeting with Noah. Together they sent out final orders to the surviving forces making up the near-Earth defense grid. There was nothing left to do but wait for the enemy to arrive.

With the Stickman forces already attacking the decoy and robot ships, the fleet admirals gave their full attention to their tactical holograms. There was a slaughter beginning to take place at the battlefront, but for once, Ruark's people, with their Dragons masked from the Stickmen, were the ones doing all of the slaughtering.

Chapter 48
Inexplicable Events

It pleased the fleet master to see the leading wave of Swarm groups beginning to engage the hated enemy forces in dozens of places, with new confrontations growing by the minute. However, after a short observation period, his tactical system revealed another baffling anomaly. In almost half the developing conflicts, the enemy ships offered no resistance at all to his swarm attacks. In those places, not a single Swarm ship became lost during their engagements, while swarm groups were utterly decimated in short order in other areas. Thousands of Hive Swarm ships disappeared each minute, if not tens of thousands! Ruark's undetected Dragons hiding near the decoys were wreaking incredible havoc far beyond what the fleet master knew the defending Seed ships were ordinarily capable of inflicting.

Adding to the puzzle, those enemy ships declining to fight back seemed practically impervious to the endless barrage of force beams with which the tormenting swarms mercilessly battered them. The procession of mysterious events was becoming maddening. All were outside the realm of his experience of multiple conflicts with this frustrating enemy. Each of those campaigns was practically indistinguishable from any former ones. He found nothing even remotely similar to those past campaigns for this sterilization mission, and his confusion and frustration intensified to an intolerable level.

With an urgent need to solve these mysteries, he chose to do something distasteful that he would normally not lower himself to do. He activated a mode of the knowledge transfer systems to recreate within his mind everything one of his swarm warriors currently saw and experienced.

Choosing one swarm warrior and adjusting himself to this enabled state of mind, the fleet master acquired an awareness of hundreds of other Swarm ships all around him as if he piloted the Swarm ship himself. Together, 'his' Swarm ship and the surrounding mass of ships began to close on one of the enormous, sphere-shaped enemy vessels.

Surprisingly, as the swarm drew closer to their target, the expected disappearances of swarm ships typically accompanying an attack failed to materialize. Either this enemy ship refused to fight, or its weapons were disabled!

The swarm warrior whose consciousness he infiltrated soon came within the enemy ship's firing range. The fleet master could feel the inherent hatred that the warrior directed toward the enemy ship and the rapture he felt as he unleashed a relentless barrage against the swarm's chosen victim. The Hive technology could not detect that the bulk of the force blasts passed harmlessly through the decoy's holographic image of a Seed ship. He found it maddening that even though the swarm barraged the enemy ship with a continuous torrent of force beams, the targeted ship simply refused to succumb.

As designed, the decoy's heavily armored ball that projected the hologram could take far more punishment from random strikes than any real Seed ship could endure, its durability allowing it to last far longer than an actual ship could. To the fleet master's perception, the decoys inexplicably took forever to succumb to the onslaughts, their indestructibility causing the final phase of unleashing the swarms toward Earth to be delayed.

Finding no helpful information from his present remote viewpoint to solve these mysteries, the fleet master shifted his perception to another warrior of a different swarm. This swarm targeted an enemy ship offering fierce resistance to the attack with unheard-of ferocity. Through his pseudo-consciousness, it appalled him to see that the surrounding ships of this swarm vanished so rapidly that the entire group became decimated before it ever came close enough to launch the first salvo. His perception ended abruptly as the Swarm ship of the warrior through which he monitored the event also ceased to exist.

Chapter 49
Deceived

"Commander Noah," Ruark called over his communication disk. "Can you hear me?"

"Noah: Of course, Fleet Admiral Ruark."

"My Super Dragons have destroyed hundreds of thousands of the Stickman Swarm ships, but our decoys have kept their attention and have advanced toward Earth to a point where you need to start sending your seed ships down to the planet. We're still a good distance away, but if we get much closer, your Seed ships might not be able to take their first harvests without interference."

"Noah: I agree, Fleet Admiral. We will begin immediately."

∿ ∿ ∿

After witnessing the destruction of an unheard-of number of Swarm ships, the fleet master shifted his remote perception again to a swarm warrior participating in an attack on an enemy ship by no less than three groups of swarms. This targeted enemy appeared to be one of those ships that made no attempt to defend itself. The firepower it already absorbed should have destroyed it ten times over. When the enemy finally did succumb, the expected nova of light and massive blossom of shrapnel and debris did not appear. Obviously, the targeted ship must have been entering a wormhole as it broke apart. Only a tiny, insignificant mass of scattered debris remained. However, the puzzle persisted as to why such a ship would subject itself to a swarm attack without a defensive retaliation.

Unexpectedly, the increasingly frustrated and confounded fleet master received an urgent alarm from his tactical system. He mentally broke free of his remotely established perceptions to turn his attention back to his tactical hologram.

As the system mentally defined the alarm's nature, the information chilled him to the core. Yet another impossible scenario presented itself in an endless, nightmarish progression of them! The tactical system

244

indicated that, even though his tactical hologram displayed no enemy ships in the area of the third planet, the power signatures of thousands of the human cities began to disappear from the planet's surface!

In a flash of rage, everything became clear. The enemy must have discovered how to mask their ships from the Hive tactical systems! Many of them were already in the process of capturing human population centers! That explained why these outlying enemy ships remained unmasked and why half of them failed to return fire on the attacking swarms. It was a strategy obviously designed to entice his swarm forces into hunting them down and diverting their attention from the humans' planet!

Infuriated by the clever deception, the fleet master immediately ordered all Swarm ships to break off their current attacks and head straight for the human world at maximum speed. The prevention of the enemy's rescue of humans was the most critical mission of all.

∾ ∾ ∾

"They finally figured it out, people! Stay on them and whittle them down!"

Ruark and his masked Super Dragons continued to give chase; their superior, Ghost-improved ship drives enabling them to outpace their enemy counterparts as they continued to send tens of thousands of Swarm ships 'elsewhere' in the process.

∾ ∾ ∾

It was a solemn moment as the McKays, Orsini, and Ivanovna watched the first Ghost Seed ships rising above the Earth with their precious cargo of population centers, then winking out of existence on their tactical screens. All of the ships were safely on their way to a second home and safe refuge for its relatively small cargo of Earth's creatures, human and animal alike.

Susan wept freely at the sight, moved by the fact that, no matter what happened, the transfer of even one of those captured cities meant the Stickman plan to exterminate the human race was already a failure. Earth's life forms would survive extinction even if it only made possible by moving them to another world.

∾ ∾ ∾

Within his Sterilizer dreadnaught, the fleet master watched in frustration as thousands more of his swarm ships vanished on their way to the human planet. Undoubtedly, masked enemy ships shadowed his swarms to maintain an assault on them. Nevertheless, his forces were vast, and with millions of ships at his disposal, the losses were insignificant to him, no more than just an aggravating nuisance at the moment.

From a long history of encounters with the enemy, the fleet master knew that once the enemy rescue ships encapsulated a population center, they would be fully vulnerable and virtually helpless against his hunting swarm packs. Those ships rising from the planet with their vile cargos were now the crucial, primary targets for his forces to seek out.

With a great sense of amusement and anticipation, he observed that the surviving Earth ships, a paltry number compared to his swarms, uselessly formed a weak protective shield around the planet. It was of no concern; with their inability to see his incoming ships on their tactical systems, every one of them would be swept aside within moments of the arrival of his vanguard. The fleet master looked forward to their eradication with pleasure as the leading wave of his swarms surrounded and bore down on the humans' planet like the closing of a giant fist.

Chapter 50
The Harvest Begins

With his space-based radar unable to detect masked seed ships, Ling Wu had few resources left to determine where Seed ships were until his headquarters began receiving reports already rising into the sky.

The holographic image Ling Wu command center relied upon to view the progress of the Seed ships winked out ten minutes earlier when the Stickman spheres distributed in EDF headquarters all over the planet detonated along with thousands of the defending EDF Dragon ships. The remotely-generated images from a Stickman tactical hologram feeding his human-engineered hologram generator disappeared along with the distant EDF spaceport that once held it. Since its loss, Ling Wu's technicians struggled to find and take control of any existing planet-mapping and surveillance satellites the multiple nations of Earth placed in orbit over the past decades.

Despite knowing what just happened to Earth's defenders and realizing the enormity of the disaster, the emotionally stricken men and women of Ling Wu's headquarters still kept to their posts. More than ever, they were determined to contribute whatever became necessary to repay the Stickmen for their monstrous betrayal. Ling Wu took great pride in them all.

"Ignacy, how much more time do you think you will need to communicate with one of our surveillance satellites?" Ling Wu questioned Ignacy Helinski, the young Polish technician working to make the connections. One of the many reasons Ling Wu's staff loved him was because he knew every one of them by name.

"I just need a couple of more seconds and . . . there! I have links established to two satellites, one Russian and one Indian," Ignacy replied. "Almost
there . . ."

Ignacy's fingers flew across his keyboard as he punched in commands. An overhead monitor lit up a moment later, showing a coastline passing below one of the satellites.

"This image is coming from a Russian spy satellite, Doctor. I should have a strong link to another satellite in a moment."

"Well done, Ignacy! We are no longer completely blind!"

The coastline showing on the monitor slowly drifted to the lower left of the screen. The rest of the image displayed the bleak, brown landscape of barren desert and mountains.

"What is that location?"

"The satellite just crossed over the northeastern coast of the Gulf of California. It's moving in a northeasterly direction. We should be able to see Phoenix soon."

Isolated roads, remote ranches, and scattered patches of green containing grids of cultivated fields came into view as the populated areas became denser. As they watched, a huge sphere passed close to the satellite's position in orbit. It quickly shrank in size as it descended on the planet.

"Sir, do you see . . ."

"Yes, Ignacy. Can you zoom in and follow it?"

"It shouldn't be too much of a problem. It has barely moved horizontally with respect to the satellite, indicating that it's coming down at a steep angle from the upper atmosphere. No doubt, it's a Seed ship, sir. That has to be the city of Phoenix below that it's descending upon."

Hearing Ignacy's analysis, control room personnel left their stations to gather around the screen to watch the view without Ling Wu's objection.

Ignacy adjusted the zoom and centered the camera on the ship just as it instantly halted its meteoric descent just above ground level in the midst of a populated area northwest of Phoenix. The moment it stopped, an encasing, dome-shaped shell formed around the ship that immediately began to expand to envelop the surrounding area.

"Can you tell us where that Seed ship stopped, Ignacy?"

The technician carefully moved a cursor over a green patch on the screen, longitudes, latitudes, and location names scrolling by on the screen until the cursor stopped. The name Sahuaro Ranch Park, Glendale, Arizona, came up.

The shell kept expanding, its surface gleaming in the sun and reflecting the color of the sky and clouds above. The object became so large that it soon filled the monitor and forced Ignacy to zoom out again to keep up with the dome's growth. Buildings, streets, entire city blocks, and the people within disappeared as the shell enveloped everything in its path for miles around.

Even though the control room staff watching the monitor knew the Seed ships were there to save people, it still horrified them to see such a large suburban area swallowed up. It was just as they'd seen an alien bubble-city disappear in the Stickman holograms. Several people wept openly.

"How much detail can this satellite achieve?" Ling Wu asked.

"This satellite is a spy satellite, sir. It can probably clearly display the numbers on a license plate."

"How much longer will Phoenix be in the range of the satellite?"

"About two more minutes, sir."

"Then, if you can, please find an edge of that shell and zoom in."

As Ignacy did so, Ling Wu and his people watched in awe. The growing dome reached nearly ten miles in diameter, the top of it rising only a mile above the city, the entire casing looking more like a broad but very squat parachute.

At the shell's edge, the satellite image revealed its steep walls encrusted with objects sticking out of it at ground level. Where it stopped, they could see people, vehicles, trees, and structures of every kind partially embedded in it.

Several struggling people partially trapped in the dome wall were frantically trying to pull themselves free. In one place, they could see someone's leg protruding from the dome wall with its foot on the sidewalk as if caught in midstride with the shell trapping the rest of the body inside of the dome.

"What's going to happen to those people?" a frightened young lady asked aloud, her voice tremulous with fear. The answer came seconds later when the dome slowly drew in everything not anchored to the ground. The gigantic disk began to raise itself off the ground only when everything and everyone embedded were fully pulled inside.

Several people gasped in astonishment. As the dome rose into the sky, it revealed its underground half, a mirror image of the half above ground. Where buildings, streets, and neighborhoods stood a moment ago, only the perfect bowl of a crater appeared that went as deep into the ground as the upper part of the dome had been high. The shell wall severed immovable buildings, trees, and other structures embedded within it with such surgical precision that it left their remaining edges with a polished appearance. The sphere carried away the missing portions captured inside.

The image flickered and winked out as the satellite moved out of range. Ling Wu's people were stunned to silence, having seen such a large chunk of land plucked so effortlessly from the surface of the planet.

Ling Wu felt heartsick. Even though the area taken was miles across, he immediately realized it represented just a tiny fraction of the area's population. The Ghost Seed ships would only save a minuscule amount of Earth's population should this battle be lost today.

"Dr. Ling, sir!" Ignacy called urgently. "I've connected to an Indian satellite coming up on the southern coast of China!"

The technician pointed to the monitor as the second satellite feed replaced the former images, this time the view coming from a Geo-survey orbiter. Far below, they could see Taiwan slipping from view at the bottom left edge of the screen. In moments, it crossed the coastline of mainland China.

"There's another Seed ship descending fast, sir," Ignacy said as he pointed at one side of the monitor.

"What is this one's destination?"

Ignacy's fingers played over the keyboard once more to zoom in. He took a reading from one of his auxiliary screens and froze, his face becoming pasty white.

"Sir, it stopped just above Mong Kok, right at the center of the city of Hong Kong a few miles from here!"

There were several gasps throughout the room. Though this satellite could not provide images to the same magnification as the Russian Satellite, those gathered in the room could still see a large part of the city and much of Hong Kong Island.

Stunned, Ling Wu sank into a chair and watched helplessly as the Seed ship's disk-shaped shell formed and rapidly expanded to roll over all of Kowloon and outward in all directions. Even though he knew the Seed ships came to save population centers, he never imagined Hong Kong would be among the first cities taken.

The control room personnel watched in shock and horror as the gigantic wall of the dome raced through Hong Kong Island toward their embedded headquarters inside Mount Cameron. While it was one thing for them to witness the people of some distant place scooped up by a Seed ship, it was quite another thing to know it was about to happen to them.

Even though Ling Wu's command center was buried deep within the mountain, the Seed ship's shimmering vertical wall easily penetrated it, shooting through the control room and passing right through and past everyone and everything in it as if it were no more than a shadow. The monitor's satellite image of the event abruptly winked out. Though they could no longer see it, the disk's expansion stopped just beyond the mountain that housed their installation. The very shell they observed growing a moment earlier now encased their headquarters within it.

As the dome covering Hong Kong solidified, the room's lights flickered and went out briefly until the auxiliary power generators kicked on to feed the emergency lighting system. Knowing what was coming, Ling Wu offered a prayer for the success of his fleet admirals and the survival of the human race. At the same time, he felt the heavy load of command lifting from him. The burden of saving the human race had just shifted from him into the hands of others.

Without warning, a feeling of vertigo washed over the EDF leader, and his body lost all sensation.

~ ~ ~

As the Seed ship lifting Hong Kong from the planet began to rise, high winds roared in from all directions to fill the void the seed ship left behind. Where the shell lifted from the sea, immense cascades of seawater thundered out over the void left behind to plunge for a mile to the crater's bottom. Ships, barges, and boats, mostly abandoned, were dragged toward the hole like debris to a storm drain. Anyone who remained aboard became unintended but unavoidable innocent victims of the Ghost's seed-gathering mission.

Chapter 51
Harvested

Sally Kwas was at work in her office near downtown Chicago as a Medical Center X-ray technician when the word raced through her office about a news bulletin declaring that the long-awaited invasion had finally arrived. Like everyone else on the planet, she understood that there were thousands of highly trained, defending forces who would be fighting alongside Earth's Stickman allies to defend the planet. Still, the knowledge offered no comfort to her at the moment. She didn't care how many warriors were out there protecting the world. Right now, Sally felt only a mother's overpowering need to find her young daughter and protect her until the danger passed.

Sally knew that if she was afraid, her daughter Sarah would be terrified, and she felt an urgent need to get to her daughter's school as fast she could. Having no means to find refuge anywhere else, she planned to race home with her daughter home to take shelter in their basement. She knew hiding there would not be enough to save them if the invaders came, but at least it would allow her and her daughter to take some small comfort from being in the familiar surroundings of their home if worse came to worse.

Sally wasted no time leaving without saying anything to her boss or fellow office workers. From the number of people rushing to get down the stairway, most likely, there would soon be no one left to tell. Caught in the exit flow of the stampeding crowd, she moved along with it until she was practically ejected from the building by the pressure of the people behind her. Once out on the crowded sidewalk, it became evident that just about everyone in the city had the same desire to leave as she did. People poured out of the surrounding buildings onto streets and sidewalks dampened by the day's intermittent rains.

A bus came to a stop a few dozen feet down the sidewalk, and even though it wasn't the bus she would usually have taken, she recognized its posted destination as just a mile or two from her daughter's elementary school. The bus was already packed, but knowing the alien invasion had begun, the driver allowed as many people to board as it could hold. Sally was fortunate enough to be among the last of those who managed to squeeze in.

The traffic intensified as the minutes passed, but at least it still flowed, however slowly. To get as far as South Troy Street, though, the usual ten-minute bus ride took over forty minutes. At that point, the bus could no longer move due to an intersection ahead blocked by a multi-car collision.

Sally and most of the other passengers vacated the bus leaving behind only three people, the bus driver himself, an elderly woman with a walker, and a man with dark glasses and a guide dog. Both passengers, undeniably frightened, had no other choice but to stay with the bus. With her daughter her only concern, Sally's heart went out to the two passengers, but she couldn't take the time to help them. It gratified her to see, though, that the bus driver gallantly refused to abandon the two helpless people and went back to sit with them and reassure them of his guardianship.

With a five-mile hike to Sarah's school from where Sally exited the bus, she knew that it would take her at least two hours to walk there, even on the best of days. She felt gratified that her occupation allowed her to wear tennis shoes; those and the comfortable scrubs she had on would make the trek more bearable.

At least the sidewalks aren't impassable yet, she thought to herself as she headed off in the direction of Sarah's school. As she hurried along, people hung halfway out from windows and doorways everywhere to gawk at the appalling traffic congestion and its accompanying din, the likes of which they'd never seen before.

The deafening blare of car horns grated on Sally's already shattered nerves, and to make matters worse, the rain started to drizzle down again to add to her misery. At every intersection she came to, drivers created gridlock in complete disregard of the traffic signals and the few policemen trying to direct the vehicles. Major and minor accidents and road rage confrontations seemed to be going on everywhere

Sally heard a scream coming from across the street and saw a Mercedes SUV had driven up on the sidewalk in an attempt to bypass the stalled traffic. Desperate to get through the traffic, the driver deliberately ran over the woman who screamed, crushing her beneath his car. Plowing forward, he continued to kill and injure others as his vehicle battered them out of the way.

Shots rang out, accompanied by more screams of frightened people as a policeman trying to untangle the traffic jam at a nearby intersection saw what was happening. He dashed to a point ahead of the car to put a stop to the driver's onslaught with three bullets through the windshield. The Mercedes rolled to a stop against a lamppost, its driver slumped over, dead at the wheel.

More frightened than ever now, Sally began to run and didn't stop until the burning sensation in her lungs forced her to slow down. She'd gone just over a mile on foot when a looter rushed out of a store carrying a widescreen, 3D television.

"Outta my way, bitch!" he shouted as he knocked her aside and sent her sprawling to the sidewalk. With scraped knees bleeding, she painfully picked herself up from the sidewalk, barely comprehending what just happened to her. Feeling a little dizzy, she felt a wetness on the side of her head and discovered a bleeding gash where the corner of the television banged into her head. She pulled a handkerchief from her purse, pressed it against the cut, and kept moving, staggering along on her way but determined to find Sarah's school.

That incident opened her eyes to the magnitude of looting taking place all around her. More frightened than ever now, she moved more cautiously along, sometimes detouring around entire blocks where she knew concentrations of mercantile businesses might be suffering even more intensive plundering.

As arduous as her trek became, she managed to make better headway on foot than any of those fighting the traffic jams though her progress remained sluggish. The rain stopped again, but her wet shoes and clothing chafed at her. Knowing an alien ship might arrive at any time to carry the city away, she ignored the discomfort, the fear driving her on that she might never see her daughter again.

Several agonizing hours later, she arrived at Sarah's school. The hour that the school day ended had come and gone. Anxious to find their children, a few other parents rushed across the schoolyard to the main entrance. At the school bus parking lane, teachers gathered students waiting for buses that would never arrive to try to herd them back into the building.

Once Sally entered the school building, she found that a small group of teachers and school administrators remained who, to their credit, refused to abandon the children as many of their associates already had done. They were trying to take the children's names who were leaving with their parents.

"Parents, please give us one moment!" the lady school principal begged. "We just want you to tell us the name of the child you are taking with you! We have to keep track for the sake of the children!"

"There's no time for that bullshit!" a woman shouted back as she practically dragged her child behind her. "The invaders are coming!"

Even though the few faithful staff standing with the principal struggled to gather a few names, they failed to get all of them.

None of the school administrators tried to stop Sally from searching for Sarah. She made her way past them all to hurry down the school corridors, knowing exactly where to find Sarah's classroom. To her dismay, she found Sarah's classroom empty. In a panic, she frantically searched classroom by classroom, calling out Sarah's name until someone told her that only a few teachers remained to round up students and take them to the cafeteria. Sally knew exactly where that was and raced frantically through the halls to search there for her daughter. When she arrived, she found one elderly school nurse watching over three dozen children of various ages.

To her enormous relief, Sarah sat among them at a lunchroom table, frightened and sobbing her heart out in fear, Sarah's teacher being one of the ones who abandoned her class to take care of herself.

Sarah's tearful face lit with pure joy when she saw her mother come through the cafeteria door. She shouted, "Mummy!" and ran to her mother's outstretched arms. With tears of relief running down her cheeks, Sally gave her daughter a huge hug that both of them badly needed.

"Sarah, you can come with me now. We're going home," she told her daughter as calmly as she could manage to try to avoid frightening her even more than she already was. She mouthed a grateful Thank you" to the school nurse, who sorrowfully nodded back as she took Sarah's hand and guided her out the door. Sally's heart went out to the children still left behind, but she knew they were in the best place they could be for their parents to locate.

Making their way through the maze of hallways, Sally and Sarah reached the front entrance to the school, where Sally shouted Sarah's name to the school principal, then dodged out of the way of parents still trickling in. Still wary of looters and anyone else who might try to take advantage of the chaos, she set out for home with Sarah in tow, walking so fast Sarah could barely keep up.

"Mummy, aren't we going to wait for a bus?" Sarah asked as her mother practically dragged her along.

"No, baby, home isn't that far away. We'll just walk this time."

Sally knew there was no point in looking for public transportation to take them home. Judging by the looks of things, there wouldn't be anything moving on the streets for a long time to come, maybe never.

Luckily, Sally and Sarah had to walk only six blocks to get to their home, a small distance compared to how far Sally had already walked today.

She never saw the Seed ship coming down out of the sky. It was too far away, with its view blocked by surrounding buildings and trees even if she'd known where to look for it. With their still only house only a few streets away, she stopped dead in her tracks when the overcast day grew even darker. Looking up, she saw a high, silvery wall rushing toward them like a great tidal wave.

She screamed, believing she and Sarah were about to be smashed to a pulp by its impact, and she reflexively crouched down to clutch her daughter tightly to her. She pulled Sarah's face protectively against her breast so her daughter couldn't see the oncoming wall and then squeezed her eyes shut, bracing her entire body and cringing in anticipation of the expected collision.

When seconds went by, and nothing happened, she opened her eyes again and turned her head back in the direction of the oncoming wall. She almost sobbed with relief when she realized the wall's advance stopped dead at the very place where she and her daughter crouched together. The Seed-ship-generated shell was so large that it appeared to rise vertically into the overcast sky above.

Unable to believe her good fortune, she tried to rise and step away from the silvery wall but found she couldn't. To her horror, she realized that where the wall stopped, it encased the bend of her elbow, trapping it solidly within. Even worse, she saw her daughter's shoulder embedded in the wall as well!

When Sally tried to tug herself free, the wall held her fast, and she wailed in fear as she too attempted to free herself.

"Mummy, I'm stuck!" Sarah cried.

Sally could still feel her entire arm and her hand, but she had no sensation of anything having a grip on her at all until something started to pull at her and realized both she and Sarah were being sucked further into it!

Frantically, she glanced about, looking for someone to help her, and spied a burly-looking man standing in the doorway of a drugstore just fifty feet away staring wide-eyed at them both. Terrified, she stretched her free arm out beseechingly in his direction and pleaded to him.

"Help us, sir! Please! Come and help us pull free!"

Staring in disbelief, the man remained frozen in place, unwilling to bring himself to move. His gaze shifted from Sally to stare up at the wall where it penetrated the low-lying clouds above and back to Sally again.

Giving up on the man, Sally screamed, "Someone! Anyone! Please help us!" With Sarah sobbing in fright at her side, she struggled desperately to free them both from the iron grip of the silvery wall. Despite her efforts, the wall continued to pull them deeper inside with ever-increasing strength. In a matter of seconds, they passed entirely through to the other side, their bodies no longer trapped by the wall's surface. Trembling badly but relieved to be free of the wall, Sally took Sarah into her arms and held the weeping child tightly against her chest.

"Mummy, I'm scared!" Sarah sobbed. "I can't see you."

The darkness inside the shell was as black as anything Sally ever experienced.

Terrified herself, she choked out a reply, "I know, baby, we'll be okay, I promise!"

Blind to her surroundings, she could still hear sounds coming from all around, the voices movements of others imprisoned inside the shell along with her and Sarah. To her relief, the inky blackness abruptly gave way to the glow of a car's headlights turning on a hundred feet up the street. Other people quickly followed suit, turning on car headlights wherever they could to illuminate the entire nearby area.

"You see, baby, the lights are starting to come on. Everything will be fine."

By the glow and reflections of the light, Sally found herself still crouched on the sidewalk with familiar buildings all around her, everything perfectly intact as far as she could see. The wall reared straight up right next to her as silvery on the inside as on the outside. Where it divided the street, she saw an empty parked car half embedded still being pulled through to the inside of the shell. It bumped into the car behind it, but the obstacle didn't prevent the wall from continuing to pull it through. The back end of the embedded car pushed aside the vehicle behind it until the last of its front end came through.

Sally reached out and pushed against the wall to see if they could get back through it to the other side, but it felt as solid as the face of a granite cliff. Just as nearly everyone else on the planet saw from the Stickman holograms, she knew what happened to the cities captured by the horrible alien monsters. She pulled her sobbing daughter close to her again and let herself slump down against their prison wall to await the terrible death she expected to come soon.

There came a sensation of vertigo lasting several seconds before it disappeared again. Sally took it as a sign of the end coming soon and became sick with fright, wondering how much longer it would take the alien ship to launch her and Sarah into the vacuum of space toward the sun. Her body trembled uncontrollably as she for their inevitable deaths.

Nothing happened for nearly ten minutes, the delay adding to her emotional torture when, to her astonishment and without warning, the wall vanished as if it never existed. Instead of being tossed into the vacuum of space, the city became flooded with bright daylight again. This time, Sally did see the Seed ship that brought them to this place rise beyond the buildings in the distance into a clear blue sky. Still in a state of shock and confusion, she felt far too disoriented to try to understand what just happened.

Blue sky? she thought numbly to herself. She believed herself to be dreaming or hallucinating. The day had been rainy and chilly when the dome of the Seed ship captured her and her daughter. Now she felt a warm, scented breeze swirling around them both. Dazed and emotionally overcome by the realization that she and her daughter miraculously remained alive, she could barely move.

"Mummy, look!' Sarah's voice seemed distant as she tugged on Sally's arm, her fright already diminished by the wonder of the strange sights around her. The sound of her daughter's voice roused Sally from her traumatized state and, still in a state of bewilderment, she glanced about while trying to get a grasp on what exactly happened to them.

In front of Sally was the same street and neighborhood she'd been standing in when the shell imprisoned them. However, where the enclosing shell had passed through buildings, only the parts enclosed remained, their walls severed with razor sharpness, their edges perfectly polished. Rooms missing their outer walls were exposed to the sunshine and open air. On the second floor of one cutaway home, an older woman stood at a doorway staring in disbelief at what remained of her bedroom, half of it gone as if it never existed.

"Over there, Mummy!" Sarah said, tugging urgently at her arm once more to get her attention. Sally's eyes went wide when she twisted around to discover that behind her and beyond where the shell disappeared, the part of the city that used to be there somehow became a sprawling pasture of velvety, tall blades of incredibly green grass. Red, blue, white, and purple blossoms of a variety she'd never seen before dotted the field as far as it extended. Less than half a mile away, a forest of craggy giant trees, most of them over a hundred feet tall, marked the edge of the meadowland. Though the trees were distant, the air was so clear she felt certain sure she could see blossoms on some of them and great, pear-shaped pink fruit growing on others.

However, Sarah wasn't pointing to the meadow and forest; she pointed at the sky. Even through the brightness of a mid-day sun, two large moons dominated the heavens, the faces of both orbs split into identical phases. The closer moon seemed slightly larger than Earth's moon, and like Earth's moon, craters pockmarked its surface. The other moon appeared twice as large as the first, and Sally could see what seemed to be tiny wisps of clouds in an atmosphere above it. In the distance, far beyond the forest, another alien ship rose gracefully into the sky.

Chapter 52
Surprise Counter Attack

A voice sounding like Jake Bennings came from the translation device Lee McKay wore around his neck.

"Noah: Fleet Admiral McKay, all of my Seed ships are gone for the moment. They are transporting nearly nine thousand of your population centers to safety, having collected them without the loss of a single ship. In just over thirty of your minutes, all of them will return to gather more. The next gathering will not go as easily as this one did since the Stickmen ships will surely be upon us by then."

"They certainly will be. My tactical tells me we have close to a million Stickman ships closing on us with a leading wave of over ten thousand individual swarms. They're coming at us in from every direction," Lee reported. "These forerunners are the Swarm ships that headed out from the moon toward outer battle zone. Someone must have ordered them to turn around to take us out."

"More than sixteen and a half million more ships are also coming in not too far behind them from their bases all over the solar system," Svetlana added unnecessarily.

"Let's not forget those big boys hanging back way out there and what they are bringing to the party too," Sue told everyone after checking the progress of the Stickman dreadnoughts. "It's a small blessing that their escort Swarm ships are holding back to protect their mother ships. The first swarm waves are approaching near-Earth space."

"Commander Noah, we will do everything in our power to protect your ships when they return," Lee promised the Ghost commander.

"Noah: We do not doubt that, Fleet Admiral McKay. Regardless of the danger, we will not abandon our mission."

∾ ∾ ∾

"It's almost time, everyone," Lee announced. "Northern Zone Admirals, the swarms are close enough for you to begin assigning targets to the Dragons of your first line of defense. The enemy thinks we can't

260

see them coming. Emphasize to your Dragons that they must show absolutely no sign of awareness of the enemy's approach until we give the command to attack! It is imperative that they hold back and pretend they're blind to them until then!" Lee mentally 'heard' Pete Orsini issue identical commands to his Southern defense zone forces.

"North and south defense zone Dragons, Fleet Admiral Orsini will be the one to order the attack for both zones, so you all know when to begin your assault together. Get ready!"

"Eastern zone Defenders, intercept any Swarm ship that makes it through the defense grid," Sue ordered her people. "Things are going to get heavy real soon!"

"Western Zone commanders concentrate your defenses over the heaviest populated areas. That is where the Swarm ships will try to break through in search of Seed ships!" Svetlana commanded.

Short moments later, the leading wave of Swarm ships came almost within weapons range of Lee McKay's and Pete Orsini's Dragons, all of the EDF ships poised just outside the Earth's atmosphere.

Orsini concentrated hard on his tactical hologram presently set to view Earth and the volume of near-Earth space surrounding it. The timing meant everything if their surprise counterattack was going to work. With the incoming ships approaching in anything but a uniform manner, the perfect time to give his signal would be difficult to determine. He knew he needed to give the order before the swarms began firing upon any single defending Dragon.

His brow broke out in a sweat from the strain of this critical task placed solely upon his shoulders. Just as the closest swarms came within their weapons range of the defending Dragon ships, Orsini shouted, "Everyone attack! Tear those bastards to pieces!"

The unfortunate Stickman swarms in the lead became the first victims to feel the brunt of the surviving Dragon warriors' pent-up fury. The swift, unexpected, and simultaneous leap forward of thousands of defending Dragons headfirst into the enemy ranks proved incredibly lethal. One moment the defending ships appeared to be sitting ducks, motionless and presumably unaware of approaching swarms, and the next moment every Dragon went instantaneously to maximum velocity to plunge with berserker fury into the midst of swarm groups of a hundred or more Stickman ships. Every swarm found itself with at least a dozen vengeful Dragons lethally laying waste to their numbers.

Swarm warriors, used to overwhelming their victims and targeting them from a distance, were at a loss at how to defend themselves against enemy ships zigzagging chaotically in every direction right in the middle of their undisciplined formations. The Dragon ships bounced, ricocheted, and constantly juked in unpredictable directions, never staying in one place for the two seconds the Swarm ships' automatic targeting systems needed to lock onto them.

Mentally directing their weapons, the vengeful Dragons annihilated Swarm ship after Swarm ship in blinding flashes of light, the debris cluttering the volume of space around the Earth and adding to the rubble of Earth's dead already destroyed by the hive master's destruct command.

In their frantic efforts to defend themselves, many of the Swarm ships blasted each other out of existence as they struggled in vain to sweep the hated humans from their midst. Only by pure luck or by the misjudgment of a Dragon ship fighter pilot who lingered too long in one place were the Swarm ships able to claim any victims at all.   The surprise attack by Earth's defenders proved so swift, chaotic, and deadly that the leading edge of the fleet master's swarms rapidly disintegrated.   However, the massive destruction did not deter the few Swarm ships that survived the onslaught. The Hive civilization biologically engineered the Stickman warrior caste to replace the instinct for survival with a greater need to seek out and destroy all alien life. The few ships escaping the slaughter of their fellow warriors raced onward into Earth's atmosphere to seek out their priority targets, the Seed ships they felt an irresistible need to destroy.

Those Swarm ships surviving the slaughter above the atmosphere ran straight into the wall of Sue and Svetlana's Eastern and Western zone defenders diligently guarding Earth's skies. Their Dragons rendered every remaining Stickmen Swarm ship into raining pieces of wreckage.

Chapter 53
Bring Our People Home!

"We just shredded over a million Swarm ships!" an elated Sue McKay exclaimed jubilantly to her counterparts.

"We must remember surprise was on our side this time," Svetlana reminded her.

"Yeah, well watch what happens when Jackson springs another surprise on them right about now," Pete told them.

∿ ∿ ∿

Jackson Ruark had his hands full, blasting Stickman swarm ships apart, one after another. He checked his tactical hologram and realized that over one million Swarm ships invading Earth's skies less than fifteen minutes ago were gone as if they never existed, the ambush pulled off by his fellow fleet admirals a stunning success.

He let out a whoop of joy, and with a vengeance, plunged right through the midst of yet another oncoming swarm, zigzagging among them unnecessarily since his ship was masked to the enemy sensors. Single-handedly, he tore the entire group to shreds.

The rest of his five thousand Super Dragons likewise continued to wreak havoc on Earth-bound Swarm ships all over the solar system. Invisibly mini-jumping among the greatest concentrations of incoming swarms, the ability of his small force to fire upon the Stickman ships became nearly equivalent to the same murder the Stickmen committed on the EDF forces.

With their intended element of surprise gone, the Stickmen learned the hard way that their Swarm ships weren't masked anymore. There was no longer a need for Ruark to hold back the reserve of the captured Dragons back in his base solar system whose pilots eagerly waited to return.

"Ghost Force Dragons, it's time to bring our people home! I want each of you to pace the biggest swarm groups in your vicinity and turn on your beacon signals for them! Our people are going to come out charging right for them."

Chapter 54
Vengeance of the KIAs

Within Ruark's base solar system, Duval's Super Dragon detected almost five thousand beacons flashing somewhere out there in the universe; the long-awaited signals from Ruark's Dragons to bring them all home came at last.

"This is Colonel Duval speaking, people. It's time for us to go! You will find yourselves coming out of your wormholes right on top of large groups of enemy swarms. You know what to do then. Make those Stickman bastards pay for what they did to us! Good hunting, and God be with you! Proceed to your jump points immediately and attack at will upon wormhole exit!"

Nearly five thousand Ghost scout ships, all much smaller than Seed ships but still equipped with the wormhole generators, waited with open wormhole gates for Ruark's captured Dragons. Duval's ship and the few Super Dragons he left behind to direct the returning forces were all capable of making the jump unaided, but the Dragons captured today could not. They would return home through wormhole gates the same way the Ghost sent them to Ruark's solar system in the first place.

By now, more than enough time had passed for the nanites to have repaired even the most recently captured ships to rid them of their self-destructs and to correct their inability to detect masked ships. No one would have to wait behind.

All the pilots waiting to go home organized themselves into nearly five thousand lines of two hundred fifty ships each, one line for each of Ruark's Super Dragons waiting to receive them, and all of them ready and eager to be sent back. Earth's surviving defenders were about to receive some very welcome reinforcements.

At Duval's command, each line of ships headed straight for the Ghost Scout ships, knowing that an invisible wormhole portal was wide open between them and the Scout. Like railroad trains disappearing into tunnels, one after another, the lines of Dragon ships advanced straight into a wormhole opening and vanished as if they'd never existed.

∿ ∿ ∿

As planned, Ruark and his vanguard of masked ships were already scattered over the solar system. Their beacons turned on as they shadowed the greatest clusters of Swarm ships, all of the swarms doggedly heading straight for Earth. Following the beacons of those ships, tens of thousands of Dragon fighters burst through their wormholes everywhere to charge into the thick of nearby clusters of Stickman ships without hesitation. As they did, Ruark and his people repeatedly gave the orders, "Weapons free! Attack at will!" until the last of the reinforcement Dragons came through.

The order was hardly necessary. With profanity-laced battle cries and an unquenchable thirst for revenge, the hordes of Dragon pilots blasted themselves into the thick of the swarms like a rain of shotgun pellets fired into flocks of birds. Between Ruarks masked Dragons and the returnees, another three million more Swarm ships were either shattered by force blasts or sent 'elsewhere' in a matter of moments.

Chapter 55
The Retreat of the Swarms

Monitoring his tactical hologram, the horrified fleet master could not believe what he saw. Nothing in his breeding for his level of command prepared him to deal with so many impossible battle scenarios as the ones that kept evolving to pummel his forces, this new disaster becoming the worst of all! Hundreds of thousands of Earth's warriors, materializing all over the solar system out of nowhere, were eviscerating his swarms. Not knowing how many more would appear drove him to near panic.

His tactical system identified the deadly marauders as the very ships the Hive gave the humans. These ships were incapable of long-distance wormhole jumps and presumed destroyed, yet over a million of them appeared out of nowhere to wreak unimaginable havoc among his forces. Astoundingly, they could only have come from somewhere too far for even his sterilizer ship's formidable tactical systems to detect!

The fleet master reacted instinctively and instantly before his losses became too severe. He ordered all Swarm ships to retreat, even those almost within reach of the humans' planet. By doing so, the slaughter ended almost as quickly as it began. He sent his swarms a set of coordinates and ordered them to withdraw and regroup en masse at that single rallying point. To protect nearly thirty-five thousand tactically valuable Eradicator ships among them, the fleet master ordered Eradicators to retreat to the center of the super-swarm core. Once the super-swarm finished gathering, he planned to fall back on the only tactic the Hive race knew how to perform efficiently; to attack the enemy planet en masse with overwhelming numbers to destroy its defenders.

Ruark observed that the swarm groups everywhere were retreating within moments after his captured Dragons returned to the solar system to commence their vengeful attacks. Their change in direction away from Earth indicated a full-scale Stickman withdrawal in all sectors. He also saw that his bloodthirsty force of unmasked Dragons continued to chase after them.

266

"Ghost Force, abort your pursuits *now*! That's an order! Abort! Do as I say immediately!"

"Jackson, what's wrong? Your people were eviscerating them. Why are you backing them off?" Lee McKay demanded, baffled by his friend's order.

"Those Dragons aren't masked, and they can't fly any faster than those Swarm ships can. If they give chase, the Swarm ships' automatic targeting systems will become effective again, and we'd be sacrificing people needlessly without any significant gain. Those Dragons would be the most useful defending the Seed ships back on Earth instead. With every swarm in retreat, we have a great opportunity to get back to Earth way ahead of them to fortify the planet's defense before they rush in on us again.

"Fleet Admirals," Svetlana called. "My tactical system is indicating that all of the retreating swarms are heading for a single point of convergence. I speculate they are planning to regroup into one massive super-swarm!"

Lee McKay swore softly when his tactical confirmed her findings. "Dammit, that's going to be one big bullet coming our way!"

"On the bright side, they'll all be coming from one direction. We won't have to spread out what's left of our forces," Susan pointed out.

"I'm not sure that's an advantage," Lee responded. "It's easier to stop one buffalo charging than an entire stampeding herd."

"At least the retreat will buy me the time I need to have my unmasked Dragons jump back to Earth," Ruark concluded. "Those Seed ships are going to need their protection soon."

"Move it then! We need all the time we can get to reorganize before they come at us again!" Sue advised him.

"Agreed! Commander Noah, are you receiving me?" Ruark called to Ghost leader through his translator disk.

"Noah: I am, Fleet Admiral Ruark."

"We need as many near-Earth Seed ships available close to Earth to activate their beacons. I'm sending them all of my unmasked ships."

"Noah: That is welcome news, Fleet Admiral Ruark. My Seed fleet will need your added protection very soon. I have several hundred ships already returned from their first rescue that can fulfill your request, but please hurry. Every second wasted is valuable time my Seed ships could be using to rescue your population centers."

"Ghost Force, we're sending you home. Rely on the nearest Super Dragon to send you back closer to Earth. Super Dragons open the gates! The Ghost Seed ships are activating homing beacons close to Earth! Push everyone through."

All of the fleet admirals watched anxiously as Ruark's reinforcements darted through the wormholes and popped back into space again far above the Earth while the super-swarm continued to regroup just inside the orbit of Mars.

Lee McKay called out to the welcome reinforcements pouring through their wormhole gates. "To all forces, this is Fleet Admiral Lee McKay. Our new, true allies told us earlier that the Stickmen would be sending swarms in such numbers that, even if we were at full strength, we could not possibly hope to protect our planet. We've already proved them wrong once. Thanks to the determination and courage you've all shown, we've already whittled the enemy numbers down significantly.

"However, as you can see from your tactical holograms, the Stickmen are gathering to strike us hard. It is inevitable they will attempt to smash through our wall of defense in one mighty blow. "I've already ordered our Dragons fighters who survived the self-destruct disaster to reposition themselves over their hometowns. I am directing all of you to do the same. Your ship's knowledge transfer devices will let you know who your area sub-fleet commander is when you arrive. Obey that commander! Trust the instructions given to you. They'll be alerting you swarms coming after any Seed ships in your areas. Those Seed ships might be the very ones bearing your families away to safety! Do everything in your power to protect them!

"Once a Seed ship makes its jump escape, go back and protect another, then another until the last of them are safely gone! When that moment arrives, there will still be defenseless people on the ground. The Ghost ships can't collect everyone, so you must keep fighting to protect those folks until we blow every last Stickman ship out of the sky! We *can* do this! Now go! Choose your battle stations and get there quickly! One mother of a Stickman swarm will be coming at us soon!"

Chapter 56
The Advance of the Sterilizers

Forty-five minutes later, Sue McKay gave an alert. "The enemy fighters are done gathering. They're beginning to advance again now, all bunched so tightly together that their power signatures look like one solid blob of light on my tactical hologram! Those twelve giant ships are still hanging back, though, thank goodness! It looks like they don't want to take any chances."

"Commander Noah!" Lee McKay called through the new communications device Jake gave him.

"Noah: Yes, Fleet Admiral McKay?"

"Do you Ghost people know of any effective defense against those giant raiders out there?"

"Noah: My people have never been this close to one of them before. There has never been a need or desire to do so since they are far larger than our wormhole gates can deal with. In the past, we Ghosts observed them only from a distance. The primary purpose of those ships is to destroy entire planets. Together they will attempt to cremate every living thing on Earth down to its last microbe when they arrive."

Sue McKay, Peter Orsini, and Svetlana Ivanovna were still without Ghost translator devices, so Lee gave them Noah's response.

"If the Ghosts have no defense against them, then we have to come up with a way of stopping them by ourselves!" Svetlana told them all determinedly.

"We will when the time comes," Lee responded with more conviction than he felt. He hoped, beyond hope, they would find the elusive miracle they needed to make that come true. "Right now, though, we can thank God those monster ships are keeping themselves safe far behind the battle lines. I think they might actually be wary of us!"

"That is most likely very wishful thinking," Orsini replied pessimistically.

"Good lord, that swarm is huge! My tactical estimates it will arrive here in fourteen minutes and twenty-two seconds. Get ready!" Sue McKay advised.

"My people and I aren't going to sit around waiting for them. We're going in to attack their flanks as they're coming in." Ruark declared, already sending the attack order to his people.

"Jackson, we can't afford to lose you! Stay behind the lines with us! Command your people from here!" Sue told Ruark.

"I have a masked, Super Dragon the Stickmen can't detect," Ruark argued, "and we need every one of these kinds of ships, including mine, to continue to shrink that swarm down before they get here. Since they can't see us, every kill we make is a freebie; it will be like shooting fish in a barrel. My ship alone might make the difference whether or not another Seed ship survives."

"You S.O.B," Orsini admonished. "Good reason or not, we know damned well you're happy about going back out there!"

"I suspect you'll get your chance too before the day is out," Ruark replied, unabashed.

"Our prayers are with you, Fleet Admiral Ruark," Svetlana told him, "Please be careful."

"Thank you, Fleet Admiral Ivanovna," Ruark replied, addressing her formally as she preferred. "We'll do our best."

He directed his thought communications system to link to his masked forces and then ordered those Dragons to wormhole back out to the incoming swarm to hunt at will. He then mini-jumped his Dragon back into battle to join them and wreak as much havoc as possible before the swarm arrived at Earth.

Chapter 57
Incoming

"That swarm mass is going to come in above China and Japan," Sue McKay observed. They're going to plow through our people like they're a cloud of smoke if we don't move our ships out of their way."

"Many more Seed ships are returning to Earth," Svetlana also added, watching her hologram. "Their timing is unfortunate. They will all be in peril! Captain Bryant," she called, unable to communicate with Noah directly, "is Commander Noah ordering his ships to avoid the path of the Swarm ships? The leading edge of the super-swarm is almost here."

"Commander Noah is setting up all of his beacon signals for the arriving ships on the side of the planet opposite the enemy approach. With his Seed ships masked, it won't be easy for the swarms to find them," Bryant responded.

"We agree," Lee answered. "Those bastards will have to visually search for Ghosts since they can't see the Seed ships on their tacticals."

"Remind Commander Noah that the enemy does not have to work that hard to find them," Svetlana pointed out. "They only have to monitor the disappearance of city power signatures to know where his ships are scooping them up."

"Look at the size of that horde!" Lee McKay said grimly. His tactical system projected that the entire mass would come down entirely inside his Northern Defense Zone." Realizing the danger to his forces, he immediately switched to general broadcast mode. "To all Northern Zone Dragons who are in the path of the swarm, you are ordered to fall back out of their way immediately and attack their flanks at will when they get here."

"Eastern Zone ground defense ships, get out from under the swarm and provide support to our air defense until it passes you. The enemy will be searching for Seed ships, and there are none on that side of the planet now.

"When the bulk of the swarm hits, there will be no stopping them," Sue McKay concluded apprehensively. "Once they're inside our atmosphere, we're not going to be able to offer any kind of organized defense against a monster that size. We're going to need every ship we have to get into the fight, including us."

"That works out just fine for me," Orsini replied with grim satisfaction. "We can all pull a 'Ruark' and join the brawl."

"I'm afraid I have to agree, but not all of us can join."

"Lee McKay, don't think for one second that I'm going to standby in the bleachers and watch!" Susan warned her husband.

"I know better than to try to make you," Lee told her. "Besides, as General Milne told us when this all began, you're probably the best fighter pilot among us."

The choice was an obvious one. Lee called out apologetically to Svetlana. "Fleet Admiral Ivanovna, you've spent most of your career in the cosmonaut corps. The rest of us started out as fighter pilots. Would you . . ."

"Fleet Admiral McKay," Svetlana interrupted indignantly, "while I have no air-to-air combat experience as the three of you possess, the knowledge transfer systems have adequately taught me how to become an efficient aerial combat fighter! However," she said unhappily, "we must have someone left to provide leadership should harm befall all of you. I agree to remain out of the fighting, but I will not like it!"

"Please don't be insulted," Lee told her. Of the five of us, including Ruark, you are the most logical and level-headed one among us."

"I *know* that!" she replied indignantly. "That is *exactly* why I choose to agree with this. I *am* the logical choice. Nevertheless, I still despise this role you are dropping into my lap!"

~ ~ ~

With five minutes left before the swarm would enter the Earth's atmosphere, Jackson and his people were already eviscerating its outer envelope. The swarm fighters were no match for the masked ships that their targeting systems couldn't even locate. If the number of Ruark's ships wasn't so ridiculously tiny compared to the massed millions of Swarm ships they attacked, their achievements, so far, could still easily be categorized as slaughter. He took tremendous satisfaction knowing each one of his masked ships continued to send Swarm ships 'elsewhere' by the dozens, and best of all, his fleet of Dragons suffered no casualties whatsoever.

Regardless of their success, the unnecessary risks he witnessed so many of them freely took alarmed him. "Wise up, people!" Ruark ordered. "Keep hammering the edges of the pack! Do not penetrate it! These assholes can barely hit the broad side of a barn unless you let them surround you!"

Ignoring his advice, Ruark jumped deep into the swarm and sent another six ships 'elsewhere' before jumping back out again.

"Practice what you preach, you dumbass!" Orsini roared at Ruark with a private communication only Ruark and the other fleet admirals could hear. He was monitoring the battle from a distance on his tactical display, paying particular attention to the activity of his friend's Super Dragon. "If not for your sake, then for mine! You still owe me money!"

"You're just mad because I'm having all the fun! Quit bothering me. I have to concentrate!" he replied irritably while simultaneously taking out another Swarm ship.

"If we survive, Karen is going to hear about this!" Sue McKay promised venomously, keeping Ruark from hearing the threat to keep from distracting him. "And I'm personally going to help her kick his ass!"

Chapter 58
Super-Swarm

Despite the massive size of the fleet master's super-swarm, his tactical system continued to report losses within it at such an alarming rate he simply could not ignore the problem any longer. Finding it impossible to elude the invisible attackers tormenting his mass of Swarm ships, he came up with a plan. He ordered his Swarm ships, millions of them remaining, to train their force weapons in all directions outside the body of the swarm and to fire continuously and as rapidly as possible.

∿ ∿ ∿

Ruark just came out of a mini-jump that took him to the outskirts of a yet unmolested part of the Swarm cloud when, to his horror, two hundred forty-six of his masked Dragons exploded simultaneously. Sixty-three more took hits, leaving them crippled or completely disabled, but only for brief seconds as the unexpected eruption of the swarm's continuous super-salvo destroyed them too.

"All Dragons retreat now!" Ruark bellowed aloud even though his order went out mentally without any level of decibels involved. "They've figured out a way to hit back! Head back to Earth!" In the short seconds it took for him to give the order and make the jump, seventy-seven more of his precious masked ships blew apart.

∿ ∿ ∿

At last, the fleet master's swarm fighters were no longer defenseless. The hundreds of blossoming flashes of light and the debris flying outward from the violent destruction of dozens of attacking ships were delightful proof of how effectively the super-swarm's bristling wall of force beams worked. The casualty rate of his swarm fighters immediately dropped to zero.

Despite the success of his counterattack, the fleet master became alarmed and shaken by the next set of readings from his tactical system. Analysis of the debris from the masked ships his swarms just destroyed revealed that those ships were not the colossal city-gathering ships of the enemy; they were the very ships the Hive gave to the humans! Somehow, these ships acquired a technological evolution that far exceeded the abilities of Hive technology! While his super-swarm managed to destroy hundreds of them, the fleet master had no way of knowing how many more of them still existed out there or where they came from.

Of the fleet master's more than thirteen million remaining ships initially forming the super-swarm, the murderous masked vermin destroyed two hundred twenty-three thousand of them over the short period of time they came under attack.

At least now, thanks to his effective countermeasure, he felt confident that the vast majority of his forces would reach the human's world without further molestation. The leading edge of his super-swarm was already within one light-second of the planet, closer than its moon. In mere moments, they would be hunting down their enemy's vulnerable rescue ships as they carried their human cargoes away.

With a watchful eye on his tactical hologram, the fleet master observed with utter contempt how the wall of human-piloted fighter ships standing before his super-swarm melted out of its way. Taking their retreat for cowardice and righteous fear of Hive might, he saw no point in maintaining the super-swarm. The fleet master ordered his massive swarm to divide themselves once more into hunting groups of more suitable sizes needed to search the planet effectively for masked enemy Seed ships. There could be no doubt that once the fighting moved to within the planet's atmosphere, the cowardly humans would no longer be willing or able to offer effective resistance.

Feeling confident in the overwhelming numbers of his forces, he ordered all Swarm ships to disregard the humans' force of ships and concentrate solely on the destruction of the enemy Seed ships. He then commanded all thirty-five thousand of his five-warrior Eradicator ships to scatter themselves about the planet not only to seek out the great enemy ships but to destroy concentrations of human populations on the ground. He could deprive the enemy ships of their victim cities to harvest by blasting and leveling all population centers they encountered. With that final command given, it was time to order his dreadnought fleet to advance.

Chapter 59
Never Give Up!

"Shit!" Pete Orsini bellowed, pale and shaken by another massive blow to their defenses. "Jackson! Are you okay?" His voice quivered with his concern for his friend.

"I'm here," Ruark replied, also badly shaken.

"Did your ship take any damage?"

"Not a scratch, but I just lost hundreds of good people along with their Super Dragons that we can ill-afford to lose, and it's my fault," he replied despondently.

"It's not your fault!" Sue reprimanded angrily. "You made use of your force the most effective way you could. Any of us would have done exactly the same thing even if we knew ahead of time what would happen. Yes, you lost over three hundred ships, but your people permanently eliminated a couple hundred thousand ships out of that swarm, ships that won't be coming here to kill us. The loss is tragic, but it's still a small price to pay for what you accomplished. Now is not the time to go blaming yourself! Get back to work! We need you!" she ordered'"

"Get it together, Buddy. Sue's right. Now is not the time for you to be losing it."

"We will mourn our dead when after we have won this battle!" Svetlana added, refusing to let herself believe in any other outcome.

"Don't worry, I'll be okay," he answered irritably. "Give me a couple of minutes to reorganize my people." With that, Ruark concentrated on his tactical hologram and began to redirect his people as best he could in the seconds left before the super-swarm reached Earth.

Holy crap, look at that!" Lee McKay called out to the others in surprise. "We're going to have to maintain our command structure after all! The super-swarm is breaking up into individual swarms again."

"Another one of nature's ways of eliminating the stupid," Orsini replied happily. Idiocy is clearly *not* a characteristic unique to the human race!"

McKay switched communications to his sub fleet admirals. "Commanders, the super-swarm is breaking up into thousands of individual hunting packs! Direct your squadrons to concentrate their defense around any rising Seed ships. Direct a quarter of your sentry squadrons to create feints to areas where there are no Seed ships to make the swarms think our Dragons are racing to protect one of them." Sue, Pete, and Svetlana echoed those orders to their sub-fleet command officers.

"Sorry, Pete, looks like we won't be able to join the party after all for now," Lee told his friend.

"Frustrating as hell, but this is a far better scenario I gladly accept. Those dreadnaughts out there are coming in faster now. Jackson, do you have any good ideas on how to deal with them?" Pete asked worriedly.

"Not a clue. We must have earned some respect, though, since they held themselves back for so long. My masked ships are probably the only ones that stand a chance against them. When they get closer, we'll be the ones to go in after them," Ruark replied grimly.

"This is Captain Bryant," they all heard a moment later. "Commander Noah wants you to know that to save as many human lives as possible, we have to concentrate solely on the protection of the Seed ships. He strongly opposes Fleet Admiral Ruark's determination to engage the giant ships. He believes Fleet Admiral Ruark will be unable to stop them and will be needlessly risking and perhaps sacrificing himself and the rest of his valuable masked fighters! Noah indicates that we don't have much time left. He told me to assure you that once those dreadnought ships arrive, they will put an end to all life on the planet within moments!"

Captain Bryant's communication sphere conveyed her emotional distress over that prediction. "Commander Noah insists that we strive to save every human being we can from the Stickmen."

While Captain Bryant's news came as no surprise, it still put an icy grip on the hearts of each of the fleet admirals.

"We . . . must . . . never . . . give . . . up!" Orsini insisted vehemently. "We can find a way to annihilate those big bastards somehow. I know we can! Forget about the odds!" He received no response, but the thought communications system echoed back the same emotional, albeit pathetic, determination from his friends that he'd just sent through himself.

Chapter 60
Eradicator Assault

The fleet master watched the progress of his enormous cloud of Hive fighter swarms disperse throughout the Earth's atmosphere. As ordered, thousands of Eradicators separated themselves from the center of the super-swarm, all of them the same type of ship that pursued Duval and his team away from Mars.

With each Eradicator having a crew of one shipmaster and four force weapon operators, the fleet master felt jubilant in knowing they would soon be wreaking havoc on unprotected humans on the planet's surface. In contrast, the humans' commanders would almost certainly commit all of their remaining fighters to protect the Seed ships. He watched his tactical display as the points of light representing his Eradicators separated themselves from each other. Individually, they began to hunt.

∿ ∿ ∿

"We have a huge group of Stickman fighter ships entering the atmosphere over India. They're bigger buggers than our Dragons by the looks of their power signatures, and there are thousands of them!" Sue McKay warned. Before she finished speaking, her tactical hologram displayed the entire group of ships spreading themselves in all directions at incredible speeds.

"From their signature readings, they're likely to be the type of ship that tried to take out Duval's squadron when he disappeared," Ruark judged. "What the hell are they up to?"

"I guess we'll know soon enough," Pete Orsini replied. "Get ready for us to have to pull another magic plan out of our butts."

∿ ∿ ∿

"And just what the hell is that thing, mate?" Lieutenant Joseph Welmsly asked his partner, Lieutenant Roland Collins, as they closed in on a lone bogey dropping down from the sky near their hometown of Kilpatrick, Australia. The large Stickman ship leveled off at an altitude of five hundred feet. Before Collins could answer, the strange-looking ship opened fire on targets below it.

Wherever their weapons struck, they smashed the surface of the Earth deep into the ground, their continuous firepower forming overlapping circular holes in quick succession. Where streets and buildings on the outskirts of Kilpatrick stood a moment ago, nothing remained but flat-bottomed craters pocking the landscape.

"That shagger is crushing everything in its path down below. It looks like giant hammers are pounding everything into the ground! Let's get the bastard!"

With the enemy vessel twice as large as their Dragons, the two men had no idea how much more powerful it was than their ships. The Eradicator altered its speed to a relative crawl, working its way to the center of Australian town below. Its weapons fired so rapidly it left behind a ribbon of squashed landscape a mile wide. Everything below, including people, structures, vehicles, and vegetation, were mercilessly crushed flat by the perpetual bombardment of force beams.

Collins opened fire first, upon which the Stickman ship immediately retaliated. "Crikey! Veer off!" Collins shouted the warning to his partner. His ship received a vicious blow from a weapon far more powerful than that of his Dragon.

Acting solely on reflex, both pilots changed course instantly and raced away, each in a different direction. To Welmsly's relief, the strange-looking Stickman ship did not attempt to pursue them. Ignoring the presence of the two Dragons, the Stickman ship continued on its path to lay waste to everything below, their advance reaching the center of Kilpatrick.

"I took a nasty hit!" Collins declared.

"Are you OK?" Welmsly asked anxiously.

Collins checked the status of his ship's systems and turned pale. "No," he replied one second before his ship exploded.

Badly shaken by the loss of his partner, Welmsly put more distance between himself and the deadly Stickman ship while, at the same time, using his thought communications system to report to his area sub-commander.

"Sir, this is Lieutenant Joseph Welmsly, Squadron Kilpatrick 2," he reported anxiously. "There's a large ship of a type I've never seen before that's destroying the town of Kilpatrick, smashing its flat with its weaponry. It took out my partner as we approached it. It's at least twice as large as our Dragons, and it's moving slowly while smashing everything below it!" Welmsly declared with a shaky voice. "Innocent people are being murdered! There's not going to be anyone or anything left before too long!"

"Standby, Lieutenant," came the reply. What seemed like an endless delay which, in reality, was only sixteen seconds before he received the following message. Welmsly was surprised to find it came from Fleet Admiral Ruark himself as a general communication to all defending Dragons.

"All Dragons, the Stickmen have thousands of heavy weapon ships that are attacking population centers on the ground. They are all five-warrior ships loaded with multiple force weapons much more powerful and longer-ranged than yours. Back off! They can detect your unmasked ships! Do not intercept and engage them! They are too low to the ground to give you enough evasive maneuvering room that you need to be effective. My Super Dragons ships will take them out. Continue to protect the Ghost Seed ships as ordered, but avoid those big bastards!"

Ruark then narrowed his communications band to connect only to his fleet of masked ships. "You all heard what I just ordered. Those assholes still can't see us. We're going to pay them back for what they did to our friends. Seek out the power signatures that are identical to the one presently over Kilpatrick and take them out. Scatter and hunt! Tear every last one of them apart and make it fast! They're slaughtering innocent people on the ground!"

Already burning with an almost rabid need for revenge after the loss of their comrades, the Ruark's masked fighters gladly went after the Stickman Eradicator ships that their advanced tactical systems easily identified and located.

∿ ∿ ∿

With tears rolling down his cheeks, Lieutenant Welmsly watched helplessly as the beams of the Eradicator ship continued crushing everything below it, half the town already annihilated. The enemy ship slammed everything into the ground in great clouds of dust, pulverizing anyone unfortunate enough to get caught in the zones of destruction.

Unfortunately for the Eradicator, its existence quickly came to a violent end. One second the Stickman ship was blasting away at the innocents below; the next second, something literally cut it in half, creating an enormous white flash and burst spewing red-hot debris in every direction.

"That should take care of that, Lieutenant Welmsly. I'm sorry I didn't get here sooner. You have my sympathy for the loss of your partner and your people below."

Welmsly was stunned to find that the thought communication system identified the voice as belonging to Fleet Admiral Ruark himself.

"Th-Thank you, Fleet Admiral. Is there any chance I can acquire a ship like yours? I want revenge!"

～ ～ ～

Ruark had less than forty-five hundred of his masked Dragons left after the counter-attack by the super-swarm. Invisible to the Stickman tactical displays, they were the only ones capable of chasing down and destroying the Eradicator ships with virtually no chance of retaliation. The Dragons worked with deadly efficiency and without mercy, taking only twenty-five minutes to hunt down and destroy every one of the thirty-five thousand murderous Eradicators without another single loss to themselves.

After witnessing what the Eradicator ships did to their helpless victims on the ground, Ruark almost wished he could restore and revive every one of those Stickman ships just so he and his team could kill them all over again.

Chapter 61
Squadron Greensburg 12

As big a city as Pittsburgh was, it was not one taken by the first wave of Seed ships. There was a Seed ship on the way now, though, with well over one hundred Dragons ordered to move into place to protect it. The defending Dragons took guard positions in a wide ring that encircled the city at a distance great enough to give the Seed ship enough room to expand its excavating shell.

Captain Ken Edwards, Lieutenant Steven Zacary, and Lieutenant James Logan were responsible for standing guard over an area outside Pittsburgh. Their assigned territory included nearby Greensburg and the surrounding small towns and villages where their families lived. Together, their three ships were too few to be called a squadron. Nevertheless, their area commander designated them as one. With many more towns in the United States also named "Greensburg," they were given the squadron identification name of "Greensburg 12."

These three young men were among the lucky ones to have survived the hive master's destruct signal that wiped out so many EDF forces. Among the dead were many of their good friends. They were distraught, bitter, mad as hell, and eager to get even with the treacherous Stickmen. Still, they dutifully obeyed their orders to seek out their hometown areas, identify themselves to the area sub-commander, and stand guard above their friends and families.

Anxious to fight, though, all three men were miffed that they weren't selected to be part of the group of defenders ordered to join in the protection of Pittsburgh. They knew the Seed ships would be coming for the large population centers, and that's where all the fighting would be likely to occur. Their small hometowns were less likely to see a Seed ship, so they watched their tactical holograms enviously as the area commander called upon others to gather near Pittsburgh.

"Just look at your tacticals! There are swarms all over the place just asking for trouble, and we're just sitting here!" Logan complained.

Edwards, the designated squad leader, replied, "And we will continue to sit here on guard, Lieutenant Logan, until . . . Hold it!" He tensed and leaned forward to study his tactical hologram more closely. What drew his attention became verified by a thought-driven communique from their area commander.

"Squadrons Greensburg 12, Bedford 3 and Somerset 1. There's a Seed ship coming down over Pittsburgh, and you have three groups of incoming bogeys of thirty to forty swarm fighters, each heading that way. They're on a course that will pass through or quite near to your positions. Take care of them! You are weapons-free!"

"You get one wish in life, Lieutenant Logan, and you just wasted yours on this!" Captain Edwards grumbled irritably as he observed a thirty-one-ship swarm heading in their direction.

"I see them on my tactical!" Lieutenant Logan replied, greatly cheered by the enemy approach and the prospect of striking back at the Stickmen at last.

"I see them too. There are thirty-one against the three of us! Ten apiece! Shall we do scissors, rock, paper to see who gets the extra one!" Lieutenant Zacary quipped nervously.

"They're not moving very fast," Captain Edwards observed. "Either they're still trying to locate masked Seed ships, or maybe they already know one is coming to scoop up Pittsburgh, and they're holding back until it becomes vulnerable when it lifts the city. Either way, this swarm will pass over Chestnut Ridge almost directly over our position. There's no way they're going to miss finding that Seed ship coming down on Pittsburgh if we don't stop them."

Edwards used his knowledge transfer system to deliver his intended plan of action without further discussion. Following Edward's orders, Lieutenants Logan and Zacary raced downrange of the swarm's route, then separated in opposite directions perpendicular to the calculated path of the swarm. With several miles of distance between them, they landed and turned off their Dragon's drive power to reduce their power signatures to a level where the swarm would not be able to identify them as Dragons.

Edwards, himself, set a course straight for the oncoming enemy ships while executing a well-practiced high-speed zigzag approach to make himself a difficult target for the Swarm ships to lock onto as his Dragon charged toward them.

Confident of his marksmanship as nearly all Dragon fighter pilots were, he mentally directed his ship's force weapon rather than rely on the much slower automatic targeting system. As fast as he could think about it, he targeted two leading ships and fired. He scored a direct hit on the first one's power plant, causing the Swarm ship to disintegrate in a brilliant ball of light with fiery chunks of debris cascading out of the sky to pepper the landscape below.

The second Swarm ship took a hit in its inertia control system just as its Stickman pilot ordered it to accelerate to close on the attacker. With the Swarm ship's inertia system disabled and no longer able to nullify its inertia, the pilot was slammed against the inside hull of his ship and splattered into an unrecognizable pulp. Without guidance, the injured ship veered away from the swarm and plowed through a quarter-mile of trees before cratering on the mountain slope below.

The moment Edwards finished firing his weapon, he juked his Dragon upward, then sideways to prevent swarm weapons from locking on his ship, then ordered an instantaneous course reversal to flee just ahead of the swarm. As he ran, he maintained the zigzag maneuvering that made the Swarm ships' automatic targeting systems incapable of locking onto his Dragon, their salvos passing harmlessly through places his ship no longer occupied.

While creating the impression of trying to flee from the swarm, Edwards led it straight between his two squadron mates who waited to perform the world's oldest type of ambush. As the swarm came alongside Lieutenants Logan and Zacary's hiding places, those two men activated their ship's power and went instantly to maximum speed to plow straight through the swarm's flanks from two different directions. Zacary destroyed five Swarm ships, and Logan killed six before coming out of the opposite sides of the swarm. Making matters worse for the Stickmen, Edwards immediately dropped his altitude below the Swarm ships chasing him and came to a dead stop. The pursuing swarm shot past him overhead, and Edwards went to maximum speed again to plow through the enemy group from behind.

Executing the effective ricochet tactics that Danny Murphy invented, the three Dragons continued to pinball themselves among the Swarm ships to make it impossible for the enemy's weapons to lock onto them. Swarm ship after Swarm ship took killing and crippling hits, most of the enemy vessels exploding in midair, others either crashing to the surface below or racing out of control back into outer space.

By the time the entire melee ended less than eighty seconds after it began, the three EDF Dragons single-handedly succeeded in destroying the entire pack of thirty-one enemy ships.

"Squadron Greensburg 12, return to your sentry positions," came the dispassionate order from their area sub-commander.

"Well, *that* gushing praise left me blushing," Edwards told his team sarcastically.

Once again, the three men returned to their sentry positions over the skies of Greensburg. Monitoring their tacticals, they were proud to see a large chunk of the city of Pittsburgh they just helped to protect rise unmolested into the sky.

Chapter 62
We Can't Save Everyone

At long last, the fleet master's forces were becoming successful in their hunt for the Seed ships with the help of the Sterilizer ships themselves. With their superior tactical systems, the Hive dreadnaughts easily mapped the power signatures of every human population center on the surface of the human planet from afar. When one of the signatures winked out as a Seed ship enclosed it, the Hive dreadnoughts directed the swarm forces closest to it to race to that location. The tactic worked. At last, Seed ships carrying the loathsome humans away from the planet began to fall from the planet's skies.

In their desperate efforts to save their cities, the vicious and deadly maneuvers the defending human ships employed continued to decimate his forces. But even though his Swarm ships took on massive casualties, the fleet master's vastly superior numbers still gave him confidence. He maintained his order for his swarms to disregard the human fighters unless attacked and concentrate on eliminating the Seed ships. It was far more critical to minimize the number of these deadly humans that the enemy rescue ships could carry away than to waste time seeking out and engaging the defending humans.

However, it soon became that, despite the efforts of the swarms, the aggressive enemy tactics allowed far too many enemy rescue ships to escape with their cargo of human population centers if he did not act immediately. He decided he could no longer afford the luxury of a cautious approach to the planet. He issued the command for his planet-sterilizing dreadnoughts to accelerate to maximum speed toward the humans' world. Its incineration would put a stop to the population rescues altogether. The sooner his Sterilizer ships reduced the surface of the planet to ashes, the less time the enemy would have to carry more of the humans away to safety. It chilled what served the fleet master as blood to know that many of the humans already taken away might someday reappear as an effective and vengeful enemy against the Hive race.

Reluctantly, he conceded to himself how dangerously formidable these Earth warriors were and ordered his Sterilizers to group tightly together to increase the density of their protective shield of Swarm ships and ensure a safe and clear path to the human world. Given their increased speed, it would not take his Sterilizer armada very long to arrive at their target.

~ ~ ~

"Too many swarms are getting through to the Seed ships taking our cities!" a horrified Sue McKay cried out in alarm. "Our people are spread too thin to guard every Seed ship effectively. We just don't have enough fighters left." She tried hard to remain calm, but the loss of entire cities and the strain of their failure to protect them began to tear her apart emotionally.

"Sue, we knew this would happen. We can only do the best we can do with the limited resources we have to work with," her husband told her, sensing through the thought transfer system how the climbing mass fatalities emotionally tore her up. "Concentrate on what you still need to do for the living, and don't think about the dead!"

All five fleet admirals, Ruark included, tried hard not to succumb to despair over the terrible loss of humanity the Stickmen were causing. In truth, they knew Seed ship losses were much lower than any of them could have dared hope for considering how many Dragon ships they'd lost to the self-destruct signal and to the endless fighting since, but that knowledge gave no comfort to any of them. Each loss of a Seed ship carrying a human population felt like a horrendous failure on their part to protect it.

"Our people are doing a miraculous job," Svetlana reasoned as she too became concerned about the depth of Susan's distress. "The Swarm ships are practically helpless against our Dragon bounce tactics, and they are ignoring our sentries in their desperation to find the Seed ships. It is a huge tactical error on their part. Our Dragons are wreaking incredible havoc on the enemy forces, but even so, you are correct; our fighters are far too few to be everywhere. There is nothing in our power we can do to change that, so we must keep fighting with what we have!"

"I know it, but that doesn't make it all any less painful. I'll be okay. I can do this, but I may need someone to put me back together when I fall to pieces if we survive this."

"We all have to keep it together! We now have less than an hour before those dreadnoughts get here, and we still don't have a clue how to deal with them," Pete Orsini warned.

"We can't possibly spare anyone to try to stop them! We can't dilute the forces left who are trying to protect the Seed ships," Orsini replied adamantly.

"We've got no choice," Lee agreed. "We have to continue to give priority to the protection of those ships! We just have to accept the fact that we won't be able to save everyone on the planet."

Chapter 63
Okazaki Defenders

The sterilizer ships were getting closer, all of them well inside the orbit of Mars. Shortly before their arrival, the fleet master intended to release the armada's protective shield of Swarm ships to reinforce his exponentially dwindling forces still hunting down the enemy Seed ships.

When his fleet reached the humans' planet, the Sterilizer armada would exercise their standard destruction sequence by positioning themselves in a ring formation large enough to encircle their world. Then, as they advanced with the planet passing through their ring, their beams of ultra-hard radiation would incinerate every living thing below with ruthless efficiency. Once they destroyed the humans' world, this solar system would be ready for the Hive to colonize it.

∾ ∾ ∾

In the early moments of the Seed ships' invasion of Earth's solar system, Colonel Hiroshi Takamura was among the first of thousands of EDF Dragons the Ghost Seed ships captured and sent to Ruark's remote base. When he learned of the deceit of the Stickmen, his need to take vengeance on the deceivers burned savagely within him as it did with the thousands of other Dragon fighter pilots captured by Ruark's forces.

He emerged from the wormhole portal into Earth's solar system with thousands of Stickman Swarm ships spread close before him like ripe fruit ready to be devoured just as Fleet Admiral Ruark orchestrated. At last, he could take revenge. Flying a zig-zag path into the thick of enemy ships, he destroyed three in seconds, gleefully marveling at their inability to deal with the Dragon ships attacking them from within their midst. The enemy swarms found themselves nearly helpless against the evasive bounce tactics the EDF adopted as its most devastating offensive tactic.

However, to Hiroshi's anguish, the Dragons' surprise attack was too short-lived. It took all of his willpower to obey Ruark's order calling off their attack just as the Swarm ships fled from Earth's resurrected Dragons.

His frustration ended when Fleet Admiral McKay issued the command for all fighters to return to their home cities to protect them. Hearing the order, he joyfully raced back to Earth and proudly stood guard over his hometown of Okazaki, Japan. Reaching his home city, Takamura welcomed ten other EDF fighters from the area who joined him in the great honor of protecting their homes, their families, and their country. Takamura, the ranking officer among them, felt doubly honored when the area commander appointed him as their squadron leader.

It wasn't too long before a Seed ship descended on the nearby city of Nagoya, encasing a large part of it within its capturing shell. Several Stickman swarms soon gathered to attack the now-defenseless Seed ship as it began to rise. In the effort to provide enough Dragons to keep the Seed ship safe, the number of protective squadrons called to defend it drained most of the already scarce sentry resources of the area. Takamura's team was a bit too far away for the area commander to include them.

As the Dragons fought off dozens of swarms protecting the Nagoya Seed ship, Takamura became horrified to find another Seed ship descending above Okazaki. From the knowledge transfers he received upon his capture earlier that day, he knew the Ghosts were not militarily competent, but he couldn't believe they were ignorant to the degree that would permit them to send another ship into an area drained of adequate protection. Worse yet, his tactical hologram revealed several more swarms altering their course in the direction of Nagoya, all of them initially drawn in by the presence of the Nagoya Seed ship. There could be no doubt that they would also discover the Okazaki Seed ship.

Takamura watched helplessly as Okazaki and a large part of the city of Anjo became encased by the Seed ship even as the Nagoya Seed ship still rose in the midst of a fierce attack. As Takamura feared, the moment Okazaki's power signature disappeared from his tactical hologram, more distant swarms also began racing in. Horrified, he watched as the Seed ship carrying his home city gradually began to rise.

With only Takamura's lone squadron close enough to provide immediate protection, the shell of the Seed ship carrying Okazaki became an enticing and vulnerable target for the swarms. It promptly fell under vicious and relentless attack, the arriving swarms mercilessly pouring ruinous volleys of force beams into it.

Knowing their families were aboard the besieged Okazaki Seed ship, Takamura's squadron fought like demons against nearly thirty times their number. They raced through and around the Stickmen swarm formations like ricocheting bullets with a total disregard for personal safety. Takamura sent out a desperate plea for help, but so many swarm fighters were still attacking the Seed ship carrying Nagoya away that none of that city's protective squadrons were able to break away to come to the aid of Okazaki. His tactical hologram displayed other squadrons coming to their rescue from a distance, but he knew they were too far away to reach Okazaki in time.

Two of Takamura's Dragons blew apart during the melee. Despite their loss, Takamura's men destroyed such an ungodly number of Swarm fighters that the sky above the crater where Okazaki stood moments before became filled with the raining debris of annihilated Stickman Swarm ships.

However, Okazaki was doomed right from the start with the number of Stickman attackers simply too overwhelming for the defenders to prevent the swarms' inflicted damage to the rising ship. Despite the squadrons' near superhuman efforts, the Ghost Seed ship, helpless inside its encompassing shell, soon began to falter. Before it could even climb halfway to the edge of the atmosphere, bolts of electrostatic discharge began to flicker all over its surface just before the miles-wide protective bubble around the city vanished altogether. The overloaded core of the Seed ship's drive blew the vessel apart in an expanding ball of light. The explosion shattered Okazaki, Anjo, and their citizens thousands of feet above the ground.

Takamura screamed in anguish and horror as pieces of his city flew apart. Charred remains rained back down to Earth over hundreds of square miles, some of the debris bouncing off the impervious hull of his ship. Nearly insane with grief and fury and feeling they had nothing left to live for, Takamura and his men redoubled their already maniacal assaults on the remainder of the Stickman swarms that committed this atrocity. They relentlessly pursued every Swarm ship with reckless abandon until the skies were wiped clean of them.

When it was over, only Takamura and seven others of his squadron survived the battle, losing only one more man during their vengeful fray. With no enemy left to fight, Takamura descended to hover his ship above the place where his city and his family existed just a short while earlier and wept bitterly as the ocean poured into the crater Okazaki's Seed ship left behind.

The area commander ordered what was left of his squadron to return to sentry duty, which Takamura ignored. Grief-stricken and overcome with shame by his failure to protect his home, to his mind, there was only one thing left that he desperately needed to do; to die in battle and atone for his failure by taking as many enemies with him as he could.

Utilizing his tactical hologram, he saw battles raging everywhere all over the planet and in the volume of space just outside the atmosphere in target-rich environments, but he knew from reports that there were more worthy targets out there. He expanded the range of his hologram and found what he searched for, the power signatures of the twelve enormous earthbound enemy ships forming the brightest group of lights in his holographic display. These were the terrible planet-destroying dreadnoughts the fleet admirals warned them about. They all protectively grouped themselves in typical Stickman fashion as they approached Earth unopposed. Zooming his tactical in on their position, he saw that their formation included a shielding forefront of several hundred thousand Swarm ships.

Driven by an insane hatred he never imagined possible, Takamura immediately knew what he wanted to do. The enormous ships were twenty minutes out at Dragon fighter speed, forty minutes from Earth given their cautious approach to Earth. He sent out a mental message to his squadron, letting them know his intentions and bidding them to rejoin the efforts to protect the Seed ships. He wished them all a farewell and then shot his Dragon upward through the atmosphere, bypassing and ignoring the hunting swarms of Stickman fighters who snubbed his presence in their quest to locate targets far more desirable to them.

Just as Takamura cleared the atmosphere, he received a mental message directed solely to him. "Command us, Takamura San. We will be honored."

His heart swelled with pride as his tactical hologram showed all seven survivors of his squadron forming up in wing formation to either side of him.

"It will be my greatest honor to die fighting in your company," he told them.

He studied the hologram for a moment, and then knowledge transferred his plan to his men. The strategy received their unanimous approval and praise for its ingenuity. All seven ships peeled away from each other, breaking up the formation that otherwise might have drawn attention.

With thousands of ships engaged in battles still raging above the Earth, Takamura's fighters went unnoticed as they planted themselves directly in the path of the Stickman Sterilizer ships just beyond the orbit of the moon. Scattered, they hid themselves within the densest clouds of debris, the remains of thousands of near-earth sentry Dragons destroyed by the hive master's destruct signal. Their tactical displays informed them of the exact time when the dreadnoughts would be where they wanted them to be. All eight men mentally commanded their ships to turn off all their Dragon's power systems to eliminate their detectable signatures. Then they simply waited.

Takamura said prayers for his lost family and home, then pulled a notepad and pen out of his pocket. He leaned back in the pilot's seat and began to compose a death poem no one but he would ever see.

∿ ∿ ∿

As thin as the EDF's defensive coverage had become, the dogfighting bounce tactics of the surviving Dragons continued to eviscerate swarm formations. The number of Seed ships escaping with their precious cargoes increased as the number of swarms hunting them dwindled dramatically.

More and more cities and towns became surgically cut from the face of the Earth and were successfully lifted into the skies by the Seed ships. A fury of fighting raged around every one of them as they rose above the atmosphere, the fortunate ones finally winking safely out of existence through a wormhole.

Earth became pockmarked with smooth, polished, hemispherical craters where the cities, towns, fields, and forests once existed. For the billions of humans still left behind, the Ghosts could do nothing to save them. They would be at the mercy, or more accurately, lack of mercy, of the Stickmen. When the Sterilizers arrived, the Ghost ships would have to abandon their rescue of the human race, and that time was rapidly approaching.

PART THREE
Never Give Up

Chapter 64
Takamura's Vengeance

An alarm from his wristwatch brought Takamura out of a state of meditation. A glance at its illuminated face told him it was time; the dreadnoughts should have gone past his position by now. He said a final prayer and waited for the seconds to count down to the exact time he ordered his men to reactivate their ships.

At last, the moment arrived. Mentally sending a command to his Dragon, its drive power leaped back to life in an instant, and the smile that came to his face would have raised the hairs on the necks of anyone who could have seen it.

As he had planned, the dreadnoughts and their advance shield of Stickman Swarm fighters protecting them passed his Dragon by and those of his squadron survivors without taking any notice of them hidden among the debris of the dead. The entire rear approach to dreadnought armada was left entirely unguarded.

Takamura sent and received back mental messages to his squadmates wishing them well. He did not have to tell them what to do; they already knew. They had only a few short seconds to act. The awakening of their ships' power sources probably already raised alarms on every tactical system in the dreadnought fleet.

Takamura and his men immediately drew precise coordinates from distant beacon ships, and they accelerated their ships through sub-light speed to mini-jumps. The tactical systems of the Stickman Swarm fighters and Sterilizer ships began blaring out their alarms when it was already far too late to try to stop the vengeful humans.

Even though the Sterilizer ships' massive automatic defense armaments automatically attempted to target the threatening Dragons, none of the weapon systems could track ships making a mini-jump through wormholes.

An instant before his death, Takamura's only regret was that there were twelve dreadnoughts and only eight Dragons left of his squadron. Each of

Takamura's squad warriors chose a Sterilizer of his own to target. An impact at near-light speeds alone would have been enough to destroy any one of the great ships, but the men set their navigation controls so their Dragons would come out of their wormholes at that incredible speed *inside* the dreadnoughts.

For the first time in Hive history, wormholes opened inside large, atmosphere-filled masses. Takamura's Dragon emerged from the wormhole in the same space as one of the massive bulkheads of the dreadnaught's structure. Combined with the inertia of its near-light speed, the collision created a super mini-nova that vaporized the entire dreadnought along with thousands of its protective cloud of leading Swarm ships.

The wormhole delivering Takamura's Dragon, needing milliseconds to fully close, was still partially open when a river of massive purple-hot plasma shot back through the opening. A spear of blinding energy poured out of the other end of the wormhole hundreds of miles away at the point where Takamura first entered it. The transported energy blast ballooned outward before dissipating gradually into a cloud of glowing gases.

Even as Takamura's ship exploded, identical explosions vaporized seven more of the great Sterilizer ships. Two of the remaining dreadnaughts were so close to targeted ships that the blast of a sister ship shattered one of them in half, while a shock wave from another explosion wrecked the power system of the other, killing most of its Hive crew and leaving it a useless hulk. Takamura and his companions would have been proud to know that they'd achieved their revenge far beyond their greatest expectations.

Chapter 65
Disbelief!

The cataclysmic explosion from the ship nearest the fleet master's Sterilizer caused the inertia control system of his dreadnought to falter momentarily. His entire ship lurched, throwing him from his feet and knocking the great ship off course. Slightly injured, he rose unsteadily as his ship's sensors pumped multiple alarms into his mind.

Panic! Somehow, the enemy managed a wholly unexpected and incomprehensible attack on his fleet once again using weapons of unknown origin, the same way the hive master's lunar base must have been destroyed! An unfamiliar feeling of terror coursed through him, clouding his ability to think clearly. In all of Hive history, no Sterilizer ship had ever been attacked!

His tactical hologram flickered and then restored itself, but judging from its display, it couldn't possibly be functioning properly. He stared at it expectantly as he waited for it to correct itself since what it depicted could not possibly be valid and had to be the result of a malfunction.

Nevertheless, the hologram display remained unchanged. It revealed eight clouds of glowing plasma filling the space where eight of his enormous Sterilizer ships used to be. Inexplicably, eight lesser masses of plasma also glowed out in space several hundred miles out from his fleet's location.

Still disbelieving the display, the fleet master turned to examine the space around him through a viewing field that followed his gaze. He jumped, startled, as the gutted, spinning half of a Sterilizer drifted past, in and out again from view, the ragged edges of its torn hull still glowing white-hot. The other half of the ship was simply gone.

As the derelict spun, chunks and pieces of debris flew out of it, flickering with the reflected light of this solar system's sun as they tumbled through space. The ejected bodies and fragments of bodies of thousands of the ship's crew flew out into space in all directions as part of the debris. Some of its crew who survived the blast still flailed weakly as they succumbed to the vacuum of space.

The fleet master's tactical system verified that whatever attacked his Sterilizer ships vaporized them entirely. The derelict of a ninth ship drifted by, damaged by the explosion of the dreadnaught closest to it. The battering it took from the violent forces of two of the nearby explosions killed most of its hundreds of thousands of its Hive crew.

Three-quarters of the twelve hundred thousand shielding Swarm ships leading the fleet also disappeared in the massive blast zones. The explosion left thousands more inoperable, their pilots killed or entombed within now-useless ships. Less than a tenth of the original guardian forces remained capable of providing protection, but only the fleet master's ship and one other Sterilizer were left for them to protect.

The fleet master's urge to continue the attack on the human planet was a powerful one, but with the planet's destruction no longer possible, his instinct to preserve the Hive was greater. Informing the Hive homeworlds of what happened here and delivering all recordings of the events for their analysis took priority. The fleet master sent a thought-driven order to the commander of the surviving sister ship. Without making an effort to help survivors of the Swarm ship derelicts, both undamaged Sterilizers opened wormholes to make the first of the many jumps back to the center of the Hive Empire. The swarm fighter and dreadnought crew survivors they abandoned were unimportant.

Chapter 66
What Just Happened?

"What the hell just happened out there?" a bewildered but joyous Pete Orsini called out to his fleet admiral counterparts. "Did any of you catch that? I checked the progress of those incoming big boys, and then the energy readings I received from my tactical suddenly went off the charts. It looks like eight of them turned into mini-novas, one after the other, within seconds of each other! There were twelve of them out there, and now my tactical system can only detect full power signatures for just two of them, and I can just barely detect whispers of a power signature on one more! If that's not surprising enough, there's only a small fraction of the Swarm ships left that ran interference ahead of them!"

"Roger that! I'm finding only two full dreadnought signatures showing on my tactical too!" Lee McKay verified. "Wait. Cancel that! Those two signatures just vanished!"

"I don't think they vanished; I think they jumped. I saw a spike in their power signatures just before they disappeared. They're retreating!" Susan informed them elatedly.

"We'll they left all their kiddies behind," Orsini said. The swarms attacking our Seed ships below aren't letting up, and what's left of the fighters the dreadnoughts left behind are all coming in fast to join them!"

"Commander Noah!" Ruark called to the Ghost Commander. "I thought you said you had no defense against those huge ships out there."

"Noah: We did not cause their destruction, Fleet Admiral Ruark. We jubilantly presumed you humans somehow managed to find a way to stop them."

"We can thank God and figure it out later, people!" Pete admonished. We still have our hands full below. That 'small fraction' of escort ships I mentioned is still a good one hundred and ten thousand reinforcements!"

"Let them come," Lee responded, "The swarms are almost as helpless against our bounce tactics as they are against Jackson's masked ships!" Don't' worry about the Swarm reinforcements until they get here. We've got to keep protecting those Seed ships! One thing we can do, though, is to give our boys a morale boost." That said, he set his thought transfer system to send a general broadcast.

"This is Fleet Admiral McKay. Those twelve super-ships that were coming in at us are gone! Nine blew apart, one other appears to be disabled or worse, and the last two are running away with their tails between their legs, and if they are running, then they must believe they've lost the battle! Against all the odds, people, we are beating them! Finish the bastards off!"

McKay's announcement pumped new life into the morale of the defending Dragon warriors. The defenders redoubled their efforts to destroy the enemy ships, their tactics and maneuvers still far beyond the capability of the enemy Swarm fighters to deal with effectively.

Jackson Ruark's Super Dragons took the greatest toll of all. To them, the Stickman ships were nothing more than target practice. With his Super Dragons invisible to swarm tactical and weapons systems, the enemy ships could locate them visually. The Dragons moved far too fast and erratically to target even when they could be seen.

With the Sterilizer ships no longer coordinating and directing swarm groups from afar to Seed ship targets, the swarms lost their ability to locate the Seed ships as efficiently as they had before. When they did find one, with no concern for their survival, the Stickman swarms threw themselves relentlessly at the Ghost ships while doing little to ward off the Earth fighters who fought viciously to stop them.

When the remnant swarm forces left behind by the dreadnoughts arrived to reinforce the remains of the hunting swarms, they made no impact on the tide of the battle. Against all the odds, the Earth's defenders were winning, and the Dragon defenders would soon outnumber the remaining attackers.

Chapter 67
Mop up

"There's not enough of the enemy left down there requiring any great strategy or direction from us anymore," Pete Orsini announced to his friends. "I'm releasing my sub-command officers to allow them to join in the battle, and I'm going down there to get a piece of the action myself." With that said, he cut the links of his thought transfer system to his friends before they could offer any form of protest.

On their tactical holograms, the remaining three fleet admirals saw Pete's ship and those of his sub-commanders streak down into Earth's atmosphere to join the melee.

"I think, for once, Pete has the right idea. How can our guys ever truly respect us knowing we sat back the whole time without tasting blood ourselves?" Lee told Sue and Svetlana. He received no reply. The two women were already racing down to join Pete, their sub-command staffs gone with them.

"I'm talking to myself," Lee muttered irritably as he released his commanders and mentally ordered his ship to race full speed toward the closest group of remaining Swarm ships.

A moment later, Lee McKay blew his first Swarm ship out of the sky above the Earth. However, in the short amount of time it took for him to accomplish that, going by the old aerial combat standards, his wife and Svetlana had already earned the title of aces in their first actual combat roles.

∾ ∾ ∾

The battle raged for one more hour. Against all odds, Pete Orsini himself obtained the honor of blasting the last Swarm ship out of the sky. He followed through with a quick examination of his tactical hologram to locate the next nearest group of enemy ships and stared in disbelief that there were no more enemy Swarm ships to be found anywhere, every one of them gone! The Stickmen were defeated, at least for the time being.

The Seed ships rising from the planet could continue to do so now unimpeded, all of them safe at last.

~ ~ ~

"We did it!" Sue cried out incredulously, tears streaming down her cheeks. "We really did it!"

"That's because we didn't give up!" Orsini told them triumphantly.

"But at what did our victory cost? How many of our people did we lose?" Ruark asked gravely as he tried to determine the answer himself from his tactical system.

"And how many towns and cities?" Svetlana added.

"Too many," Lee McKay responded solemnly. "It looks like nearly all of your Super Dragons survived, Jackson, but only about four hundred fifty thousand Dragons still exist of the nearly three million we had before the Seed ships began the invasion. I have no idea of how many Seed ships fell during the attack, but I know there were many."

"And for each Seed ship destroyed, the tens of thousands of people they tried to save died with them," Svetlana choked. Her strict nature and rigorously formal attitude wilted away, and she began to sob so hard she couldn't stop. With the stress of command finally over, the hard exterior shell she always tried to present melted away from the tragedy of it all.

As Svetlana wept, the rest of the fleet admirals said nothing for a while. The enormity of what they'd all gone through and the shock of achieving a victory none of them ever really believed possible left them all mentally and physically drained.

Lee McKay broke the silence. He set his thought communications system for general broadcast. "All forces, this is Fleet Admiral McKay," he said wearily. "The fighting is over. We've wiped out every last one of the enemy swarms."

He let the news sink in before continuing. "The courage you all exhibited today will be remembered forever! Against all odds, you defeated an enemy force vastly superior to ours, one that should have been impossible to overcome. We, your commanding officers, are honored to have served with you.

Lee paused again as he searched for words. "Our planet is gravely wounded, and we've lost many people, warriors, and civilians alike. Pray for them and thank God that there weren't more of them, and pray that you all find your loved ones safe and sound either here on Earth or wherever the Ghosts took our people to safety."

Lee looked out through his viewing field down to his planet and sighed sadly. "You must all remember that we've only won a battle. We haven't won this war as long as the Stickman Empire is still out there. The Stickmen will return even though it won't be today, tomorrow, or even next week. When that time comes, we'll need to fight again. Please be ready!

"For the time being, go home. Find your families and take them to the safety of the Ghost ships. For those of you who have lost loved ones, friends, and comrades, our hearts go out to you. We will forever share your grief. Go now, and take care of your people, but do it quickly. The evacuation of the planet isn't over. There are still billions left who need you. Be ready when you hear us call you back to duty; I doubt if it will be too long before the need arises."

He mentally switched his communications back to private links to his wife and three friends. "Sue and Pete, go find your families and make sure they're OK. I imagine they'll be anxious to see you too. We can regroup on Noah's ship later."

Without a need to hear that order twice, Sue and Pete set a course for home to search for their loved ones.

"Svetlana, is there anyone you need to find?"

"Like you, I have no family, Lee," she said, calling him by his first name for the first time.

"Then let's go join Noah. Our problems are far from over."

∼ ∼ ∼

At long last, there were no Swarm ships left for the Dragon pilots to fight. Most of the surviving Dragon pilots flew their ships straight home to see if their homes still existed. Susan McKay headed for home from the Gulf of Bothnia, where her last dogfight took place off the Swedish coast. By then, the tides had turned dramatically; the EDF Dragons outnumbered the remaining Swarm ships.

Anxious about her parents, Susan sped over the Arctic Circle to get to Seattle. As far as she could see, the meteoric debris of destroyed ships, friend and foe alike, rained endlessly down all over the planet. Flying high over the Yukon, she saw little evidence of Seed ship activity, but as she approached the border of Canada and the United States, their former presence became evident in dozens of places where gigantic craters pocked the surface of the landscape.

Reducing her Dragon's speed as she approached Seattle, Susan cruised in closer to the ground. She found an enormous crater centered over what used to be the most populated area. So much of the city remained behind, though she knew most of the population would die if the Stickmen reappeared too soon.

Susan examined her tactical hologram, which registered the power signatures of several hundred Dragons in the areas below, all of their pilots checking on the welfare of their families. With dozens of Dragons parked along the edge of the crater, she deduced the Seed ship must have taken the homes and families of those pilots, and she wondered if those pilots realized that even though the seed ships took their families away, they were the lucky ones.

A few miles beyond the crater, Susan came to a gentle landing to park her Dragon above her parent's front lawn. They were waiting for her.

Chapter 68
Reunions

A grim Pete Orsini raced high above the atmosphere toward his family. Having fought most of his aerial battles over Australia, he didn't know if they were dead or alive. Seconds after crossing the Californian coast, Pete could see far across the United States. With the ability of his ship's communication system to contact anyone within line-of-sight," he called out to them after commanding his communications system to connect only with them.

"Melissa, Nick, Danielle, he called out anxiously. It was a long shot, but he hoped that at least one of them might be outdoors without anything that might block his ship's line-of-sight to them.

"Oh, Daddy! Is that really you?" Danielle cried out excitedly.

"It sure is, sweetheart," Pete answered, her voice bringing tears to his eyes. "Are you all okay?"

"Yes, Daddy, we're fine!" Pete didn't realize until that moment how tight the knot in his gut felt. He practically wilted with relief, knowing his family came through the conflict unharmed. "I'm on my way home, honey. You must be outside somewhere. Are you close to the house?"

"Yes," she replied, but the thought communications system relayed her emotions of joy and relief from hearing his voice and discovering he survived the battles.

"Go get your mother and Nick and tell them to come outside to where you are now." He waited patiently while Danielle went to get them. Since the Ruark family disappeared, Pete sent his family to their farm to take care of it and keep the livestock fed out of respect. Before the revelation that Jackson Ruark and his family were still alive, they planned to help settle the estate for their friends.

"Peter, can you hear me?" Melissa called to him. He could sense her relief coming through the communications system.

"I can, dear, and I'm on my way to you now. Nick, are you there?"

"Yeah, Dad, I'm here." Pete raised one eyebrow at the boy's tone. The boy sounded sad.

Pete created a temporary private channel with his wife. "Is Nick alright, Melissa?"

"We have a lot to tell you. Come home first, Peter."

"I have a lot to tell you too. I'm coming, but now that I know you are all okay, I'm going to take a bit longer than planned. I need to recon some of the damage below on my way."

"Please don't be long."

"I won't. I promise!"

Pete dropped down low over Nevada to fly across the Southwestern landscape.

Passing just north of Las Vegas, Pete slowed his Dragon to get a closer look. Las Vegas was gone, really *gone*, not rescued. When multiple swarms blew apart the city's rescuing Seed ship, the debris of the ship's cargo not only fell back into the crater it came from but also rained down and into the remaining part of the city and surrounding countryside to cause even more death and destruction.

Pete spotted dozens of Dragons parked along the crater's edge and scattered throughout the remainder of the city. He knew some of those pilots grieved for their loved ones who died with the Seed ship. The others had to be searching for family among the ruins outside the boundary of the crater. The spectacle tore at his heart and fanned the flames of his hatred for the Stickmen to new heights.

Crossing over the desert and into the plains, the exodus of refugees he saw remained consistent. Everywhere, people were still trying to distance themselves from the population centers. Cars and trucks crammed full of people filled secondary and country roads that would typically be empty. Many people walked in cities and towns everywhere, their vehicles unable to make progress through traffic jams. Some pushed carts, some carried suitcases, while others led children by the hand or carried them across their shoulders. Their endless lines spread outward along highways and roads radiating from every population center. Pete guessed very few of the evacuees knew where the EDF had refugee centers prepared, and with that realization, he sent out an urgent message to Lee McKay and Svetlana Ivanovna.

Pete did recognize one EDF refugee center by concentrations of refugees, the ones who did know its location. They flowed toward it from all directions, the camp already bulging with them. He passed over another evac center several minutes later that was unrecognizable. Earlier in the day, a Stickman Eradicator smashed it into the ground along with everyone in it.

As Pete passed over Dallas, he felt gratified that an unblemished crater sat in the center of the city, the absence of debris indicating at least part of Dallas would live on somewhere out in the universe.

At last, he crossed into Alabama, anxious to see his family. As he approached Jackson Ruark's farm, he turned ghostly pale when he saw the debris of nearby Montgomery lying within a crater with much of its remains scattered about the countryside just as Las Vegas had been. The destroyed Seed ship missed carrying away Ruark's farm along with Pete's family by a little over a mile.

When Pete landed at last in Ruark's farmyard, he raced from his ship to group-hug his wife and children. Still holding on to them, the enormity of what they'd all been through hit him hard, and just like Svetlana, he sank to his knees and wept.

～ ～ ～

Hours later, Sue met her husband in person again for the first time in days aboard Noah's command ship, which would become the regular meeting place of the Ghosts and humans. Lee was already working there with Svetlana and Jackson. Megan Bryant, Noah, Jake, and the Ghost, Pat, were with them.

Sue ran to her husband when she saw him and gave him a huge hug, not having been with him since days before the invasion began. Lee lifted her off her feet with his embrace, squeezing her so hard it made her ribs ache.

Pushing herself away from him, she beamed a huge smile at him. "Lee, I found my mom and dad. They're OK!" Her eyes welled up with joy as she told him about it. The others in the room gathered to welcome her warmly too. She was so glad to see everyone she hugged them all, even Jake, whom she had never met before in person. When she wrapped her arms as far as she could around the trunks of each of the two tall Ghosts, she triggered another one of their spasms of untranslated patterns of heat and rippling color patterns.

Pete Orsini arrived a few hours later, his entire family in tow. His wife and children went wide-eyed when they saw their first Ghost beings.

"Ruark's farm, where I told them to go, was just a few miles outside the range of the Seed ship that took Montgomery," he explained. "Several swarms attacked the ship and destroyed it along with the city it carried. I almost lost my family and didn't know how close I came to it! I'm not letting them out of my sight ever again!" he said defiantly.

Melissa Orsini looked gaunt, and both she and her daughters' faces appeared swollen from very recent tears. Jackson and Lee noticed that about Orsini too but pretended not to. When Melissa saw Jackson Ruark, whom she thought to be dead, she burst into tears again and ran to give him a huge hug. Between sobs, she managed to ask about Karen.

She's OK, Melissa. Really, she's fine," he comforted her.

Sue went to Melissa's side and put an arm around her. Pete's daughter, Danielle, hung onto her father's arm as if she would never let go again. Pete's son, Nick, stood to one side and slightly behind his father with an angry scowl as severe as his father's, his anger his way of dealing with his grief and with everything he and his family had gone through.

"The kids made a lot of new friends in Montgomery," Pete informed the group privately through the chamber's thought communications devices. Nick lost a girlfriend he met a few weeks ago whom he was beginning to care a great deal for."

After Pete's family settled in quarters provided by the Ghosts, it was a somber group that gathered together again several hours later.

"This murderous attack by the Stickmen brought about the most disastrous loss of human life in Earth's history," Svetlana told everyone. "We will never know exactly how many souls were lost, but we must be thankful there is anyone left at all, and extra thankful we still have each other to continue to plan what needs to be done next."

"We are indeed lucky to have anyone left," Jackson acknowledged, "but our mission is as urgent as ever, and as Lee told our troops earlier, the war is far from being won."

"Thanks to Fleet Admiral Orsini's message warning us that most of Earth's population still believed the Seed ships to be the invading enemy, Fleet Admiral McKay and I succeeded in rallying several thousand Dragon pilots. Most of them are either those who have families taken to safety or no longer have families at all.

Without knowing for sure if knowledge transfers would work the same way our thought communications line-of-site functionality, we ordered them to distribute their Dragons high above the planet and send knowledge transfers to the civilians on the ground. It was imperative to let them know the truth about the Seed ships to put a stop to their flight away from their towns. Fortunately, the transfers do work just like the communications systems. Our Dragons remain aloft to blanket the world continuously with our message. Civilians are returning to their homes once more."

"That's good news," Susan responded. "We have to reconcentrate our populations in a hurry to maximize the number of people the Ghosts can carry before the Stickmen return." She frowned as she thought about the battle and added, "We've learned something significant about these Stickmen; they demonstrated such a maniacal determination to destroy the Ghost ships, it became obvious their personal survival did not concern to them at all, and an enemy that doesn't fear death is the most terrifying kind of enemy."

"A frightening characteristic indeed, nevertheless, one that actually worked in our favor," Svetlana countered. "I believe their lack of self-preservation contributed to our victory just as much as the courage of our fighters who took advantage of it. They practically let us shoot them down in their rabid determination to destroy the Seed ships rather than defend themselves properly."

"You all seem to be forgetting something. Dozens of active Stickman bases remain all over the solar system. Our enhanced tacticals are revealing the power signatures of all of them. They may not have any ships left, but the bases they came from still have support personnel left behind. It's time for us to make them disappear too! We can't leave their foothold in the solar system intact!" Pete told them venomously.

"Noah: Fleet Admiral Orsini, I apologize, but I must respectfully disagree with you in the strongest of terms. You *must* understand the Stickmen will be back in overwhelming numbers. The time we have for rescuing Earth's population is extremely limited. The obsession of the Stickmen to destroy all life forms is an unquenchable thirst for them. Now that the human race has proved to be a formidable threat to them, the first they've ever encountered, their ultimate priority will be to come back with a truly irresistible force to hunt your people down and destroy them.

"I believe they will try to do so with a ferocity and disregard for their lives that will go far beyond what we have ever seen before. When they return, there will be no stopping them this time!

"You must also remember that we Ghosts have a minimal number of Seed ships that have never before been tasked with rescuing the population of an entire planet. The number of your people we Ghosts have already transferred is only a tiny fraction of the concentrations of human population centers still scattered all over the planet. The magnitude of rescue work needed to save everyone on your world is still quite beyond our capability to achieve within the amount of time I believe we have left before the enemy returns. Our task has barely begun. For the sake of collecting every innocent life we can possibly gather, you must ignore the former Stickman swarm bases for now and use this precious time to help us save your people."

"I agree with Commander Noah," Jackson said. "We have to take full advantage of the time left to us and do everything we possibly can to transfer people to safety."

With a scowl, Orsini reluctantly nodded in agreement.

"Looks like it's unanimous," Lee replied. "Commander Noah, do you have any idea how much time we have before the Stickmen return?"

"Noah: With their primitive wormhole drives, it will take several days for them to reach their homeworlds, but you must remember their thought communications systems are instantaneous, and their range of communication can span most of the galaxy. The death ships that survived do not have to return to their homeworld to deliver the news of what has happened here. I assure you that their homeworlds are already reacting to their report.

"We estimate that if the Stickmen gather their forces from just their nearest colonies, their return could come in as little as nine days. If they gather their fleet from all the worlds of their empire, it may take as long as thirty-seven of your days. When they arrive," he reemphasized, "I truly believe they will be unstoppable!"

"Noah," Ruark asked the Ghost Commander, "can your Ghost people reconfigure the ships we have left to the same level as my masked Super Dragons?"

"Noah: Yes, Fleet Admiral Ruark, but that will render each ship undergoing the change to be inoperable for one full day of your time. It is a day we can put to better use by commanding your small fighting ships to help locate and gather your scattered people and shuttle them to safety. Through the remarkable skills of your people, your small force of Dragon fighters has inconceivably managed to destroy many times their number of swarm fighters, but when the Stickmen return, they will number thousands to one against you. You cannot prevail a second time!"

Those gathered said nothing, none of them able to dispute the truth of Noah's words.

Jackson Ruark broke the silence. "We need to come up with a new plan quickly, people," he told them, stating the obvious. "We'll need some extraordinary ideas on how to maximize the use of the Ghost's technical talents."

"We need Dr. Ling back," Svetlana concluded for him. "The power signatures for both Hong Kong and Ling Wu's command center, I know, are gone. Commander Noah, can you help us find out if Hong Kong survived one of your Seed ship's attempted rescues and, if so, where that Seed ship transplanted it?"

"Noah: We can do this, Fleet Admiral Ivanovna. I will gather this information immediately."

Chapter 69
Transplanted

"Dr. Ling, are you alright?" Ling Wu heard a concerned voice ask as he rose unsteadily out of his chair to his feet again. He raised a hand to his forehead as the overwhelming feeling of disorientation and the bit of nausea he felt briefly began to fade. The question came from Ignacy, the same technician who, earlier, called his attention to the view of Hong Kong's capture and who presently stood over him with a concerned expression.

Ling Wu's staff began to stir, the ones less affected by the transition through the wormhole helping those slower to recover.

"I felt light-headed momentarily, but I'm fine now. Thank you for your concern, Ignacy," Ling Wu said with a pat on the technician's shoulder as the young man helped him rise out of his chair.

Backup emergency lighting dimly lit the room. The backup generators kicked on to restore limited power throughout the base when the center's sensors detected the absence of external power sources.

Ling Wu glanced about the control center. Monitors and communications equipment were coming back online, but there were no longer any signals to receive or satellites to feed them images. His base and the captured city of Hong Kong remained encased by the Seed ship bubble as it traveled toward its destination.

"Everyone, please, check on the well-being of those near you. Search the base for anyone who may be injured," Ling Wu called out. "Afterward, please I want all personnel to gather here at the control center." A communications technician went to a nearby console and announced Ling Wu's requests via the base public address system.

Fortunately, no one was injured and, soon al two hundred EDF support personnel managing Ling Wu's headquarters gravitated to the central command center. The control room became too jammed for everyone. Latecomers had to stand just outside the control room entranceway. Ling Wu saw that, without exception, the faces of those around him displayed

314

expressions of fear, uncertainty, and apprehension of what their future held. He waited until the last of them gathered before he addressed them.

"My loyal friends, we are among a fortunate few who have been taken to safety from our world, all of us rescued from the slaughter that our Stickman enemies would have inflicted upon us. We saw from our satellite feeds that the expanding shell of the Seed ship that now carries us scooped up a large part of Hong Kong and swept toward our base, presumably enclosing it along with the city, as evidenced by our lack of power.

"We don't know where the Ghost people are taking us, but I know that wherever it is, we will be far from the Stickmen's reach. Please be patient until this lifeboat of a protective bubble releases us. We'll determine what to do next then."

Instead of returning futilely to their posts, most of the headquarters' staff chose to linger near the control room together. Their first view of outside their sealed headquarters would come from there. Although diagnostics indicated that all external cameras were functional, the monitors tied to them displayed nothing but inky blackness.

Just over ten minutes later, the time it took for the seed ship to approach the sanctuary planet and deposit its Hong Kong cargo, the monitors lit up again. The base perimeter became flooded with daylight once more now that the Seed ship's encasing shell was gone as if it never existed.

"Doctor Ling, it appears we've arrived," a technician called out needlessly.

Ling Wu focused his attention on the monitors to see for himself, the base personnel crowding around to view the monitors with him. To their confusion, they saw nothing more than what the cameras displayed before the shell encased the base.

"Can you manipulate the outside cameras?" Ling Wu asked.

"Yes, but they only cover the approach to our area and everything from the entrance to the gate. No one saw a need to expand their range of view any further."

"Then we will see nothing more than we normally have in the past," Dr. Ling concluded. "We must remember that many square miles of our planet have been carried away with us, and while we are almost certainly on the outskirts of the section taken, we are also inside a mountain that obscures our view in the direction closest to the edge. To see anything more, we must go outside." He gestured toward the exit hallway, and, as crowded as the room was, the people parted to allow Dr. Ling to lead the way.

With the main entrance to Ling Wu's headquarters carved into the side of a mountain, the installation's only point of entry and exit, barring its several emergency escape tunnels. Entry into the heart of the complex required passing through a large set of extra-thick metal doors designed to withstand the blast of a nuclear explosion. The doors were ordered sealed shut since the Seed ship invasion began.

Ling Wu gave the order to open the doors. They slid sideways to provide passage to the externally attached security building where headquarters personnel and visitors were obliged to identify themselves to access the buried command center. Ling Wu preceded his people through the security building and into the open.

Outside, a strange and beautiful sight greeted the group. Most of Hong Kong, its surrounding countryside, and more distant urban areas could be seen from the headquarters' high vantage point as base personnel were accustomed to seeing. However, where the familiar landscape ended, the panorama beyond had changed enormously. While a large part of Kowloon appeared below, gone was the sea that separated it from Hong Kong Island. The parts of the sea captured with the city were now salt-water lakes contained within the new crater where the Seed ship deposited its cargo. At the moment, there was no way for Ling Wu and his people to know yet how much of the island of Hong Kong the Seed ship had scooped up.

The Ghost ship took a bigger cut out of Kowloon than Hong Kong Island to maximize the number of people to save. Now, where the cutaway part of Kowloon ended, a pristine forest stood instead of the sprawling city that used to be there. The forest ran with a gradual upward slope to the foot of a majestic range of snow-capped mountains standing a good seventy-five miles away.

Even with a bright sun midway between the horizon and the highest point of a deep blue sky, two pale moons sat close to the skyline and remained bright enough to share the daylight sky. Ling Wu and his people could see what they thought to be bodies of water on the surface of one of the moons as well as clouds above it. The group couldn't tell if the orbs were rising or setting; several more minutes would answer that question.

Ling Wu's people could see the shining lozenge-shape of a Seed ship's enclosing shell dropping down out of the sky Far off in the distance. Its enormous shell made swirling mists out of clouds banks it pushed aside as it lowered itself to the ground. The size of the ship was a fearsome thing to behold even though they knew it brought more refugees from Earth.

People continued to point out features of the distant landscape to each other, their voices filled with wonder. However, despite the planet's pristine beauty, Ling Wu could see that those among his base personnel who had family in the city below were far more interested in finding them than viewing the far-off wonders of their new planet.

Calling loudly out to the crowd, he told them, "I know all of you are all concerned about your families and friends. We must pray that your families are among those brought to this haven for those of you who have homes in other cities and other countries back on Earth. For any of you fortunate enough to live near our base, you are free to go and search for your families."

Colonel Kang, the base security commander, stepped forward and held up his hands to stop anyone from leaving.   "Dr. Ling, sir, we have been transferred to a whole new world, one we know nothing about. From what we can see beyond Hong Kong, it's certainly beautiful out there, but we have no idea what dangers might exist. I recommend we all stay in place until we can send out several scouting teams to find out what we are facing."

"Colonel Kang, as sound as your advice is, I am certain our new alien friends would not take us from harm's way to place us in danger on another world. I must also remind you that most of what is around us for many miles is still a large piece of our own planet. Please allow our people to pass so they can find their families and discover for themselves what this new world has to offer."

The Colonel considered the matter, then grudgingly nodded and stepped aside. "As you wish, Dr. Ling."

Nearly eighty of the command center's two hundred personnel, including four of Colonel Kang's men, had families stationed with them near the base.

Those leaving exchanged well wishes with those staying, and with tears parting handshakes, the two groups separated. The Colonel himself remained at Ling Wu's side.

"Are you not going with them, Colonel? If I recall correctly, you have family in Kowloon."

The Colonel could not meet Ling Wu's eyes, embarrassed by tears forming there as he enviously watched the lucky ones disperse to find their cars and trucks. In a husky voice, he replied, "My family lives in Tseung Kwan O. It is on the other side of the Black Hill Ridge. The Black Hill Ridge did not come with us."

Ling Wu put a sympathetic hand on the Colonel's shoulder. "I'm truly sorry, Colonel, but please do not give up hope. More ships are coming carrying our people." The Colonel gave a curt nod, unconvinced his family would be among them.

Ling Wu knew the man needed something to take his mind off his separation from his family. "Colonel Kang, the people in the city below must surely be frightened and confused. Our EDF ground force headquarters in the city will surely be overwhelmed trying to maintain order. Would you and those still left of your men please consider reporting there? I want you to place yourselves at the disposal of General Forsyth, the area commander there, and help him try to maintain order. There are several former soldiers still left among my remaining staff who can protect us if we still need it."

Clearing his throat with a cough, Kang replied, "We will do so immediately, Dr. Ling." With that, he began barking orders to his men as he led them to the site's parked security vehicles.

With just over one hundred people left of his base personnel remaining with him, Ling Wu knew they, too, needed something to take their minds off their families. He led them back inside and set them to work to establish communications with other transplanted cities deposited on this beautiful new world.

Chapter 70
Ling Wu Found

Nearly a day later, Earth time, Ling Wu's people already made contact with the sections of London, Brisbane, Marseilles, Oklahoma City, and dozens of other cities, large and small, brought to this world. His staff created a makeshift map of the planet from the information they gathered. The map consisted of a series of circles devoid of geographical features. It simply represented hemispherical depictions of the new planet on which his staff plotted the roughly calculated positions of captured cities with respect to each other. As Ling Wu reviewed their progress, the lights flickered and grew brighter.

"Dr. Ling, sir," one of the control room technicians called, "External power has just been restored somehow! The generators just went offline."

Seconds later, a very excited staff member burst into the control room. "Dr. Ling, please come outside. You will certainly want to see this!"

His curiosity piqued, Ling Wu followed the worker back through the security building and outside again, most of his staff trailing along to see what caused the man to be so excited.

The light was fading, and the clouds in the twilight sky were gorgeous with orange, pink, and purple hues of the alien sun already set below the horizon. Those already gathered outside pointed excitedly to the chunk of Hong Kong and Kowloon below them in the distance. In some sections of the city, the lights were on! As they watched, entire city blocks began to light up one after another.

"All the power lines coming into the city were severed! How can this be happening?" someone asked.

Ling Wu watched in awe as the rest of the city lights came to life and silently berated himself for needlessly agonizing over how the transplanted cities would survive the loss of all basic utilities. He should have realized that the new Ghost allies would care for their needs through their advanced technology.

When Colonel Duval reappeared at Lee McKay's headquarters, he explained to him the Ghosts' use of nanites, but he failed to grasp the depth of how powerful a tool those microscopic machines could be until now.

"Dr. Ling, over there!" One of the control room officers called to him, pointing to the sky in the direction where the sky still glowed the brightest.

A Dragon ship raced in their direction out of the twilight of a turquoise sky, the light of the sun well below the horizon reflecting off its mirrored surface to make it glow a bright orange. In a few heartbeats, it closed the distance to the Hong Kong base and came to an immediate halt directly above the small group of people below.

When the ship lowered itself to hover three feet off the ground, a portal opened, and a ramp formed that barely touched the ground before its pilot emerged, gazing all around as he strode down the ramp. He turned and beckoned to someone inside the ship, which then disgorged the members of six large families, consisting mainly of children, who had all been crammed inside. Satisfied they were all accounted for, The Dragon's pilot spotted Ling Wu among the small gathering of his base personnel and walked quickly over to him, breathing a visible sigh of relief as he snapped to attention to salute the doctor.

"Sir, I'm Lieutenant Commander Joshua Harkins of the EDF Northern Defense Zone. I was one of Fleet Admiral McKay's fighters, but I currently serve under Fleet Admiral Ruark. I am truly honored to meet you, sir. However, the fleet admirals urgently request that you return to our home system."

Ling Wu reached out and shook Harkin's hand. "I believe I can guess why you've come to find me. I held great hope but little confidence that someone would eventually come. Can I joyously presume, then, that our Dragons have somehow managed to prevail against the Stickman forces?"

"Yes, sir, at least for the time being." Joshua took the time to give Ling Wu a summary of the critical events of the battle, the Ghost's contributions to it, and the outcome.

Finishing his review, he noticed the doctor looking toward the families Joshua brought. Josh glanced over his shoulder and, with a tilt of his head toward his former passengers, he said, "All of the Dragons are bringing people here, sir. My mission was to find you, but no trip to this planet goes to waste.

"Very efficient, Lieutenant Commander.

"We knew you would approve, sir. But if I may say so, we owe our lives to you as much as the Ghost people. It was your genius behind the orchestrated development of Earth's defenses. You are still the one person the world authorized to make decisions on the entire planet, and we need you back again! Will you please accompany me back to Earth? We desperately need your guidance again back home."

Ling Wu was surprised to see that the young man seemed anxious as if half expecting Ling Wu to refuse the request as if he would! "Of course, I will return to Earth with you. Please be at ease Lieutenant Commander."

"Commander Noah, the Ghost commander of the Seed ship fleet, assures us the Stickmen will be returning with an unstoppable force soon. We don't know how long we have, but we believe it will be a least a couple of weeks." Joshua looked around, clearly puzzled. "Is this your entire headquarters staff, sir?"

"The fortunate ones among us have families in the transplanted part of the city below. I dismissed them all to go find them."

A frown formed as he pondered what Harkins told him. "Two weeks," he muttered distractedly to himself. "The Seed ships must have certainly brought thousands of our towns and cities here, but most are just very small pieces of them. How do we even begin to gather those who are left?"

"That's just one reason why we need to bring you back, sir," Harkins told him. "The Ghosts neutralized the Stickman self-destruct inside my ship, so there's no need to worry about that. Are you able to immediately return to Earth with me, sir?"

"Lead the way, Lieutenant Commander Harkins. I must warn you, though, that I've never flown within one of these remarkable ships."

"I promise I'll take good care of you. Please follow me."

Ling Wu took several moments to locate the most senior ranking officers of his staff to give instructions for the care of the newly arrived refugees and, with a promise he would return when he could, he followed Harkins up the ramp of his ship.

Ling Wu went to a seat that rose out of the deck for him. It bore a resemblance to an enormous, silvery, upside-down mushroom cap. When he gingerly sat upon it, he marveled at how it formed itself around him, even though from reading the report about Dragon ship studies, he expected the seat to adjust to his body shape. The ship's walls became transparent the moment Harkins took his seat, and the clarity of the view astounded Ling Wu as it created the perfect illusion of no wall existing at all between the two men and the outside of the ship.

Harkins glanced over at his passenger to satisfy himself that Ling Wu was settled comfortably.

"Are you ready, sir?"

Ever cautious and conscious of detail, Ling Wu replied, "You are clearly a very fit and healthy young man, Lieutenant Commander Harkins, but I would not like to be unprepared for the extremely remote chance that you become ill or incapacitated while we are in transit. I understand this ship can teach me how to control it?"

Harkins smiled and said, "No problem, Dr. Ling." Joshua sent a mental command to his ship. Ling Wu's first knowledge transfer experience left him filled with wonder.

Chapter 71
Returned

"I've ordered to head for the Ghost command ship," Harkins told his important passenger moments after his fighter ship latched on to a beacon signal and popped back into near-Earth space.

"I am quite excited, Lieutenant Commander," Ling Wu confessed as he looked out through the viewing field of Harkin's ship. "I have never seen one of these Ghost beings except through the holograms the Stickmen provided us,"

Through the Dragon's viewing field, he marveled at the beauty of his homeworld that grew larger as they approached. At a half-million miles out, the moon added to the beauty of the vista spread before him. In the clarity of the vacuum of space, Ling Wu perceived a haze around the entire planet whose origin puzzled him momentarily until he mournfully realized that it was composed of the debris of hundreds of thousands of shattered ships belonging to both friend and foe alike. Shreds of that wreckage would continue to rain down through the atmosphere in fiery trails for years, and perhaps even for centuries to come, as Earth's gravity pulled the remains out of orbit.

"I have wondered if these Ghost people truly look like the Stickmen presented them to us via their holograms, or if their distasteful appearance might yet be another part of their deception."

"I assure you, sir, they do look exactly like they did in the holograms," Harkins replied. "Don't worry, though, sir. I've worked alongside them at our remote base with Fleet Admiral Ruark. They're terrific folks!"

Ling Wu smiled at Harkin's comfortable familiarity with the Ghosts to enable him to think of them as 'folks.'

Harkins paid close attention to his tactical hologram for a moment and announced, "Commander Noah's ship is just ahead, sir."

A silvery dot in the distance came into view and quickly grew to a size that dwarfed Harkin's Dragon as they drew closer.

323

"That silvery surface you see isn't the ship itself," Harkins explained, "It's just a protective outer shield of some kind. We're going to pass right through it, so don't be afraid. We're not going to collide with anything solid."

"Thank you for telling me, Lieutenant Commander. I suspect our approach would indeed have caused me a moment of anxiety without that advanced warning."

As Harkins approached the Ghost command ship, the Earth filled much of the viewing field just a thousand miles away. Even at this distance, Ling Wu could easily see pinpoints of light rising out of Earth's atmosphere and others descending. He knew those lights were the Ghost Seed ships still working tirelessly to gather Earth's population. With a sorrowful heart, it reminded him again why his fleet admirals wanted him back.

Harkins slowed his ship, and despite knowing the outer sphere wasn't solid, he gingerly approached its surface and slowed to a crawl as he made contact with it. Continuing forward, his ship passed through its boundary as though it were nothing but a mirage. In the pitch-blackness of the shell's interior, light spilled out into the darkness not too far ahead, growing brighter as a hangar portal opened fully on the hull of Noah's command ship.

As Harkins expected, something took control of his Dragon to tug it toward the opening. Once fully inside, the ship was placed in a parked position three feet above the metal deck, and Harkins sent a mentally directed command to open his ship's exit portal and extend the exit ramp to the deck below.

With the Dragon ship's viewing field still active, Ling Wu looked out into a massive hangar bay where six other Dragon ships floated in parked positions next to each other. "We are not the first to arrive," Ling Wu observed.

"No, sir, and as I said, I know everyone is quite anxious to have you back."

As Ling Wu accompanied Harkins down the ramp of his Dragon, an opening appeared in one of the internal hangar walls, and a reception party emerged. Ling Wu recognized all five of his fleet admirals and their first missing-in-action officer Colonel Duval. Two other humans accompanied them whom Ling Wu did not recognize, a bearded young man in civilian clothing and a young woman dressed in the tunic of an EDF Lieutenant.

Even though he knew the Ghost people were allies, Ling Wu's heart beat a bit faster when he saw the two tall white alien beings accompanying the group of humans.

"They do look exactly like the Stickmen presented them to us, Lieutenant Commander."

"Yes, sir, and as I said, they are great folks! Dr. Ling, I won't be joining you. I have to leave. You are in good hands. My Dragon is needed back down on Earth."

"Of course, Lieutenant Commander Harkins, and thank you for the extremely educational journey." Ling Wu held out his hand for a handshake, and Harkins took it, beaming him a huge smile.

"Anytime, Dr. Ling. Maybe you won't need anyone's taxi service anymore since you know how to fly one of these Dragons yourself now." With that, Harkins saluted and returned to his ship.

Lee McKay led the approaching welcoming committee and was the first to greet Ling Wu, offering his hand to the EDF leader. "Dr. Ling, welcome! I can't even begin to tell you how delighted we all are to see you safe and unharmed."

"Thank you, Fleet Admiral McKay. Ling Wu gladly accepted the welcome and the outstretched hands of the other fleet admirals, too, accepting a hug from Susan McKay instead of a handshake.

"Fleet Admiral Ruark, I was overjoyed to learn you are still alive. I can't possibly convey my admiration for the brilliant tactics and strategies Colonel Duval you and the rest of your staff conceived and executed. Absolutely ingenious! Back on Earth, we never dreamt that the people we lost to the Ghost ships during battle could still be alive! Without your inventiveness, our world would already be lost forever to the deceptions of the Stickman race."

"Thank you, sir, but it was the examples of your planning methods that inspired us," Ruark responded, self-conscious of the praise. Not wishing to dwell on further accolades, he immediately redirected the conversation. "Doctor Ling, may I introduce Jake Bennings and Captain Megan Bryant, both of whom proved to be invaluable assets to us during the most intense period of the conflict?"

Cheeks flaming with embarrassment, Megan Bryant shook Ling Wu's hand. Jake Bennings also took the doctor's hand next when his turn came, wide-eyed at meeting the most powerful leader Earth the people of Earth ever appointed.

Lee McKay had the honor of making Ling Wu's introductions to the Ghosts. "Dr. Ling, we would like you to meet two very important friends and allies. This is Noah, Commander of the Seed ship fleet, and the Ghost Chief Scientist, Pat," he said with an arm extended in the general direction of the two Ghost people and deliberately leaving out which was which. Despite all of his interaction with the Ghosts, he still couldn't tell them apart. He hoped no one noticed.

"Noah: I am delighted to meet Earth's greatest strategist," came a voice out of a small sphere that hung around Jackson Ruark's neck. Ling Wu noticed that all of the humans present wore such a necklace. Ruark stood closest to him, the device around his neck that 'spoke' in a very monotone voice sounding exactly like Jake Bennings.

Forewarned by Lieutenant Commander Harkins, Ling Wu already knew the Ghosts preceded their words with the prefix of their name when they spoke. The fact that they all sounded like Jake Bennings came as something of a surprise, though, something Lieutenant Commander Harkins neglected to mention.

"Pat: I, too, am very pleased to meet you, Dr. Ling. We have heard much about you, and we are quite anxious to work with you as soon as possible." Once again, the voice sounded exactly like Jake's voice. Ling Wu could also feel small bursts of heat coming from the two alien beings as each one 'spoke.'

"If you'll allow me, Dr. Ling," Sue McKay said as she stepped forward and pulled a chain with a translator device from one of her flight suit's pockets to place around Ling Wu's neck.

"It's both a Ghost-improved thought communications unit for use among ourselves and a translation device we use to communicate with the Ghosts, even over great distances. You'll need it when we begin our meetings with them."

"Thank you, Susan. Commander Noah and . . . Pat, I am genuinely thrilled to meet you. Without the courage and sacrifice of your people, the human race would now be extinct. On behalf of the human race, I must tell you that we will never be able to thank you enough. However, I have been informed that the danger has not yet been eliminated, and I witnessed your Seed ships still at work on our planet as we approached your ship. That can only mean one thing."

"Noah: Your implied conclusion is correct. Dr. Ling. We are all in need of your extraordinary strategic and organizational knowledge once more. We believe we only have only a short time before the Stickmen return with an irresistible force of destructive vessels. We Ghosts have just over six thousand of our Seed ships left out of an armada originally numbering over eight thousand; a fleet that, even at full strength, has never before been tasked with saving all the creatures of an entire planet. Your Dragons have joined in, packing their Dragons with evacuees to maximize the number of people we can save."

"We're so relieved that we were able to find you and bring you back to help us," Susan told the Doctor.

From the hopeful expressions of the people looking back at him, Ling Wu found it evident that they were counting on him to deliver miracles he had no idea how to produce. The burden of saving lives came down once more to land on his shoulders. With a sigh of resignation, he said, "We have much work to do and little time to prepare. But before we do anything, I wish to see the present state of our world for myself."

~ ~ ~

In silence, Jackson Ruark flew Ling Wu over some of the world's former great countries and cities. The devastation, carnage, and human suffering Ling Wu witnessed left him heartsick as Ruark passed above the planet. Despite his best efforts to coordinate the planet's defenses, he felt as if he failed miserably.

Ruark told him dejectedly, "You know, Doctor Ling, I saw a lot of this going on below us during the fighting as it occurred, but in the heat of battle, the magnitude of it all didn't hit me like it's hitting me now. The damage to Earth's civilization and ecology seems beyond salvage."

"Perhaps, in a matter of weeks, even this world may no longer exist, Fleet Admiral Ruark. I must confess I feel helpless to a degree I've never felt before, but somehow, someway, we must find a way to save our poor, battered planet. These horrific scenes below us must be used as a source to ignite a reinforcement of determination in us all."

"Noah told us the numbers they send against us this time will be uncountable."

"As Fleet Admiral Orsini is fond of saying, we must never give up, no matter what the odds; it is our solemn duty to the survivors below. While we live, there is always hope."

Given Ling Wu's confession of helplessness, Ruark wondered if the doctor truly believed that himself.

"Shall we head back to Noah's ship then? As you said, we have much to do."

"Before we return, take me to a place near Hong Kong called Tseung Kwan O. There is something I wish to do there, and I will need to make use of your ship's thought communications system.

Ruark couldn't imagine what the doctor wanted to do there but didn't question his commander. As ordered, he turned his Dragon toward Hong Kong, or at least toward what remained of it.

~ ~ ~

Many hours later, a Dragon dropped out of the sky of the planet holding Earth's refugee cities. It landed near the center of transplanted Hong Kong and Kowloon. Joshua Harkins used his thought communications system to locate Ling Wu's former security commander, Colonel Kang. To take his troubled mind off the loss of his family, Kang kept himself working almost non-stop to help direct and settle previous Dragon loads of evacuees. Ghost nanite construction made housing seem to grow from nothing on the city's outskirts.

Finding the Colonel helping direct a group of refugees, Joshua called out to him via his communications system. "Colonel Kang, my name is Lieutenant Command Harkins. We met when I came for Dr. Ling. Could you please meet me when I arrive? I have another ship full of evacuees to deliver to your care."

"I will do so, Lieutenant Commander. We are ready to accept them."

Wearily, Kang watched the incoming EDF Dragon float gracefully above Kowloon to come to a stop one hundred feet above him, then gently lower itself into a parked position and extend its ramp. Nearly three dozen passengers filed out from their crowding on the main deck and below in the living quarters of Harkin's Dragon. Kang's wife and two daughters were the first ones down the ramp.

Chapter 72
Mystery Solved

Landing inside Noah's Seed ship, Ruark led the doctor to the ship's conference room where the remaining fleet admirals, Pat, Noah, and Jake Bennings, were already gathered. As Ling Wu expected, its metallic walls and floors were without adornment or decoration. It surprised him, though, to see an ordinary-looking conference table and comfortably cushioned chairs indistinguishable from human furniture at the head of the table and along one side.

Taking note of Ling Wu's surprise, Ruark informed him, "This is all Jake Bennings doing, Dr. Ling. He's spent many months among the Ghosts and has long since instructed them on the details of human needs and comfort."

Ling Wu nodded appreciatively and took the seat at the head of the conference table, the remaining humans seated along one side and the two Ghosts standing, as always, on the opposite side.

Ling Wu began the conference. "As you all know, with Fleet Admiral Ruark's assistance, we assessed the damage to our world in the aftermath of the conflict. The number of civilians and Dragon fighters killed in this conflict is horrifying. Millions of our civilians died from the Stickman attacks on the Seed ships carrying away our cities and their direct attacks against our people on the ground.

"Regretfully, despite the best intentions of the Ghost people, thousands of additional casualties resulted from the environmental disasters caused by the huge craters the Seed ships left behind. Seas and oceans poured cataclysmically into the new craters, and, in some places, magma pools became exposed by the mile-deep excavations made by the Seed ships. The resulting seismic and volcanic activity its toll on the surrounding populations."

"Noah: We deeply regret the loss of innocent human lives. While we were aware of an unavoidable loss of human life, you must remember that we also believed that the remainder of the human population would soon

329

be incinerated along with your entire planet, as yet they may be. Some of our seed ships are restoring landmass to the volcanically active craters to prevent further suffering and loss of life. If the Stickmen were not returning, we could repair much more of the damage to your world, but in the short time remaining to us, we must rescue as many of your people that we possibly can before they arrive."

"We knew, upfront, casualties would happen, Noah," Jackson Ruark assured the Ghost commander. "We are not so backward in our understanding of physics to believe that there would be no consequences to removing major chunks of our planet; no one holds that against your people. On the contrary, we realize that no one would be alive right now if it weren't for the intervention and sacrifices of your people to help us. The only thing that matters now is our urgent need to defend ourselves once more against another inevitable attack."

"Defend ourselves with what?" Pete Orsini protested. "The Ghosts have already told us, without a doubt, that there will be millions upon millions of Stickmen ships coming to finish us off. We have only a few hundred thousand of our fighters left!"

"Fleet Admiral Orsini, is it not you who have always insisted that we must never give up?" Receiving an embarrassed scowl from Orsini in return for having his motto turned against him, Ling Wu looked over the rest of the faces of the others for any other signs of surrender. Finding none, he said, "Let us begin then. We have very little time and much work to do. Commander Noah, what is the current status of your Seed ship fleet?"

"Noah: Our Seed ships continue to gather the growing concentrations of refugees returning to collection point cities all over your planet," the Seed ship commander informed Ling Wu and the fleet admirals several days after their previous meeting.

"That's positive news. Thanks to the knowledge transfer broadcasts of our Dragon ships, they know the evacuation of Earth may be the only thing that can save them," Ling Wu responded. "However, while the total evacuation of our population before the Stickmen return is imperative, we must also accept the reality that it is impossible!"

"Noah: Regretfully so. To determine how much time we have left, I've sent hundreds of masked Ghost scout ships to every known Stickman star system to watch for a gathering of their forces. With the closest enemy star system nine days distant and their furthest system seventeen days away, we must hope that all Stickman worlds contribute to their retaliatory forces. The time needed for all of them to gather would grant us several extra days to continue to rescue as many of your people as we can.

"Every available Dragon ship is working night and day to transfer refugees to the new planet or to help locate and shuttle every remotely situated group of people they can find to collection points," Lee McKay reported. "The knowledge transfers the Dragons keep broadcasting are key to convincing even the most primitive peoples of Earth's population to leave their villages and join the mass exodus."

"Noah is right, though," Pete Orsini concluded dejectedly. "No matter how the next Stickman attack unfolds, given the paltry few EDF defenders who have survived, we'll only be able to save a fraction of the billions of our world's population. I can't bear the thought of abandoning them when the time comes."

"Must I quote you, once again, Fleet admiral Orsini, about giving up?" Ling Wu responded with a grim smile. He then turned his attention to the rest of the group. "I'm told that, somehow, eight great ships of the Stickmen were destroyed. Have we learned how this happened?"

"We have, Dr. Ling." Svetlana went straight to the facts as she held the undivided attention of everyone in the room, Ghost and human alike. "In just over a day since the battles ended, we've had multiple research teams, with the help of the Stickmen's technology, scouring and analyzing the records of as many tactical systems we could locate that might contain clues regarding the mystifying destruction of the great Stickman extermination ships.

"We were able to conclude without a doubt that a group of eight Dragon ships executed the attack single-handedly. Useful information proved very difficult to uncover since their entire attack on the super-ships lasted only a few short seconds, with the Dragons involved proving to be invisible even to our enhanced tracking capabilities. That is why it took so long to piece together the information we currently have."

The findings left everyone in the room stunned. "Eight lone Dragons? How is that even possible?" Orsini interrupted. "Those ships had no masking capabilities whatsoever, and their weapons would have barely dented those monster ships!"

"Working together in a coordinated manner, the pilots who flew those Dragons placed themselves adrift in space among the debris and wreckage of the thousands of our Dragon ships demolished by the Stickman destruct signal. Then these eight courageous people simply turned off all of their ships' power systems and played dead, leaving no power signatures any standard or enhanced tactical systems could have detected!"

Orsini nodded to himself appreciatively. "Absolutely brilliant!"

"It was very painstaking work, but we managed to trace this group's activities from the point in time where they hid among the debris, back to their participation in defense of a Seed ship attempting to carry away the Japanese town of Okazaki. Originally, they were a squadron of eleven, and we speculate Okazaki must have been their home.

Unfortunately, a Seed ship captured nearby Nagoya just moments earlier, and most of the available area defenders were already busy protecting that ship. The Seed ship carrying Okazaki fell under heavy attack by overwhelming numbers of Stickman Swarm ships that were just too many for the eleven Dragons to prevail.

"I must tell you, though, the level of devastation those eleven men wrought upon the enemy in defense of their city is nothing short of astonishing! Nine of the defending ships remained unscathed when the Stickman swarms destroyed the Seed ship carrying Okazaki despite their heroic efforts. Those nine pursued and relentlessly dispatched what remained four swarms of Stickman fighters. Together they destroyed every Swarm ship that participated in the destruction of the Seed ship carrying Okazaki. In doing so, they lost only one more of their number.

"When they finished, one of the eight surviving ships immediately abandoned the fighting on Earth and set a course directly for the dreadnought ships. The remaining seven followed him. They all scattered away from each other some distance beyond the moon, placing themselves directly in the path of the oncoming super-ships. There they remained hidden until the dreadnoughts passed them by."

"But how did eight small Dragon Fighters take out ten dreadnoughts?" a baffled and intrigued Orsini demanded once again.

"With their power signatures gone, the Stickman super-ships couldn't detect the hidden Dragons any more than any of us could even with our enhanced tactical systems. When the dreadnoughts passed their locations, all eight ships activated their ship's drives within seconds of each other. That is the point where our enhanced tacticals once again picked up their power signatures. The last thing the tactical recordings revealed to us is that each one of those Dragons went to sub-light speed then to mini-jump drive, charging directly toward the dreadnaughts. The recorded images show each of them entering one final wormhole from which none of them visibly emerged again anywhere.

"Our irrefutable conclusion is that all eight Dragons directed their ships to come out of their wormholes *inside* one of the dreadnoughts. At the near-light speed they traveled when they emerged, the devastation they caused was horrendous. Not only did each Dragon totally vaporize the ship it targeted, the energy released by the internal collision created eight mini-novas which damaged or destroyed two more of the remaining super-ships unfortunate enough to be too close to the others. Only two hundred ninety thousand survived intact of the more than one million Swarm ships providing a leading shield for the dreadnaughts. Of those, just two hundred twenty thousand remained functional, the rest rendered helpless derelicts."

The group met Svetlana's report with stunned silence. It was Noah who spoke first.

"Noah: In all of the centuries of opposing the Stickmen, never has a Stickman super-ship been attacked, let alone destroyed. I assure everyone that the critical turning point of the entire battle came directly from the sacrifice of those eight brave human beings. The number of Ghost and human lives they saved by their selfless act is incalculable."

"Svetlana, do we know who those people were? Were you able to identify them?

"Unfortunately, not yet, but we will! But for them, our world would be lost. We have all paid a high price," she continued sadly. "So many civilians and warriors, Ghost and human alike, killed by the Stickmen. So many places were destroyed and in ruins; our planet in tatters. We have less than a quarter of our original forces left, and God alone knows how many people perished on the ground."

"There are heroes, humans, and Ghosts alike, whose names and selfless acts are the equal of what those eight people carried out, but we will never know who they are. We must always remain grateful to them all," Ling Wu told the group. "Most of all, we must not let any of these sacrifices be in vain. Those eight people proved to us that nothing is invincible. The miracle we are looking for may lie in the selfless act of those eight Dragon pilots. Let us study their actions more closely. If eight lone Dragons are capable of causing so much harm, perhaps we can find something we can use to defend ourselves more effectively from this evil race."

Chapter 73
A Ray of Hope?

With time running out, despite their adopted official motto to 'Never give up,' it was a grim, frustrated, and troubled group of humans and Ghosts who were near the end of yet again strategy meeting aboard Noah's ship. After brainstorming for over twelve hours, no trace of hope existed in any of their haunted expressions that they would find a way to keep another Stickman invasion at bay, especially knowing the predicted size of their forces. The group could not conceive of a single defensive scenario that could prevent the inevitable loss of thousands of additional lives among what remained of Earth's population and its Dragon defenders.

~ ~ ~

Susan McKay's hair was in disarray, and her eyes occasionally went unfocused as she struggled to keep them open. Another yawn escaped her as she stared stupidly at her cup from which she'd been gulping coffee. She distractedly wondered, once again, how the Ghosts kept it always filled and steaming hot. Svetlana Ivanovna mirrored Susan's state of fatigue

"Please replay the hologram once again," Ling Wu directed. His request met with several groans around the table.

"Dr. Ling, we've already played and studied the recording of the destruction of the super-ships over a dozen times," Pete Orsini whined. "We've beaten every possible defensive scenario to death, including this one, and we keep failing to find anything that will keep the Stickmen from rolling right over us when they return."

Ling Wu ignored his protest. Something displayed within the recordings continued to nag at his subconscious. So much so that Orsini's complaint didn't register enough to break his concentration. He knew there was something significant about the event which, oddly enough, nagged him more in his exhausted state than it did when he was fully alert, yet he couldn't quite grasp what it was. Once more, he studied the replay of a recorded hologram taken from a great distance that caught the moment the eight ships came out of hiding right up to the massive destruction of the super-ships short seconds later.

To Ling Wu, when the Dragon ships emerged from their wormholes at near-light speed, the mini-novas created by their collision with the dreadnoughts did not surprise him. What nagged at him was the appearance of eight secondary novas hundreds of miles away from the dreadnoughts at the points where each of the eight Dragons entered their wormholes for the last time.

Finally, the missing piece of the puzzle fell into place, and Ling Wu slowly nodded his head as he began to grasp the significance. There certainly could be something *very* useful there.

"Friends, we all know that the Dragon ships the Stickmen gave us are capable of traveling vast distances by employing frequent but relatively microscopic wormhole jumps compared to Seed ship capability, do we not?"

"Noah: That is correct, Dr. Ling."

The mentally exhausted team of strategists conceded several weary nods of agreement. Though weary of rehashing the same information repeatedly, they waited respectfully while Ling Wu tried to finish piecing together the idea forming in his mind.

When he spoke again, he asked, "Commander Noah, when your Seed ships use their wormhole weaponry on the Stickmen, please explain to me once again how the weapon works."

"Noah: Gladly, Dr. Wu," the tireless Ghost Commander replied. "While you humans still insist on calling it a weapon, it is simply a device that projects an opening or portal in space. If you'll permit me to use an overly simplistic example, imagine, if you will, a sheet of paper with a dot at each of its furthest edges. Metaphorically speaking, our wormhole generator folds that piece of paper until the two dots touch each other and then creates a portal. It works on the same principle your Dragon ships use to generate wormholes to make their jumps, as you call them. The difference between the Stickman portals and ours is that ours can span any distance within the universe with a single doorway.

"That is how we send the Stickman ships elsewhere, and it is also how we send your Dragon ships very precisely, with the help of beacon ships, to chosen destinations. Hopefully, Dr. Ling, this is a satisfactory explanation for why we do not consider this technology a weapon? It merely creates a doorway. Weapons kill; doorways do not."

"I understand perfectly, Commander Noah. Thank you for that very clear explanation."

"Dr. Ling, while this lesson in wormhole physics would be fascinating under normal circumstances, we've drifted from the subject of how we can defend the world without the need to have us all perform a 300 Spartan re-enactment," Orsini growled impatiently.

"Fleet Admiral Orsini, I agree we've spent many tedious hours examining and re-examining dozens of innovative ways to deploy the forces left to us, but none project endings that give us enough time to transport Earth's remaining population. Do you truly believe more hours spent searching for additional deployment strategies will eventually provide one that will take us beyond the impasse that we are simply overwhelmingly outnumbered?"

Pete's shoulders sagged in defeat. He knew Ling Wu was right. Wishing for a solution didn't mean one existed.

Ling Wu told him sympathetically, "Even if every one of our people were capable of the same self-sacrifice made by those eight heroes, there would still not be enough of us to destroy the armada expected to arrive soon. Therefore, the '300 Spartan re-enactment,' as you called it, is not a feasible solution in any case. As we discussed earlier, even if we created robotic missiles to perform the same task, the Ghost people are incapable of producing the number of missiles we would need to defend ourselves within the time we have left."

Ling Wu sighed deeply. "In the past, my friends, when I've reached an impasse such as this one, I've found it is best to look in other unlikely places for new straws to grasp, no matter how small."

Pete reluctantly nodded his head in surrender, his lips pressed together and his shoulders sagging in bitter disappointment.

"Commander Noah, please tell me a bit more about how this 'portal' device of yours operates."

"Noah: When under attack, a Seed ship crew will project a doorway in front of a Swarm ship no matter what direction it is traveling. Once the target has passed through the boundaries of the wormhole event, the doorway closes immediately. The time it takes from the firing of our weapon, as you call it, and the time we take to close it again is milliseconds. To the perception of an outside observer, the opening and closing seem to be instantaneous."

"Is there a reason for the short duration of the opening's existence?"

"Noah: A wormhole generator can only open one doorway at a time. We must close it again as quickly as possible to enable us to retarget another enemy ship; otherwise, we can leave such a portal open indefinitely."

"Are you considering using a wormhole weapon to stop the Stickmen somehow?" Jackson Ruark asked. "You already know that when my group of Super Dragons tried, we couldn't take out nearly as many of the super-swarm ships that we needed to for us to make a significant enough reduction of their numbers. Besides, the Stickmen already devised a counter-strategy to drive us off."

"Fleet Admiral Ruark, even though the Ghost wormhole weapon is an effective device, there are not enough of us to send the anticipated great numbers of enemy ships 'elsewhere' even if we converted all of our ships to Super Dragons." Ling Wu made sure he used the 'elsewhere' term that the Ghosts favored. "However, please bear with me for a few moments more, everyone," Ling Wu asked, holding up a hand to halt further debate and argument. He sat staring, unfocused, at a point on the conference table, deep in thought for several moments.

Lee McKay glanced over to Ruark and Orsini. Ruark shrugged his shoulders to indicate he had no idea where this was leading, and Orsini just shook his head as frustrated as ever.

"Commander Noah," Ling Wu said slowly, trying to formulate the right question, "when a Swarm ship passes through a wormhole, do they emerge in a direct line from the opening at a point somewhere else in the universe?"

"Noah: Once through the opening, there is no straight-line tunnel or shaft to the exit point; on the contrary, the opening simply causes two distant places to briefly touch each other, allowing an object to pass from one space to another.

"The wormhole generators can create an exit point anywhere, even in the opposite direction of travel of the ship that enters it. Curiously, even though the transition of moving from one space to another is instantaneous, the more distant the connecting spaces, the greater the sensation is of a long transition time experienced by the traveler.

"I must remind you, Dr. Ling, that the created doorway must be able to encompass the target completely. If you are thinking of using our wormhole gates to send the Stickman dreadnoughts elsewhere, these ships are far too large for any wormhole generator in existence to send them anywhere. Contrarily, while we cannot project overly large wormholes externally, wormhole generators can create openings around our seed ships that completely encompass them and their encasing shells as long as the wormhole generator is an integral part of those ships. Even then, only a massive internal power system can carry a large body through one of those openings."

Ling Wu stared, once more, in the direction of the hologram projector and sent a thought command to replay, once again, the scenes of the dreadnought destruction and the distant plasma flares that resulted.

"Fleet Admiral Ruark's Super Dragons have integrated into them the identical wormhole projection devices your Seed ships utilize, do they not? This is why, just like the seed ships, they can send the ships they target to the unknown distant points in the universe you refer to as elsewhere?'"

"Noah: Indeed. As I have instructed your fleet admirals, they can also precisely project a wormhole opening anywhere in the universe provided there is a beacon ship within at least a light-month of your miles from the desired exit point."

After working closely with Ling Wu, the group recognized that he was becoming excited about something. Everyone in the room focused on him with varying expressions ranging from impatience to budding hope that the good doctor might be on the verge of a workable idea at last. All waited anxiously for what he would say next.

"My friends," he said gravely, "we know we simply do not have enough defense ships left to survive a face-to-face encounter with the number of enemy ships expected to arrive. We all believe our Dragon ships would be swept aside by the anticipated Stickman force to the same degree a hurricane would sweep leaves from the ground. I do believe, though, there may be a way we might prevail."

That comment regained the room's full attention, this time the light of hope shining in everyone's eyes for the first time in days.

"Commander Noah, do I recall correctly that the modification of a Dragon fighter takes twenty-eight hours to convert it to the same enhancements as Fleet Admiral Ruark's group of Super Dragons?"

"Noah: That is correct, Dr. Ling. However, to do so, the ship must remain inactive as we make the modifications."

"Commander Noah, while I recognize the desperate need for as many of the unaltered Dragons as possible to remain free to help gather the vast remains of our population still on Earth, we must take a necessary risk. How long would it take for your people to generate the nanites needed to convert all of our ships into Super Dragons?"

"Noah: Our nanites are self-generating, and as they reproduce more of themselves, newly-produced nanites, in turn, produce even more. Their numbers increase exponentially as long as they have enough material to construct more of themselves. In a matter of hours, we can simultaneously infect and modify every Dragon ship in your possession to Super Dragon equivalency. As you correctly indicated, approximately twenty-eight hours are needed to complete their upgrades."

Ling Wu did some mental calculations as he pondered the information. "My friends, we have over four hundred thousand surviving ships. I am ordering half of them to be grounded immediately for conversion to Super Dragons. As soon as their reconstruction is complete, I am ordering the second half of them to be modified. By the Ghosts' most conservative estimates, the Stickman fleets could begin sending their armadas from their home solar systems at any moment. That said, we have at least nine days left to finish formulating an effective plan before the first of them arrive."

"Noah: We will do as you ordered, Dr. Ling, but I still fear this temporary incapacitation of your Dragons will result in the loss of many of your people who, otherwise, could be saved."

"I am well aware of that possibility, Commander Noah, but I ask you to trust me. Please issue the orders necessary for your people to begin converting our ships immediately."

Ling Wu looked off to his right where Jackson Ruark sat. "Fleet Admiral Ruark, you are most familiar with the capabilities of these Super Dragons. I will need the services of you and some of your people to help familiarize our pilots with the new capabilities their ships will soon have, but first, there is an experiment I want you to perform." Ling Wu then revealed his plan to the group.

Chapter 74
How Much Time Left?

Lee and Susan McKay sat aboard their newly upgraded ships parked side-by-side high above the Earth's atmosphere. They took in the beauty of their home planet far below and wondered how much longer it would exist.

"Thousands of chunks of our planet were taken away by the Seed ships, and you can barely tell from up here," Sue told her husband.

"It's still a world teeming with life. We could keep up the transfer of Earth-born life for another hundred years, and we still wouldn't be able to save it all."

"The Ghosts never intended the Seed ships to save everything on an entire planet, especially with just a few thousand Seed ships in their fleet. Until now, their sole objective has simply been to prevent total extinction of any alien species."

"Do you think Ling Wu's plan will work?"

"Against potentially three hundred fifty Stickman worlds? It's the only plan we have, but it's a damned fine one!" he replied with conviction.

Both of their hearts ached with the thought that humanity's birthplace and much of the human race itself might soon be gone if Ling Wu's strategy failed. The two lingered a while longer in silence until a message from their thought communications system interrupted their wistful admiration of Earth.

"Noah wanted me to inform you that the Stickmen are coming, Fleet Admirals," announced the voice of Captain Megan Bryant, presently reassigned to direct Ling Wu's communications staff.

～ ～ ～

Wasting no time after hearing Captain Bryant's message, all of the fleet admirals hastily gathered on Noah's flagship. They met with Ling Wu and Noah to piece together the final details of their plans based on the incoming information from the distant reconnoitering Ghost scout ships.

340

"How many are coming, and how much time do we have?" Jackson Ruark asked grimly.

"Noah: Our scout ships indicate that every one of the three hundred fifty Stickman worlds appears to be preparing for a retaliatory attack against your world. The vessels from the more distant worlds are already en route. However, this is to our benefit. With each of those enemy worlds contributing one of their great extermination ships, it will take longer for the more distant ships to arrive. We ascertain by their actions so far that the Stickman worlds are staggering the launching of their dreadnaughts to arrive in Earth's vicinity together at approximately the same time.

Svetlana Ivanovna blanched at the news. "Bozhe Moi! Three hundred fifty of their great ships as well as the swarm fighters they carry!"

"Noah: That would be a minimum of one hundred thousand Swarm ships apiece; thirty-five million in all. It appears that they are taking the threat your species poses to them quite seriously."

"That has to be one of the great understatements of all time!" an equally alarmed Lee McKay exclaimed, the staggering figure leaving everyone stunned.

"Noah: We project from the current paths of the convoys already on the way that they intend to converge at a single gathering point several hours outside the orbit of the planet you call Pluto. The number of their combined forces far exceeds the number of retaliatory ships that even we Ghosts anticipated. They will become the first swarm of planet-destroying super-ships that we Ghosts have ever seen."

Ling Wu rested his elbows on the conference room table and leaned his head on his clasped hands. He gazed with an unfocused stare at a point beyond the conference room table as he assessed this new information.

Slowly he nodded his head and surprised them all by saying, "Under the circumstances, I believe we could not ask for a more favorable development. It is fortunate that we took the time to modify all of our remaining Dragons, given the enormous size of the enemy fleet. We can now finalize our defensive plan and make the final adjustments as the last of the enemy ships arrive at their gathering point. Timing is the critical factor.

"In the meantime, in case our plan fails, our surviving forces must redouble their efforts to bring what remains of Earth's population to the designated gathering points. With the entire Hive Empire contributing to this vast armada from even their most distant solar systems, we have the good fortune to have at least another seventeen days until all of the approaching ships reach their gathering point. We must make the most of

341

the remaining time to continue with the evacuation of Earth's population before their armada arrives. Put ever Dragon we have to the task!"

Chapter 75
Hive Retribution

On the seventeenth day after the first of the Stickman Sterilizers began its journey to the edge of Earth's solar system, one great ship after another began to arrive at the predicted rendezvous point within hours of each other at a location just fourteen light-hours from the sun.

Each shipmaster ceded overall command to the grand fleet master, the first-ever in Hive history to oversee such a huge armada of Sterilizer ships.

The grand fleet master paid close attention to his tactical hologram as each Sterilizer ship arrived, one from each Hive star system. He personally directed them to pre-assigned positions to create a huge, spherical formation. Within that array, the distances between ships were more than enough to prevent the potential destruction of one ship damaging another should the same weapon be used against them that destroyed the previous Sterilizer fleet. This precaution came from one of the lessons learned after the careful evaluation of information brought back from humans' solar system by the surviving two Sterilizer ships.

Weeks earlier, the news of the astounding disaster that befell the Hive forces horrified the leadership of the Hive Empire. The Hive leadership disregarded the detailed information sent ahead by the fleet master returning from Earth's solar system. In their arrogance, they ruled that the vermin race of humans could not possibly have defeated the legion of Hive Swarm ships based within their star system. They deduced, instead, that the defeated fleet master must be a vastly flawed vassal of the Hive Empire, and they immediately reclassified him as a life form even lower than that of the humans. They also declared the fleet master's ship and its occupants contaminated by his presence. As the fleet master's Sterilizer entered its home solar system, Hive artificially intelligent control systems remotely overrode its navigation system and sent the great ship directly into its homeworld's sun. The last surviving ship was allowed to return home.

Afterward, Hive analysts attempted to study the recorded information brought back by the surviving ship's tactical system, but to their frustration, they found most of its memory damaged from the attack. The analysts knowledge-transferred what little useful information they harvested to every fleet master assigned to join the great extermination armada organized to return to the human's solar system.

The Hive Empire would never acknowledge that the size of the retaliatory armada they planned was equivalent to an admission of fear of the humans. They maintained that every Hive solar system sending one Sterilizer ship each fulfilled a great need for all Hive planets to participate in the Empire's craving to avenge the Humans' affront to their empire.

~ ~ ~

With each arrival of a Sterilizer ship, the grand fleet master's spherical formation became more solidified and formidable. Every ship received orders to release its entire flotilla of Swarm ships to both surround the sphere formation and fill it to protect their mother ships, thus making the armada stronger by the hour. The grand fleet master's positioned his Sterilizer ship safely in the center of a sphere packed with the Swarm ships that would doubly ensure his personal protection.

With the safeguarding of the great ships against the enemy's mysterious new weapon in place, the fleet master would soon order the Armada to go to near light speed to its target as soon as the last of the Sterilizer ships arrived.

No matter what weapon the enemy used to destroy the former armada of ten ships, the grand fleet master felt confident the humans would not dare confront his massive assault force. From the last known number of the Swarm ships the Hive gave them, they barely had the strength left to defend themselves against five Sterilizers, let alone hundreds. Soon the Hive would wipe the filthy life forms of this solar system from the universe.

Chapter 76
They Are Coming

"Ghost sensors indicate the last Stickman convoy of super-ships will be joining their great armada in two more hours," Ling Wu told his fleet admirals via a thought transfer sphere from the bridge of Noah's command ship. "The Ghost beacon ships are masked and in place near the Hive Armada's gathering point. Their beacon signals are already active."

"Noah: The remainder of our Seed ships is leaving Earth for the final time before the arrival of the Stickman fleet. No matter what the outcome of this encounter will be, the progeny of your planet will live on. We were truly gifted with the extra time we have to remove most of your human population. Still, there are several thousand Dragon fighters assigned to remain behind to continue to shuttle more of your planet's population up to the very last minute should our defense fail.

"We Ghosts have done all we can do. What happens next, Dr. Ling, is in the hands of your fleet admirals and their defending forces. The Ghost people offer you their hopes that the Great Creator will aid us all in bringing an end to the Stickman destruction of his wondrous works."

"We pray so too. Thank you, Commander Noah, but if we fail, know our people will always be in your debt for what you Ghosts have done for us."

Ling Wu turned his attention back to his commanders. "Fleet Admirals, let us begin."

∿ ∿ ∿

A half-million miles out from Earth, Pete Orsini, for the last time, stared out through his ship's viewing field, wishing, once again, he could see the positioning of his ships with his own eyes. Not only were they all too far away to perceive visually, their newest innovation of light-absorbing, jet black hulls would have made it difficult to spot them even if they floated right next to his ship.

Pete and the remaining four fleet admirals had ninety thousand fully enhanced Super Dragons assigned to them to command, nearly every ship

Earth had left to its defense. Pete turned back to his tactical hologram, where he could observe his nearby fleet's power signatures, verifying for the tenth time they were all perfectly in place. "Fleet One is ready to jump," he declared over his Dragon's thought communications system.

"Fleet Two ready," announced Sue McKay

"Fleet Three also is ready," Svetlana Ivanovna said.

"Fleet Four ready," Lee McKay confirmed.

"Fleet Five all set," Jackson Ruark finished.

"God be with you all," Ling Wu broadcast to the entire fleet from Noah's command ship. "Fleet Admirals, deploy your forces."

Chapter 77
Dragon Deployment

With their enhanced drive and navigation systems, the Super Dragons didn't need to rely on Ghost ships to push them through a wormhole gate to the super armada's gathering place. They could accurately cross the fourteen light-hours distance unaided with a single leap. However, to come out precisely where they wanted to be and to maintain a semblance of their formation at the exit point, they made use of the signals of beacon ships the Ghosts put in place near the gathering Stickman Armada.

When the fleet admirals gave the signal, all five attack fleets jumped seconds apart. Each massive fleet emerged in five separate volumes of space very near the gathering Stickman forces and well outside the calculated path of the last Stickman Sterilizer due to arrive shortly.

As ordered, the five Super Dragon fleets remained stationary at the point where they materialized while their fleet admirals studied every sensor at their disposal to uncover any sign that the enemy might have detected their EDF fleets.

"I'm getting nothing," Pete Orsini first reported after examining his tactical hologram and absorbing the mentally fed information his ship's sensors gave him.

"I, too, find no sign of detection," Svetlana confirmed. The readings Ruark and the McKays took confirmed both conclusions.

"I'm seeing three hundred forty-nine super-ships present and spaced in a ball formation approximately five hundred miles in diameter. They have a single Super-ship at the center of the formation; no doubt their brave Fleet Commander's ship."

"Dr. Ling, are you picking up this information?"

"I am," the Doctor confirmed. "I find it quite remarkable how your transmitted thoughts are as clear as if you were speaking right next to me despite the vast distance between us. Commander Noah indicates that the last arriving enemy ship will be there within thirty minutes. It should be in the range of your tactical systems very soon."

"Dr. Ling, please tell Commander Noah that I am sending him the exact size and position of every vessel in the enemy armada. We will be ready to receive the calculations his people make to optimize our attack." Svetlana Ivanovna called

Ling Wu's response came back in seconds. "It is done. The Ghost people sent individual positioning and targeting information to each of your Super Dragons."

"All forces, shift your Super Dragons to the coordinates you've received and direct your weapons."

As pre-planned, five attack fleets of over four hundred and fifty thousand masked Dragons drew toward each other, combining to create one massive gathering. Once they completed their maneuvering, they formed a curved curtain of ships, wrapped one-third of the way around the Stickman Armada, much like an enormous, bowl-shaped Centurion interception formation.

" Dr. Ling, we are in position," Sue McKay reported. "Every Super Dragon is poised at the maximum distance their wormhole projectors can reach their targets. The Stickman armada is so huge that we can see the enemy formation through our viewing fields, even from our distant position. The Stickman dreadnaughts have grouped into a spherical formation densely packed with Swarm ships inside and outside the sphere. The entire collection looks like a monstrous Christmas tree ornament reflecting the light from the sun."

"Commander Noah believes once the final Stickman super-ship arrives, their completed armada will need only moments to solidify its formation," Ling Wu warned. "There will be only a very brief integration period before their entire fleet begins its advance upon our solar system. You *must* strike before they activate their jump drives!"

"Roger that," Sue once again spoke for all of the fleet admirals. At the same time, Lee ran another set of calculations to generate a unique set of wormhole target coordinates for every Super Dragon present.

"All ships, make sure your wormhole projection points are programmed into your weapons systems to include wormhole entrance and exit point coordinates," Lee announced. "The final few target points will be assigned and delivered when the last arriving ship is in place. Be ready and do not hesitate to fire your weapons when I give the command! Turn off your viewing field systems immediately and be ready."

They waited less than six minutes before their tacticals picked up the last Sterilizer ship approaching. Like snipers waiting for the perfect moment to strike, the EDF Super Dragons waited patiently as the final

Hive Sterilizer popped into space several light-seconds out from where its sister Sterilizer ships waited for them.

Chapter 78
Chastisement

As the last Hive Sterilizer moved into position, the grand Fleet Master monitored its Swarm ships' deployment to complete the sphere formation. The final journey to obliterate the humans' world would begin in moments.

A minor alarm, mentally implanted, warned him of an anomaly. He gave it brief attention. Apparently, the light pattern from the myriads of stars in view on one side of the command ship changed slightly. Something, many somethings, individual masses, seemed to be blocking part of their light. He dismissed the warning as a nuisance alarm. Such warnings were common in the fringes of any solar system. They were triggered by constantly moving rivers of debris left from a solar system's formation. He turned his attention back to the final maneuvering of the last Sterilizer and its newly deployed swarms.

~ ~ ~

The EDF fleet admirals wasted no time triggering their ambush. If Ling Wu's plan failed, Earth would be left fully exposed and unprotected.

"All ships, open fire!" Lee issued the command to all forces while, at the same time, projecting the wormhole entrance and exit points of his Dragon's weapon system toward his own target.

All four hundred and fifty thousand Super Dragons peppered the entire Stickman sphere formation. Multiple wormholes opened up deep inside every one of the gigantic ships, with hundreds of thousands more opening within and just without the armada formation

~ ~ ~

Weeks earlier, when Ling Wu began to reveal his plan to his group of strategists, he directed them, once again, to watch the hologram of the eight Dragon ships attacking the Stickman super ships.

"This recording has troubled me since I first saw it," he told them. "I finally realized why. Carefully watch the point where each of the eight ships makes its last jump into the dreadnoughts they targeted."

The group obeyed, studying the scene with renewed interest and concentration as they struggled to comprehend whatever it was Ling Wu saw that they didn't.

One by one, over a matter of a few short seconds, the colossal enemy ships exploded, as evidenced by the massive energy signatures of the resulting mini-novas. As they'd seen many times before, eight small, secondary novas formed consisting of white-hot plasma ejected back through the wormhole openings like bazooka exhausts. All emerged at the last jump point of each of the self-sacrificing Dragon ships.

"The ejection of plasma appearing at each of the eight entry points of the wormholes makes it obvious the wormholes are bi-directional!" Ling Wu explained excitedly. "Matter can pass through from either direction once an opening forms." Ling Wu looked expectantly at the faces before him. Somewhat disappointed, he saw no sign of enlightenment dawning there.

Lee McKay confirmed their continued lack of comprehension. "Where are you going with this Doctor Ling?

"Do you not see how the great explosions launched the plasma back through the wormholes to where the eight Dragons entered them?

"Yes, but how does that help us?"

"Each side of a wormhole can be both an exit and an entry point. Given this indisputable conclusion, can you imagine what would happen if we project a wormhole near or within one of our targets and make the exit point the center of a sun?"

～ ～ ～

The fleet admirals immediately put Ling Wu's revelation to the test. Knowing Stickmen still survived on bases throughout the solar system who might witness and report the planned experiment, they asked the Ghosts to choose a site in a distant corner of the universe where they could conduct it. Ruark volunteered to perform the test, with Lee McKay serving as an observer.

Thousands of light-years from the nearest galaxy, Jackson Ruark generated a wormhole opening as far away from his ship as his weapons system could reach, just over two thousand miles away. He projected the wormhole's exit into the core of one of the hottest stars the Ghosts could identify from their maps of the universe.

The results left both men pale, shaken . . . and elated.

～ ～ ～

Obeying Lee McKay's order to fire, four hundred fifty thousand wormhole openings were simultaneously projected inside the Sterilizer

351

ships and throughout the enormous spherical formation of Sterilizer and Swarm ships. Each wormhole ejected hellish jets of plasma with temperatures of over 377,000 degrees Fahrenheit; jets so fiercely brilliant they would have blinded the attacking Dragon ship pilots if they hadn't shut down their viewing fields ahead of time.

Even though with the wormhole generators programmed to keep the portals open for less than a second, the plasma jets erupted with such ferocity that they spanned far beyond the edge of the Stickman formation by tens of thousands of miles. The entire armada became engulfed.

When it was over, every Dragon warrior in the fleet waited anxiously until the plasma's brightness dissipated enough for their viewing fields to reactivate automatically. They were all prepared to leap forward to give everything they had left to destroy any remaining ships.

When their viewing fields and tactical systems came back online, every man and woman in the fleet became stunned by what they saw. The armada was gone. The plasma jets from the star vaporized every Stickman ship, large and small, down to their component atoms. Thirty-five million Swarm ships and three hundred fifty dreadnoughts were gone as if they never existed. Where the mighty armada of enemy ships stood moments ago, only a vast cloud of gaseous, ultra-vaporized matter remained, propelled away from the target area by the fury of the solar hellfire that created it. The EDF attack on the armada erased close to a billion Hive warriors from the universe without a trace.

Chapter 79
The Promise

The homeworld of the Hive race shared the same arm of the Milky Way Galaxy as Earth's solar system. Located almost five hundred light-years from Earth, it stood at the center of an ever-expanding Hive Empire composed of star systems that once teemed with billions of different forms of life. Those star systems, all long sterilized of their native life forms, now held vast underground Hive cities and fledgling Hive colonies from which future underground cities would evolve.

The all-master, the ultimate ruler of the Hive Empire, rarely left the unadorned, glassy-walled command chamber serving as his underground living quarters and the hub of his reign. He spent most of his time there in a state of semi-awareness of his surroundings as transferred knowledge continuously poured into his mind to keep him informed of the events of his realm. He sent out his governing commands to the empire in the same indirect manner.

Because of the constant need to mentally monitor and direct his empire, leaving his chamber was largely unnecessary thanks to the Hive civilization's efficient command and caste structure. Many layers of subordinate Hive masters served the all-master, who in turn were served by layers of subordinate hive masters and fleet masters of a lower caste, all of them bred to carry out, without question, the all-master's directives to the many worlds of the empire.

While the direction of his empire was his primary concern, the startling and unbelievable destruction of ten of the Hive Sterilizer ships by obscene lower life forms became a huge secondary concern that he found to be both disturbing and distracting. On this day, though, while he impatiently awaited word of the final destruction of the race of humans, something never before experienced by the Hive race occurred to distract him even further. A lone ship of unknown origin inexplicably appeared just beyond the outskirts of the homeworld solar system. Its presence triggered security alarms all over the Hive solar system that warned of a potential alien life form contamination event.

Long-range sensors quickly dispelled the possibility of alien contamination when they identified the ship as a lone Hive Swarm fighter. It remained poised in deep in space right where it appeared. Inexplicably, the mysterious ship did not attempt to travel in the direction of the homeworld, and the mystery deepened when the scans indicated that, though the ship maintained a full-strength power signature, it contained no life forms of any kind. It arrived pilotless.

The all-master's curiosity became piqued, and since nothing like this ever occurred in the entire history of the Hive race, he could not depend on a subordinate to deal with it. Only an all-master retained the power to decide how to cope with unprecedented events outside the experience of the Hive race; therefore, the matter required his personal attention. He disconnected his mind from the supervisory demands of his empire and brought himself back to full awareness of his immediate surroundings.

Once his mind cleared to focus solely on this extraordinary matter, the all-master ordered a Sterilizer ship placed at his disposal. He summoned ten additional Sterilizer ships to serve as his guardian escort. For the first time in seventy-eight Earth years and for the second time in his entire life, the all-master then left his command quarters, and for the first time in his life, he left the surface of his homeworld. For future reference, the Hives of every planet of the empire would monitor his investigation and the resulting decisions he would make to deal with this anomaly. This way, they would know the proper response to any similar future event, however unlikely.

The Sterilizer ship carrying the all-master reached the anomalous Swarm ship in less than two hours' travel and came to a halt mere yards away from it, a behemoth confronting an ant by comparison. The all-master activated a viewing field to see this mystery ship for himself and was startled to see the image of a creature embedded in its impregnable hull with some form of symbols forming a line of characters underneath.

The all-master hissed in shock and recoiled at finding himself in such close proximity to an obviously contaminated ship and reflexively sent out a self-preserving mental command. In response, his Sterilizer ship leaped away from the mystery ship. Simultaneously, its devastating force weapons annihilated the tiny Swarm ship, tearing it apart in a brilliant flash of energy.

With the images of the contaminated ship recorded, the all-master ordered his ship's systems to search the vast Hive databases and archives to identify the symbols it held. As he waited for the results, he studied the recorded holographic view of the intruding Swarm ship.

On the ship's hull, there was a depiction of green serpentine, winged creature with clawed forearms reaching outward from its scaly body as if about to attack. The open jaws of its long snout displayed rows of needle-sharp teeth and a long, forked tongue. From the sides of its head, two long, ragged-edged ears hung down, and glowing red elongated slits of an iris gave the illusion that the creature's hate-filled, yellow eyes focused on him.

The all-master's ship's databases soon identified the glyphs underneath the image of the frightful creature. They were the characters humans used to record written messages. The symbols read, *We are coming for you!*

Infuriated and deeply affronted by his near contamination and an insolent threat from a lower form of life, the all-master ordered an immediate report of the super armada's progress on its mission to destroy the foul humans who dared to send such a message. The cleansing of that vermin race from the distant solar system could not come soon enough.

The report he requested should have come back instantly. Instead, an alarm came through. Of the three hundred fifty thought communications systems aboard those ships, the alarm message indicated no such ships existed!

With the shock of that revelation, the all-master's breathing became labored. The Hive super armada was gone, vanished without a trace and without communication to the homeworlds of any kind. For the first time in his long life, the all-master felt fear.

Epilogue

A year passed since the destruction of the mighty Stickman armada. Instead of building another force to send to Earth, the Stickmen did something unexpected. Thousands of their Sterilizer ships, each capable of establishing a colonial foothold in any solar system, scattered in all directions like the Hive spores they were undoubtedly now meant to be. The Ghost and EDF leaders knew that the Sterilizers would invade and infect the more distant reaches of the galaxy. They might even attempt to reach other galaxies.

Behind them, they left the populations of every planet in their empire discarded and undefended. Tracking down all of the fleeing Sterilizer ships among the billions of stars could take the Ghost-Human alliance years, if not centuries. Nevertheless, the allies pledged to each other a commitment to find every one of them no matter how long it took.

~ ~ ~

Over the past year, the Earth Defense Forces fleets had grown to over twelve million Super Dragons. The Ghosts transported the Stickmen's factory ships left behind in Earth's solar system to this new solar system to continue Dragon production. The transfer of the factories proved to be an easy task for the Ghosts. While the Stickman factory ships were too large to send through wormholes, Ghost Seed ships effortlessly encased them and transported them to this new solar system like they carried the Earth's cities.

Nanite construction stations replaced what the Ghosts considered to be primitive manufacturing machinery within the factory ships. With the factory upgrades completed, almost nothing remained of their original manufacturing systems except the shells of the factories themselves. Since then, the Ghost-refurbished factories autonomously continued to pump out thousands of Super Dragon ships.

People with the same gift of imagination as Danny Murphy found marvelous new ways to put the Ghost technology to good use, resulting

356

in the construction of new Super Dragons with even more capability than their original predecessors.

The EDF soon possessed more ships than men and women to pilot them. The cream of Earth's warriors was gone, and the citizens of Earth who survived the Stickman attacks had their dead to mourn, their lives to restore, and a new world to build. There would be a shortage of Dragon warriors some years, but the hunt for the Stickmen had already begun. Millions of other planets and civilizations existed that would need protection.

∿ ∿ ∿

With the evening light fading, Lee and Susan McKay walked arm in arm through a parklike meadow at the edge of the transplanted city of Savannah. They talked in the low tones of lovers as they enjoyed the evening breezes and the sight of the brightest stars starting to show themselves in the darkening purple skies to the East.

"Lee, look," Susan said quietly as she pointed to another couple approaching and enjoying a leisurely walk of their own. L.C Duval, fleet admiral of the newly formed Hunter-Killer Force 6, and his wife, retired Fleet Admiral Svetlana Ivanovna, walked toward them, arms around each other's waists and Svetlana's head resting against Duval's shoulder. The two officers discovered a mutual attraction during the strategizing sessions for Earth's defense. Six months after the Stickman defeat, Svetlana resigned when the two became engaged, and they married two months after that.

Svetlana straightened when she saw her friends approach and whispered to L.C., who shifted his hand from Svetlana's waist to hold her hand instead as they greeted the McKay's. L.C. held out his free hand to grip Lee's in a warm handshake.

"A beautiful evening for a walk," L.C. commented, letting go of Svetlana's hand so she and Sue could hug their greetings.

"Couldn't be better," Lee returned.

"Do you know whether it will be a boy or girl yet?" Sue asked Svetlana, noting her friend unconsciously rubbing the bulge in her belly.

"We wish to be surprised," Svetlana replied with a smile. "I so look forward to it. I barely remember what it is like to have a family."

"Thank God, we are safe now to be able to raise our families again and start new ones," L.C. commented. "We all miss Earth, but this new world the Ghosts picked for us to settle upon and make new homes is a magnificent substitute."

"It's still a comfort that Earth still exists, and knowing its native life will thrive there again with the help of the Ghost people reversing the ecological disasters resulting from the war. Do you think you'll ever go back there?"

"We're going to make this our home now," L.C. answered. "It's a paradise to raise our children in, and with the help of the Ghosts, we can keep it that way by learning from our past ecological mistakes. Besides, Svetlana and I can't help but think of Earth as a memorial to the millions of us who died trying to save it."

On that sad note, Sue changed the subject. "Lee and I are heading back to town. Would you care to walk with us?"

"We would love to. Perhaps we can discuss possible names for our baby," Svetlana replied. "L.C. and I are still undecided."

The couples continued to converse as they strolled back to town when Sue stopped suddenly and said, "Listen! I hear music!"

From somewhere nearby came the strains of an orchestra. Their curiosity aroused, the four followed the sound until they came across a new amphitheater. There, to their surprise, they found several hundred humans gathered with over a hundred Ghost beings scattered among them. All of the Ghosts stood still as if frozen in place as the strains of Beethoven's Pastoral Symphony, Movement Number 1, played over the theater's loudspeakers. A large white blank screen stretched across the front of the stage.

"What in the world is going on," Susan asked rhetorically. "The Ghosts can't be listening to the music. They can't hear the sound!"

Lee spotted Danielle Orsini sitting at a table on the otherwise empty stage of the Amphitheatre. The two couples worked their way through the crowd to join her on the amphitheater stage. On Danielle's table sat the equipment that produced the music. While distractedly keeping an eye on several digital gauges on a control box sitting in front of her, hands folded on her lap, she focused more on enjoying the sound of the beautiful music herself.

Danielle acknowledged the appearance of her father's friends with a smile as they approached. As they all continued to listen, they noticed dozens more of the Ghosts entering the area, each of them abruptly becoming very still as if mesmerized as they came within sight of the stage.

When the music ended, the humans in the crowd applauded their appreciation of Danielle's concert. From what Lee and Susan knew of the Ghosts, most of them displayed the signs they'd come to recognize as excitement as the Ghosts' bodies rippled with heat and the pink color patterns of their communication with each other. The Ghost, Pat, whom the group of friends saw nearby but of course couldn't recognize from all the other Ghosts, separated himself from his companions and approached Danielle, ignoring the fleet admirals in his excitement.

"Pat: Please, Danielle Orsini, continue to generate more of this phenomenon. We find it to be incredibly pleasing! We have never encountered anything like it in the universe, nor have we imagined such a wonder could exist! What is this called?"

"It's called music. Do you like it?"

The alien visibly displayed his excitement. "Pat: 'Like' is not an adequate word. Our race has never encountered anything as beautiful as this, and yet you humans manufactured it! Once again, confound us! How is it be possible for any beings to create such a wonder? You are the most baffling and enigmatic race we have ever known. We are astounded!"

"What in the world did you do," a bewildered Susan McKay asked. "They can't hear sounds. They have only a mathematical concept of sound based on their study of us. All of their communication is via infrared light."

Danielle beamed with a huge smile, thrilled with the success of her presentation. "I asked Pat for some help in understanding the Ghost sense of vision and communication." She glanced up at the Ghost scientist with genuine affection. "With Pat's aid, I determined the full range of infrared light frequencies they are capable of seeing. I found out their translator disks convert the sounds the human voice can produce and then scales them proportionally to the infrared range their visual organs can detect. The translator disks convert sound to infrared light for the Ghosts and infrared light back to sound for us.

"When I found out how they transform sound to light, I wondered how they would react to our music. On a whim, I set up this experiment. With the help of my Ghost companion, we converted a version of their translator disks to take in the full range of sound frequencies and the magnitude of volume we humans can hear. Then we scaled those ranges proportionally to the full spectrum of infrared frequencies and light intensity that the Ghosts can see just as they convert the sound of our voices. Afterward, we devised a means to project the infrared light onto the screen on the stage.

"This is the first time I tried to run sound of music through my infrared light converter publicly. You came just in time; the Beethoven piece was my very first selection. Most of the Ghost audience out there heard about my experiment and came here out of curiosity."

"It appears your experiment is a huge success." Lee complimented, incredibly impressed with her ingenuity.

"Pat: You all do not understand the significance of what you perceive as just a successful experiment," the Ghost interrupted, "Observe the ship in the sky above us." The three humans looked up to see a Ghost science vessel glide silently into place above the amphitheater. "Your music is a phenomenon we find to be wondrous. It has completely enchanted us. The science vessel above will duplicate your set of patterns and deliver them to every member of our race scattered throughout the universe. Please, will you repeat the pattern for us?"

"I can provide many such patterns for you."

Pat remained motionless for a moment as if contemplating her words. "Pat: You have more than one of these wonderful patterns?"

Danielle giggled and beamed with delight. "I can give you thousands upon thousands of such patterns. Humans have been creating music as long as they've existed."

"Pat - Thousands? How can this be? Truly, you humans have embedded within you the most incredible mix of contrary and normally incompatible characteristics we Ghosts have ever encountered. I suspect that if your species hadn't devoted so much time to your warring nature, your technological and artistic accomplishments might already be nearly as advanced as ours."

"Sad, but true. However," L.C. countered, "if we never developed that tendency to fight among ourselves, we would never have developed the military expertise we needed to defeat the Stickmen."

"Pat: Whether or not we perceive the reasons why, there is a purpose for all things, Fleet Admiral Duval." The Ghost paused again, this time to communicate with the ship above. "Please, Danielle, the Ghost people anxiously await another such presentation."

Danielle touched the "Play" button on the music storage system on the desk. The voices of the Mormon Tabernacle Choir began the first verses of the "Hallelujah Chorus." Almost as one, Ghosts, scattered throughout the audience, froze in place and, once again, became spellbound.